Praise for
Careless

'Astounding. Heart-breaking but hopeful,
and a fresh new voice'
Pandora Sykes

'Moving and beautifully-written – a voice and a story that need
to be heard'
Libby Page

'Sharp, sensitive, and powerful. A book that is this thoughtful,
this well-crafted, and this intelligent, without being preten-
tious, is a rare thing. The literary equivalent of gold dust'
Benjamin Zephaniah

'I felt this book in my gut! It's funny, it's emotional, and at
times definitely heartbreaking, but Bess is a hero you can
believe in'
Jendella Benson

'I am so proud of my super-talented former student, Kirsty
Capes. I'm so impressed with how her writing has flourished
with the cracking characters and energetic prose of her
fantastic debut novel'
Bernardine Evaristo

'Vivid, bold and beautifully observed'
Abbie Greaves

Kirsty Capes works in publishing and, as a care leaver, is an advocate for better representation for care-experienced people in the media. She recently completed her PhD, which investigates female-centric care narratives in contemporary fiction, under the supervision of 2019 Booker prize-winner Bernardine Evaristo. *Careless* is her first novel.

Follow Kirsty on Twitter @kirstycapes to find out more.

CARE LESS

KIRSTY CAPES

ORION

First published in Great Britain in 2021 by Orion Fiction,
an imprint of The Orion Publishing Group Ltd.,
Carmelite House, 50 Victoria Embankment
London EC4Y ODZ

An Hachette UK Company

1 3 5 7 9 10 8 6 4 2

A CIP catalogue record for this book is
available from the British Library.

ISBN (Hardback) 9781398700086
ISBN (Trade Paperback) 9781398700093
ISBN (eBook) 9781398700116

Typeset by Input Data Services Ltd, Somerset

Printed in Great Britain by Clays Ltd, Elcograf S.p.A.

MIX
Paper from
responsible sources
FSC® C104740

www.orionbooks.co.uk

For my mum, Dawn. Thank you for everything.

Chapter One

The long and short of it is this: it's the kind of day where the heat sticks plimsolls to tarmac and I'm standing in the toilet in the Golden Grill kebab shop with a pregnancy test stuffed into my backpack.

I'm waiting for my best friend Eshal. The toilet is not a cubicle but a single room with dirty magnolia tiles that need regrouting and oily lipstick smears on the mirror. The metallic smell of periods is clogging the air and my forehead is damp with sweat. My face watches me from the mirror, distorted by the cherry-coloured imprints of puckered lips, my skin the colour of tiles, too much eyeliner smudged around my eyes and a thin sheen of moisture coating my upper lip.

The first thing I ever learned about my biological mother is that she was very into astrology. The zodiac. I have a pattern of freckles on my lower back, which, if you look at in a certain way, resembles the Big Dipper, and I wonder whether she has the same constellation on her own body.

When I was born, I was already dead. I left the womb with my umbilical cord wrapped around my neck. Had my mother hoped I would never come back to life?

I wonder whether or not it's time to do the pregnancy test; whether I really counted the days right, whether I'm even late at all, or if this is some gross trick my brain is playing on me, addled by the smell of chip fat in the kebab shop. I turn the limescale-encrusted taps back on and splash water over my face.

I think about Boy. What he would think if he saw me now. Sometimes Boy drives us to Chertsey, one town over, and we climb up to the spot on St Ann's Hill with the bricked-in observation deck, and we make bets about who can get down faster, and we run so hard I feel like my legs will swing out from under me and I'll break all my teeth on the ground, and he always wins because his legs are so long and much stronger than mine, which are pudgy from too much sleep and too many kebabs. And when it's autumn, he picks up leaves and twirls the stems between his thumb and forefinger before giving them to me. But we haven't done that for a while now.

I rattle my backpack, listening for change, and realise that I spent the last of my money in the chemist's, and now I have none for chips. The small frosted-glass window in the bathroom is open, and outside I can hear Bora, or one of the other guys, dropping a rubbish bag into the industrial-sized metal bins.

The time is 3.04 p.m., according to the Hello Kitty wristwatch I stole out of my foster sister Clarissa's jewellery box at home. I unzip the front pocket of my bag and take out the long box I got from the pharmacy. I open it and one of the two plastic sticks inside clatters to the floor. I gather it up quickly, embarrassed despite my total aloneness. I ease my denim shorts down to my knees and wait as the build-up of liquid in my bladder streams out. I hold the pregnancy test that didn't hit the floor between my legs, clumsily, dousing my hand in my own hot urine as I do so. I wonder whether it's wet enough. When I pull it out from between my thighs, the applicator on the end is a stark artificial pink, the colour of kids' toothpaste, pale yellow droplets discolouring the white plastic.

2

I think about pulling my shorts up, but for the moment it seems like too much effort. I think about my biological mother, how she might have found out she was pregnant. Her waters broke in the cinema, three weeks earlier than expected. She was watching *The Karate Kid*. I don't think about my biological dad at all; I think he was a one-night stand. The social workers told me she never knew him. But I feel like these other things ought to be important: me, with the Big Dipper on my back. Her, watching *The Karate Kid* (Who was she with? A friend? Was she alone?). And then me again, deciding enough was enough and fighting my way out of her body, ripping her open so that while I was being resuscitated in intensive care, nurses violently rubbing my body, she was being stitched back together. She was so sure I would be a boy because a palm reader told her. After they sewed her up and took her to see me, in my little transparent plastic box, she asked them, tripping out from the gas and air maybe, where my penis was. The nurse who was with her gently told her she had had a girl. She didn't believe I was her baby. She thought I'd been swapped.

All these stories told in therapy at the Family Centre, to make me feel as though I knew her my whole life. To pre-empt any signs of *behavioural deficiencies, attachment disorders, sociopathic tendencies* associated with *early childhood trauma*. The case file turned into fairy stories that would make sense to me in ways the truth would not.

The pregnancy test is positive.

I see the pink cross and I can't see the off-white sink, the tiles, the slimy lipstick kisses, the permanent-marker love notes and pentagrams. I concentrate and strain my eyes until they burn and everything disappears from sight, except that little pink cross.

If I screw my eyes shut and open them quickly, the tiles make psychedelic patterns in purple and blue. I check my watch again and, impossibly, it's only been five minutes.

In two months' time, there's going to be a total eclipse.

My skin is salty. I think about cockroaches surviving a nuclear winter by curling up into the foetal position in the mud. I tug my feet up to my knees, mindful of the puddles of urine and God-knows-what-else on the floor.

I wonder how I am going to survive a nuclear summer.

I wonder what on God's green Earth I'm going to tell Boy.

My bum is stuck to the plastic toilet seat. I haven't shaved the backs of my thighs and the hairs are poking into my skin.

When I was ten, I went through a phase of compulsively banging my head against the wall. When I was twelve, I tried my first cigarette and I was so ashamed of myself that I hit myself in the face until, I swear on my life, the shape of my skull changed, my forehead flattening, like one of those pre-homo-sapiens.

I wonder if I hit myself in the stomach enough this will all go away. Wonder if the shape of my body will change. Stupid of me, because of course it will.

I'm fifteen years old.

The test might be wrong.

It's probably not wrong, though.

My muscles aren't working properly. The pee stick slips from my fingers and clatters onto the floor by my feet. I pick it up, plus the second from the box, nestled in with the paper instruction leaflet. I take my litre bottle of Coke, which is perched on the windowsill, and finish off the dregs. I sit back down on the loo, manoeuvre the second stick between my legs. I catch sight of myself in the mirror, my arm awkwardly bent between my legs, my hair in a lopsided ponytail, long, ratty and full of split ends, in dire need of a cut. My eyes are tiny little black bugs in my steaming face, which has a different kind of shine to it now. A fearful shine.

4

I pull up my damp shorts, buttoning them so my stomach strains against the waistband. I recently learned what a muffin-top is, after hearing a group of girls at school talking about it in the changing rooms, comparing their non-existent belly fat with one another, each of them competing to have the biggest, the most obscene, pinching their flesh violently, leaving red marks, which turned slowly pink, their sing-song self-detriment so naked and fake in the dim strip lights. I could see all their hip bones. They took too long to put on their shirts to be ashamed, their lacy A-cup bras scooping their boobs together into artificial cleavage, and Eshal and I mocking them the next row of benches over, her prancing around on tiptoes, pressing her boobs together, rolling her hand at the wrist, high above her head, mimicking the royal wave. Me, snorting with scornful laughter, but being sure to button up my own shirt the quickest, untucking it to obscure the bulge brimming over the sides of my skirt. Now, here, in the Golden Grill toilets, it's more pronounced than ever.

I cap the second stick, stuff it into the front pocket of my bag along with the first, without checking for the pink cross. I wash my hands slowly, taking time to lather the spaces between my fingers with the sliver of soap balanced on the hand dryer. I grab my bag and bike helmet and leave the bathroom.

Eshal has just walked in. And she is like:

Hey. All right? as she spots me coming out of the loo.

And I was hoping she wouldn't see me.

Bora, the kebab shop guy, is peeling strips of meat off the skewer with a long double-handled knife. Fat particles steam up the air. I imagine that I can feel them landing on my face and burrowing into the pores of my skin.

Hey Bora, I shout across the shop. One of the pensioners from the Greeno Centre, enjoying a portion of chips at a yellowing

5

table, looks up. I tell Bora, That's got to be a health and safety violation.

What are you talking about? Bora shouts back over his shoulder. You know we don't do that health and safety shit here, Bess.

I'm talking about Bora's knife. He holds the knife like a bicycle handlebar, each hand firmly gripping either end of it, the wooden handles stained with fat and sweat. He lifts the knife high above his head and drags it over the meat, pulling it down and towards him in a practised motion. The knife gathers momentum under the pressure of Bora's pull, and when it breaks free of the meat, it stops inches from Bora's stomach, every time moments from slicing into his abdomen. Bora is lean, but I can see the sinewy muscles in his shoulders working under the strain of it. The blade of the knife is sharpened to a razor's edge, but the colour is dull beneath the strips of meat it pulls away.

I walk over. Bora sets the knife down on the counter and wipes his hands on his shirt. He reaches under the counter and hands me and Eshal a lollipop each. Mine is orange flavour. I unwrap it carefully.

I say to Eshal, I've got no money.

What, for chips?

I shrug. For anything.

And I feel so desperate. And I hold my breath and think of Boy, while she watches me, chewing on her lollipop.

That's cool, she says, I'll front you. She reaches into her back pocket and pulls out a fiver.

Inside my rucksack is the pregnancy test, fizzing against my back like a hot poker, and inside me is the feeling of being a cockroach, and the air is hazy and my lollipop sticks to my tongue, all sour.

I say, Nah, don't worry. I was just leaving.

6

Are you fucking joking? I just got here. I've got money! She waves the fiver in my face, fanning me.

Sorry! I say. You were late, anyways! Turn up on time, dickhead, and maybe I'll let you buy me chips. I'm trying to joke around, but Eshal notices the manic note in my voice.

Wait, what's up, Bess?

I can't look her in the face. I'm thinking about cockroaches and Boy's dick poking into my back and the permanent-marker message on a broken sink tile in the Golden Grill toilet that said CARRIE IS A SLUTTY SKANK BAG and another one in pink that said CALL BELINDA FOR HOT SEX with a scribbled-out phone number and how the heat wobbles off cars and roofs and what am I going to tell my foster parents and, Jesus, what about Boy and everyone, and I think about being a baby in a plastic box in St Peter's Hospital, being choked by my placenta. I think about all the water contained in separate concrete cradles across all of the Pits, the reservoir by my house hovering fifty feet above my head while I'm sleeping. If the reservoir broke its banks now, we'd be at the epicentre of the flood, like when stars implode and cave in on themselves.

I can't tell Eshal. I can't. I stare at her, trying to convey how serious I am without having to announce my situation to the whole of the Golden Grill. Then, I don't know why, but I stick my tongue out at her. It seems to work.

Fine, she says, her eyebrows knitting together, just go. And as I'm leaving, Eshal turns back to Bora and I hear her ask him if he's got any weed.

Chapter Two

The town where I live is cut up by the M3 and circumvented by the Thames. Shepperton is famous for its film studios and parakeets. I've lived here since I was four years old and I've never seen a film star. My house is on the Studios Estate on the edge of town. Not an estate like someone inherited it and there's a mansion and acres of land; estate like council estate, and Studios because we're on the edge of the film studios, with all the stage buildings looming over the houses. Wherever you go on the estate, you're in the shadow of Stage H. Although it isn't a stage like you find at the theatre; it's a big old ugly warehouse with corrugated-iron walls and roof, the size of two football pitches end-to-end. Even so, they still guard it from us, the people who live on the estate. Just to get to any of the stages, you have to pass through three security gates and the fences are covered in barbed wire. My neighbour Billy has been trying to hop the fence for years.

I remember when I first arrived here, on Studios Estate, the social worker driving me to my new home pointed out the stone gargoyles on the roof of Stage H. My fingernails scratched at the seat belt as I watched them. Six of them along each side of the building, black silhouettes against the clouds, teetering on the lip of the roof as though the smallest nudge might push them to their deaths.

My foster mother Lisa tells me that the parakeets escaped from the film studios when they were filming *The African Queen* in the late forties. I don't know whether that's true, but I like to take photographs of them and imagine the escape. The whole world stretching out beneath them, a huge new openness in their ribcages.

From my bedroom window on the estate, I can see the park, with two big horse chestnut trees on the green where the parakeets roost. The parakeets have dark orange beaks, the colour of dried blood. I can also see Stage H. And the long sloping sides of the reservoir, just beyond the farmer's fields, but none of the water inside it. If I climb out of the window and sit on the porch roof facing in the opposite direction, I can see the River Ash Woods, where everyone goes to fly-tip and inject heroin. And then the tin houses, which are what everyone calls the pre-fabs, from after the Second World War. The houses were supposed to be temporary but they were never demolished. That's where the kids who are too poor for the Studios Estate live, the ones who come to school with holes in their trousers and scabby chins and stains on their shirts. Behind them are the Pits, which used to be gravel pits once upon a time, but I guess whoever owned them didn't need the gravel any more because they're all filled up with water and shopping trollies now, with mounds of the leftover gravel peeking out of the waterline and forming little brown islands overgrown with weeds. There are footbridges that connect the islands together and they're so high up that when you jump from them into the water, your toes graze the bottom of the lake.

The ceiling in my bedroom is speckled with loads of tiny puckered nipples of paint. I wake up and count them, look for faces in them. I do this all the time. It's like the faces are watching me, waiting for me to pick them out.

We've been out of school for four weeks already, on study leave. I've just finished Year 11; I've had my last exam. And now when I wake up, I forget for a moment that I'm done with school forever, and I listen to the washing machine downstairs. The window is open and the air is like cold milk on my skin.

And for a moment, yesterday doesn't matter – the Golden Grill, Esh, the pregnancy test – and the whole summer is stretched out before me in the sky outside my window. And one of the houses across the road has a rusty old swing in its front garden, someone's dumped it there. And it's like *Ferris Bueller's Day Off* and I'm thinking maybe today me and Esh can steal that swing and paint it, or maybe throw it into the Pits. Or I could find Boy and see if he'll drive us to St Ann's Hill and let me put my head in his lap and pretend to sleep and he'll stroke my hair and then I'll pretend to wake up and kiss him long and hard and he'll fall in love with me again. And then I remember that I'm pregnant and I look out of the window and there's a dead fox in the road and my foster dad Rory is scraping it off the concrete with the metal shovel that my foster mum Lisa uses to dig weeds out of the gaps in the patio slabs.

I should tell someone. I can't tell *them*. Rory and Lisa. I can't tell my social worker Henry, who is useless. I ought to tell Eshal, and probably Boy. I climb through the open window onto the porch roof with my Pentax, the K1000, one of the most reliable manual cameras commercially available, roll a cigarette, and shoot my neighbour Billy (two years below, collects Pokémon cards) as he tries to throw the rope of a tyre swing over a low-hanging branch of one of the horse chestnuts on the green, but fails because he's too short to reach it. The shadow of Stage H looms over him from behind the barbed-wire fence.

I shower quickly, and watch myself in the mirror while I wash. I stand so my reflection is in profile, the water running over me.

There are so many parts of my body that could be better if I just tried a bit harder. I could have a body like Hannah Barrington's if I stopped eating chips all the time. And now I'm going to get even fatter, this thing growing inside me. My belly button is going to turn inside out.

I wonder how many weeks I am. I don't even know what that means. It's just something pregnant women say.

I practise saying it.

I whisper it: I'm pregnant. I'm having a baby. I'm *with child*. I'm expecting. How far gone am I? I'm not sure. If I were to hazard a guess, I'd say that I am pretty far gone. No one can save you now, Bess.

I wander downstairs and Lisa is hoovering the living room. She turns off the vacuum cleaner as I enter, strands of her blonde hair stuck to the sides of her face, her earlobes red.

Afternoon, she says.

Funny, I reply.

The lunchtime news is on the TV. The picture is showing a crudely put-together diagram of how exactly the total eclipse is going to happen. And how, soon, NASA's going to land the *Lunar Prospector* on the moon and find water. Guaranteed.

Let's hope we all survive the end of the millennium.

What are you doing today? she asks me, but not in a conversational tone.

Mum has this habit of fluttering her hand to her neck when she's nervous, and on her upper arms she has these little chicken-skin bumps, called keratosis pilaris, where the protein molecules get stuck in the hair follicles.

She says, Can you get your shoes off the carpet, please.

I take my shoes off and put them on the table.

It's bad luck to put shoes on the table. Not to mention disgusting.

Wow, thanks, Lisa, I reply, and she touches her neck in that nervous way, her eyes pale and liquid, because she hates it when I call her Lisa.

Now she's saying something about keeping the house clean because she has a student she's tutoring coming over in half an hour.

I'm not listening to her. I'm looking at the fridge magnet with a picture of Rick Astley on it and wondering whether Boy has been fucking someone else.

Mum goes: *Bess.*

Everything in our house is pink because that's her favourite colour. She says pink is the colour of luxury. I always thought it was the colour of femininity and sex and weakness. Purple is the colour of luxury, because it's royal.

She is still trying to dislodge me from the kitchen. Clarissa, my sister, joins us and pours herself a beaker of squash. Clarissa says, in her know-it-all voice, It's only bad luck if it's new shoes.

We both give her blank looks, Mum's hair falling across her face.

On the table. Shoes on the table. Only bad luck if it's new shoes.

There you go, I say, looking at Mum.

Clarissa is ten and the sparkling, legitimate, blood-related daughter of the family. When Lisa brought her along to the Year 10 parents' evening at my school, Our Lady of the Assumption, no one could believe that, with my dark hair and moony cow face and beetle eyes and her dusty blonde ringlets and brown eyes the size of UFOs, she was my sister. Well, not really my sister. But she kept trying to hold my hand and introduced herself loudly to all the teachers as my sister.

I'm the Other Child.

Mum and Rory had Clarissa about a year after they fostered

me. I am their first and last (so far) foster child. I think they felt a bit guilty thinking about the prospect of putting me back into care after Mum got pregnant with Riss. Maybe they were worried I would have attachment issues. Foster kids get that sometimes, because they haven't been nurtured properly in their early childhood development. I read that in a pamphlet Mum left in the loo once.

Rory's not too bad. He tends not to talk too much, which suits me fine. He doesn't make me call him 'Dad', like Lisa does with 'Mum', which I must admit is a big relief. I'm sort of indifferent to him, and he is to me. He has just come in from scraping the fox up and Mum is telling him off for washing the fox guts off the shovel in the kitchen sink. I catch Clarissa's eye and she is trying not to dry-heave, I think.

Mum is saying, Can you not do that with the hose in the garden, for Chrissakes? I've got a student over *any minute*.

Yeah, Dad, it is pretty disgusting, Riss says.

Which student? Rory asks Mum, ignoring her thing about the shovel.

Mum answers that it's Hannah and I say that I'm going out.

There's a surprise, she responds.

Can I come? Clarissa asks.

I shake my head, just as Mum says no.

I traipse back upstairs with my shoes to grab my bag. While I'm up there, I call Eshal from the house phone. I hear the doorbell go. Mum opens it and Hannah Barrington's voice fills up the hallway, bouncing off the walls, which are in a shade of pink called 'crêpe'.

Hannah is in the year below, half Spanish and very thin. Fun fact about Hannah Barrington: when I was in Year 8, she cut a chunk of Eshal's hair out with some child-safety scissors during assembly. Then, in November last year, Eshal and I bumped into her and her sister Mary Beth on the bridge by the golf course. Mary Beth is four years older and apparently Eshal had slighted her in some way or other because she dragged Esh through the fence onto the eighteenth hole and beat the shit out of her. Mary Beth held her face into the grass long enough that she made Eshal's limbs spasm and twitch because she couldn't breathe. Hannah was there too. She held Mary Beth's stuff while she kicked Esh so hard in the stomach she coughed blood for a week afterwards.

Mum tutors Hannah for Maths and English, and a couple of other kids from the year below, when she's not working at the opticians. So, I get to see Hannah in our dining room once a week looking for the hypotenuse.

I try to sneak out the back door. My stupid clunky boots echo off the walls in the stairwell.

Mum's all like, Bess, where are you going? Are you actually going out wearing that?!

I ignore her.

Mum tells me to bend over. She wants to see if she can see my bum in this skirt. This is the test. If she can see my bum when I bend over, I have to go and change.

I look at Hannah, who is smirking.

She's still saying bend over, I need to see if your bits are on show.

Nahhhhh.

Mum says, For crying out loud, just do it, Bess.

I tell her to stop objectifying me.

She waits. I bend over, pretending that Hannah Fucking Barrington isn't in this room and isn't going to tell all her gal pals about how much of a joke my life is. I want to punch my mum in her stupid face.

Mum's like, Bess, I can see your ovaries from here, put

something decent on before you go out please.

Are you fucking joking, Mum (I don't say this out loud, just in my head). And I turn around and I can see her looking at me, her eyes all watery-pale and her jaw square and her neck mottled pink, and I plonk back upstairs and change into a pair of jeans. I stash my skirt in my bag.

Halfway down the woods, on my way to meet Eshal at the pub, I dip into the undergrowth, propping my bike against a tree, and change back into my skirt.

I stick my headphones on and press play on my Walkman. The song is 'Strawberry Letter 23' and it makes me feel invincible. My neighbour Billy rides by on a bike. He lets out a low wolf whistle, except because he hasn't quite mastered it, it comes out a bit pathetic. I say, WHY ARE YOU FOLLOWING ME, loud enough to make him pedal faster. I spit at him and miss.

I cycle towards the high street, which is a mile to the east of my house, over the motorway bridge and onto the other side of the M3. The Pits are to the south, behind the Studios Estate. The further east you go in Shepperton, the posher it gets because it's closer to the river. On the actual riverbank, near Manor Park, the houses are worth millions of pounds and the grass is always mown in neat straight lines like a cricket pitch. There's no McDonald's, but there are two pharmacies because everyone is old and they're always getting sick. Luckily for me and Eshal, there are plenty of pubs and no one bothers to ask us for ID. We spend all our spare time together. Or we used to, before Boy.

It's 2.30 p.m. I'm not supposed to be in the pub.

I'm sitting in the farthest corner next to the fruit machine, a dirty sofa with a sticky brown table. Eshal's gone to the toilets to fix her wonky fake eyelashes. I am on my third lager and lime, and my belly is starting to bulge out between the waistband of my skirt and my crop top. Now I *look* pregnant as well as actually being real-life pregnant.

Eshal is tottering back to our spot in her platforms, eyelashes fixed but eyeliner smudged so badly it looks like she's been socked.

Eshal is the only Asian girl in our school. Well: she was until our last exam. Now the whole of Our Lady is pasty white and the Hampton lot need someone new to pick on. My bet is on the tin-house kids.

I take out my camera, my favourite of the four I own, a Diana Mini I nabbed from a car-boot sale for a pound. I wind it up and snap a quick picture of her, while she's making fish faces into a hairbrush compact mirror, still poking at her eyelashes.

I know that look you've got on, she says.

I feel my cheeks warm, a little ashamed at how easily she can read me. Am I so transparent to people? Or just Esh? I got my period for the first time in the middle of biology when I was thirteen, and I was too scared and embarrassed to go to the school office to get sanitary towels. So I went to the toilets and wadded up a load of tissue and shoved it in my knickers. When I came back, she looked at me and knew immediately what had happened. Esh is just like that, a mind reader. I didn't have to say a word to her. And when class finished, she went to the school office and got pads for me, pretending they were for her, and we crawled under the fence at the back of the rugby pitch and ran to her house, and we skived the rest of the day off and watched *Kilroy* and ate Magic Stars until we felt sick, until her dad got home from work and made me call Lisa to come and collect me.

She snaps the compact closed and leans forward, close enough that I can smell the soap she uses on her hands.

She's still looking at me, her eyes beady, with her pointy chin jutting out the way it does when she wants the dirt. She knows me like the back of her hand. She knows almost everything about me, and I her. We're soulmates, me and Esh.

Come on, what is it? Is it Boy?

I feel small, like Billy trying to hook the tyre swing over that big conker tree a hundred years older than him.

Kind of.

She leans back in her seat and rips off a hangnail swiftly. I see a little bubble of blood appear there. She says, I should've known it would have something to do with Scumbag of the Year.

I shrug and chew at my own fingernails, chipping off the nail polish with my teeth.

You're not pregnant, are you?

Her comment is flippant, half-joking, but she can read my mind just by looking at me. She watches me go very still. And she knows that she's bang on the money.

I tell her everything.

Chapter Three

The thing about Boy is it's not a love story.

Sometimes when I stare at the ceiling in bed finding faces in the dots, I imagine him outside my house like John Cusack in *Say Anything*, blasting Peter Gabriel out of a boombox. Him climbing through my bedroom window, coming to save me. Except I'm not Diane. I'm not even Molly Ringwald in a John Hughes movie. I'm Allison in *The Breakfast Club*. The one with dandruff.

One time, after I'd been hanging out with Boy for a few weeks, Eshal asked me, Is the L word on the cards? And I imagined a deck of cards and the letter L was on all of them. I imagined drawing the edge of a playing card across my skin, the thin line and the beads of blood it would leave behind. That is what it feels like with Boy.

The me now, a year on, hasn't spoken to Boy for weeks and it's the same feeling – like falling in your sleep and waking up thinking you're dead. He doesn't belong to me any more, except for the piece of him growing inside me.

Here's how I meet him. It's summer 1998.

I rent *I Know What You Did Last Summer* from the Apollo video store – mainly to see whether it really *is* an almost shot-for-shot rip-off of *Scream* (it is) and only because they *still* hadn't managed to get *Titanic* in. I make Clarissa watch it with me and then she starts getting nightmares about a fisherman crashing through her bedroom window coming to murder her. I don't know why I even bothered renting it – I hate slashers, they're so predictable – really I should've just waited an extra week and taken out *Titanic* to corrupt Riss with that Kate-Winslet-meaty-hand-slap-against-car-window bit instead. But anyway, this is what gets Mum mad initially, and we start arguing. I can't remember a time – except maybe when I was tiny, at the very beginning, when I first came to live with them – that Mum hasn't been irritated with me. It's like I can't do anything right. I think she's way too harsh on me. So I argue back, because it's not fair, and this makes things worse. Every time Mum and I have a row, Clarissa goes really small in a corner somewhere and Rory watches but never says anything and sighs a lot and rubs his forehead, pinching the skin between his eyebrows and taking off his watch and cleaning it with a corner of his shirt. And when I can't listen to her shouting any more, I leave the house and I walk or cycle to Eshal's house, or wherever Eshal might be if she's not at her house, like the Pits or Manor Park Green, which is at the end of the high street and slopes onto the banks of the Thames.

So, I've been at the Manor with Eshal, our bikes lying down on the grass by the river, sharing a spliff and listening to the *Black Caesar* soundtrack on my Walkman, which she hates but she has no choice because it's my player, my rules. Now I'm on my way home. I'm on Squires Bridge Road at the top of the actual Squires Bridge, a Victorian thing with big ornate pillars on either side. Tree branches claw at the sky. It's almost dark, and silent because there's no traffic around here after dusk. Only trees stirring in the breeze and squares of light from the houses illuminating the pavement.

Behind me there's a roaring sound, like an engine revving to the point of breaking. It's getting louder and closer. Ahead is the church of St Mary Magdalene. The church is glowing under floodlights, the old overgrown gravestones casting long shadows across the walls.

A little silver Ford Fiesta skids past me over Squires Bridge, whipping around the corner towards the church. A thumping Prodigy bassline spills out of it as it passes. And a noise between surprise and annoyance escapes me as the car narrowly misses knocking me off my bike. I feel the wind rush through my legs in the wake of the car, and it liquefies my bones. And I get the feeling like I've missed a step on the stairs, like something awful is going to happen.

I watch it happen like it's all in slow motion. People say that all the time, but it really is true. As the car smashes into the church, I see every tiny detail, like the old newspaper dragging itself across the road in the low breeze, Tony Blair's face crumpled across the front page, and the houses on Squires Bridge Road with orange lights on in downstairs windows – in one of them I can see the TV is on, showing the Argentina v. England World Cup match.

The car careers from one side to the other, the exhaust bouncing off the road, the tyres slipping across tarmac, leaving scorch marks and the smell of burning rubber. It knocks itself up the kerb and slams into the low brown brick wall at the perimeter of the church. The sound of the brickwork splitting and crumbling under the impact of the car is deafening. Much louder than you would expect. Then, after it comes to a stop, the car hisses loudly as the wreck smokes in a pile of rubble where the wall used to be. The only thing I can think is that the whole thing would look incredible on film.

The Mary Magdalene church is eight hundred years old (some of it, anyway) and someone just smashed into the side of it.

I am setting up the shots for a film noir in my head.

The passenger door opens and a boy stumbles out in black and white and my vision is complete. He is probably nineteen or twenty, all cut up and bleeding from the crash. He is Boy, but I don't know that yet. The smell of hot metal and melting plastic fills up the road, displacing the dead air. The boy is stumbling in the middle of the street, rubbing his head. He's wearing a light T-shirt and dark jeans, but that's all I can see from here. He's pale and looks tall, maybe six feet, and his hair is dark and longish. He has a narrow face. He keeps moving his hand to brush his hair out of it.

An elderly woman wearing a dressing gown has opened her front door on the opposite side of the road.

Do you know how bloody old that church is? she screeches.

The boy shouts something back, but I don't know what it is. I'm dazed, dizzy like I was in the car with him when it crashed. I watch him stagger back towards the Fiesta and assess the damage. He tugs gently at the passenger door – the side facing me – and the door falls off.

The woman in the doorway shouts again.

She yells: Is that your car, young man?

And then: I'm calling the police.

He stumbles up the road in chunky black lace-up Docs.

I'm thinking maybe he's drunk or on drugs or something and I should probably just cycle away, but he's walking towards me and I can't move.

Give me your bike, he shouts from fifty yards down the road.

And I'm like, Nah, mate, and the tone of my voice is an octave lower and it wobbles as I speak, and suddenly I can feel my fingertips throbbing with my own rapid heartbeat.

I can see him more distinctly now. Close up, he's even taller than I thought, maybe six-two or six-three. He has the appearance of someone who has recently had an unexpected growth spurt and doesn't quite know what to do with all the extra length on his limbs. He looks like one of those house spiders that disappeared behind the sofa six months ago and has re-emerged with knees. Behind him, his fucked-up car is billowing black smoke into the sky so that the church spire is hidden behind it.

He's coming towards me. And I notice other things about him, like how even though he's got a smirk on him like he doesn't give a shit about anyone or anything in the whole world, he has these brown eyes which are almond-shaped and shiny as though he is about to cry. He's got dark features and a mouth that looks like it could turn persuasive. His face is scratched up from the crash and on one side there is a layer of grit embedded into his cheek. And his jaw is very square, his cheekbones jutting out like he doesn't get enough food.

And he's watching me. I'm suddenly conscious of the blackheads on my cheeks, and the cheap cracked lipstick I'm wearing, which I haven't bothered to reapply and that's now probably sweated halfway down my chin. I've always had trouble maintaining eye contact. One of Mum's attachment-theory books suggests that it's because I can't form meaningful attachments with other humans due to being deprived of basic nurturing during my key developmental phases as a baby.

The air is still.

The boy is slowly advancing towards me.

I'm like, Bess, come on girl, get your shit together.

The boy says, What? very loudly and for a moment I wonder whether he heard my thoughts. But that's stupid.

Nothing, I say.

The boy is now directly in front of me, his feet planted firmly on the pavement, blocking my way forward. He stops and pulls a tooth out of his mouth. He winces as he does it. I watch him, trying not to flinch or make some involuntary noise of disgust. Who pulls their own teeth out? It's very hardcore, I have to admit. I'm impressed by it.

I say to him, Is that supposed to scare me? Is that a threat?

He says, No, sorry. I think I hit my mouth on the steering wheel.

He opens his mouth wide, and despite myself I look. I get close to his face and peer into his mouth from below, and I feel his hot breath on my cheeks, and I smell the blood. The gum from where the tooth was pulled is now pooling with bright red blood, filling up his whole mouth. He moves away from me and gobs a load out on the ground by my front wheel.

He says: Give me your bike.

Are you having a laugh?

No.

The woman who was shouting now has an old-style Kodak camera and she has padded out across the road in her slippers towards the wreck of the car. She is taking pictures like she's a forensic scientist.

The boy yells back over his shoulder, What the fuck are you doing, woman?

She shouts back, still flashing the camera, Stay there, please, the police are on their way.

He takes one long step towards me from my perched spot by the bridge. I can't move. He grabs the handlebars and shoves them hard, his grip surprisingly firm despite his skinny frame. I reckon I could ordinarily take him in a fight, but my arms feel weak, and I'm trembling and I can't tear my eyes away from his mouth, which I know is still filling up with blood.

He says, Give me your bike.

I say, What are you going to do if I don't, hit me? And then I feel like this was the wrong thing to say. Maybe I have just given him an idea he didn't think of before.

He smiles a bloody grin.

I decide that I don't want to risk it. I pull my leg over the saddle and step off.

And he's all like, Thanks, babe.

And that's it.

That's the meet-cute.

That's Cary Grant and Katharine Hepburn in *Bringing Up Baby*. It's Leonardo DiCaprio seeing Claire Danes for the first time through a fish tank in the loos at the Capulet party. It's Gene Kelly jumping into Debbie Reynolds' car in *Singin' in the Rain* – except he's jumping onto my bike, not into my car, and he's stealing it, not hitching a ride. And he's doing it because the only other car available has been smashed into a church. By him.

I have to tell Mum and Rory about the bike. It was a new one too. Me and Esh went round town all last summer washing cars and split the cash we made down the middle. Eshal bought a bunch of books about animals and I got the bike.

Mum says, This is why *we* don't buy you nice things, Bess. Because you don't look after them.

She's lying. I know the real reason they don't buy me nice things is because the social only gives them an extra thirty quid when it's my birthday.

Rory says, Come off it, Leese, she's just been mugged, give her a break.

I just think you ought to be more careful, Bess.

She rubs her head like she's got a migraine. I pretend to watch TV, but I can tell she's looking at me, trying to piece together something to say to me.

I wait until I can't stand the feeling of her eyes on me and say, What is it?

You never bring home good news, Bess, she says, her hand hovering at her neck.

Mum's always had this general sense of pissed-offness around me. It's like she's gone to a fancy restaurant and ordered the lobster but they've brought her fifty hard-boiled eggs instead, and now someone's force-feeding them to her, like in *Cool Hand Luke*. I'm the hard-boiled eggs of her otherwise orderly and well-maintained life. These days, the hard-boiled eggs have been pickled, too. I think she might be wondering why she bothered dining out at all.

She plods upstairs for a bath and Clarissa buggers off to her room soon after and I'm left with Rory, who is intensely interested in the end of the England v. Argentina match.

I say to him, Do you have any martial arts moves left over from the army?

He says, I'm an engineer, Bess. I don't know any martial arts. They don't even teach martial arts.

Okay, what about guns. Do you have any guns?

You're not shooting your mother.

I wasn't planning on it, I say wryly. He flashes me a quick grin.

What I know about Rory and the army: He was supposed to be in for maximum tenure, which is twelve years. He was in Argentina for a bit, and then, when that was over, he got sent to Kuwait. Except he took a short cut one time on a training exercise. He was driving a HGV full of expensive equipment, worth hundreds of thousands of pounds. He decided to drive up a hill rather than take the longer road route. Halfway up the hill, the engine got clogged with so much dust that it cut out and the lorry rolled back down the hill, and all the equipment inside got bashed up and ruined. Rory got put in military prison for three days and in the end he missed the whole of Desert Storm. He got deployed in Northern Ireland for a few months, then he came home to my mum and me, a four-year-old foster daughter he'd never met before. Eleven months later, Clarissa turned up. I think the whole reason I got fostered in the first place was so Mum could have someone keep her company while Rory served out his twelve years in the army. In the end, I think he only did five or six. He never talks about it, except for when there's stuff on the news about Afghanistan or Al-Qaeda in Yemen, he mutters stuff under his breath about quote-unquote Arabs and calls Tony Blair a cunt a lot.

I lie on my bed and try to find faces in the dots.

Sometimes I give the faces names and personalities. I'm not a freak. There's just nothing else to do here. My two life choices are either to do really, really well at school so I can get out of Shepperton as quickly as possible and study film in London, or become one of the locals in the Crossroads who drink so much that all their teeth have fallen out.

I could go either way right now. I just need to get through this year at school and I can get out. Apply to a good college, work hard, get into university, move away. Me and Eshal are going to do it together, because Eshal wants to be a vet, she's already picked the vet college in Basingstoke she's going to get into, and after that she's going to the Royal Veterinary College to get her degree. After uni, she'll be a super high-flying top vet with loads of awards and her own documentary TV show, and I'm going to be the director, following her round with a camera crew while she saves all the animals, performing impossible life-saving operations on budgies and rabbits and horses and stuff. It won't be like that crappy daytime TV documentary shit. It's going to be cinematic, unflinching, hard-hitting. And I'll win a BAFTA for it. It's going to be called *Eshal Bhandari: Animal Whisperer.* We've got it all planned out.

Mum has put Clarissa to bed. Everything is quiet again.

I think about the sounds of the boy who crashed into the church. The sound of his Doc Martens crunching over the shattered glass and crumbled-up brickwork as he manoeuvred his way out of the car. Heavy feet. The sounds his hands would make if he put them on different parts of my body: hair, back, shoulder, face. The sound of his voice, low, and his speech becoming less enunciated as his mouth fills up with blood.

Chapter Four

It's not until the day of the Shepperton Fair that I see him again.

Shepperton Village Fair is probably the only cool thing that ever happens in this town. It's on Manor Park Green, but it spreads up the high street too and into the shops and the residential roads and suddenly the whole of Shepperton is a fair.

Eshal and I are watching the birds in the beer garden in The Three Horseshoes. I point to the birds and she names them for me like this:

Common quail, *Coturnix coturnix*.

Grey partridge, *Perdix perdix*.

Common moorhen, *Gallinula chloropus*.

I point at the parakeets above us, their green wings blurring against one another.

Eshal says: They're from India. Did you know that? They're immigrants. Indian rose-ringed parakeet, *Psittacula kramre manillensis*. Did you know that they escaped from aviaries in London during the Great Storm?

Not what I heard, I say, wrinkling my nose at her. Haven't we had this conversation before?

The parakeets dart and swivel above us.

We're tucked around the side of the beer garden because Eshal's brother Anwar is at the fair today and if he sees her in the pub he will tell her parents and there'll be trouble. Eshal's family are from Bangladesh; her parents grew up there and migrated to the UK in the seventies. They're not *strict* strict, but they're definitely a lot stricter than Rory and Lisa. Eshal is grounded a lot, especially if she misses her curfew. If she ever got bad grades, she'd be grounded for that, too, but she never does. Obviously Mr and Mrs Bhandari don't know that Esh smokes and drinks on the sly. That's why if Anwar sees her at the pub it's a BIG problem. Hence us being hidden at the edge of the pub garden.

The best thing about the fair is the raft race. The idea is you make a raft out of old shit you find in your garden and paddle it down the Thames from one end of Shepperton to the other, starting at Ferry Lane and ending at Manor Park just before the river curves under Walton Bridge. This year the theme is 'Countries of the World' and Billy's been building an Antarctica raft in his back garden since March. Antarctica is not a Country of the World. I can see the raft on his patio if I lean out of the bathroom window far enough. The main feature of it is a load of cardboard boxes stacked on top of each other with a white sheet and cling film draped over it, the pointy bits painted with blue paint. It's supposed to be an iceberg, but it looks like a giant blue marshmallow.

Me and Eshal are watching the high street to see if we can spot Anwar when I notice Billy's giant blobby marshmallow bobbing up and down in the crowd.

Holy shit, he's actually going to sail his iceberg.

What? says Eshal.

I explain to her about Billy and his raft.

We must see this, Eshal says. She downs the rest of her drink and drags me onto my feet.

29

We make our way onto the field, hopping over the metal barrier. The trees that border the green give way to tents and gazebos, food vans smoking, and people everywhere. The air is thick with the smell of people and food, and fairground rides line the edges of the field.

We find a patch of grass on the riverbank that hasn't already been claimed and sit down.

So, who is it we're looking out for? Eshal asks for the third time. I think she might be a bit drunk.

Billy, you know, my next-door neighbour? Every time I see him, he shouts GOTH at me and makes a cross sign with his fingers. He's riding that giant blue marshmallow we just saw.

We wait for ten minutes or so as more rafts cross the finishing line to smatterings of applause from the sunbathers on picnic blankets, all announced by megaphone from a woman further down the bank perched precariously on a borrowed lifeguard's chair. She announces each raft with increasing enthusiasm.

This is raft F-six, which is Hayley, Jemima, Ellen and Darcy, who are all in Year 2 at Littleton C of E, and they've decided to do their raft up as China! How adorable.

Kimonos are Japanese, I say, not Chinese.

Cue four dots in geisha kimonos (Japanese, not Chinese) trying to paddle the Jade Palace up the Thames. Their kimonos are so waterlogged they can barely lift their arms.

What is it about people in this town and their flagrant disregard for basic geography? Eshal asks, her eyes still fixed on the China/Japan raft.

Who needs geography when Shepperton is the centre of the universe, don't-you-know, I say in a hoity-toity voice, making her snort. She does the royal wave.

Oh look, the megaphone woman chirps, here comes Pakistan, raft F-twenty-two, which is Brian and the three Johns from the Barley Mow pub on Watersplash Road! Good effort, boys!

The boys are men, all pudgy and dressed in white, paddling their raft with cricket bats. They're being overtaken by a Scout group on raft F-one who have dressed their boat as Italy and have managed to do a papier-mâché Colosseum, which the announcer tells us, breathlessly, took them three months to construct.

One of the Scouts pulls out a water pistol and starts firing at the Pakistanis. John number three pulls his cricket bat out of the water and taps it on the boy's head. A hundred metres down the bank, a woman with a toddler strapped to her chest stands up and screeches a string of profanities at Brian and the three Johns.

You realise he's an eleven-year-old boy, you twat?! she shrieks at the cricketers. They spot her and make a performance out of laughing at her.

She keeps screaming until the woman with the megaphone comes down from her lifeguard chair to shut her up. Except the mum wrestles the megaphone out of her hands and begins shouting through that instead. Now everyone on the bank is watching.

The woman shouts: LIKE TO SEE YOU DO THAT TO SOMEONE YOUR OWN SIZE JOHN MARSHALL I KNOW WHERE YOU LIVE I KNOW WHERE YOUR WIFE GETS HER NAILS DONE I'LL FUCKING HAVE BOTH OF YOU HE'S AN ELEVEN-YEAR-OLD BOY WHAT SORT OF MAN ARE YOU YOU TOSSER

John number three turns around, pulls down his creamy white cricket trousers, and moons the entire bank.

I'm going to make a photo series called 'Trouble in the Village', I tell Eshal.

That's not even funny, she says. Do better.

Meanwhile I've spotted Billy's raft through my camera lens, paddling past Pakistan and Italy, both of whom have come to a stop a few metres away from the bank as the woman continues to scream amplified abuse at them.

Eshal picks up a half-eaten Chinese takeaway carton. The slimy noodles inside are leaking grease. We stand up, brush the grass off our backsides and edge slowly towards the bank, level with Billy and three of his nerd friends. Eshal has expert aim. She nails her first shot and the takeaway box hits Billy's raft square in the centre of his marshmallow. The noodles leave a nasty orange residue before they slide slowly down the cling film covering the iceberg.

I pick up a half-full carton of chips, drenched in ketchup and mayo. I'm aiming for the tip of the iceberg, but I miss and the chip carton smacks squarely onto the back of Billy's red buoyancy aid. Billy turns around to see what's hit him and then roars when he sees all the ketchup and shit dribbling down his back into his arse crack. His eyes search the bank and land on me and Eshal, who are low-fiving on the edge of the river. Billy shouts at his friends, who all start paddling faster. I can see that some of the chips and ketchup are in his hair.

I attempt to throw another discarded chip carton, but it's too light and the wind catches it so that it blows harmlessly into a bit of dead water near the opposite bank.

One more, says Eshal, and she pulls a can of Dr Pepper out of the front of her backpack. She shakes it and lobs it at Billy's raft. The can cracks against the wooden stern and explodes, drenching the two front paddlers in sticky fizz.

A man standing next to us with his kids starts tut-tutting and giving us evil eyes.

Time to go, I say, and we hopscotch over the people on their picnic blankets back towards the fair.

Somewhere behind us, I register that someone is shouting Eshal's name.

I tell her, Someone is shouting your name.

She turns around, her eyes searching the crowd for a familiar face. Then she blanches.

It's fucking Anwar, isn't it?

She breaks into a run and yanks me with such force that I almost trip over her. We're back in the middle of the fair and there's a brass band by the Girl Guides tent. They're playing 'Geno' by Dexys Midnight Runners.

Eshal feels me slowing to watch the band and yanks my wrist again.

Come on! she hisses.

I follow her, keeping pace as she weaves through the aisles of baked goods, barbecues and knick-knacks.

We're almost at the road. I look back over my shoulder. I can't see Anwar anywhere.

Can we stop now, please? We've probably lost him, I tell her, panting.

Eshal's eyes are wild.

He's a sneaky fucker, she says, he'll pop up anywhere.

I say, Let's just stop for a minute and catch our breath.

I'm not as fit as Eshal. She does cross-country every Wednesday with the school and she goes kickboxing at her mosque's youth club in Ealing every Saturday morning.

We reach an empty picnic bench next to a burger stand and sit down. I count the silvers in my pocket and buy two cheeseburgers and a can of Coke to share between us. Eshal asks me whether the meat is halal and I start to laugh, but then I realise she's being serious. The very white, very skinhead-looking man who is flipping burgers in the van glares at Eshal like she just kicked his dog. Eshal sets her burger down in front of her and watches me eat. It's delicious. Proper meat. The kind of cheese that melts in your mouth.

Sorry, I say, my mouth full of cow meat, I forgot.

You're a shitty friend, she says, and I think (hope) she's joking.

Eshal spots something over my shoulder and she ducks her head under the table. I glance behind me to see what's caught her attention, but I kind of already know. Anwar is striding towards us, his eyes narrowed and his mouth turned down, which is a shame because Anwar is pretty buff-looking when he's not angry.

He arrives at our picnic bench. Eshal is still under the table, pretending she doesn't exist. Anwar stares at her.

I say, Hi, Anwar, are you enjoying the fair? How's uni?

Anwar glances at me.

He says, Bess, please can you tell Eshal I can see her.

I say, Eshal, Anwar can see you.

She says, Sup, Anwar.

Anwar says, I hope that's a veggie burger. He means the cheeseburger Esh shoved off the table onto the ground when she spotted Anwar coming.

I say, How's your mum, Anwar? How's your fiancée?

Shut up, Bess.

I smile my biggest, sweetest smile up at him.

Eshal, what are you playing at?

Well, I didn't eat any of it, if that's what you're asking.

I saw you throwing food at that boy on the river!

That wasn't us. That was our doppelgängers.

You think this is a joke?

34

You think this is a joke? Esh parrots back at him.

Eshal!

That kid is *evil*, Anwar, I'm not kidding, I say.

Anwar mutters something in Bengali under his breath and grabs Eshal's arm.

What are you doing? Get off me.

Anwar tells her, I'm going to have to explain to Mum. Honestly, Esh, what's wrong with you? He looks at me like he's asking me the same question. I look away.

He hauls Eshal up and, ignoring her protests, marches her along the walkway back towards the road. Anwar is such a snitch. I find it strange that he's always taking such an active interest in Eshal's life – I can't ever imagine telling on Clarissa for messing about at the fair – but that's kind of just what the Bhandaris are like. I wave them off and pick Eshal's burger up off the ground. There's no dirt on it. I take a bite. There's a girl with a *Little Mermaid* balloon watching me from the picnic bench along. She's watching me eat the floor burger.

THAT'S DISGUSTING, she yells at me. I poke my tongue out and cross my eyes at her.

I wander back towards the road, planning to start the thirty-minute walk home. I light a cigarette by the fence before hopping back over. On the other side of the war memorial, a familiar flash of red catches my eye. I look over and see my bike leaning casually against the fence by The Three Horseshoes.

I stop, squinting past the roundabout. It *looks* like my bike. I cross the road to get a better look. Yep. The yellow APOLLO logo across the frame is all scratched up. The bike is chained to a road sign. I can't believe it. He steals my bike and then has the cheek to lock it up?!

Because God forbid someone steals your already-stolen property.

I look around. I can't see him anywhere. I remember his face so clearly – a square jaw with a dusting of stubble, with straight white teeth, even though he was missing one and gargling blood. Big black eyes with thick eyelashes. The kind of guy who steals your bike and you don't even mind. My mouth is dry just thinking about it.

I don't know what to do. Should I just wait here until he comes back and confront him? Should I try to work out the combination on the lock, or just wrench it open? Should I take the quick-release front wheel off and make a run for it?

I'm about to test the lock, mortified to see he's scratched the initials B. M. into the frame – who the fuck does he think he is? – when I spot the thief bouncing across the road. He walks with long, loping strides, his knees bending gracefully with every step. He's looking behind him, his neck bent awkwardly, watching something further down the street, so he hasn't seen me yet. I panic. What exactly am I going to do when he gets over here, demand that he gives my bike back? He'll laugh in my face.

He is turning around now. I step over the wall ringing the flower beds in the pub garden and duck behind a petunia bush a few metres away, turn my face. He draws level with me, totally oblivious, and bends over to unlock the bike. I think about this dickhead cycling round on my bike for three weeks while I've been walking everywhere and scuffing my platforms so badly that I actually had to rub them down with Rory's shoe polish.

The thief sits astride the bike and pushes off – in fifth gear.

The gears click and strain under the pressure.

And I'm thinking, Does he even care about what he's doing to the derailleur?!

Of course he doesn't. It's not his bike. He stole it. From me.

I jump out from the petunia bush and make a grab for him. He catches sight of me and a flash of recognition crosses his face, but by then it's too late and I shove him hard, angry, with all my weight behind the movement. He wobbles and crashes onto the pavement, crumpled under my bike.

He looks up at me, there's grit stuck to the side of his face, just like outside the church that day.

What the fuck?! he shouts.

The rage that made me push him over is already gone and I realise exactly what I've done: attacked him in the street. I stare at him, frozen, my ears throbbing.

He lifts the bike off himself and stands up slowly. He leans over, holding his knees, breathing heavily. I think I winded him.

You stole my bike, I tell him.

You let me have it.

His response takes me off guard, but I carry on.

I tell him, I'm taking it back now.

He straightens up and I pick the bike up off the pavement. I wheel it past him, ready to leave. I want to say something cutting before I make my exit, but I can't think of anything, so I stare at him, gormless, for a moment before I pedal away. I click the gears back into first.

What's your name? he splutters. Were you *hiding* in that bush?

I say, You've got dirt in your eyebrow.

He scrubs at his brow with the heel of his hand.

He says, I'm Boy.

I say, That's nice for you.

I want to go. I look up to the flats above the kebab shop. There's a magpie sitting right on the edge of the roof. I've got a horrible sense of vertigo just looking at it. The sky is burning orange behind it, so bright that the magpie is just a silhouette.

I look back at Boy. He's still waiting for me to tell him my name. I still feel dizzy, but I'm not looking up any more. I give him the dirtiest look I can muster and turn back towards the high street, kicking the bike into motion, my feet pumping the pedals in perfect time with my heart pumping loudly in my head.

Chapter Five

When I see him next, it's the last day of Year 10. It's a year before I'm pregnant with his foetus. I still barely know him.

Eshal and I are mooching out of the gates of Our Lady, an earphone each plugged into my Walkman. Today it's The Temptations, 'Ain't Too Proud to Beg'. Eshal is saying, *Please*, for the love of God, can we just for once listen to Oasis? It's the last day of school, let me have this. And I say, Okay, where's the tape then? And, of course, she doesn't have it, and she pouts and I grin and sing the words back to her.

Our school is the seventies kind, with flimsy windows, the metal frames painted with chipped white paint, underscored with cheapy plastic green panelling. We walk out into the fore-court, with kids cramming onto the school bus, squirting water bottles at each other and soaking their shirts. Some moron from my Chemistry class gets me and Esh with lukewarm swilled-up water from his sports bottle as we're leaving. Even the teachers on going-home duty look more chilled out. It feels like the end of *The Breakfast Club* and we are all John Bender.

I've told Eshal all about Boy and my bike and what happened after she left the fair. She's just as intrigued as I am. She was grounded for a week after Anwar ratted her out for throwing food at Billy and eating beef, even though she didn't. Eshal's parents, Mr and Mrs Bhandari, are thrilled that Eshal wants to be a vet and go to university. But it also means they're very strict about *making time to study* and *being responsible*. Every time Eshal pulls some stupid shit like at the fair, Mr and Mrs Bhandari have a 'family meeting' where they talk at Eshal about her future and how she needs *to be more serious* and *stop embarrassing the family*. They don't even really shout at her, but whatever goes on in those meetings does the trick. Eshal studies harder than anyone I know and has about four million extracurriculars and mosque and her paper round on top. Imagine if they had *me* for a daughter. They're lucky. Or maybe they didn't luck out, maybe they just taught her how to work hard.

I suddenly think I see Boy as we pass the school bus. Today, Our Lady has a big empty blue sky behind it, the same colour blue as a swimming pool. The sunshine makes me feel giddy. Seeing Boy standing on the pavement opposite school, leaning casually against the railings, looking a thousand per cent badass, might be my imagination. I see him everywhere these days. I stop walking and stare at him, tugging the earbud from Eshal's ear and she turns around to look at me.

Is that *him*? she asks me, once she follows my gaze.

I don't know. I only saw him twice.

That's a lie, obviously. I remember all of it. The blood, especially. But I don't want Eshal to know that.

And the overly long hair on the person on the other side of the road staring unnervingly in our direction certainly looks like Boy's hair. The way his arms hang limply by his side, as though he's not sure how they got there or what they're supposed to be doing, look like Boy's arms.

He's staring at us, I say.

I'm going to kill him.

Eshal says that, not me.

I grab Eshal's arm and pull her back to me just as she takes a stride forward, a determined look on her face.

Just leave it, I say. He's not worth it. I got my bike back. But even as I say it, I can feel myself growing tense, though not in the same murderous-rage way as Eshal. I feel a little *ashamed* to see him. Me, here in my school uniform, shirt soaked through with backwash from someone's water bottle. Nails bitten down, eyeliner streaking. I am aware of my whole body.

But it's the principle, Eshal says. Her eyes are fixed on him, blowing the stray strands of her hair away from her face and then sucking them back in a pendulum motion, like she's about to go Super Saiyan in *Dragon Ball Z*.

Eshal says, He needs some retribution.

No, he doesn't. He's not worth our time at all. Let's just go the other way home.

I can feel the heat in my cheeks. I should be angry too, but I'm not, really. I'm just faking it.

I say to Eshal, Let's goooooo. And in my ear The Temptations are still singing.

She's not having it. Her pointy witch's chin sticks out.

I take her arm again and steer her around to the other side of the school bus so that we're out of possibly-Boy's line of vision. We round the corner and practically slam into Hannah Barring-ton and her sister Mary Beth.

Mary Beth is smoking a cigarette and leaning lazily on the handles of a toddler's pram. Inside the seat of the pram is Jay Jay – I don't think that's his real name – Mary Beth's little boy. Mary Beth is having some sort of argument with Hannah. She waves her cigarette and stabs it at the air as she punctuates each point.

I can feel in the tenseness of Esh's arms that she's either ready for a fight or ready to run. She still hasn't got Mary Beth back for beating her up on the eighteenth hole at Sunbury Golf Course. Mary Beth is big though. When she shifts her body, I can see her stomach hanging out from the bottom of her belly top.

Eshal still can't close her left eye properly because of Mary Beth.

I say to her, Come on. But her legs are locked to the ground. Her fists are balled up so tightly that I can see her knuckles turning white.

They haven't spotted us yet. There's still time. I glance back over to the other side of the road and possibly-Boy is still standing there, watching us, his long, lanky arms folding neatly across his chest.

Mary Beth has spotted us. She turns around, her face puffy and pink from the shouting she's been doing at Hannah.

Hey, Hannah, look who it is, Paki Girl and Demon Goth.

Apparently, they are united against the sight of me and Eshal, the argument forgotten.

When I was in Year 9, I made a pizza in Food Tech and Hannah Barrington chased me down the A-corridor until she caught up with me and stole my pizza right out of my hands. She unwrapped it from its tin foil and cream-pied a wall with it, slamming it like a pancake against the yellow-painted brickwork on the staircase. Even after I'd cycled all the way home, I was still crying, and Mum asked me why and I told her and she rang Hannah Barrington's mum and had a *right go*. Which obviously made things about four million times worse, and the next day at school not only was there still a faded circle of tomato sauce on the A-corridor wall, which someone had written 'Bess's shit pizza' next to in biro, but Hannah Barrington was holding court in the playground, mimicking the pinched nasal voice my mum does when she's really angry. It was a good imitation, to be fair to Hannah. But it was still embarrassing. Everyone knew what happened and that Bess's mummy, who's not even her real mummy anyway, had to fight her battle for her. Eshal saw the *Bess's shit pizza* wall art too, and saw Hannah doing the impression of Mum, and she got one of the big waist-high bins from the quad and dumped it over Hannah's head. After that, I didn't cry, I just followed Eshal's lead and threw my stationery at people.

Eshal says to Mary Beth, What are you doing here, still trying to pass your SATs, Mary? I thought you would've got the hint by now.

Mary Beth's forehead wrinkles.

The hint that you're dumb as shit, Eshal elaborates.

Hannah says, Go back to Curry Town, *Eshal*. Go back to the cult, *Demon Goth*.

Full of purposeful steps today, Eshal takes another one. Towards Mary Beth.

It's so lucky that your kid didn't inherit those pig-nose genes you've got going on, Eshal says.

Shut your fucking mouth. I can smell your curry breath from here, Mary Beth retaliates.

Eshal's neck is tense. I can see what she's thinking. She's imagining how Mary Beth held her arm behind her back until she screamed. And how Mary Beth sat on her chest and let a globule of saliva slide slowly from her mouth, until the string of spit connecting it snapped and the globule landed on Eshal's face. Eshal hates it when she's called a Paki, even though she does a *really* good job of hiding how much it gets to her. I think she would actually rather have another fist fight with the Barringtons. Esh told me that when she was little, she realised crying doesn't make racists feel sorry for you. So you have to be tough instead. Sometimes I think I've got things bad, and then I hear what people call Eshal to her face, in the broad light of day, and I think, fuck that. She's the strongest person I know.

Hannah pushes Eshal from the side, slamming her into the bus. The force of it knocks Eshal aside easily and the metallic thud rattles the side of the vehicle. A couple of Year 7s sitting on the bus glance out of the window, their eyes big.

Mary Beth pulls Jay Jay out of the way. The pram gets caught and almost topples, but Mary Beth catches it at the last moment.

She says, Hannah, what the fuck?!

Hannah ignores her.

Eshal is still pinned against the bus under Hannah's forearm.

I say, Just leave it out, Hannah. I want to sound aloof and annoyed, like the whole thing is beneath me, and I've got somewhere to be, better things to do. But my voice comes out like a squeak.

Eshal almost shoves Hannah out of the way, but Hannah pushes Eshal back onto the side of the bus with the palm of her hand on her chest.

Mary Beth stands next to me, watching Eshal struggle against Hannah's arm. My face is so close to hers – Mary Beth's – and I can smell her breath. I can see that the sweat on her back has soaked through her navy crop top and made a dark patch on her clothes.

Eshal's eyes are glassy. She looks at me.

I try again: Hannah, stop being such a cunt. Get off her.

Mary Beth interjects, Actually, yeah, Hannah, I've got places to be. I don't have time for you to be playing who's-the-biggest-slag with Curry Breath.

Eshal shrieks, SHUT THE FUCK UP MARY BETH and her voice is out of control and for one horrible moment I think that she's going to cry.

Hannah grudgingly relaxes her grip. She releases Eshal and shoves her one more time for good measure and Eshal's head bangs against the side of the bus, making a hollow metallic sound.

You're a fucking know-it-all bitch, you know that? she screeches at Eshal, almost hysterical, almost like she's going to cry herself, and what I see in her pale freckled face is hatred, or maybe fear, I'm not sure which. I wonder how it got to this.

I grab Eshal and yank her away before she goes for Hannah. I repeat our mantra to her as I tug her away.

Not worth it. Not worth it. Not worth it.

One of the Year 7s has gone and blabbed, and now Monsieur Alain, our French teacher, has just rounded a corner.

He says loudly, Does someone want to tell me what's going on here?

I take in Eshal's blossoming pink neck and her hair all in knots. She is panting hard. She sneers back at Hannah and Mary Beth.

Fucking council-house scum, she shouts at them. I want to tell her, no, that's too far, but after what they've just said to her, who can blame her?

Monsieur Alain starts, Eshal, language, you girls come with me—

We don't wait to hear what else he has to say. We dodge around the side of the bus before either of them has the chance to retaliate and sprint out the front gate. No time to get our bikes. We keep running down the street, weaving through the masses of schoolkids ambling down the road towards the train station. Monsieur Alain is patting Hannah's shoulder. She's turned on the crocodile tears. Further down the road ahead, one of the PE teachers whose name I don't know is listening to his walkie-talkie. He glances in our direction as we head towards him. I wonder what they told him. *Apprehend the brown girl and her fat friend.*

We stop.

Esh looks at me, genuine fear now on her face, more genuine than when Hannah had her against the bus.

The last time someone called home about Eshal getting into fights, her mum grounded her for a whole summer.

Which is bullshit, because most of the time it's some racist brute hassling Eshal, and there's nothing she can do to avoid it.

This is not fucking happening again, she says loudly. She turns around and strides back towards the school. I follow her, unsure of what her plan is.

Eshal crosses the road and I understand.

She hops over the metal barrier which is supposed to stop cars mounting the pavement. She crosses the road without looking. I follow her. She strides right up to Boy, who is still leaning against the fence. Up close, I can tell that it is definitely him. I wonder whether he saw what happened with Hannah and Mary Beth. I wonder why he didn't come and try to help us, or stop them.

Boy watches us come to him.

You're Boy, right? Eshal demands. He is head and shoulders taller than her. I think you owe my friend Bess here a favour. She indicates me with a thumb over her shoulder. He looks up to meet my gaze and I can feel a lump forming in my throat. The houses swim around me.

What are you actually doing here? I ask him, still too shrill.

Eshal says, It doesn't matter. What matters is that he owes you.

Boy looks like he's going to laugh. Instead he turns around and says, Come on.

I nudge Eshal, indicating that I think that this is a bad idea and maybe we should just get caught and accept our punishment.

Eshal understands all of this wordless communication. She says, under her breath, I don't care if he's a psycho, there is no fucking way I am spending another summer in my bedroom revising Advanced Biology and reading aloud to myself from the Qur'an.

So, we follow him and I feel like I can't breathe.

And we're already in his car. A bashed-up blue Ford Sierra. Not the car he wrote off at the church, a different one.

It's parked by the gates to the Greeno. I don't think the teachers saw where we went. Eshal sits in the front seat. I sit behind Boy, on the bit that doesn't have the deep crater of a cigarette burn in the seat. The whole inside of it smells like stale smoke. A troll doll with bright pink hair hangs from the rear-view mirror.

Boy takes us to his house. The whole time we're in the car he says barely anything, despite Eshal's relentless questioning:

Is this your car or did you steal it like you stole Bess's bike? Did you steal the car you crashed into the church? How come you crashed a car into a church, have you got a grudge or something? Were you high? Tell the truth though, you were high, weren't you? Are you high right now? Should you be driving? Do you even have a licence? Are you old enough to have a licence? Where are you taking us? Is it your house? Where do you live, is it on Green Lane because that's where I live and we can't go down there in case my parents see me? Do you have any cigarettes?

Boy says that he is nineteen and that is the only one of Eshal's questions he answers, indirectly. I wonder why he chose to answer that one, of all of them. I'm embarrassed by my own surge of disappointment that he's too old to like me. We drive towards the Studios and pass it. Boy is slamming on worn brakes that groan as we pass the speed camera, towards the BP garage and over the A308 junction into Ashford, on School Road. He pulls into a driveway with two overflowing wheelie bins on the pathway.

Do me a favour and move those bins, he says, turning to Eshal. I forgot how deep his voice is. It sounds just like how toast smells.

Eshal gets out of the car.

All right? he says, once we're alone.

It's not a *hello* all right, it's an *are you okay with this* all right.

I don't know if I'm okay with this, so I say nothing, shrug and try to communicate something meaningful with my eyes alone. The window in the back seat is smeared with tiny fingerprints the size of a small child's, but not handprints. Like someone has rested the tips of their fingers on the window for just a moment, a hundred times over.

He opens the door and steps out, and I follow his lead. He doesn't use a key for the front door to the house, he just turns the handle and it pushes open. I follow Eshal inside, pulling her back to let Boy walk a little ahead so I can whisper without him hearing.

I hiss at her, We are staying five minutes and then we are leaving.

Duh, you think I want to stick around? This guy is a total creep.

Boy can't hear us because he is in the kitchen at the end of the hallway, looking in the fridge. The carpet in the hallway is dark and musty, bits of fluff and dust trodden into it. The word COCKZ is spelled out in plastic magnet letters on the door. Somewhere in the house, or on the street outside, it sounds like there's a baby crying.

We stand awkwardly in the hallway, watching Boy close the fridge door and walk out the back of the kitchen into the garden, which is overgrown, with broken fence panels and an ancient rusted flat-pack metal shed entangled in the undergrowth. Some cheap plastic white garden furniture is arranged in a U-shape on the tiny patio. We follow Boy and perch ourselves on the edges of the plastic chairs.

Boy lights a cigarette.

What now? I ask the garden.

Boy shrugs and exhales a plume of smoke.

You can stick around for a bit if you want. Watch some TV or something. Or I can take you home.

I imagine Boy dropping me outside my house in his bashed-up Sierra, my mum twitching at the curtains, the tirade of questions that would follow.

Clearly Eshal is thinking the same thing because she goes, Uh, no thanks.

I can't think of anything to say, so I ask Boy how he sleeps with all the noise from School Road outside.

He says, That's the least of my problems when there's a baby.

I feel my mouth scrunch up involuntarily.

Eshal, forever the tactful one, thinking for both of us, screeches, You have a BABY?!

My feeling of being very, very young intensifies.

Boy shakes his head, No, my sister's baby. She lives on the first floor.

Where are your parents? Eshal asks.

Boy shrugs and blows smoke rings at the sun.

And we sit and wait for something to happen, someone to say something, each of us not wanting to be the person who does, and none of us do, so we look everywhere but at each other.

That evening, I take the 400 bus home and I watch the shiny, molten surface of the reservoir through the window, milky pinky-blue sky behind it. As the bus rounds the corner onto the estate, I look up at Stage H, thinking someday I'll be in there, making films. And I spot a tall man striding along the pavement and I think it's *him*, and his chin turns in my direction and our eyes meet for half a second, and I feel my whole body throb in that moment, locked in that glance through the bus window, which is grey with exhaust fumes and scratched up with graffiti. And then I realise it's not him at all, I remember that I've just left his home and he's still there, and it takes me a while to regulate my breathing and I wonder what is happening to me.

When I get home, Mum has had a call from school already about our altercation with Mary Beth and Hannah.

She shouts.

She is going to call Henry about my behaviour. Henry is my social worker.

She doesn't call anyone when Clarissa is playing up. Because Clarissa doesn't have a social worker.

This is the fundamental problem with our little family set-up.

I say, Why don't you just fucking deal with it like a normal mother instead of threatening to send me away every time I mess up?

I know I don't need to swear, but I do it anyway because she hates it. And I hate when she uses social services against me like a weapon. She's been doing it more and more as I get older. I hate that so much.

She calls Henry anyway and tells him that she can't cope. I open my bedroom window as wide as I can so I can hear her talking on the telephone through the open window downstairs. I hear words like *unacceptable* and *difficult* and *attitude*. I think I hear her crying.

Later, when I'm sleeping, she comes upstairs with too-sweet tea for me. She says sorry for shouting and she is trying to be a good mum, her hand hovering at the back of her neck and sometimes mine. We don't hug. We're not allowed to. It's one of those things they teach you when you're training to be a foster carer. I say sorry for being a moody teenager and I will try to be less angry and not get in fights. And we both know that it is so much more than this, whatever it is that is going on between us.

It's been building for years. We pretend that it's just about being *good* – a good mum and a good daughter – like we are actors playing parts, and when she leaves, I feel like I haven't eaten in days.

On the weekend, I walk to school and get my bike back from the bike lockers. I cycle to Boy's house on School Road and think about knocking. But I don't. I have this jittery feeling in my tendons and I feel like something terrible is happening to me.

Chapter Six

And now it's later in the summer holidays, just before we start Year 11, a year before I'm in the Golden Grill loos pregnant with his foetus, my boobs all weird and achy. The grass and the trees are turning brown, the sky is dark and angry and Boy and I are on the edge of something, but I don't know what it is yet.

I'm in Manor Park, waiting for Eshal to come back from the shops with cigarettes, thinking to myself, I spend my whole life waiting for Eshal. The grass is dewy wet and the river is choppy. The boats moored further along the bank rock as the water slaps against their sides.

Manor Park Jesus is asleep on the bench.

Everyone in Shepperton knows Manor Park Jesus. He deals weed and pills out of the flat above the bookies in the high street but for some reason prefers to sleep under the trees in Manor Park rather than under a roof. Me and Esh share a joint with him on Sunday afternoons when the weather's nice. He's been arrested in every pub in Shepperton and probably most of the ones over the bridge in Walton too. He's been a permanent fixture of Shepperton for as long as I can remember.

The first time I properly met him, though, was when he was being arrested outside The Three Horseshoes. Manor Park Jesus was yanking against the handcuffs, which were already strapped around his wrists. His earring was on the floor – a slim scratched-up gold hoop. As Manor Park Jesus struggled, the police officer kicked the earring around the pavement. When they moved a little further down the road towards the patrol car, I slipped through the crowd that had gathered and picked up the earring. Jesus saw me do it. I saw that his left earlobe had been split in two and blood snaked down the side of his neck

He shouted over his shoulder as the policeman tried to force his head into the car.

Look after my earring, he yelled at me.

I was ten. I'd escaped my foster parents for a moment as they stopped to get cold medicine for Clarissa in the pharmacy. Things were just starting to change. Mum was starting to get angrier and angrier at smaller and smaller things. I was starting to talk back.

He shouted again. Look after it.

I closed my fist around it and held it high in the air, showing him.

His face relaxed and he let the policeman put him in the car.

On the way home, I took the earring out of my pocket and examined it. It was smooth but scuffed-black and the thin bit that goes through the earlobe was the colour of rust. Mum noticed.

What is that? she asked me, twisting round in the passenger seat, the seat belt cutting a tight line across her bony chest.

I said, It belongs to Jesus.

Mum said, For Chrissakes, don't be ridiculous, Bess.

She took the hoop from between my fingers and threw it out of the open car window.

The smallest thing of all, that earring. Such a small thing to get angry about.

When Manor Park Jesus got out of prison a few weeks later, I went to see him on his bench by the river after school one day.

I told him I had lost the earring. I thought he might hit me. Or stab me. Instead he just laughed.

Today, he's having a bad day. He's asleep on a bench and he's lost his shoes. It is almost the end of the summer and Manor Park is dead compared to how it was a couple of months ago, on Fair Day. I sit down by the river and pick up a stick. I ping it at Jesus and it flicks him in the cheek. He wakes up.

Only me, Jesus, I tell him.

What's that for, you little shit?

The sky feels like it is too close, and today the river itself is a dull charcoal grey.

I sit down and let the wet grass soak into the seat of my jeans. I watch the kids on the island stoke a makeshift barbecue. The air smells of rain and woodsmoke and blood.

Eshal finally arrives with cigarettes and we light one each. Jesus wanders over from his bench and bums one too.

We sit quietly for a while, and then Jesus says, One day you will see that I'm a genius and you'll marry me.

Eshal ignores him and asks me if I have a crush on Boy.

She wants me to say no, I can tell. Esh and I have never bothered much with boys. On the whole, we think they're stupid and dirty. We tolerate a few of them as acquaintances – the ones who play Dungeons and Dragons in the library at lunchtime and don't make comments about our tits. We've always agreed that *boyfriends* as a concept is all a bit pathetic. But then, there's never been anyone at school who I've properly *fancied*. I think Eshal liked a boy once, in Year 9. He was this rugby-player type in the year above, Daniel Tyler. I caught her writing his name in her daybook in Maths. She had this habit of staring at him with this stupid dreamy smile on her face, especially when he was making a fool of himself in assembly, trying to be the centre of attention. I teased her about it and she wouldn't talk to me for a week afterwards. That's when she told me that her parents would be arranging her marriage for her when she was old enough.

Are you taking the piss? I asked her. Isn't that, like, not allowed?

You're fucking dense sometimes, Bess. Of course it's allowed. It's what happens all the time in Bangladesh. Most of the time, it works better than a love marriage. My parents had an arranged marriage and look how they turned out.

It's true. Eshal's parents are probably the most solid out of all the parents I know. They are very obviously properly in love. You can just tell because of these little acts of kindness they do for each other. Like, every morning at the crack of dawn, Mr Bhandari goes to the bakery on the high street and gets Mrs Bhandari a cherry strudel, hot, because she likes them best when they're piping. When I stay over, Mr Bhandari gets hot pastries for us too, which is another bonus of hanging out at Esh's house.

The point is, Eshal told me, even if I *did* like Daniel Tyler – which I *don't* – it wouldn't make a difference because my parents are going to pick me a husband, like they will pick a wife for my brother. And I'll tell you for free that my husband is *not* going to look like Daniel.

But what if they pick the wrong one? I asked her.

Eshal shrugged.

What about true love? I continued dramatically, hands over my heart. What if you never get to meet your Leonardo Di-Caprio? We'd recently seen Baz Luhrmann's *Romeo + Juliet* and were both obsessed with it. I spent a full six weeks with Des'ree in my CD player on repeat.

She rolled her eyes.

It's just tradition, she said. In Bangladesh, getting married isn't about two people falling in love. It's about two families forming, like, a union. And it *works*, that's a fact. My parents, for one.

And my cousin Aisha in Dhaka had an arranged marriage when she was eighteen and she's like the happiest person I know. Her husband is a *concert pianist*.

And that settled it. I had to admit being married to a concert pianist would be seriously cool. And then Daniel Tyler started going out with another girl in his year and Esh stopped writing his name in her daybook.

Boy is different from the boys at school, though. He's older, for one: way more mature. He has a house, a car, probably a job. And that day when I saw him outside school, I don't want to admit to *anyone* – not Esh, not myself – what kind of weird backflip my appendix did when my eyes landed on him standing across the road. That feeling is the first time I've ever wanted to keep something from Esh.

I don't answer her straight away. I remember taking the bus home at dusk, the day we met him and he took us to his house, and looking out the window at the sun dropping down over the Pits, turning the sky pink. I think about all the things that are wrong with me, things that he will hate.

I say to her, Whenever I'm alone, I imagine that he's watching me.

I say, Whenever I'm somewhere busy, like the high street or on the train, I imagine bumping into him. I create these conversations in my head between us. I keep seeing him everywhere.

Eshal tells me I need to sort it out.

I know, I know.

Also, Eshal says, this guy is nineteen years old. As much as you're amazing, hot and cool, there's no way he is going for you. You've only just turned fifteen.

I know.

She says, You're letting him define you. Don't do that. Don't ever let a boy – don't let *anyone* define you. You should learn yourself first before you learn another person. Don't forget, Bess. Don't let him know you until you know yourself.

Her face is apologetic as she says it.

Who died and made you Cher? I ask her.

She looks so earnest. I start on at her with a pitchy rendition of 'Walking in Memphis' and she smacks me on the head until I stop.

I don't see Boy for the rest of that summer, but even so, I imagine he's watching me constantly. From car windows, from tall buildings, through the bathroom mirror. I test the limits of my feelings in daydreams, imagine him telling me to do things and quietly assessing my reaction as to whether I would or not. This is how I learn that I would cross live train tracks for him, if he told me to, but I wouldn't murder someone.

In October, Clarissa wakes up in the middle of the night screaming. My bedroom is down the hall from hers. I hear her before Mum and Rory do so I get to her first. She has fallen out of bed in the night and her right elbow juts out from the joint, pushing so violently against the skin that it threatens to break it from the inside. She won't stop screaming.

Rory comes in next and kneels by Clarissa's bed.

I ask Clarissa if she can show me her arm and she does, her eyes great big flying saucers, like Uma Thurman on coke in *Pulp Fiction*.

Rory examines the arm. It's definitely dislocated, he tells us both.

Clarissa says, Am I going to die?

I say, For crying out loud, Riss, you're ten years old, get a grip.

Rory makes me sit with her while he goes to wake Mum. Clarissa's all twisted up in her bed sheets, hot and snotty and tearful. The bedroom is blue from the moon coming through the slatted blinds. Rory comes back in. We're going to take her to the hospital.

I heave Clarissa out of her bed, with effort, just as Mum comes in.

Mum screeches, Put her down! What are you doing? Let Rory do it!

She hisses at me. Put her down. Don't touch her.

Clarissa is crying again. Rory lifts her gently from my arms and holds her gingerly. I can see he's trying to stop himself from looking too panicked and scaring her. Riss cradles her arm.

Mum decides that she will go in the car to the hospital with Rory and Clarissa.

I sit down on Clarissa's bed and listen out for the door to slam. It's 2.43 a.m. I climb out onto the porch roof through my bedroom window, and light a cigarette. I watch Stage H in the dark. It looks like it's alive, stirring. I make up a scene in my head. A car crash. Very old-style, 1950s or earlier, like in *A Streetcar Named Desire* (the Marlon Brando one). Except the streetcar isn't a streetcar at all, it's a Ford Fiesta crashed into a church. And Marlon is climbing out of the wreckage, screaming out for Stella like his life depends on it.

The air is warm. A car pulls into the driveway of the house opposite, headlights on, booming house music, and a man approaches the driver's window, hands over money, takes a baggie and then the car reverses out and drives away.

I take my bike out of the shed and cycle along Old Charlton Road towards Boy's house in my pyjamas. At the speed camera, about halfway, I realise what I'm doing and turn back.

When I do eventually see Boy, it's because I'm in his supermarket. The Tesco in Sunbury. I'm collecting some film I dropped in to get developed. They've started playing Christmas songs in the shops, even though it's not even December yet. It's been months since I last saw him. I'm alone, because Eshal's grandmother is dead, and she's gone to Dhaka for the funeral. In the chocolate aisle, Boy is stacking shelves in a blue shirt.

It takes me a moment to realise what he is wearing and doing. He works here. His long hair is pulled into a scruffy knot. He looks even lankier in the black uniform trousers. He turns to face me and I duck around the corner of the end of the aisle. When he moves away a little, I follow him. He looks tired. His arms are thin and pale. They look as though they might be malleable and could curve around each other until they are tangled like Stretch Armstrong.

I follow him around Tesco for twenty minutes before a security guard approaches me and asks me if I'm planning on buying anything. I pick up a Kinder Egg and pay for it with the copper coins that have fallen through the holes in my pockets into the lining of my coat.

Whenever I look in a mirror, I've started practising facial expressions to use on him. Secret faces that only he will know about. I imagine that he can read my mind, that he's getting all the messages I'm sending him in my head. I wait for him in places no one else would think to look, because I know he knows where I am and he'll come soon. I can't explain how I know this.

Lisa knows something is wrong. We sit at dinner and I feed Clarissa with a spoon, because although her arm is almost healed, it's not ready to come out of the sling yet, and she can't use cutlery with her left hand. She's not a baby any more; she's probably playing it up. But Mum insists.

When I drop a spoon of peas down Clarissa, each one bouncing off her sling and landing in her lap, for the fourth time, Mum loses it. Starts yelling. What the hell is wrong with you?

Nothing, I say, just tired.

You've been tired for weeks.

I shrug.

Are you listening to me, Bess?

When I don't answer, she slams her fork down on the table. It clatters against the side of her plate. We all jump. Me, Clarissa and Rory. The table jerks with our collective wince. For a moment I wonder whether she's going to hit me. But weirdly I don't feel afraid of her. When she talks to me, it's like she's at the other end of a swimming pool. Eshal isn't back from Bangladesh and I've been stuck in this house for days.

And eventually, one day in December when I leave my house for school, he's there on the street. I mean, he is actually there, sitting on the bonnet of his bashed-up Sierra smoking a cigarette and watching the sheep on the fields that slope up the sides of the reservoir.

Right outside.

Thank God you came. Thank God because I was suffocating.

I don't say this, but I think it.

I stop and watch him for a moment. He's staring at me. He lifts his arm high above his head and holds it there.

The pavement is dry and smooth. The sky still feels too close.

I shout at him, as loud as I can without alerting Rory inside.

What the fuck are you doing here, you creep?

He says, I got you a Kinder Egg. You like those, don't you?

Of *course* he didn't hear my thought-messages to him. Of *course* he didn't realise that I had been waiting for him and that it was now time to come.

I feel like if I move he might jump on me and beat the shit out of me because he knows. He knows I stalked him at his job. That *I'm* the creep, not him.

He says after a moment, I'll give you a lift to school.

He's wearing his Tesco uniform. I walk slowly to the car, listening to the slapping sound my girlish school shoes make against the concrete. Boy already has the engine running. I slip into the passenger seat, slam the door, glancing one more time through the living-room window as I do, half-expecting Rory to be watching my every move.

He's not there. Boy does a U-turn and pulls away.

We don't go to Our Lady in the end.

We end up by the river. It's all very *Dazed and Confused*.

Luckily, Manor Park Jesus isn't asleep on the bench today so he can't rat on me to Eshal.

I smoke Boy's cigarettes and he sits in silence, stripping a blade of sedge grass of its seeds with his fingernails.

Eventually I say, Sorry for following you round Tesco. I didn't mean to. Really. I didn't even know you worked there. I just saw you and couldn't help it.

I hear the words as they come out of my mouth and realise what I sound like. *Couldn't help it.* Desperate. I wait for him to pick them apart.

He doesn't. He says, It's fine, really. You're a weirdo, though, do you know that?

I say, Yes, I know.

Then I say, Look at it this way. If you didn't steal my bike, none of this would've happened. So, really, it's *your* fault that you've got a weirdo following you around.

He laughs, but it sounds forced. He's wearing sunglasses, even though it's December and it's cold and the sun is hidden behind thick black-grey clouds. The light is waning even now.

He stretches back on the grass, and I think about doing the same thing, stretching out like that, but I can't because my body is rigid and I'm hyper-aware of every single move that I make and what he will think of me, the way I hold my arms, the way my body looks sideways, how the light hits my face.

On the weekend, he picks me up again. I see the car from my bedroom window when I glance out. I've just got out of the shower. I'm wrapped in a ratty old bath towel, tiny globes of water dotted across my shoulders like freckles, yesterday's make-up streaked down my face. He doesn't see me at first. I stand there, watching him, for far too long, until the water droplets have all dried into my skin. And I try not to breathe, in case he hears me. Of course, he won't hear me, but still. I will him with my mind to look up, into my window, to see me. And, eventually, he does.

We go to his house and I help him paint the walls in the living room, which is also his bedroom. The bed is a Z-bed folded into a sofa. The whole time we are painting, I'm so nervous I imagine myself vomiting all over the walls.

I say, Do you not have any friends to help you do this?

He says, All those guys at Tesco are like forty. They all live in their mums' basements. Wanking all day.

Where are your parents?

He is standing on a chair by the window, poking a paintbrush into the very top corner of the room.

My dad's in Brighton. My mum's not around. It's just me and Keris here. Keris is my sister. And obviously her kid.

I don't ask anything else. Think of my own parents, Lisa and Rory, and my biological ones – my mum with her waters breaking in the cinema and my nameless, faceless, one-night-stand dad who I've never been much bothered about. Wonder whether I should tell Boy about them, whether he'd even be interested. The TV plays an advert for a loans company. Lombard Direct with the cartoon blue phone. I don't tell him.

When we're finished painting, the walls and ceiling are a bright white, like new bed sheets. I have a glob of paint on the inside of my nostril and it whistles as I breathe out. I try to breathe through my mouth instead, but my throat is so dry it has closed up. I alternate between loud mouth-breathing and whistling air past the paint in my nose.

Boy says, What the fuck is that noise?

I show him my nose. I have a paint bogey, I say.

His face splits into a huge grin, his teeth all glittery. Come here.

I come here and he shoves his thumb up my nostril. The pad of the thumb is rough against the inside of my nose, but the fingernail is hard and smooth. He pulls the glob of paint from my nostril, yanking out several nose hairs with it.

He holds up the paint bogey. I position my index finger between his and flick it as hard as I can. It bounces off the window and disappears behind the sofa.

You're disgusting, he says.

I throw my hair back like I'm a L'Oréal shampoo model.

A few days later, he rings my house phone at 4 p.m. Mum answers the phone and calls me to collect it.

She says, There is a man asking for you on the phone. You don't know any men, do you? Her hand drifts up to her neck.

I shrug and take the phone to my bedroom and lie on my bed.

Boy says, 'Sup, weirdo.

How did you get my number? I ask him, watching the dots on the ceiling morph into faces.

I need you to get this gum out of my hair. Keris said she won't do it because Zack's got injections. I'm starting a shift at two. I can't turn up with gum in my hair.

How the fuck did you get gum in your hair?

Zack did it. Keris has this shitty habit of leaving gum in receipts everywhere. Who the fuck leaves gum lying around when there are toddlers in the house?

I say, Boy, I've got no clue how to get gum out of hair.

Can you at least try? It's right at the back. I can't do it properly by myself.

As I go downstairs and put the phone back in its cradle on the windowsill, I wonder why he's not asking anyone else to help him.

I start to pull on my boots and Mum asks me where I'm going.

Just to a friend's. Do you know how to get gum out of hair?

Which friend? Eshal is still in Bangladesh, isn't she?

A new friend.

Who?

No one special.

I drag my bike from behind the bins in the back garden. Mum watches me leave through the kitchen window. I pretend I can't see her.

We end up cutting the gum out. Boy hates that there's a huge chunk of hair missing at the back of his head.

It looks uneven, he says. I look like a Furby.

Nah, it looks intentional. For sure.

He says, Don't patronise me, but I think he's joking.

I say, Fine, and pick up the scissors. I cut the rest of his hair to the same length as the chewing gum patch.

He stares at it in the bathroom mirror. I hold a second one taken from Keris's bedroom so he can see it from all angles. He looks like Shakespeare or something, with an awkward short bob. It's completely ridiculous.

The bathroom sink is full of black hair.

I say, I'm not cleaning up this mess, okay?

Boy is still watching his reflection, the crease between his eyebrows disappearing and reappearing as his jaw works. He opens the bathroom cabinet and takes out a set of clippers.

Just get rid of all of it, he says.

You're not serious.

I'm deadly serious.

I shave clumps of his hair off, holding fistfuls away from his head and letting the clippers slide effortlessly against the roots. I pull his ears back to get the clippers behind them, going all the way to the bottom of the back of his neck to get the downy fuzz reaching into his shirt collar.

When I'm done, I tell him, You look like a convict.

He runs his hands over his head, rubbing the tiny hairs protruding from his scalp.

It's a very strange sensation, he says.

He offers his bald scalp for me to feel. I place my hands on his head and slowly begin to circle the crown. I rub my hands round and round for what seems like hours. I imagine the bathroom darkening into night, the world turning without us, the end of humanity in a nuclear apocalypse, and I am still here rubbing his head as he kneels before me.

You're right, I say. It's like I can feel your brain through your skull.

I slow my hands to a stop. He is quiet.

We catch each other's eye at exactly the same time.

Chapter Seven

Christmas is quiet because Eshal is still in Dhaka for her nanuji's funeral and Ramadan. On Christmas Day, we visit my uncle Jason, Mum's brother, who lives alone in a flat on a shitty Brentford estate that's even worse than ours. When you go inside though, he's decked the place out like it's a palace. Everything is cream with gold and black bits. Even the sofa is a kind of chaise longue with a gold-painted frame. Clarissa and I sit on the edge of it, our shoes not touching the floor. Jason has tried to serve us mimosas three times, but Mum keeps telling him no. Now Jason's asking Riss about school. Riss is a straight-A student. She tells him about a science project she's been doing, something to do with a papier-mâché volcano and baking soda. I pretend that I'm not listening, but the way she describes it makes it sound really cool.

Impressive, Jason tells her, and takes another sip of his mimosa, which Mum says is honestly just glorified Buck's Fizz.

And what about you, Bess? he asks me. Any plans for after you finish school? Are you heading off to college?

Bess doesn't like to plan, Mum says, smirking, and I make a note of the tone of voice she uses so I can mimic it back to her later.

I want to go to film school, I tell Jason, ignoring her. I like

Jason. He looks me in the eye when I talk to him. He makes the kinds of noises when I speak that make me think he cares about what I'm saying. He makes me feel like I'm more important than Riss, not the other way around, like it is with most of Mum's and Rory's family.

What sort of films are you into? he asks me.

My favourites are Tarantino, I tell him, and John Hughes. Have you seen *The Breakfast Club*?

It's one of my all-time favourites.

We have a long conversation about whether or not Molly Ringwald should have ended up with Bender at the end of the film. I think the moment Claire gives Bender the earring is the most romantic thing in cinema, ever, I say. Jason says straight men are only romantically interested in women they don't respect.

He opens up a cabinet underneath the TV set and takes out a VHS case. He hands it to me.

Limited-edition director's cut, he says.

Holy shit.

Bess, language, please, Mum says.

Can I borrow this? I ask him.

Keep it.

Holy *shit*.

Bess!

Give her a break, Leese, Jason says, rolling his eyes comically.

You're going to tell me how to raise my kids?

He doesn't answer and after a moment she looks away.

I suddenly feel like an intruder, an outsider eavesdropping on a private family dispute. My face is burning red, I can feel it. And then Rory says, Jason, do you need a hand with anything in the kitchen? And Jason, whose whole face relaxes, says, Yes please, Rory, that would be great. And they both go into the kitchen, which is really only a section of the same room with a plasterboard wall separating it, and Mum, Riss and I sit in silence for a while, *The Breakfast Club* still in my sticky hands.

After Christmas dinner, we open our presents. My dead biological grandmother, who is called Emelie, has sent me fifty pounds from beyond the grave, care of Henry my social worker. This is a yearly tradition that's been happening since she died, like some kind of staggered inheritance, and I'm pretty sure she has delegated enough fifty-pound notes to send me for every birthday and Christmas until I retire. She even picked out all of the cards herself and wrote messages in them. I don't know too much about her apart from what she writes to me posthumously. This year she has sent me a poem by Emily Brontë, called 'Love and Friendship'. She had lung cancer, and I think it was a slow dying. After I got taken into care when I was four, I stopped seeing her. Stopped contact is what they call it. Stopped contact with anyone from my birth family, actually. And then, when I was seven, she died. My social worker at the time took less than thirty seconds on the phone to give me the news.

The things I remember about my gran are: a huge farmhouse in the countryside with a tree house and a garden so big and complex that it felt like a maze; an unidentifiable perfumed scent which I have never found in any Superdrug or Boots or Debenhams despite sniffing every single bottle and spritzing my wrists until I'm a cloud of flora, which is usually when a pissed-off beauty-counter attendant asks me to buy something or leave; a sit-down lawnmower that she drove through the maze-garden while I sat on her lap. That's all I remember, apart from the fact that after I went into foster care she refused to talk to my real mother. So now I suppose she sends me the money to make up for something that she never did wrong.

For Christmas, Jason has bought me a load of film for my

cameras, and some film soundtracks on CD, including the original John Williams score for *Close Encounters of the Third Kind*. Mum and Rory (Mum picked it, bought it and wrapped it. Rory probably has no idea what it is) have given me a leather-bound scrapbook. It's beautiful. I say thank you.

Later on, I can hear Jason in the kitchen asking Mum in a hushed whisper whether that was all they got for me, look at all the stuff Clarissa got, it was so much more, do you not see how unfair you're being to her, and Mum replies something angrily which shuts him up quickly and they come back into the living room, where the rest of us are watching the *EastEnders* Christmas special and eating mince pies, and I can't stop my face from turning bright red again, and Mum looks at me and she knows that we all heard them and then she tells us it's time to go. And that is our Christmas.

When Eshal comes home from Bangladesh in January, just in time for the start of the spring term, she wants me to tell her all about Boy. She's been away for half a term of school. It's weird her being back. Every time I try to tell her, I can't bring myself to do it. I want to keep the things Boy and I do together private and that's the first time I've ever felt like keeping something from Eshal.

I realise that she is my only friend, apart from Boy. And I'm not sure he even counts.

She says, So what's he like?

I tell her I don't know.

Bullshit, she says.

We're in Art, finishing up our projects before the final exam in May.

It's true. I don't know anything about Boy, still.

Eshal leans close to me so her long wispy hair is tickling my shoulder and goes, in a stage whisper, You're not *fucking* him, are you?

She says *fucking* like it's a dog that just took a shit on her new platforms.

Oh my God, Esh, get a grip.

I'm just asking!

She waits for me to answer, and when I don't, she says, Well, are you? And I realise that I've got something that she hasn't for the first time in, like, ever.

The idea of *fucking* Boy, as she puts it, sends a shiver up my spine, but I'm not sure whether it's excitement or fear. Wonder whether he even thinks of me like that. I'm still not sure he does. I feel as though I might shatter into a million pieces if he looks at me that way. I wink at her, not exactly lying but not telling the truth either, like I'm cooler than Eshal for once, as Miss Turvy comes over to check our work. And Esh widens her eyes at me. And for the rest of the day things are weird between us and we can't quite keep a conversation going.

It's February now and no one wants to think about exams, but we all are, all the while pretending like we don't care. I tell Eshal I can't hang out on weekends any more because I have to revise for Physics or English, but really, I'm with Boy.

I ask him, What is your most secret fantasy?

He says, If there was guaranteed no repercussions, I would eat a human being.

He asks me what mine is. I tell him when I was little, I always wanted to be an astronaut.

I don't tell him that now I want to make movies about astronauts instead, Ridley Scott-style.

I'm thinking maybe being as far away as possible isn't the best way to understand things. Maybe being as close to them as possible, long-lens-style, panoramic, or zoomed in on all the ugly bits. Maybe that's how you really, truly get to know something.

On the weekends, Mum thinks I'm in my bedroom most of the time, but I'm climbing through the window onto the porch roof and shimmying down the drainpipe. No one notices I've gone.

It's been a while since Eshal got back from Dhaka and I still haven't seen her outside of school. I know she was doing some work experience at a cattery, but that was only one weekend. She's probably fuming that I haven't asked her about her nanuji and the funeral, but I try not to think about it. Eshal has a love-hate relationship with Bangladesh. She hates that her Bengali isn't as good as everyone else's, that people look at her funny and can tell straight away that she's not a local, even though she practises all the time. But there are things she loves about being there, too. She loves getting spoiled by her cousins, who fuss over her and treat her and Anwar like minor celebrities. She likes cycling the length of Gulshan Lake near her grand-mother's old house with the heat of the sun on her neck and the smell of the markets and the street-food vendors drifting across the water. She probably wants to tell me about her cousin Aisha, who is a notorious shopaholic and always takes Eshal on a huge spending spree when she visits, no expense spared. She loves Dhaka. But then other times, she says, It's like I'm not good enough for here or good enough for there. So where is it that I will be good enough?

I climb out onto the porch roof, to take the drainpipe route to Boy's. Shivering in the frost, I can see the top of the warehouses and a tiny bit of the reservoir behind them.

I sit there for a moment, watching Billy trying to get over the barbed-wire fence into the Studios, his small breaths coming out in pale clouds, his nose sticking out, red as a glacé cherry, from the collar of his parka. He can't get his leg high enough to hop it. I daydream about how one day they'll let me in through the front gate, when I'm making my own films. I'll build a spaceship inside the Stage H warehouse, and I'll make a film about heartbreak in the vacuum of the solar system. And I'll stand on the other side of that fence, the inside side, and give Billy a hand up.

Eshal rounds the corner by the park and spots me on the porch roof. She says, What the fuck are you doing up there?

I motion for her to shush, and point at the living-room window, where Mum is marking homework in front of the telly.

I get off the roof by way of the drainpipe and motion for Eshal to follow me around the side of the house towards the woods.

When we're out of the way, she says, What the hell, Bess? What are you playing at? Where've you been?

I look at her and I'm not sure how to answer. Weak February sunlight filters through the horse chestnut trees lining the footpath in the woods.

My nan died. I got back three weeks ago, and you haven't come round. I thought it was because you're grounded, but clearly that's not stopping you.

I say, uselessly, I'm sorry.

You've just got more important places to be.

She says it like it's a fact, not a question.

She's angry. Her chin juts out like Clarissa's used to when she was about to throw a tantrum. She lets her hair fall across her face, something she only does when she doesn't want me to see that I've upset her. Her nose points through a parting of hair.

Where are you even going?

I shrug, and my stomach is hot.

You're going to Boy's, she says. Statement, not question.

I don't answer.

Fine, she says. I'll come with you.

She looks exhausted.

Eshal, I say, I'm sorry, all right? Fucking get over it.

She doesn't answer, and I hear those words leave my mouth and realise how I sound, how truly awfully selfish I am.

She power-walks ahead of me, shoulders tensed up, and I trip along behind her, half-jogging to keep up, like a sad puppy. She's so mad at me. But it's a long walk to Boy's. After a while, her shoulders drop and she slows her pace, and I catch up with her and link my arm in hers, and I say I'm sorry again, but this time sincerely, and she says, I'm worried about you, and I say, I'm worried about me too.

When Boy opens the door and sees me, his face grins, all glittery, an expression with which I'm becoming very familiar. Then he sees Eshal next to me in the driveway.

Eshal wanted to say hi, I tell him.

She pushes past me into the house, and I can tell from the bend of her elbows that all that hostile energy she's been directing at me, now it's all for him.

Hi, Boy, she says. She marches into the kitchen and opens the fridge. Boy watches her do it and says nothing. She takes a carton of orange juice out of the fridge and unscrews it. She swigs.

That's really unhygienic, I say from the doorstep, but my voice is small and she doesn't hear me.

She closes the fridge and takes a seat at the little kitchen table, kicking off her trainers. On the table, there is a deck of cards. She opens the packet and empties the cards onto the table.

Boy isn't your real name, is it?

Boy sits down at the other chair across from her and picks up a card, spinning it between his two index fingers.

Eshal asks Boy if he has any cigarettes.

I'm sorry, I tell him.

Eshal looks up at me, bewildered, Why are you sorry? she asks, too loudly. Am I embarrassing you? she says. Am I? She tells Boy, I'm her bodyguard, okay? I'm her mum.

I don't answer, but for some reason I feel like crying.

The boiler turns on upstairs and we hear footsteps.

Someone shouts from the hallway: Have you seen Zack's mittens?

Boy shouts back, No, try the airing cupboard.

Who's that? Eshal asks.

My sister, Keris.

Cool. Shall we go and say hi?

She'll be down in a minute. We're going out, actually, so you're going to have to shove off soon. Thanks for the social call, though.

Boy looks at me when he says this.

Where are you going? Eshal asks, flicking her hair back, her eyes blazing under her eyebrows.

I turn away and rearrange the letters on the fridge door.

We're going to see my dad.

Thought you said you didn't have a dad?

I say, What kind of a question is that, Eshal?

Well, he might have come into existence through mitosis. Like in Biology. Bacteria. We're revising for that in school, Boy. We've got exams. Bess really wants to get an A in Science. Don't you, Bess?

Sure, I say.

Keris comes down the stairs with Zack in front of her on uncertain feet, chattering loudly about something. When they reach the kitchen, he stares and clutches at her legs. Keris isn't at all what I expected. She is almost as tall as Boy and just as skinny, but instead of dark hair, she has a bushy ginger mane encircling her head like a halo. Her face and bare arms are scattered with dark freckles. Zack is, by comparison, a chubby two-year-old with a slobbery thumb in his mouth, but with exactly the same shade of copper-bronze hair.

Oh, cool, Keris says, which one of you is Bess?

Eshal points at me, and I'm kind of flattered that Boy thinks enough of me to mention me to his sister.

You're the one who did that to my brother's hair? she asks me, gesturing to Boy's bald head. It looks *so* much better.

You guys have to go now, Boy tells us, his voice a monotone.

What, you're not coming with us? Keris asks. Zack climbs onto Boy's lap, yanking at his T-shirt, casting wary glances at me and Esh.

Boy says, Zack, mate, say hello to Eshal and Bess. But the kid turns his face into Boy's neck and makes a protest noise.

They're not coming to Brighton, Boy tells Keris.

Oh. Okay.

We can come, Eshal says loudly.

That's okay, I say.

No. Seriously, it'll be fun.

Keris says, I don't see why not. Our dad lives in Brighton. Is that okay?

We love Brighton, don't we, Bess?

I haven't been to Brighton since I was nine. I picture miserable kids dropping ice creams on the pavement and screaming to get off the merry-go-round.

Sure, I say again. I say it to Boy. I look at him and he looks back, his eyes boring into mine. I briefly think about the CD that's playing on my stereo in my bedroom with the door closed, surely by now on its third go of *Close Encounters*. Mum will be getting suspicious soon.

And then I'm like, fuck it, I don't care.

And I don't.

Eshal asks to use the phone and dials a number.

She says: Dad? Dad, I'm staying at Bess's late tonight. Revision. Yeah, okay. Love you too.

And she hangs up.

I'm still looking at Boy, and he's looking at me. And there's that sensation again, that feeling of being incredibly fragile, like Boy is holding me in his hands and that any slight movement in the wrong direction will smash me to smithereens.

Zack stares at us both, suspicious, his eyes all round and shiny.

Chapter Eight

We all squeeze into Boy's bashed-up Sierra, which turns out to
be Keris's, I realise, as she slides into the driving seat.

We share it, Boy explains.

No, we don't, Keris clarifies, I own it and Boy steals it because
he smashed his own into a church.

Boy says nothing. I sit in the back with him and Zack strapped
into a baby seat, while Eshal gets in the front passenger seat and
asks Keris a million questions about herself and Zack.

How old are you?

I'm twenty-three.

How come you guys don't live with your parents?

We never knew our mum and we don't get on with our dad.

So why are you going to visit him?

Because I wanted to introduce him to Zack. He hasn't met
him yet.

Where's Zack's dad?

Hit-and-run.

Oh my God! Did he die?

No, although it might be better if he did. I mean, he hit *me*
and ran. But he's also in prison for traffic offences.

What did he do?

Hit-and-run.

Oh.

Yup.

So, do you have a boyfriend?

Nope. Just me and Zack. And Boy, I guess, too.

Keris beams over her shoulder at Boy and I understand that their smile is hereditary. I wonder if their dad's got it as well. Wonder if *I've* got *my* dad's smile.

Keris bombs the car down the M25 at a speed that pushes my head back against the headrest. She's got *The Lion King* soundtrack shoved into the tape player and Zack mumbles his way through most of the lyrics, Keris sometimes joining in with him. But when the chorus for 'The Circle of Life' kicks in, both Zack and Keris suddenly start screeching along to it at the top of their lungs. When the tape finishes – the last song being 'Can You Feel the Love Tonight', Keris rewinds the tape and we start all over again. Then she reaches over Eshal to the glove compartment and pulls out *The Little Mermaid*. She switches the tape over and winds it forward until she finds 'Under the Sea' and the whole process begins again. The whole time she's doing this, her eyes on the tape player and not the road, we are hitting eighty-five miles per hour on the motorway. When we get further out of London and closer to the coast, she eases up a little bit on the accelerator and I see Eshal visibly relax

I look out at the fields with the window rolled down and even lean out and take a couple of pictures with my Pentax, fortifying myself against the icy winter wind. The sun is low and orange, making long slim shadows of the trees lining the motorway. Zack bashes his little hands against the window, going LOOK MUMMY when he sees the sea, leaving trails of saliva against it like snail tracks.

As we arrive in Brighton, Keris winds the front windows all the way down, even though it's February and it's freezing. The

Nothing new to report, David answers.

Nothing new in three years? says Keris.

Not really. What about you? You've been busy, clearly. David points at Zack, who just glares at him again.

Clearly I have, Keris replies, beaming, and I realise that she is one of those people who doesn't have a bad bone in her body. This is Zack, she says, gesturing to him. Zack, that's Mummy's daddy, that's your granddad David, say hello to your granddad.

Let's have a look at him then, David says, holding out his arms.

Zack starts to cry and nestles into Keris's neck.

What's all this nonsense about, little man? David says to him, putting on this awful baby-talk voice that makes me cringe.

He's a bit shy with strangers, Boy says, his lip curling.

David looks up, as if only noticing Boy just now.

And how is the boy? he asks. Still stacking shelves?

Nothing new to report, David, Boy says. Just like you.

Just like your father, David agrees, but the way he says it is loaded, like it's not a good thing for Boy to be like David, and it's not a good thing for David to have Boy be like him.

Go on, let him down so he can have a play, David says as Zack tries to climb off Keris's lap again, his face going red with the effort.

Where can I put him? Keris asks, looking around the flat.

Just stick him on the floor. He'll be all right.

Keris looks at the floor. Eshal and I look at the floor too. I notice there is an unemptied ashtray on the carpet next to the sofa. I glance up at Keris and catch her eye and her face is so open, it's so easy to see what exactly she thinks of letting Zack play on this floor. David doesn't notice because he hasn't properly looked at any of us yet.

Keris says, He'll be all right for now.

Zack says, I WANT TO PLAY THERE MUMMY, pointing at the kitchen, wriggling around on her lap.

We're not staying long, Boy says.

What? David turns back to him. Come all this way to see me and you're only here five minutes?

Well, we actually came here with our friends, Boy says, gesturing to me and Eshal. And we want to take Zack to the beach.

I haven't even made you all a cup of tea yet! Silly me. Where are my manners? David slaps his bald head comically and tries to catch my eye. I think he's expecting me to laugh, so I do, high-pitched and irregular. Eshal looks at me with a stricken expression and I know she feels as weird as I do about this whole situation.

Actually, I think we'll go now, don't you, Keris? says Boy.

Keris looks relieved and the more time I spend looking at her, the more I think that she is completely incapable of masking her emotions. She says, Yeah, okay.

Come on, Boy says to me. Let's go.

Nice to meet you, Eshal says half-heartedly to David, but Boy already has the door open and is pulling me out by my sleeve.

David doesn't say anything. He just stands in the middle of his living room and watches us leave one by one through his front door.

Outside, Keris says, I'm sorry, that was a mistake.

Boy says, It's okay. And he pulls her into a hug.

Keris says, I thought he might have changed. He sounded so – ordinary – on the phone.

People don't change, Boy says.

We walk along the seafront up to the pier and Boy buys chips with shrapnel from his coat pockets. Keris lets Zack toddle around on the beach and we watch him try to fit rocks into his mouth. He is fascinated by the sea, never looking away even as he bangs pebbles together in his fat hands or eats chips out of Keris's. But when Boy takes him right up to the edge of the tide and lowers him so that the water splashes against the soles of his shoes, he screams and doesn't stop until Boy lifts him out and gives him back to Keris.

Eshal watches the horizon with a philosophical look on her face for a long time before announcing: This is the weirdest day ever. And your dad is a total fucking creep. Sorry.

Keris says, Don't be. He is.

I follow Boy back up to the edge of the water and he slides his hand into mine. It's like we are in *The Piano*, waiting for our piano to arrive on the beach, and he is the mum and I'm the daughter. And I feel like this is progress, from him flinching at me. His hand is rough in mine and it's making my fingertips go fizzy.

I say, Sorry your dad's a jerk.

He says, It's all right, everyone has fucked-up parents.

The tide throbs against our feet and then pulls away gently, displacing the tiny stones beneath. The sensation of the water tugging at me makes me feel brave.

I tell him, My biological mother tried to kill me when I was a toddler.

He turns and looks at me, and I look right back at him, determined not to break the moment. He chews the inside of his cheek. His hand is damp with seawater and it is still in mine. And my cheeks burn with the cold. And everything feels and smells and tastes a little sharper.

I've never told anyone that before, I tell him.

He says, I'm really sorry, Bess. And I shrug and screw up my face to show him that it's okay and that I don't want to talk about it. I just want to show him that we're kind of kinspeople.

I say, You know you're never going to get to eat a person, right?

He nods. And you'll never be an astronaut. You'll never get out of here. He spreads an arm wide in front of him, showing me the beach, the pier, the sea, the world.

And I say, No, not an astronaut. But I'm going to make it out. Bet you anything. You can watch me do it.

Later, we go to a small pub called The Bear, a little bit away from the seafront. Keris orders drinks and we tuck ourselves into a booth. I sit three seats over from Boy, and Eshal and I try to guess what his name might be. His mouth is an Andrew, but the way he moves it when he talks is a George. His cheekbones are Jasper and his skin is the colour of warm bone china like a Harry. If I were to give his hair a name, now that it's all shorn off, it would be Christopher.

Boy doesn't answer and Keris refuses to give it away, a smile playing on her mouth. Zack falls asleep on her lap. We drink wine and our guesses at Boy's name become more and more unlikely. Barnabus. Fitzpatrick. Julie. He shrugs at each sugges-tion, neither confirming nor denying.

Eshal's words become slower and less pronounced. I'm trying to catch Boy's eye and to communicate the sensation that is slowly gathering in the pit of my stomach, like a storm in July. The parting of the Red Sea in reverse. I know he can read my thoughts. I know it.

And I'm following Boy out of the pub, leaving Keris and Eshal behind to talk about birds and dads, and the sharp air pierces every pore of my face. The sea spray is salty in my mouth and on my fingertips.

We go down the verge towards the sea. He has snatched the bottle of wine from the table, offers me a swig from its remnants.

I shake my head, which is swimming. Keep it.

He smiles thanks and returns to gazing at his shoes, fiddling with the label on the bottle.

I wait for him to say something, that feeling in my gut intensifying.

Every single part of my body is hyper-aware of every single part of his body. The way he sits down on the pebbles. The way his legs are crossed at the ankles, one over the other. The way he's leaning back casually on one elbow, the way the collar of his jumper grazes his collarbone, underneath twin moles on his neck. His nails are so bitten down that the skin is red-raw and swollen.

He shifts slightly and I try to work out whether he's turned towards me or turned away.

Is this what love feels like?

He looks like he might say something, but he still doesn't.

I think at him, Say something. Say something. He doesn't notice.

I feel like I'm about to lose him, so when the silence is at its most oppressive, I say to him: Well. This is a fucking dive, isn't it?

All casual, but my voice is wavering and too quiet against the waves.

What? he says.

I don't answer. And I think something needs to happen now. I need to make it happen. It might be the only chance I'll ever get.

So I say, Come on, weirdo, my voice still squeaky and pathetic. But I'm already doing it, I can't stop. I pull off my boots and stand up on the pebbles, waiting for him to do the same.

A questioning look. The sea is black and loud. I suddenly feel very brave.

We're going for a swim, I tell him.

We sprint into the sea, losing sight of the pub and thrown

back by the throb of waves as each one hits us like a slap in the face. I push myself into the cold. My dress absorbs the salty water and clings to my body, the parts I would rather hide suddenly on display, and I'm not so sure, but I think to myself, For fuck's sake, Bess, you've come this far. You might be in love. Just get on with it.

Boy is a few metres behind me, hovering closer to the shore, shirt on and only waist-deep.

Come on! I yell at him.

He does. He unbuttons his shirt, throws it back onto the beach and wades in with his jeans still on, inhaling sharply as the cold water and grit hits the upper part of his body.

I step backwards into deeper water, facing him, taunting him to follow. So cold I can hardly think. Like in *Titanic*.

Eventually he steps towards me. I stop, treading water now, and he's so close that I can see the water pooling in the concave bit of his chest.

He watches me watching him.

He says, What?

I say, What? But the sounds of our voices disintegrate in the wake of the tide against the pier.

He moves closer to me as the waves tug at his middle, and then sways away again, all the while watching me watch him. It's like he's having some kind of internal struggle, an argument with himself. And something momentous is about to happen. I can feel it. In my head, there is a voice that might scream.

I'm gasping for breath. I know he's listening to my thoughts.

I tell him in my head, It's like *Titanic*.

And he laughs aloud like he heard me and he kisses me. His mouth is warm and there is salt on his lips.

A proper kind of kiss. My first.

How do you feel? Don't you feel free? he says, speaking the words into my mouth.

I think how it feels like he's taken hold of the fragile glass part of me and wrapped it up, tucking it away somewhere safe that only he knows about. And I feel like I'm Leonardo DiCaprio in the film and that we're living through a historically significant moment. Like he's the door in the freezing-cold ocean and I'm clinging on for dear life.

I pull away and the storm has broken and now it's raining. Not actually, but like it's raining in my brain and my chest and my belly – and I look at him and my face is like, *Is this really happening* and with his face he's saying, *Yep, yeah, yes, it is.*

And we turn and wade back to the shore, the waves foaming at our waists then our knees then our ankles as we near the beach, and the lights of the promenade beaming bright ahead.

Chapter Nine

Boy doesn't say a thing to me on the ninety-minute drive home. We are both wet and shivery in the back of Keris's car and the feeling of being a precious thing, safe in the palm of his hand, ebbs out of me like the tide shrinking away from the shore, and I'm certain he could dash me to the ground and shatter me into a thousand pieces if he wanted to. And that feeling grows and grows, the longer he refuses to look at me, the longer he holds his body stiffly away from mine so as to avoid touching. Eshal glances back at me from the front seat and gives me a weird look, like she knows something big has happened.

Esh knows I've never kissed a boy before. She knows how much I've risked coming to Brighton: the inevitable shitstorm that is waiting when we get home. And it's all been for nothing. All of the euphoria of being in the sea with Boy, of the feeling of his lips as he kissed me, is slowly ebbing out of me like the tide going out. I feel sick and giddy with all the wine and my clothes are cold and wet and now I'm wondering if I imagined the whole thing.

Keris drops Eshal off first, then me, and when I get out of the car, Boy's asleep, like it all meant nothing to him. Keris says goodbye and he stirs but doesn't open his eyes.

Keris hesitates, as though she wants to say something but

shouldn't. I wait, but she just waves me off as she pulls away from the kerb.

When I get in the house, Mum is in the living room in her dressing gown. I consider just going straight upstairs and ignoring her, but that would only make the inevitable row worse, so I take off my boots by the stairs and head into the living room. Mum is waiting, holding the remote control in one hand. The TV is on mute, Mum isn't watching it. She's watching me as I come in. She doesn't look as angry as I thought she would. She looks tired.

I sit down on the sofa and wait for what feels like an age.

Finally, she says, *Well?*

I wait. In a small voice, I say, Sorry.

Sorry? Is that it?

I shrug, say nothing.

Are you going to tell me where you've been all night?

It's 1 a.m., so all night is an exaggeration. I went out with friends, I needed a break.

Trust me, Bess, your whole life is a break.

I don't answer.

You know what won't be a break? I'll tell you. When you fail these exams and you can't get into college or get a job because no one will hire you, and you'll be forced to stack shelves for the rest of your life.

Her voice rises in pitch and volume as she speaks. I think of Boy stacking shelves, and how I followed him round Tesco. It feels like years of things have happened since then.

These are the most important exams of your life and you are pissing them away to go and mess about with Eshal. Why is your hair wet?

I think of Boy's mouth, all salty, on mine in the middle of the sea. I'm silent.

Mum says, You're throwing everything away you've worked so hard for to go and piss about in the Pits.

I say nothing.

Is it a boyfriend?

What? No! Of course not.

I can tell when you're lying to me, Bess.

It's not a boy.

Who rang the house phone for you the other day?

No one.

No one. What do you take me for? One day, when you've developed some common sense, you're going to realise that no boy is worth your future, your education or career. But at the moment it seems you're happy to be slutting around and not bothering with school.

I think, What I'm doing with Boy is not slutting around. Not in the slightest.

Mum says, I don't know why I'm even surprised. I should've known you had it in you.

I stand up, my face hot and prickly. I know I'm going to cry. I turn away from Mum and go to head up the stairs. Rory is sitting on the middle landing section.

Having a good snoop, were we? I sneer at him, but my voice is small and cracks slightly.

Mum shouts from the living room, Don't you dare talk to him like that!

I sprint the rest of the stairs and slam my bedroom door, like a child. I throw myself onto the bed and feel the hot tears spill from under my eyelids and dampen the pillow.

Should've known you had it in you.

I know what that means. That's code for, I should've known you were born bad. I should never have taken you on. I knew this was coming. I should have expected it.

90

I lay there and listen to Mum and Rory's voices distorted through the floorboards, wait for them to pad slowly up the stairs and close their bedroom door before I switch out my light.

On the Wednesday after our Brighton trip, Henry is waiting for me in the school office when lessons end for the day. I say good-bye to Eshal and go to meet him. In the eyes of social services, I'm classified as 'settled' due to my *permanent care placement*. So the only time I ever see Henry is when I'm in deep shit and Mum has called him.

Henry is tall and skinny, in his late twenties, fresh off the boat in social worker terms, with neat blondish hair and, sometimes, the remnants of poorly removed blue or pink nail polish on his fingernails. When we get coffee, he asks for *soya milk*. I have a theory that Henry might be a drag queen in one of those big gay bars in Soho on the weekends.

Henry takes me to Café Mocha in the high street.

What the hell is going on, Bess, he says, without bothering with our usual niceties of asking how I've been over the last six months.

I hate it when he's like this.

I say, I'm not going to talk to you if you treat me like one of your case kids.

You *are* one of my case kids, Bess.

Henry is here to tick his boxes, ones that say I'm not into crime or hard drugs, or being bullied or feeling suicidal or anything. I'm such an easy case. Most kids get totally fucked by the system, end up in eight different care homes in as many months and then therapy for behaviour disorders, or in jail for robbery or GBH. When I was younger, I always felt like I was the luckiest kid in the system by getting placed with Lisa and Rory. Foster parents for life. But sometimes I feel like I have the worst luck ever.

I always wonder what it would be like if Lisa wasn't my foster mum, if I'd never been taken into care. What kind of person I would be now. I wonder what it would be like to have a mother who loves you unconditionally, like how Eshal's mum loves her.

I'm not saying Lisa doesn't love me. She does, I think. Even if she doesn't say it. Even if she's not allowed to. But there is a disclaimer on it. There are caveats.

I asked Henry once why Mum and Rory don't just adopt me, seeing as it's agreed that I'm never being rehomed (rehomed, like a dog), and he looked super uncomfortable and said something vague about money. I worked out afterwards that Mum and Rory don't get paid to adopt, but the local council pays foster carers. Not much, but enough to make it worth your while. When I was younger, I didn't understand why they always saved the receipts for food shopping, or petrol if we went out somewhere, or the hairdresser's, dentists, all that kind of stuff. When social workers visited, they handed them over. Took me ages to realise I was being *expensed*.

I asked Lisa about it. Asked her why they never wanted to adopt me. What the receipts were for. Whether she claimed back for the heating and water I use, too. And her neck went pink, and her fingers fluttered to her throat, and she told me I was being ungrateful, shouted it, really, and there was a roaring in my ears like I was listening to the ocean through a seashell. Later on, when I was in hospital, they told me I'd hit my head so hard against the wall that I blacked out. After that she stopped giving receipts to social workers – or she doesn't do it in front of me any more, at least.

Henry says, I thought we had an understanding, Bess, pouring two sugar sachets into my big coffee.

The best thing about having social worker visits is that they always take you somewhere nice and pay for your food.

We do have an understanding, Henry, I reply, copying his condescending tone.

What are your grades looking like? he asks me.

Fine, I say.

And what are your college applications looking like?

Fine, I say again, but they're not. I haven't so much as picked up a prospectus from the school library. I'm thinking about going into the military, I tell Henry.

Bullshit, he says, taking a sip of his latte. He tells me this: It's obvious that you're dying to get out of care at your first possible chance. We're not going to move you to a new placement when you're so settled here, just because you're bored or angsty.

I'm not angsty, I interject.

Your options are either to get on the housing register and wait about five years to get anywhere, and then be a slave to the system for the rest of your life – or find a job that is going to pay well enough to help you get out of your foster placement, or go to university. Both of those things require getting a good education.

Yes, I say.

What do you want to do with your life, Bess?

I think of Boy at nineteen-almost-twenty, stacking shelves in Tesco.

I want to get educated, I tell him. I want to make films. I want to make *the* films. Can you name a female film director off the top of your head?

Henry thinks for a moment. No, I can't.

Exactly. I'm going to be the name that pops into your head when someone asks you that question. And after I've done that I'm going to be the name that you think of when someone says think of a film director, *any film director*. That's what I'm going to be.

*

Henry drives me home, but I ask him to stop and drop me at the church. The wall that Boy crashed into is low, hip-height, and someone has re-bricked it where the car damaged it. I wander around the graveyard and look at the headstones for each grave, imagining the lives of the dead people.

And someone behind me asks, Anyone you know?

An elderly woman is standing by the church door, in the archway. She's watching me.

I shake my head no.

I remember you, she says.

Really?

I worry, stupidly, that the woman is a ghost. I wonder if I'm dreaming.

That boy stole your bike. The one who crashed into the church.

I look at her face properly and remember. The woman who yelled at him and called the police.

Hello again, I say awkwardly. I didn't recognise you without your dressing gown.

She laughs and asks me whether I ever got my bike back.

I wonder whether this is a trap. I feel all curled up and rigid, like a woodlouse when you poke it with a stick. I look for something to kick, but the only nearby thing is a headstone and that seems inappropriate.

She says her name is May and she runs the women's group at the church.

We do beginners' knitting classes on Tuesday nights, she says pointedly.

Sounds great, I say.

You should come.

Maybe.

I'll see you on Tuesday night, then.

I don't say anything. I'm suspicious of her, suspicious of why she's being so nice to a stranger.

You should probably get out of the graveyard now, May prompts me.

Yes. Sorry.

I leave, stepping carefully over the graves, feeling her eyes on my back the whole time, my cheeks hot.

When I get home, I call Boy, a knot forming in my stomach. He answers on the third ring, his tone irate. Then he realises it's only me and his voice relaxes. I haven't spoken to him since we snogged in the sea in Brighton. I've been doing this thing where I imagine him bursting into my bedroom in the middle of the night, picking me up like I'm a little kid and taking me away in his car, to somewhere, anywhere that's not here. But I know he's probably not even thinking of me. He's probably already forgotten the kiss.

That was the first time I've ever kissed anyone. I sort of assumed that he would want to be my boyfriend afterwards, but I'm realising how it was stupid to think that. Of course he doesn't want anything to do with me. He hasn't called me, has he? He hasn't turned up at my house like he used to before we kissed. I've ruined everything. I came on too strong. No one likes a girl who's too confident. No one likes a slut. I need to make myself believe he's not interested, otherwise I'll go crazy, madwoman-in-the-attic style, like in *Jane Eyre*. Although I wouldn't be as skinny or have the incredible hair of the Maria Schneider 1996 version we watched in English class.

But still, I'm here calling him with this sickly feeling in my throat, wondering why I always have this sense of dread when I speak to him. Why there's always a part of me screaming *Please like me*. So needy. No wonder he's not falling over himself to see me again.

What are you doing tonight? I ask him, pathetically.

Nothing, but I need to scrape together some cash quickly, so I can't really hang out.

Why? What's going on?

Not much. My dipshit of a boss underpaid me and now we haven't got enough for rent.

I can tell he's fobbing me off. But I can't stop myself.

How much?

Eighty or so. We need it tonight, too. We're already a week late.

I can hear Keris shouting in the background for Boy to get off the phone, and Zack crying, and I realise again how young I must seem to him. What's rent to a kid like me? Social services pay my rent. I never realised what a luxury that was until now.

Listen, Bess, I've got to go. But we'll get together soon, okay? Tomorrow?

He hangs up without waiting for me to respond. And I catch sight of Mum watching me from the door to the kitchen. I don't know how long she's been there. I put the phone back in its cradle. I'm gutted, but I try to make my face look casual.

Who was that? she asks me.

No one. Just Eshal.

I wish you wouldn't lie to me, Bess.

Who says I'm lying?

I wasn't born yesterday.

Rory is in the kitchen making tea, but I hear the tinkle of the spoon against china stop as the hysterical note in Mum's voice rises. Clarissa is on the living-room floor doing home-work, but she stops too and stares at the two of us with her big glassy eyes.

I say, I can see where this is going, so I'm going to leave before we have another screaming match, okay?

I step over Clarissa and walk up the stairs. I hear Mum shout a reply, but my ears are ringing so loudly that I can't decipher what she's saying.

Upstairs, in my room, I open my desk drawer and take out a photo album. In between the last two pages, there is an envelope full of the money that my dead grandmother Emelie sends from beyond the grave every birthday and Christmas.

The envelope has written on it in cursive script, 'To Isabelle, lots of love, Nanny Emelie'.

I count out the notes in the envelope. Altogether there is eight hundred and fifty pounds. The number surprises me, even though it makes sense, considering the number of years I've been in care.

I count out two notes, a hundred quid, and slide the rest back into the envelope and the drawer. The money feels strange to me, like charity from a stranger, even though I don't need any charity, and if I ever spent it, it would be on stupid, material things that run out, like food and make-up and clothes and film for my cameras. It makes sense that I should help Boy out with it.

I cycle to Boy's and knock. He opens the door, holding Zack, his eyes wild. Zack is crying. He looks like he's trying to explode.

Boy goes, I thought I said don't come round?

He doesn't say it. He shouts it over Zack's screams. Partly to be heard and partly because he is angry. I feel like I'm shrinking.

I think I can help you, I tell him.

What?

I said, I CAN HELP YOU.

Boy still looks mad, but he moves aside so I can get in. I go to the kitchen and find Keris sitting at the table with a jar full of coins in front of her. The coins are being extracted and arranged into piles to make up pounds. She looks up as I come in.

Hey, Bess, now's not a great time, she says, and despite everything, she manages to smile.

I sit down opposite her and take the money out of the front pocket of my bag. I place the fifties in front of her like an offering, like two halves of a whole. A very expensive cake.

Boy has followed me into the kitchen.

Where the hell did you get that? he says.

Keris stares at the money, and then at me, her eyes wide with shock.

She says, Bess.

I say, You'll have to pay me back, obviously. But not, like, quickly. Just when you have the money.

Bess, you have no idea what this means. We were about to get evicted. The housing association has been calling all morning. Boy was just about to sell the TV and the microwave.

Where did you get it, though? Boy says again.

It's just savings, I say, and I turn around in the chair to look at him. His eyebrows are even more furrowed than they usually are, and his face is blazing.

We can't take this, Boy says to Keris, I'm going to take the TV to Daley's and see what they'll give me for it.

Boy, don't be stupid, Keris says. She takes my hand across the table.

I nod. It's no trouble, really. I wouldn't do it if I couldn't. You know?

Boy nods. He picks up the money.

This is more than enough to cover it, he says.

Good.

I'm going to call Eric.

Our landlord, Keris clarifies to me.

Boy takes the phone from the kitchen wall and dials a number. He puts it to his ear.

I'm paying you back as soon as I get paid, he says to me, his eyes boring into mine. I nod. Then Eric answers and he says, I've got your money, you fucker.

I don't know why, but I feel like I've crossed a line that has always been there, but I've only just realised that it exists.

Eric the landlord turns up half an hour later and he and Boy have a very loud argument on the doorstep as he hands the money over. Keris won't stop hugging me and calling me a lifesaver. I'm light-headed.

Later, Keris and Zack go to sleep upstairs and I help Boy plug his TV back into the wall from where he'd boxed it up to sell it. He can't get the aerial right, though, so the picture is fuzzy and keeps cutting between two channels.

Boy doesn't say anything to me for a long time. I feel like it's his turn to try to tell me something meaningful, since it's always me doing the talking. I realise, sickeningly, that I've basically paid him to spend time with me. What does that make me? Desperate? And he still won't even look me in the eyes? I wait and wait and wait and still nothing. Finally, I say to him:

Are you giving me the silent treatment?

He doesn't answer immediately, and then he says, No, I'm watching this programme.

Yeah, right.

I wait again, but he doesn't continue. Outside, it's getting dark and I want to curl up into a ball on the corner of his sofa bed and go to sleep and never wake up.

I imagine picking up the TV and throwing it through the bay window so all the glass smashes.

I say, I feel weird about what happened in Brighton.

He turns to look at me properly, and our elbows are touching.

I know, me too, he says.

I can't do another whole conversation where I make statements about things that are important and you just say *I know*.

He grins and says, I know.

Because this is important, Boy.

I know.

I laugh despite myself.

He says, I'm sorry, I'll be serious now.

I reach out and 'get' his nose between my index and middle fingers.

He says, I really like you, Bess.

I feel like I'm going to throw up all over him.

I say, I like you too.

He says, I think you are sweet and funny and kind and thoughtful.

I say, same. High-five?

We high-five. And then he kisses me again. Hesitant at first, like in Brighton, and then harder. Properly. His hands on my face and then my back and then my hips and then my legs.

The TV is almost completely static.

Chapter Ten

After that, that's it.

I can't stop thinking about him. I see him every night after school and all day on the weekends. Sometimes we hang out in his room and sometimes he drives us to high-up places so we can see far away and make up stories about the people who live in the tiny patchwork houses, in a haze of pollution and pylons. Or we sit on the railings of the bridge at the Pits and throw stuff – sticks and bits of moss and dirt – into the water, black crescents underneath our fingernails.

I steal one of his jumpers and wear it under my blazer to school every day until a teacher confiscates it.

Eshal kicks me under the table. Is that Boy's? So are you guys a thing now?

Yeah. We're a thing.

Eshal doesn't like it. She frowns at me and mimes puking.

Sometimes I catch myself touching my own face softly. I ask him, Am I your girlfriend now?

He says, Come on, Bess, what are we, twelve?

One time. he rings the house phone on a Saturday morning and Lisa answers it before I can get to it.

She says, Please stop calling my daughter, and then hangs up. *Mum!*

She tells me, There is no way in high hell that you are having a boyfriend when you're just about to start your exams. No. Bloody. Way, Bess.

I walk out to save having the argument.

Boy thinks it's funny.

Your mum's scary, he says.

I say, You have no idea.

Henry calls to check up on me.

Lisa says she barely sees you any more.

She's paranoid.

Have you filled out your college applications?

Yes, of course, I say into the phone as I stare directly at the untouched pile of papers on the floor.

I tell Boy almost – *almost* – everything. I don't think anyone knows as much about me as he does, now. He knows what they wrote about me in my case file. We wrap his duvet around us and our legs tangle together as I tell him these things in a small voice. He watches my mouth as I speak. We are so close that his breath warms my face and I can smell his toothpaste.

He says, Are you a virgin?

And I reply, Of course not, but I'm lying.

I feel like I'm constantly teetering on the edge of being a child to him.

Sex hangs in the air between us and neither of us want to talk about it because it would be like looking directly into the sun. It is so bright. I wonder whether he would even try anything with me, because I'm so much younger. But every time I see him, things get more and more intense. He takes my shirt off and slides his hands into my trousers and I mimic him clumsily. I think of the girls in the P.E. changing rooms at school – the girls like Hannah Barrington – who wear thongs and push-up bras and hang around in shopping centres with their money and mobile phones and expensive lives like Alicia Silverstone in *Clueless* and shave not just their legs and armpits.

I love those bright lacy bras they wear, the ones you can see through a white school shirt. They look beautiful and dirty at the same time. Their birth-control pill packets peek out of their make-up bags accidentally-on-purpose when they reapply their foundation in the A-corridor toilets. They always know the right thing to say to a boy, the right kind of look to give him.

In March, I have a dream that I'm the *Lunar Prospector* – not that I'm inside it, but that I *am* it, a silver-coloured cylinder with cranes for arms. I'm orbiting the moon and as I'm spinning around and around in the vacuum of space, the Earth is imploding below me, burning up like a big old supernova, melting, dripping off the edge of the galaxy, and here I am, all the way up here, and I'm okay.

And now I'm staring at the mirror on Boy's wardrobe and wanting to break it. We are in Boy's bedroom and I can see myself lying on his sofa bed, unfolded, and him lying on top of me, through the mirror. He has one finger inside me.

I feel like I could still give more of myself to him. I want to tell him something real. I say, Did you know my real name is Isabelle?

He is frowning at the wall behind me, concentrating on his knuckles under the denim of my jeans, but now he is looking down at me, bewildered.

Of course I knew that, he says.

I know for a fact that he did not know that. It's one of the few things I didn't tell him.

He says, Why are you talking about that now?

I say, Why not?

I say, Don't you think it's weird that both of our names are secret?

He says, Well, yours isn't a secret now.

His fingers are clawing out my insides. I don't think that's how it's supposed to feel. His fingernail digs into something inside of me and I wince.

You okay?

Yeah.

I wonder if there's something wrong with me. Maybe my vagina doesn't work like other people's. Maybe this is supposed to feel nice, but I don't work properly, so for me it just feels gross.

Boy kisses me hard on the lips. His teeth bash against mine. He takes his hand out of my underwear and unpops the button of my jeans. As he pulls them down, I help him by wriggling my legs out of the fabric.

He positions his body over mine.

He is still fully clothed and I am in my underwear.

I notice that there is a clump of pubic hair escaping from the side of my knickers, black against the paleness of my thigh. It looks like a spider perching on my leg.

And I think, Wow, this is really happening, isn't it.

The sun is cold and it is making everything in the room look whitewashed like the walls.

I look back at the mirror and notice that the way my head is resting makes me have a double chin. I reposition my head to a more upright position, so he doesn't see how ugly I can be, but the position is unnatural and it sends a shot of pain up my back.

What are you doing? Boy asks.

Nothing.

Why are you twisting your head like that?

It's comfortable.

Isabelle is a much nicer name than Bess, Boy says. Why did you change it?

I didn't change it. I just shortened it.

He snorts and tries to kiss me again. He's talking into my mouth.

He's saying, Isabelle doesn't shorten to Bess. It's a whole different name.

He hesitates, then reaches under me and unclips my bra. As it falls away, I bring my arms up to my chest, self-conscious. It's too light in here. Boy can see every part of me.

Boy asks me what I'm doing. I don't answer. My mouth has gone really dry. I look up at him. He gently tries to pry my arms away from my chest, but I lock my elbows and refuse to let him.

I say, Can't you close the curtains or something?

Why would I want to do that?

He is propped up on his elbows, but this time when he kisses me, he lets his full weight rest on top of me. For someone so skinny, he's surprisingly heavy. All of the air is squeezed out of my lungs.

Boy says, You look really pretty in this light.

He looks nervous, or something.

I think, Does that make me look not pretty in other light?

He never calls me pretty or anything like that.

He's watching my face and I'm not making eye contact. I'm watching the mirror and the ceiling and the window.

He kneels up and takes off his jeans. His hands might be trembling, but I'm not certain. Then he pulls off my underwear, unhooking them from my ankles, so now I am completely naked.

I close my eyes and try to control my face. I still have my arms crossed over my chest, utterly rigid.

I feel his weight leave the sofa bed and his desk drawer open. I keep my eyes closed. He slides the drawer shut and opens the one below it. I listen to the wood scraping along the metal fixture. He moves the stuff in the drawer around. And then his weight is back on the bed, over me. And I crack one eye open an inch to see him rolling a condom onto his penis. I've never seen it (his dick) in the light before. I've only ever felt it in the darkness of the back of the car or under his duvet.

Boy asks me if I'm cold. I'm not, but I nod anyway, hoping he'll let me get under the blanket. He doesn't offer and instead clambers on top of me again. His arms snake under me, wriggling to find the space between my back and the mattress, and pull me up to him. With his legs, he parts my knees and lowers his hips towards mine.

I say, Can you close the curtains please.

I can see people walking their dogs past his house. I can see cars driving by.

He obliges, gets off me and draws the curtains.

I'm thinking This is it, this is it, this is it.

I thought I was going to die a virgin. I must be the last virgin left in my year at school, apart from Eshal, but she has a legitimate, Allah-related reason to be.

Boy reaches down and repositions his dick. I watch the ceiling. I feel him press into me. No, against me.

I wait.

In Sex Education they said it would hurt, but I can't feel anything.

I look at Boy, who is still concentrating very hard. He reaches down again, this time brushing his hands against the inside of my legs, at the top. He leans back and pushes my knees out further in opposite directions. He leans down for a better view.

Oh my *days*.

He puts two fingers halfway into my vagina and opens them up.

Like, he is prying me open.

It's unpleasant.

I feel like maybe I should have shaved like Hannah Barrington, worn some Ann Summers knickers or sprayed my crotch with perfume or deodorant or something.

Boy is breathing heavily. There are actual beads of sweat rolling down his forehead.

I imagine that I am drowning. I hold my breath, hoping Boy will notice that his breathing is the only noise in the room. He doesn't.

I say, Shall I go on top?

I feel like that is something people who have sex say.

Boy exhales and disengages himself from my legs.

I'm 99.99% sure that penetration has not yet occurred.

Maybe there really is something wrong with me.

Boy lies on his back and I get on top of him, straddling him. We've done this a million times but always fully clothed, and not with the intention of sex in mind; at least not for me. I take hold of Boy's penis and position myself on top of it. I *know* that this is the right position. I found one of those top-shelf magazines in the woods on the way to school once and I'm doing it exactly like the girls in the pictures are. I let all the strength out of my legs and push down on Boy. But something won't give. I'm stuck hovering above him, like I'm squatting to pee on the floor.

Boy is looking at me expectantly. I can't make eye contact with him, so instead I'm looking at the *Godfather 3* poster behind his bed, which is slightly wonky, and suddenly I want to cry.

He says, Are you sure you've done this before?

I'm like, Of course. Are *you* sure?

There's no need to be such a bitch about it.

I *dismount* and lie down on my back next to Boy.

This is so stupid.

I wonder if God is watching me now. I wonder if Eshal's dead grandmother is watching me now. If *my* dead grandmother is watching me.

Boy reaches for the remote and switches on his TV. I take his cue that our 'sex' is over. I scramble to collect my clothes from the floor around his bed and dress myself. I feel horribly ashamed. I wonder if he'll ask/tell me to leave. The sun is ebbing through the curtains, leaving a soft orange light illuminating the dust mites.

There is a football match halfway through on the TV and the commentators are discussing Fulham's offensive strategy.

In the hallway, the front door slams and Keris shouts a hello.

I look at Boy. He's putting his boxers on. I sit up straighter.

A moment later, I can hear Keris walking through the hallway, dropping her keys on the sideboard in the kitchen, putting Zack in his high chair. She pokes her head around the side of Boy's door, which is slightly ajar.

Hi, you two, she says.

Hi, Keris, I say.

Boy says nothing. He is back next to me, one arm draped over my shoulder.

I stare at the TV.

Keris says, Where are your trousers, Boy?

Boy shrugs.

I catch her eye and Keris raises her eyebrows at me. I shrug too, imitating Boy. She leaves and shuts the door with a sharp click behind her. I look at Boy again. He is watching the TV screen, chewing the inside of his cheek. I don't know what to do, so I close my eyes and pretend I'm falling asleep. I shrink into him and he lets an arm slide around me so I can get closer.

The commentators are shouting because someone has scored. I think about mirrors. I imagine the mirror on Boy's wardrobe, smashing.

It gets darker.

When Boy shakes me awake, it is totally black. He is whispering my name. My hair is stuck to the side of his face; it's too hot and the duvet smells like sleep. Musty. In the darkness, his mouth finds mine and we are kissing. He pulls me closer to him.

He says, I'm so sorry about earlier.

I say, It's okay.

He kisses me again.

I say, Just so you know, I was lying. I'm a virgin.

Boy says, It's all right, I kind of guessed.

I put my head on his chest and listen to his heartbeat.

He says, Just so you know, I've only done this, like, twice before, so I'm not exactly an expert either. We don't have to do anything, he says, we can just hang out and watch TV.

My skin feels prickly. I'm still wearing my jeans.

I say, Come here.

And he does.

After the first few times, it gets easier, like we've worked out how our bodies fit together. On the fourth time, I come and I understand what people were going on about. I'm on top of him and he looks extremely pleased with himself.

After, I can't stop looking at him. He says, What?

Nothing, I say.

No, seriously, tell me.

Just that I understand now. Why everyone talks about how good sex is.

He grins at me again, his eyes black and glittering in the darkness of his bedroom.

I tell Henry about Boy – not about us having sex, just about *him* – because I can't not tell anyone. Eshal won't talk to me any more, because I flaked on her too many times. I'll call her and make it up. When I tell Henry about Boy, he's pleased for me.

Look at Bess. All grown up with a boyfriend.

I beam at him. We are in Mango Café eating Thai green curry on a Friday after school.

What's he like?

He's interesting. He knows these random things that no one else knows. Like, did you know, that there is a thing called spontaneous human combustion and it's when you randomly burst into flames. For no reason. And the only thing left of you is your shoes. It actually happens.

So how old is he?

Maybe when the eclipse comes around in a few months everyone is going to spontaneously combust, right?

Right. So how old is he?

I mash up my sticky rice and make it swim in the curry sauce.

Bess?

Don't freak out, all right?

How old is he?

He's older.

How much older?

He's nineteen, right, but he's a young nineteen, okay? And I'm an old fifteen. You know that, Henry. Don't be a dick about this.

Henry leans his heads back and his lips move like he's praying.

He says, For fuck's sake, Bess.

What?

You know what.

Of course, he tells Mum and Rory. Mum freaks out and the whole thing is so predictable. Step one: Mum shouts for a long, long time while Rory and Henry stay very quiet and occasionally nod and go 'Mmm' to punctuate Mum's points. Henry sips tea out of one of our fancy mugs. Step two: I have to stay in my bedroom until they decide what to do with me. Mum shrieks with a voice that sounds like she's about to cry, but she never actually does. Step three: I am grounded all summer and I am not to see Boy any more, not that they even know his name, but Mum did say *that boy*, which is alarmingly close to the real thing. Step four: everything goes quiet and while they all believe I'm thinking about my actions and repenting, I'm actually dry-humping the drainpipe into the front garden and sprinting towards the reservoir.

When I get to Boy's, I tell him about Henry and Mum and Rory.

They think you're a pervert, I tell him, expecting him to laugh, but he doesn't. They wanted to call the police, but Henry said there's nothing they can do when they don't even know your name.

When *I* don't even know your name, I think.

You'd better not hang around outside school, I tell him, still trying to get a rise, you're on a list.

Are you *joking*?

Course I am. Well. No. Henry did ring the school. But it's fine. It's paperwork and bullshit. I'll probably get a note on my file and that's it.

I'm underplaying it, of course. Henry said I have to have an interview with a safeguarding person at school to make sure I'm not being exploited or trafficked or anything. They'll probably try to get details about Boy out of me so they can caution him or something. Mum's all about pressing charges. I want to tell them, it's *Boy*, for fuck's sake. He's harmless. But of course, I can't.

Can I stay here for a while? I ask him.

What, like, for the night?

Like, a week?

He looks at me, and I can see already that his whole face is closing up. He folds his arms.

That's not a good idea, Bess. Stay here for a night or two. But I've got to get on with my life, you know? And so have you. You can't run away from your parents every time you have a row.

I know that, really, he's right, but it still stings. I feel like he's putting himself deliberately out of my reach, like I'm a child and he's hiding the big bad world from me because I can't take it. I realise that he knows so much more about me than I do about him, and that's what makes him so much more powerful than me. He can give affection and take it away as the wind takes him. When I try to do the same, he doesn't seem to care. I want him to draw me into him and hold me, but his arms are still folded and now he's turning away to go into the kitchen.

Running away from your parents because you don't get on with them, I say to his back. Hang on, where have I heard that before?

He tucks one of the kitchen chairs under the table, but it slams against the edge and makes a racket.

Wow, that's harsh, Bess.

I'm sorry. I'm just frustrated.

It's cool. But I can't put you up, all right? You've got to get through it.

I nod and then he pulls me into a hug, his mouth finding mine. We stand in the hallway and kiss until his hand slides down my back and back up under my shirt, then we go to his bed and have sex, then sleep all night.

When I wake up, Keris is in the garden spooning mushy green food into Zack's screeching mouth. It's warmer now. Zack is only in his nappy. The sky is still a diluted shade of blue, still not quite in full-on summer yet.

I say hey to Keris and she murmurs a greeting as she successfully deposits another spoonful of food in Zack's mouth.

Zack must be hard work, I say to Keris.

Yeah, he's worth it though, she replies. And she smiles, more to herself, not to me, like she's remembering something happy.

We sit quietly for a while. Someone a few doors down is mowing the lawn and the air is full of the smell of cut grass.

Then she says, What the hell are you doing, Bess?

She doesn't shout it, like mum or Henry does, she says it quietly and sadly, like she knows that it's a bad idea to say anything before the words are even out of her mouth.

What?

With my brother. I know he's a nice guy, but look at him. He's got no future. He works in Tesco. He can't pay his own rent. You're so young. You don't need to deal with all that shit. You're clever, right? Why aren't you focusing on getting into college and stuff? Boy said you want to make films, right? Why aren't you concentrating on that stuff instead of bumming around with him?

I look at her, a little stunned.

Keris, what the fuck?

She shrugs. I know, I know, it's none of mine. Keep my nose out, not my place to say and all that. But I'm just putting a disclaimer on it, all right. On this. This whole thing. She gestures around her with the spoon, indicating the house, the garden. The world. I can tell she thinks of me as a kid, too. For a moment I hate her for it. Some of the green goop falls from the spoon and lands on her shirt.

A few weeks later, I'm in bed watching the faces moving on the ceiling, their eyes boring into me, their little mouths contorting, and he knocks on my window. It scares the shit out of me and I have to stop myself from yelping out loud. He's crouched low on the porch roof, his limbs all gangly and wrapped around himself. He looks like a cat burglar with a brown beanie pulled low over his eyebrows. When he sees that I've seen him, he flashes this glittering kind of smile that makes me want to cry.

I skip out of bed, conscious that I haven't showered and all I'm wearing is an old Brentford football shirt and these babyish Groovy Chick knickers with holes in them and my hair is all greasy, pulled back into a ponytail. It's almost midnight and everyone's in bed. I push the window open and shush him as he climbs in, knocking the stack of CDs on my windowsill over with his foot.

What the fuck are you doing? I shout-whisper at him.

I wanted to see you.

What? Why?

I just did, all right?

And he pushes me onto the bed and I understand what he means. He wants to have sex. So we get wrapped up in my duvet and he lets me take all his clothes off and we are quiet and gentle with each other so as not to wake anyone, and it's actually quite beautiful, and my heart is singing.

And afterwards, I say to him, *Say Anything* much?

And he says, What?

And I say, Don't worry.

And after a moment of silence, I say, I thought you were going off me, anyway.

He doesn't answer immediately. He's going through my drawers. My wardrobe, my bookshelf. Pulling stuff out, amused at himself, at the things I keep in my bedroom, the things that I believe to be precious

What made you think that?

Boy. You basically told me you didn't want to hang out any more.

I never said that. When did I say that?

He's reading one of the birthday cards that my dead grand-ma Emelie left me, with their poems and little inspirational quotes and psalms. He's pulled them all out of my bedside-table drawer.

He asks me, Is it hard being in foster care?

I think about it for a moment, and tell him, It's not as hard as some other people have it. At least I've got people looking out for me. At least I've got a roof over my head.

He puts the stash of cards back in the drawer and climbs into bed with me. It's cold, but we wrap ourselves around each other and soon we're matted with sweat. When I wake up again – at three or four in the morning – he's already gone, left the window wide open. I hop out of bed, goosebumps covering my body, and pull it shut with a soft click.

I go to see Eshal. I haven't seen her in too long. I'm worried about what she'll say to me. She'll almost certainly make me feel guilty. She's so good at doing that.

Eshal's mum, Mrs Bhandari, opens the door and gives me a big hug. She insists I come into the kitchen for a biscuit before I go up to Eshal's room.

Mrs Bhandari is in her fifties but she looks much older. Her hair is almost completely grey and her knuckles are big, like doorknobs. The skin on her hands is papery thin and shiny. She always looks worn out, but she never stoops. Her back is straight and she lifts things much heavier than herself, things that you wouldn't expect her to be able to carry. She's always moving her furniture around. Eshal has inherited this secret strength from her, too.

How's revision, Bess? How's mum and dad?

All good, thanks, I say, my mouth full of chocolate digestive.

Mrs Bhandari puts the kettle on and drops two teabags into mugs.

I heard you've been up to no good, young lady. Gone a bit AWOL, I heard.

What? Where did you hear that?

Eshal tells me things.

Does she? Not everything, I hope.

You two girls are just as bad as each other.

She says it jokingly, but there's a hint of worry in her smile too. Eshal *does* tell her parents a lot, way more than I would ever dare to tell Lisa and Rory, even though she can't stand how strict they can be with her. Every time there's a big row at my house, mostly between me and Lisa, Mrs Bhandari somehow gets wind of it. It must be nice to have someone you don't have to hide things from. They're all very close. Even Anwar, who is a bellend most of the time, and obviously takes the big-brother role a bit too seriously. I hope that Esh hasn't told them everything about Boy.

You need to stick together, you two, after school, Mrs Bhandari says. When Eshal goes off to college in Basingstoke, she won't be around as much. But you're always welcome here for a chat, Bess. Even if you and Eshal aren't talking. You've always got a family here when you need it.

Her sincerity catches me off guard, and tears prickle at the corners of my eyes. I rise from the kitchen table and let her pull me into a hug.

I bring the tea up to Eshal, nervous. She's in her bedroom, splayed out across her bed in a fan of textbooks, scribbled-on pieces of paper, flash cards, Post-it notes and the rest. She looks up when I come in.

What the fuck do you want? she hisses at me.

I sit down on her bed, taking care to avoid knocking all the revision stuff onto the floor. I give her my best eyelashes, blinking rapidly.

What? she says.

Sorryyyyyyyyyyy.

You're a shithead, Bess.

Yes, I am, I reply.

You know this woman's got me in here six hours a day working on this shit? She gestures through the floor at Mrs Bhandari downstairs and then at the fan of work surrounding her. I notice an unfamiliar book under her knee.

What's that? I ask, pointing at it.

Nothing, she replies, and she quickly grabs it away from my reaching hands and shoves it under the corner of her duvet.

But I already saw the title, *Marriage Among the South Asian Diaspora: Preference and Choice.*

I need to get out, Bess. I'm so sick of revision.

I can help you, I tell her.

You could've helped me weeks ago. Where have you been? Actually, don't answer that. I already know where you've been.

Sorry, Esh.

Nah you're not. It's cool, everyone has that one guy they ditch all their friends for. At least you got it out the way early, eh?

I shrug. I think about the hundred quid I gave Boy, wonder whether it was silly, like me giving myself over to him. Wonder whether my grandmother Emelie would approve. In her birthday cards, she always leaves a note about how God is watching over me.

I ask Eshal, Do you believe in heaven?

What?

You know. God and heaven. Do you believe in them?

Of course I do, Bess. I'm Muslim.

I didn't think you took that stuff too seriously.

She looks at me, perplexed for a moment, and snorts.

What? You're always moaning about having to go to some function at the community centre. When your parents make you do Qur'an studies.

She glances up at her own Qur'an, which is wrapped in a piece of linen and stored on top of her wardrobe.

We've known each other a long time, Bess. But sometimes I feel like you go out of your way to not know me at all.

What do you mean?

My religion is a big part of my life. I know I don't follow all the rules. Like, smoking and drinking and swearing and stuff. My family is pretty lax compared to some of the people we know from Mosque and youth group. But that doesn't mean I don't have faith.

Faith in what?

She shrugs. Faith in God's plan for me, I suppose. And faith that He's looking out for me. And my family. When I'm reading the Qur'an or doing salat, I can feel God with me. I feel Him with me all the time, actually. I complain about that stuff sometimes, but I don't know what I would do without it.

Do you think your grandmother is watching you?

I don't know. Maybe. I know that I miss her, though. So much.

I say, Esh, I'm so sorry. I've been a shit friend.

Eshal says, Yeah. You have. But I'll let you off.

She flashes me a huge toothy smile and I match it.

Anyway, seeing as you haven't been around, I'm actually going to boss the Chemistry exam next week. Because of all the extra revision I've been doing.

The Chemistry exam is next week? I interrupt, and she's registering the look of panic on my face.

Oh, Bess, she says.

There's something else though. The Chemistry exam is next week, which means I have six days to revise two years' worth of science. But it also means my period is late. Like, weeks late.

That's how I end up in the Golden Grill with a white plastic stick stuck between my legs, hands covered in my own pee. And then the pub and Eshal doing her make-up and guessing it, because she knows me better than I know myself.

Chapter Eleven

After the Chemistry exam, after I've told her everything, in the Crossroads, Eshal wants me to do another pregnancy test.

Just in case, she says.

Just in case of what? I ask her. Just in case the first two were playing a hilarious joke on me? Just in case the fertilised egg fell out of my vag while I was taking a piss?

We are lying on the grass in her back garden. Mrs Bhandari is in the kitchen, so we're keeping our voices low. Through the open window, we can hear Mr Bhandari coming home from work. He pops his head out of the kitchen window and waves at us. We wave back.

You haven't told them, have you? I ask her, nodding at the open window.

She raises her eyebrows at me. Don't be ridiculous.

We listen to Mr and Mrs Bhandari talking in the kitchen, something about Anwar, who is still at uni in Glasgow finishing up his summer internship.

Pregnancy tests can be wrong, you know, she says.

I ask her why she's got that stupid look on. The corners of her mouth upturned, her lips pursed, her left eyebrow cocked. Eshal has an extremely angular face, with a pointy nose and a pointy chin, like someone pinched them and pulled them forward. She says nothing this exciting has ever happened to her.

Glad you're enjoying this, I tell her.

She rolls over and stretches lazily in the grass, ignoring me.

The Bhandaris' garden is a broad oblong shape with a water feature and a big picnic table. The grass looks like it's been spray-painted with something artificial. Eshal's dad takes a lot of pride in it, I think. Mr Bhandari has a good job in the city, something to do with finance.

My favourite thing about the Bhandaris' house is their big black and chrome winding staircase in the lobby. Everything is very modern and chic, so different from my own house. Lisa likes shagpile carpets, stripy wallpaper and plates with pictures of Princess Diana displayed in floor-to-ceiling glass cabinets.

I lean back on the grass and watch two birds chase each other across the space directly above us.

What are they? I ask Eshal. This is a routine we commonly have.

Eshal opens her eyes a fraction to watch. They're flying circles around each other, spinning upwards towards the higher branches of the sycamore tree in next-door's garden. Eshal says they are blue tits.

Bit late for them to be breeding, though, she says.

What do you mean?

Most birds are done with their breeding season by late May or early June. I'm guessing they failed; they're trying again.

Gross, I say.

Could be worse. Sparrows and swallows wait for the mother to leave the nest and then they sneak in and kill all the baby blue tits. No one really knows why they do it.

There's a knot that has formed in my abdomen. It's been tightening ever since the Golden Grill. That was a week ago now. The thought of the birds killing those chicks makes it constrict even more.

Eshal holds my wrist now, her fingernails digging into my forearm.

You know you've got to sort this out, don't you? she says, her thick eyebrows knitting together as she looks at me.

I know, I know, I know.

Well, let's sort it out, then!

I imagine all of the acid in my stomach burning through the fleshy lining and dribbling down through my muscles into my legs. That's how I feel.

We hit the pharmacy in the high street again, and Eshal has to lend me the money because I spent all mine on the last pregnancy test a week ago. We watch people walk in and out. There is a mother with twin toddlers in a double pram. I watch her pay for Calpol through the shop window. As she leaves, a man in his sixties ties a brown spaniel to the lamp post outside the pharmacy and wanders in. Eshal goes over to the lamp post and pets the dog. She lets it lick her hand and talks to it in a baby voice: *Who's a good boy? Are you a good boy?* The dog's owner exits the pharmacy and gives her a dirty look as he unties the dog and walks away.

The pharmacy is empty now. We go in and Eshal walks to the exact right spot, without having to search. She picks a box from the bottom shelf and marches to the counter. I hover behind her. The cashier is the same one who served me when I bought the first test. Her eyes dart from me to Eshal and back again. She's trying to work out whether I'm the same girl who came in last week, and if I am, whether Eshal is pregnant too or she's here on my behalf. I think I recognise her from school; she was a few years above us. I think she left when I was in Year 8. I think her name is Sheri. I know she's judging me; I can see it in her face.

The pregnancy test is in a paper bag and it crumples loudly as Eshal shoves it into her backpack. I look around guiltily again, even though I already know that we're the only customers in the shop.

When we get back to Eshal's, she makes me stash the pee stick in the waistband of my jeans and go into the toilet when her parents are looking the other way.

I sit down on the loo and stick the pregnancy test between my legs, my hand twisted so I don't end up urinating on myself like before. I'm becoming an expert. I stare at the wallpaper pattern, which is green with blue ducks. Above them is a framed photograph of Eshal and her family. It's a formal portrait, placed in front of one of those ugly watercolour backdrops. Mrs Bhandari's face, with her straight white teeth and thin lips like Eshal's, looks like it is about to stretch sideways and slide right off her skull. Esh is only eight or nine in the picture, and she is still wearing a hijab. She stopped wearing it when she started secondary school. Mr Bhandari is round-faced with silver threads of hair at his temple. He wears thick-rimmed glasses and has a long, pointed nose like Eshal's. Anwar, who is six years older than her, must be about fifteen in the picture, the age that we are now, except he looks way younger than any of the boys in my year at school, all buck-toothed and messy-haired. He has big thick eyebrows too, but unlike Eshal he hasn't tried to tame them, so they crawl across his forehead and meet in the middle.

I put the cap back on the stick and balance it on the sink while I wash my hands. I shake it a bit because that's what they do on American sitcoms. I put it back in my jeans waistband. I feel like Molly Ringwald in *For Keeps*.

I wonder why they even put a family picture in the bathroom in the first place. At home, we don't have any family photos. There's a school photo of Clarissa on the mantelpiece in the living room. And Rufus our grumpy old tabby cat who died years ago. Come to think of it, I don't think there're *any* pictures of me up at home. In the Bhandaris' house, you can't move for different iterations of Eshal and Anwar staring down at you from the walls and shelves. It's like walking through their biographies. Baby newborn Eshal with curious dark eyes and a shock of fine black hair, foreshadowing the waist-length shiny mane she has now. Buck-toothed Eshal at seven or eight and then Eshal with pink-rimmed glasses and a mouth full of metal wire at twelve. And her latest school portrait. She's aged gracefully. She gets embarrassed by how over-the-top her parents can be, but I think it's kind of cute that they're so obsessed with her.

Isn't the toilet a weird place to put a family photo? I ask Eshal as I sit down next to her.

She rolls her eyes and mutters something about her mum.

So, what does it say? Still pregnant? she asks me.

I haven't looked yet, I tell her. It's still cooking. It's in the oven.

So, you're going to get it out and flaunt it around my garden? Are you an imbecile?

I pull my waistband away and glimpse the pregnancy test.

What are you doing? Eshal asks.

I pull it out a bit further, exposing the papery bit of the applicator to the July sunshine, so I can see better. Yep, it's still there. That little pink cross of doom.

Fuck this, I say loudly to Eshal.

How about you shut up before my mother comes out here and kicks your behind, Eshal says.

The whole situation is almost laughable now, in this harmless patch of grass behind Eshal's pretty little house, on a quiet residential road in a quiet residential suburb, in a nice part of town. How could I be pregnant? Why does this stuff always happen to me? There will always be some drama to stop me going where I want to go: bad grades, unreasonable foster parents, stupid local council legislation, unplanned pregnancy.

I say to Eshal, This is the icing on the cake for a, broadly speaking, shit existence thus far.

Mr Bhandari comes out onto the patio, holding a glass of iced lemonade, asking us if we want some. He wanders over to us, tousling Eshal's hair affectionately as he crouches down on our picnic blanket. It takes him a while to get down here, all his joints and muscles telling him no. He's not a skinny man. But he does it. Mr Bhandari is young at heart.

Just so you know, Duck, we've set a date for the wedding. Anwar's wedding, that is.

Duck is the Bhandaris' pet name for Eshal, on account of her laugh as a baby, which sounded like a quack.

Eshal asks her dad when Anwar's wedding is.

Early next year. In the *desh*.

In Dhaka? *Dad*, we only just got back.

Mrs Bhandari has joined him now, with the jug of the rest of the lemonade and glasses for all of us, pulling up one of the deckchairs from the patio.

We got back in January, silly, she says. It's a lot cheaper to fly *us* home, instead of paying for all of your cousins and aunties and uncles and all of Maheera's family to fly over here for the wedding. We can make it a holiday too. You can go to the markets and get all your tapes and hoop earrings and denim skirts and what have you.

Eshal says, I'm just surprised it's even going ahead. Those two have been engaged for, what, three years? I thought after this long, it wouldn't happen.

We like Bengali weddings and long British engagements.

And the two of them clink their glasses, satisfied with

themselves, and Esh and I both laugh. I get the impression that this is something they say a lot.

Speaking of which, Mr Bhandari says, did you hear any more about that *boka* from your kickboxing class?

Who's this? I ask, intrigued.

Habib Chowdhury, Esh says. He was engaged to this girl – arranged marriage, you know, like Anwar – and a month before the wedding, he went missing. Turns out he ran away to Krakow to marry this Polish girl he met on his gap year.

Embarrassing, Mrs Bhandari says.

I think it's sweet, Eshal replies, and I agree with her.

Their love was too strong to keep them apart, I say, thinking of Boy.

Yes, and it humiliated his entire family, and the poor girl he was meant to marry too. Now none of them will talk to him. They've completely cut him off.

Mr Bhandari nods along, his brow knotted up, and the vehemence in Mrs Bhandari's voice is surprising.

Can you imagine if you or Anwar pulled something like that? Mrs Bhandari says to Eshal, kind of laughing at the absurdity of it.

Eshal laughs too, nervously, and the mood changes ever so slightly, and I can't tell whether Eshal's mum is joking. And I don't think Esh can either.

Well, it's a long way off to be worrying about all that, Eshal says, shrugging, dragging her fingers through the grass.

A long way off? Silly girl. As soon as Anwar's wedding is done, we're calling the matchmaker.

Indoors, the phone rings and Mrs Bhandari goes in to answer it. Eshal's dad isn't far behind her, moving the deckchair back to the patio and complaining that the ground is too hard for his knees.

Once they're inside, I glance over at Eshal, and there's this stricken look on her face that I've never seen before.

Engaged by next year, then? I ask her.

Well. Looks like it.

And you're all right with it?

Of course I am, she snaps. It was always going to happen. It's not like it's a big surprise to me.

I nod slowly.

I just thought, she says, pausing. I thought I would have more time. That's all.

You could ask them for some more time, I suggest.

That's not how it works, Bess.

I can tell she's in a bad mood, so I don't push the point any further. But for the rest of the time we spend in her garden, it feels as though a rainstorm is coming, even though the sky is blue and endless and full of sun.

Anyway, Esh says after a while. You need to focus on your own *situation*, remember?

My thoughts turn to the test, still in my waistband, the pink cross burning a brand onto my hip.

I let myself imagine the possibility of having a baby.

Maybe I can talk Henry into not being a totally useless case worker for once and see about getting a council flat; I knew this boy, Jonathan, who I was in respite with for a while. Respite is when they stick you in a different foster home for a while to give your foster carers a break from your difficult behaviour, or so they can go on holiday without you. Lisa and Rory sent me to respite for six weeks when Riss was born. It was a group home with a padded 'quiet room' and locks on the fridges, and all the house parents had training on how to restrain a child without being accused of sexual assault. Jonathan was a bit older than me, and he had what adults liked to call 'challenges' so he was moved around loads of different foster placements before they just gave up trying to settle him somewhere and let him live on his own in a flat. When I knew him, we were five and seven, and he's been moving from place to place, never staying more than six months, ever since. He got put into this programme for looked-after children (that's what our social workers call us) with problematic behaviour, and I think it straightened him out a bit. He stopped getting in fights and starting fires in public places. They even gave him, like, a thousand pounds so he can buy a washing machine for his flat and stuff. Maybe Henry can sort me out with one of those deals.

If I can get somewhere to live, a council flat, I can find a job doing something low-maintenance with enough money. Maybe I could work in Tesco like Boy. He seems to hate it, but at least he has money most of the time. Maybe we could move in together. Maybe he would be okay about the whole pregnant thing.

I remember that there was a day last year when he made me meet him after work and took me onto the roof of the multi-storey car park and he'd lain out a blanket and a picnic with shitty wine and cocktail sausages and a disposable barbecue and he made us melted-chocolate-bananas wrapped in chargrilled tin foil, and he let me put my head on his chest and he gently traced the outline of my lips with his fingers, the lightest of touches, while I told him about the constellations. Ursas Minor and Major, and he said quietly, after a while of just lying there, You really are something, you know that? And he kissed me long and breathless and it was so perfect.

What are you going to say to him? Eshal asks me, like she knows what I'm thinking, like always.

I can't think of an answer. The truth is, I honestly don't know. He's been so weird and distant lately. The last time I saw him was when he climbed through my window in the middle of the night. And that was weeks ago. Probably that's the time I got pregnant. He hasn't even tried to call me since. I've phoned his house more than once and Keris always picks up and tells me he's not in. The one time he *did* pick up himself, he said, Sorry, I'm busy, and hung up. Not even a hi or bye. It felt like being punched in the back of the head. So unexpectedly painful.

Is he being deliberately cruel to me? Where is he all the time? Is he seeing another girl?

Since *sorry, I'm busy,* I've stopped myself from calling him, every time I've gone to pick up the phone. Sometimes I go as far as dialling his number and listening to the first few rings before I panic and slam the receiver down. I never thought I would be that person.

I'm going to wait and see, I tell Eshal.

Wait and see for what? Wait until you're showing? Wait until you're in *labour*?

Shut up, I say to her, you're making me feel sick.

Bit too early for morning sickness, isn't it? She looks pointedly at my belly.

Shut *up*.

I knew this was going to happen, Bess. I warned you, even, didn't I? I said, *Don't fuck with a boy like him.* He's a total waste of space. I bet he's on drugs. I bet he's fucking some other poor girl. I bet he doesn't even brush the roof of his mouth when he brushes his teeth.

Just leave it, please.

We look at each other, and I can sense that she's exhausted from thinking about it, like me, and it's ruined, this perfect day, by making the things we're imagining become real. Or maybe I'm ruining it by being pregnant. Or maybe she's ruining it by being almost-engaged.

She pulls me into a tight hug, her hair tickling the bottom of my chin. Our skin sticks together, tacky from the heat.

What's happening to us, Esh? I ask her.

I don't know, she says, and when we pull away for a moment, she looks so desperate that I have to turn away.

Instead of going straight home, I go to the Pits. I cycle extra fast because if I pedal hard enough, I can't concentrate on anything else except regulating my breathing. It's kind of exhilarating. At the top of the footbridge, I lock my bike to a tree and walk down the overgrown path to the edge of the water. I sit down, dangle my feet over the edge with my shoes off, let the evening sunlight warm my shinbones. Out there, all that calm blackish water looking like glass, all those birds, the overgrown islands that populate the vastness of the lake, those thick trees with their leaves that sound like the wind, the M3 over there behind them with its dank-smelling concrete, I feel like I'm becoming embedded in this place. I don't know how to get out. I don't know how to stop my mind from cycling so fast, like full-pelt down the motorway bridge, to slow down enough to work out what to do. I feel like I'm running out of time.

When I get home, I take a too-hot shower and let the water run all over my body, leaving raw pink skin in its wake. I sit down under the shower head, in the bath, and let the water run cold. Mum will be mad that I emptied the tank. It's an old boiler so it takes ages to reheat. Clarissa starts banging on the door, wanting to get in. I wrap myself tightly in my towel, and open the door to her.

About time, she says, staring at me. Her blonde ringlets are sat on her narrow shoulders just so. I don't get how she can get her hair to do that with so little effort. She doesn't need make-up to look pretty either, because her skin is the colour and texture of milk and her eyes are so big she looks like Sailor Moon. And I am Queen Metalia, that black and purple cloud mass with slitted eyes and pointy teeth, engulfing all the good things in Sailor Moon's world and rotting them away.

I shrug and shove past her. In my bedroom, I put James Brown into my CD player – the *Black Caesar* soundtrack – and crank up the volume. I open all my windows. I spin around and around and let myself fall onto the bed, watching the ceiling spiral as though on an axis above me. Mum and Rory aren't home. It's Saturday. I vaguely remember a conversation about me being home by six to babysit Riss because they had some birthday dinner to go to. Another thing for Mum to be mad about.

I climb out of the biggest window onto the porch roof and light a cigarette as 'Down and Out in New York City' kicks in on the CD player. Over the top of the reservoir, I can see the Chubb tower. Behind me, the Pits are sparkling in the evening sunshine. A parakeet lands on the porch roof by my foot. I shoo it away.

It takes a long half-hour for the sun to sink into the woods, but there's still a pinkish glow along the horizon. I have the feeling that I'm being watched and it takes me a moment to realise it's because Clarissa is standing at my bedroom door.

I jerk my head round. What do you think you're doing in here?

She shrugs. She's wearing one of Rory's old AC/DC T-shirts, her little skinny arms poking out of it like twigs. Can I try it? she asks, gesturing to my lit cigarette.

Get out, you're ten.

I'm eleven now.

I'm eleven now, I mimic her, flipping my hair and fluttering my eyelashes.

You're actually such a cow sometimes, Bess, Clarissa says, and turns to leave. I suddenly have an overwhelming urge to tell her everything.

Hey, Riss, wait, I call after her.

What?

I'm pregnant, I think. I wonder what her reaction might be. I think she might be impressed; it's the kind of thing she would find cool and interesting, she who exclusively reads Jacqueline Wilson books, even though she's probably too old for them now, and who thinks *EastEnders* is the most dramatically gripping thing on television. Either that, or she would view me in the same way I think of Mary Beth Barrington, who will probably smoke or eat herself to death in front of daytime TV.

Nothing, fuck off, I tell her.

She mutters something back, turns to leave. I'm still sat on top of the porch. Billy is cycling down the road towards us, towards his house. Sunshine lighting his bike up like halogen. The CD player clicks and now we're listening to 'The Boss', and I say, Riss, come here a sec.

And she huffs and does, crawling through the window to join me on the porch, her skinny white legs muddy with bruises.

I say to her, lifting my sunglasses, Look, it's Billy.

So?

He's looking up at us. He waves.

I shout at him, WHAT, BILLY?

And I see his face blossoming red, from all the way up here. He wasn't expecting a response.

And then Riss, getting it, goes, ARE YOU SPYING ON US, BILLY? YOU'RE SO CREEPY.

SOOOOO CREEPY, I agree with her, and she laughs.

BILLY, IF YOU WANT TO ASK ME OUT, YOU SHOULD JUST SAY SO, Riss yells, even louder. Across the road, one of our neighbours has popped his head over the fence to watch us. Billy slows to a stop at the front of our house, dismounts his bike and wheels it up the garden path of his next-door, not looking at us.

After Riss is gone, I climb back through the window and into bed. I fall asleep imagining that my head is in the crook of Boy's arm and that he is falling asleep beside me, and that there is no seed embedded in the lining of my womb, slowly beginning to germinate.

Chapter Twelve

Mum keeps looking at me funny, like she knows something's going on. Every time I sit down to watch TV or to eat a meal, she casts sideways glances at me, like she's waiting for me to spontaneously combust, her thin hair drawn back tight, stretching her face across her cheekbones.

She says, You're round the house a lot more these days, and I nod and shrug and try not to make eye contact with her.

In the evenings, I watch the six o'clock news with Rory and Clarissa. I try to ignore the silence that clogs the air between us. I ask Rory questions about Iraq, even though I already know he won't answer. He takes long seconds to speak and when he does, he gives one- or two-word responses. Sometimes we watch *The Simpsons* afterwards. No one says a word to Mum. I try hard, but I can't bring myself to care enough about it, this thing that is happening between us, where she has at least a mild distaste for everything I do.

It didn't used to be like this. She used to treat me more like she does Clarissa, like her kid. But things have been changing for a long time – years, even – without me realising. She seems very far away to me. Maybe the novelty of fostering has finally worn off. When she talks, I can't hear her over all of the buzzing in my own head. Her thoughts don't seem as real or as acutely painful as mine are. I can't imagine her feeling things the way I feel them, with the same intensity, with the same kind of taste of illness in my mouth and the bad feeling wriggling around my belly like a tapeworm. I feel as though we're trying to communicate underwater. You know when people say, That's it? Like, that's it, I've had enough, I've had it. I've always wondered what 'it' actually is. I think she's finally sick of me. I think the list of things she doesn't like about me has been growing and growing and now it's at capacity. I think I've done 'it' for her.

Eshal and I are no closer to getting a resolution for my predicament, and every minute we stall, I think I can *feel* the thing inside me growing and moving.

I know that's impossible. It's probably a kidney bean or something right now. But that's not to say it won't get bigger soon. I haven't been to a doctor; I don't even know how many *weeks* I am. I know you can only get an abortion up to twenty-four weeks; we learned about it in Biology. We watched this super-graphic video of a woman giving birth. She actually let a camera crew come in and film her squeezing it out. It's so gross. I don't understand how a whole human being can come out of that tiny little opening between your legs. I have what mean girls in gym changing rooms like to call 'childbearing hips'. At the end of the childbirth video, the bit of skin between the woman's bum and her vag split open, and all this blood gushed out. The baby was all slimy and grey-looking. Not pink like everyone says, *grey*. It came out so fast that the midwife had to make a dash to catch it as it slipped its way out of there. The dad was there too with a surgical cap on, and when he held the baby, he cried. This pale girl called Amy in my class fainted and smacked her head on the radiator as she went down and Mrs Franks had to call an ambulance.

I sneak out and cycle to Boy's house. I think again of him

wrapped up in my duvet, the last time I saw him, his legs all tangled up with mine, and that feeling – remembering how special it was before – it's like a penny dissolving in stomach acid. I don't know if it's even cool to turn up at his house unannounced, even though I've done it a million times before. But I can sense that things have changed between us. *Sorry, I'm busy.* Dial tone. I feel like something terrible is going to happen and there's no way for me to stop it because I don't know when to expect it or even what it is. I breathe in metallic summer air and watch the long dusty grass comb itself with the wind through the wire-mesh fence. I look up and watch the moorhens dithering on the breeze, heading towards the river, their little wings flapping violently against the upthrust, and I am slowing to a stop, pulling up onto the pavement, and inside I feel this overwhelming sense of dread.

When I knock, he opens the door.

Jeez, about time, stranger, I say to him, trying for casual and unfazed, but my voice comes out as this stupid pipsqueak noise. He is scruffy, in a crumpled dark grey T-shirt and loose jeans hanging below his waist, with no belt. His hair is still buzz-cut short. It's strangely comforting to see him like this, like nothing has changed. I don't know what I was expecting, really.

I push past him into the hallway, not looking at him because I'm afraid of what I might see in his face. I think, If I can just act like nothing has changed, maybe that will make things normal between us.

He seems to be playing along.

Want a drink? he asks, closing the door behind him and following me into the kitchen. Zack's pram is not in its usual place by the back door, so I guess Keris has taken him out somewhere. We're alone. The kitchen is in its usual state of disarray, with the worktop dirtied with splashes of milk, cereal, dry pasta pieces, breadcrumbs and used cutlery. On the square wooden table, there is a stack of opened envelopes and a half-eaten bowl of tomato pasta. On the fridge, the alphabet magnets have been rearranged to spell:

BABY ZACK

MVMMY

B4BY B0Y

Why are you Baby Boy, not just Boy? I ask him.

I don't know, he says, distracted. Did you want a drink, or no?

He wanders over to me and opens the fridge, takes out a Tesco own-brand bottle of fizzy orange from the shelf on the door and offers it to me.

No thank you, I say, imagining how ugly I'll look drinking in front of him.

I go to the back door and head out into the garden. I sit on one of the plastic garden chairs. I listen to him pottering about in the kitchen, opening and closing cupboards, washing his hands, pouring the drink into a glass. He's stalling.

One of Zack's toy trains is half-buried in the long grass beyond the patio. I pick it up and wipe the dew onto the lap of my jeans.

Boy wanders out and pulls another plastic chair from under the table. There is water in its seat, so he tips the chair forward and lets it run off onto the concrete.

What's up?

Not much, I reply, thinking I'm pregnant, I'm pregnant, I'm pregnant. Any false move, I think, and he'll see me for what I am. A little girl, really, just a kid, with a slight lisp, damp skin, the return of acne on my shoulders, another human growing inside me.

He offers me a cigarette from a crumpled packet he takes from his back pocket. I let him light it for me and it feels romantic. I watch him as I smoke, determined not to be the first to initiate a conversation. He is looking absent-mindedly at a spot beyond me, above next-door's garden. Maybe he's watching the birds. I don't want to turn around and check what he's looking at because that might seem offensive, like I'm suggesting he should be looking at me. I guess he *should* be looking at me; we are having a conversation after all. Or trying to. I wonder how Eshal would behave if she was in this situation. She would probably flick him between the eyebrows and go, Oi, dipshit, I'm over here, don't be rude. After a silence that becomes more and more embarrassing as it gets longer, I give up.

What have you been up to? I ask him, feeling like a child.

Not much.

I called you a few times, I say.

I try to underplay the enormity of my desperation. The countless times I picked up the house phone and dialled his number, the times when I was halfway to his house on my bike before forcing myself to turn around.

He rubs again at his stubbly head. As he does, I change my mind about how it makes him look. I used to think short hair made him look more dangerous, but I've realised that it's not dangerous at all; it's alien.

What would you do if I was pregnant? I ask him in my head.

He glances up at me suddenly like he actually heard me, like I said it out loud.

You're being weird, he says to me.

Erm, no. *You're* being weird, I reply, aware of how I sound. I haven't heard from you in ages.

He shrugs, I'm not obligated to keep in touch with you.

What?

He doesn't look at me, and shrugs again.

I think about it for a moment, picking out the words I want to say carefully. Each silence between us stretches out longer than the one preceding it. The green paint on the door to his kitchen is peeling away at the bottom, exposing the damp, mildewed wood beneath it.

I think about what Eshal said, about not letting a boy ever know you until you know yourself.

I say, Whatever's going on between us, Boy, you're still a shit friend.

He finally looks at me. I try to stop my eyes from watering.

He says, What do you mean, whatever's going on between us?

You *know* what, I say, and my voice has stopped with its high-pitched shrillness. I feel angry. And he's looking at me now. And that makes me even madder. Don't fucking pretend you don't know, I tell him, gesturing vaguely at the air between us, at the concrete slabs that make up the patio.

What is going on here? he asks.

I pick at a scab on the second knuckle of my left index finger.

You know what, I say again. And by the look on his face, it's obvious he knows. He is far away, though. I want him to remember the gentleness with which he made little plaits in my hair, running his fingers through them until they unravelled in his hands. The way he touched quiet parts of my body – the backs of my knees, my earlobes, my ankles. When we climbed a tree at the Pits and got stoned in the branches, laying on top of each other, our limbs all tangled up together, and he told me he could feel my heartbeat through his belly, the way I pressed my head against it.

I want to tell him how at night I close my eyes and imagine him sleeping next to me, snoring lightly with one arm draped across my body, and his presence puts us both in a little bubble where no one can reach us. I imagine that he is watching me from above and through mirrors wherever I go, that he is always thinking about me when I think about him, that when I look at the moon at night, he looks at it too and he knows that we are both looking at the same thing. I want to tell him how I know he can hear my thoughts. But it's all wrong.

I stand up to leave.

He tells me to wait and stands up with me. He holds out his hands to me. I look at him, and at the garden, the fence panelling which is rotting like the green door.

I step forward and let him pull me into a hug. I breathe in the smell of shaving cream on his face and stale cigarette smoke embedded into the fibres of his clothes.

I'm sorry, he says, his voice tickling my ear because his mouth is so close to it.

It's fine, I say, it's fine.

I leave because I don't want to annoy him by being there too long, though he has that look on his face that means he wants to have sex. I know what will happen after: he'll turn to face away from me until I gather my things up and leave, making the effort to click the front door shut quietly even though no one is sleeping. I wonder whether he's just been having a bad few weeks and this deep sensation of shame filling me up to the brim, the feeling that he can't bear to look at me, is in my imagination. The way he touched me at the end was intimate.

As I cycle back towards Shepperton, I spot Keris in the Ford Sierra driving towards the house. It looks like someone has reversed into the front of the car, or maybe Boy or Keris hit something, because the bumper is all crumpled up like a piece of tin foil, and the left headlight is hanging out of its socket. She spots me and I wave at her. She doesn't wave back, just flashes me a tight smile before returning her attention to the road.

I keep going, past the farmers' fields and the reservoir and Stage H.

I stop at the top of the road and touch my belly. I wonder if it's got fatter or I'm just imagining it. I cycle to Eshal's.

She opens the door and she is wearing her hijab, something I haven't seen her wear except in old pictures and when she goes to visit her uncle in Walthamstow. She's not wearing any make-up, either. She looks unfamiliar without it, and with none of her hair showing.

What's going on? I ask her.

We're going to see a friend of my mum's. A matchmaker.

A what?

She looks exhausted.

Can you go, Bess? We're about to leave.

I stare at her, not sure what to say. We're still standing at her door. Mrs Bhandari comes into the hallway holding her handbag.

You ready, Duck? she asks, and then noticing me, Hello, Bess, darling.

Hi, Mrs Bhandari. You're going to see the matchmaker?

Isn't it exciting! My little girl, finding a husband.

And she comes up behind Eshal and squeezes her shoulders, and Eshal turns around and smiles up at her mum, this big fake smile that doesn't reach her eyes.

I'll be two minutes, she tells her, and Mrs Bhandari goes back into the house.

You haven't told her you don't want this, I say. Not a question but a statement.

I *do* want it.

You might be able to lie to your mum, but you can't lie to me. I can see it in your face.

Don't start, Bess.

Why are you shutting me out like this?

Because I know what you'll say. I know what you'll do. You've got this habit of whitewashing things, you know?

What the fuck is that supposed to mean?

She goes to say something but seems to change her mind.

Just shut up about my shit and focus on your own, okay?

She extends an index finger and jabs me, hard, in the soft pudge of my stomach. Dumb, I look down at the spot where her finger connected, just above my belly button. It is an aftertaste kind of pain, the kind you feel when you apply pressure to a bruise.

Last year, before I met Boy, me and Esh got invited to this party at some kid from Esh's cross-country club's house. It was our first ever party – like, proper party with alcohol and people getting fingered on the trampoline and stuff. Esh didn't want to go, but I was desperate. I made her lie to her parents about visiting her cousin for the weekend, and then she came to mine and we got ready together. We shared a bottle of vodka mixed with flat Coke on the bus – except I drank three quarters of it. Then, when we got there, the party was shit. No one talked to us. Turned out the boy whose party it was, Christopher, was expecting to shag Eshal, and she wasn't interested. So, she spent the majority of the night helping me throw up in the bathtub and politely telling Christopher to fuck off in fifty different ways. And then, when we got home, Lisa and Rory thought she'd got me drunk, thought it had all been her idea, so Mum rang Mr and Mrs Bhandari and spilled the beans, and she got grounded for the whole summer and wasn't allowed to go to this kickboxing camp that she was really excited about. It was all my fault.

Fine, I say.

She shuts the door without saying anything else. I stand there for a moment staring at it, so close that my nose and my waist are almost touching it. Mum always tells me that my posture is bad, I stick my belly out and slouch my shoulders. Through the frosted glass of the door, I see the shape of Mrs Bhandari moving back and forth, her silhouette visible against the light coming through the kitchen. I turn away and wheel my bike out of the driveway.

I cycle around aimlessly for a while, stopping at high points like the M3 motorway bridge to watch the landscape below, the farmers' fields that were once orchards before the First World War, before the soil went bad and no one could grow anything there apart from long reedy grass. Now there are a few old cob horses grazing lazily, each one wearing a sheet-like jacket across their backs, their tails swishing to keep the horseflies away. Further than the fields, beyond the reservoir, is Heathrow Airport and the Chubb tower in Sunbury, black against the orange of the sky. It's almost dusk. This day feels like it's gone on forever.

I cycle back towards the Studios but don't turn down my road. I go towards the Pits, over the motorway bridge and past the church. I pump the pedals through the overgrown footpath, with tree roots sticking out of the hard soil. At the top of the bridge, I lean over the wall and watch the sun go down, turning the black water orange.

The railings are cold against the soft palms of my hands. My face feels itchy in the gentle breeze. I lift my hands up to scratch both cheeks. Down below, in the water, I can see a mildewed shopping trolley, its limbs poking out like a skeleton. I have a sudden urge to throw up.

I think, *I need to get out of here.* Not just the Pits. Not just Shepperton. Like, I need to be *rid* of this place and everything about it. I don't just need to be out, I need to be *away.* But now, there's a thing growing inside me, and it's going to tie me to this place forever.

I think, *I need to get it out of me.*

I need to get it out of me. Sooner rather than later. I look around me, as though an answer might appear out of the trees. A doctor might saunter up the bridge to meet me, a spoon in each hand, ready to scoop the foetal matter out of my womb and into the water. Then I wouldn't feel so heavy, as though my abdomen is weighing me down like an anchor. I would feel light, like a bubble, and I would float up, up, up into the atmosphere until the air becomes too thin to sustain me and I would pop, and tiny droplets of me would sprinkle down towards the M3. A light shower.

I need to get it out of me. I need to kill it.

I prop my bike up against the wall and climb over to the other side of the railings, sit on the ledge.

I look down to the water. It's about twenty feet below me. I place my right hand on the metal railing, coated with flaking plasticky black paint. The steel is cold. As I lift my hand away, I see that little flakes of the paint have stuck to my palm because it's sticky with sweat.

Maybe if I hit the water really hard, belly-flop style. Maybe that'll do it.

I look down.

Maybe I can do it like this.

Easy.

I lean back on my heels and propel myself forward.

I feel the pit of my stomach drop. Like there is a hook in my navel that has just been yanked upward, like that feeling you get when the car drives too fast over the hump in a bridge. The black stains against light concrete, the long angular shadows cast by the bridge, the darkening trees, the skeleton in the water, they are all a blur.

I panic. Let out an awful, embarrassing, garbled screeching noise.

And then I am in the water, and it's up my nose and in my armpits and soaking into my shoes and my clothes. And I hurt all over. I feel so stupid. I propel down, down, down before my body slows and I stop sinking. I swim long strokes to the surface and break free into the night air, my teeth chattering, the rank smell of Pits water all around me. I grab onto the trolley to keep myself afloat. A weird whimpering noise is coming from me.

I wait a moment for the ripples around me to settle a bit. And then I drag myself, my clothes leaden, over to the side of the lake. I crawl up onto the bank, the soil sticking to my hands and my knees, the smell of pine needles in my nostrils. The M3 roars with traffic.

I scream again, my eyes burning, hit myself on both sides of my head twice. How could I be so stupid? How could I let someone do this to me? Let *Boy* do this to me? I want to cry, but I don't deserve to. I don't want to give myself the satisfaction. I can almost hear Mum going, It's your own fault, Bess, your own fault for being so careless. *Should've known you had it in you.* I warned you. But you're too clever to listen.

But she's not here, and nor is Boy, and nor is anyone. Just me and the black water, and the foetus.

And my thoughts are as follows: That's it. I've had it. I'm getting rid of it.

Chapter Thirteen

A few days after the Pits, Eshal and I sit on the riverbank and pull fistfuls of grass up from the ground and sprinkle it into the water below us, watching the colour of the blades darken as they become saturated with water.

How was your engagement party? I ask her, only half-joking.

How's your pregnancy?

I kick her in the shin.

But really . . . what's going on? You and I both know you don't want an arranged marriage.

I *do* want to get married, Bess. I want to do this. It's important to me, and you need to understand that. I just thought . . . I don't know. I thought it was a long way off. I didn't really believe it was going to happen until it actually started happening, you know? And I kind of had this idea – I don't know, it's silly – I thought maybe I would meet someone first, someone who *I* liked, and who my parents liked, and I wouldn't have to have a matchmaker at all.

Someone like Daniel Tyler, you mean?

Don't be ridiculous.

You're not being honest with yourself. Or with your parents.

How can I be honest with them?

I raise my eyebrows at her. She frowns and shakes her head,

trying to dispel a bad memory, and flops back on the grass, exasperated.

My parents have done everything for me. *Everything.* When they came here from Bangladesh, they had nothing. Even though they were educated, came from good families, four languages between them, no one would give them a chance. That's *multiculturalism* for you. That's *integration.* My dad has a master's from the University of Rajshahi; he graduated top of his class. And when he came to the UK, he couldn't get a job for the first year. No one would hire him because he was foreign. The number of interviews he turned up to where they thought he was the tea boy, or the post boy, or they wouldn't let him past the receptionist. He legally changed his name from Pradeep to Richard when I was four. How messed up is that?

And my mum, back home, she was a typist. But when she came here, she never could get a job. *Ever.* She's never worked in this country. No one ever gave her a chance. All my dad wanted to do was go home and try again in the *desh*, but my mum wanted to stay, wanted to raise their kids here. So, he put up with it and he worked twice as hard for half as much, to give us the life he felt we deserved. Him and my mum, they're the most inspiring people I know. That's why I study so hard, right? Why I don't mind them pushing me to work harder. To be better. Because we know what happens when you're an immigrant. It's what happened to my parents. They're doing all right now, but trust me, Bess, it took years, and knockbacks, one after the other, for them to get remotely close to comfortable in this country. And I can't do this one thing for them, when I know it means so much to them, and it's really the only thing they'll ever ask me to do apart from get an education? It's selfish. It's like I'm taking all of their hard work, all their sacrifices, all the racist bullshit they've had to put up with, and I'm throwing it back in their faces. It's like I'm saying, *Fuck you and fuck Bangladesh.* Can you imagine? They'll disown me, excommunicate me, like Habib's parents did when he broke off his engagement.

They would never do that. They *love* you, Eshal.

You heard my mum say it to my face, even. I wouldn't blame them for it, either. It doesn't matter. This is just the way it has to be.

I wait for her to say more but she doesn't. And when the silence between us is too much, I say, lamely, I'm sorry, I didn't know that stuff about your mum and dad. How hard they had it.

Well, you never asked, did you?

I'm embarrassed that I never did.

Well . . . now you know.

Yeah.

And now you understand why I have to go through with the engagement.

Oh, Esh.

I want to say more, but I know I shouldn't. Can't possibly feel the enormity of what is on Eshal's shoulders, a responsibility the weight of generations of the Bhandari family. The history of it. The obligation she feels towards them is something I'll never feel myself towards my own family.

But . . . we're not here to talk about my problems, Eshal says after a pause.

I give her a sheepish look.

Turns out Eshal has been in the library at Walton. She chose Walton Library because it has internet computers installed and Shepperton Library doesn't. Also, less chance of detection the further away from Shepperton you go. She's been doing some reading and looking on the web for some information. Information about pregnancy.

There are a few options available, she tells me. Most of them involve having to tell your parents.

Nope, I cut her off. That's not going to happen. Not even remotely. Not a chance in hell.

Have you actually thought about what you want to do? Like, are you actually going to *have* it? Or are you – you know – going to . . .

Get rid of it? I finish for her.

Well. Yeah.

I lean back and stretch my neck out so I'm staring straight up at the big blue sky.

I haven't told Eshal about cycling to the Pits and jumping in the water. It's embarrassing. All of my resolve from that night is gone in the daylight, and suddenly, looking up into the sunlight, I'm less certain again. I can't believe this is happening to me. I can't bear it.

Have you ever thought about what it would be like to go into space? I ask Eshal.

Don't change the subject, Bess.

If someone gave you the chance to be an astronaut, would you do it?

I don't know. Listen to me.

Eshal talks about doctors and clinics. There is an impartial advice service that you can ring up on a Freephone and they let you know what your options are. Options, options, options. Like choosing which panini to have from the cafeteria. Like deciding whether to wear the red or the black shoes to the party. God.

I think about Boy saying I would never be an astronaut. It's true. I won't be. I looked it up on Careers Day. You have to have twenty-twenty vision and be extremely physically fit. I have glasses for reading and, well, I'm not exactly Denise Lewis, either.

Do you want to have a baby? she asks me.

My stomach feels like it is twisting tighter and tighter, like water being wrung out from a wet flannel. I think about jumping off the bridge. I think about what my future will look like if I have a baby now.

I wouldn't be able to go to uni, or even college. I'd never be able to make films. No one is going to employ an uneducated teenage mum. I would be a walking statistic. Another example of why foster kids are such catastrophic failures. Which I am, no doubt about that. But it's not because of *me*. It's not *my fault*. I could be happy and functional if only I had people who *belonged* to me, and I belonged to them. Like Eshal and her family.

I would be broke forever with a baby. I would never be able to afford to move away. I'd be stuck on benefits, like Mary Beth Barrington – like Keris, even – not working, not getting educated, not going places.

I'll probably have to stay in Shepperton with Lisa and Rory for a long time. She wouldn't be in charge of only me, she'd be in charge of the baby, too.

I think about what Boy would say. He would never forgive me for doing this to him.

Well? Eshal asks me. Do you want it or not?

No, I say. There's no way I'm keeping it.

Well, then, she says. If that's your decision, we need to get cracking.

She starts talking about adoption services.

No way, I say. I'm not putting it into a system.

I think of being four years old and being taken to live with Lisa for the first time, driven to an unfamiliar house by an unfamiliar person and being left there with a stranger who made me call her Mummy. Scared to sleep in case Cruella de Vil from the

Disney movie came to get me, too scared to let Lisa wash me in the bath in case she drowned me.

I stand up and then sit down again. I need to get an abortion, I tell Eshal. I feel as though if I look her in the face I'm going to cry, so instead I look at the grass, pluck out a daisy, pinch the stem until it's pulverised between the pads of my finger and thumb.

She doesn't say anything, and I can tell she's waiting for me to say something else. It's cooler now, as the sun is dipping behind the trees on the opposite bank. There are kids on the island, on the other side of the river, swinging on a tyre tied to an overhanging tree branch and launching themselves into the murky water below, completely oblivious to their own self-preservation.

There's a clinic in Brixton, Esh says. That's the closest one to us. I worked out the train journey. But you have to go to the doctor's and get it signed off.

If I go to the doctor's, will they tell Lisa and Rory? Social services?

I don't know, Bess.

I look at her, thinking maybe she's being deliberately patronising with her tone, but I see my own desperate expression staring back at me.

According to this website I saw, there are certain herbal medicines you can use which supposedly force you to have a miscarriage. We could try that. Or we could do it the old-fashioned way.

What's the old-fashioned way? I ask, kicking my feet against the concrete.

Well. Coat hanger in the bath, right? That's what they used to do in Victorian times.

As *if* they did that!

They did. On my life. It was on the website I was reading.

And what if the website told you to walk in front of a bus, Esh?

Shut up. If you're serious about this, we need to find a way to get the medicine that we need and try it that way first. I'm going to Holland & Barrett on the weekend . . .

God, they're hardly going to sell abortion pills in Holland & Barrett!

Well, I don't know, do I!

I make this exaggerated exasperated noise at her and lie down on the grass, staring up at the sky. We sit in silence, pissed off at each other, but neither of us willing to leave. After a while, she slips her hand into mine and we sit there like that, together, until the sun goes down and the first stars begin to emerge.

On my way home, halfway towards the Crossroads, I spot Hannah Barrington walking out of the Mango Café with a guy. For a split second, I think the guy she's with is Boy, and my body goes heavy, and suddenly everything is momentarily sharper, like I am taking everything in more acutely than I ever have before, and I'm replaying frame-for-frame, shot-for-shot, the last conversation we had, in his garden, *don't fucking pretend you don't know*, except I'm some sort of Jennifer Connelly lookalike and I'm saying it with much more conviction, and he's desperately sorry for ever upsetting me, and then I realise that the boy with Hannah is a couple of inches too short. And Boy would never wear a puffer jacket.

Hannah spots me too and I become tense, ready to throw something back at whatever spiteful thing she is going to shout at me. But instead she just waves.

Sometimes I wonder if I died, how long it would take for him to realise I was missing and try to get in touch with my parents or

Eshal to find out where I'd gone. Would he come to my funeral? There's something satisfying about picturing your own grue-some death and imagining how devastated everyone you know would be.

I would fucking *haunt* him.

When I get home, I call Eshal.

I want to do it, I say to her.

Do what?

I'm in my bedroom, but I lower my voice anyway: I want to do the abortion. The old-fashioned way. Whatever you read on that website, I want to do that. No clinics. No social services or parents. Just us.

I believe the correct grammar is to *have* an abortion, Bessie.

Just, shut up and tell me what I need to do.

Well, I really don't fancy sticking a coat hanger or a crochet hook up your foo foo, Eshal says, and her words make my belly button tug at my stomach like I've just missed a step on the stairs. And I'm still for a moment, listening to the static on the phone, her soft breathing, the way my own heart is thundering away in my ears.

And I say quietly, Well. What then?

Supposedly it's quite effective if you just take a super-hot bath and drink a bottle of gin.

And where did you read this?

On the World Wide Web.

You know anyone can write any old shit on the internet, right?

There's plenty of other ways to do it, you know. I could punch and kick you in the stomach repeatedly. Or you can ask Boy to run you over in his car. Or you can douche yourself with bleach. That tends to get you into hospital, though.

Let's do the bath thing.
Good idea.
I trust her completely.

Chapter Fourteen

Esh calls me again and asks me to come over to her house. Her parents are out visiting relatives all day and Anwar's gone out with some of his uni mates. When I get there, the kitchen is empty. The quiet is unnerving. Eshal sits me down at the table. She places a tray with different compartments in front of me, and each compartment is filled with a different foodstuff.

Here's one I made earlier, she jokes, posing with the tray like the guy from *Art Attack!*

Some of the food is easily recognisable, like the sesame seeds and ginger. But there are others that look and smell unfamiliar.

What's all this? I ask her.

She meticulously details the properties of each type of food to me, and explains how each one can induce a miscarriage.

The orange stuff is carrot seed soup. There are also papaya and parsley leaves there too.

It's mostly about Vitamin C, Eshal tells me. Vitamin C causes the uterus to contract and the cervix to dilate. Or the other way around. The cervix contracts and the uterus dilates. I can't remember. But, basically, stuff with Vitamin C induces miscarriage.

She places a small pill bottle in front of me. I pick it up and check the label. Vitamin C pills.

Take all of them, she says.

Are you sure about all of this? I ask her.

Of course not, numbnuts. The only way to be sure is to go to a clinic and get it done properly. But you're not willing to do that because you'll probably have to tell Rory and Lisa. So, this is the next best thing we have.

She sits in silence opposite me, picking at her nails, and I realise that she has big dark shadows pitted under her eyes. If I look closely enough, I can see the hollow eye sockets of her skull defined in the shadows of her skin. She looks exhausted and I suddenly realise how horribly ungrateful I have been. I steadily make my way through the food she has prepared for me. She closes her eyes and says something quiet under her breath, so fast it's almost as though she didn't do it at all. She's praying.

Do you feel anything yet? she asks me as I finish the last spoonful of soup. It has an unpleasant nasal taste to it, like celery.

I shake my head no.

How long is it supposed to take? I ask her.

I have no idea.

I feel full from all the food. My belly protrudes like there's something stuffed under my dress. I look pregnant.

Eshal sits down opposite me again – she has been fussing in the kitchen and nervously pacing while I've been eating – and touches each of her fingers together, one by one.

I suppose I should run you a bath, she says.

And you've got gin? I ask her.

Yes.

She looks worried.

This is the last time I'll pay for you to get pissed, she says, half-joking.

Mate, I owe you several nights out after this, I say, trying to match her tone, but the tremor in my voice makes me sound like

I'm going to cry. Despite it, I feel calm. It almost feels as though this isn't happening to me, like I'm watching it happen to someone else and therefore I don't have to be emotionally invested. My voice seems very far away from me as I speak, like it doesn't belong to me. Eshal makes sudden, darting movements like she is a trapped bird.

She sits me in her bedroom while she runs the bath. I pass the time by leafing absent-mindedly through the pages of one of the books on her desk. We still have a few hours before her parents and Anwar get back. It is a science textbook, and each page is laden with beautiful and intricate diagrams of the anatomies of birds. I choose a page at random and come upon an illustration of a sparrowhawk, cross-sectioned and meticulously labelled in an antiquated script. *Accipter nisus.* The pages are thick and heavy. I run my fingers along the grooves in the paper. One passage discusses the sparrowhawk's talons and how they have been developed to become effective tools for snatching prey from the ground. On the next page, there is an osprey. I flick through a few more pages and realise that all the birds in the book are predators.

Eshal comes back into her bedroom.

I stand up slowly, the palms of my hands flat on my thighs.

Did you bring a change of clothes? A swimming costume?

I shake my head no.

Eshal pulls open one of her drawers and takes out a baggy T-shirt with a picture of a dolphin. Put this on if you want.

It's weird that, considering how much Eshal knows about me and what we're about to do, I'm shy about changing in front of her. She senses this and steps out of the room, closing the door. I take off my dress, and pull the T-shirt over my head, leaving my knickers on but taking my bra off. I leave them in a messy pile on the bed. Eshal's bed sheets are patterned with tiny starfish and seahorses. I look in the mirror and draw my hair back into a ponytail. My cheeks are flushed. My legs are soft and pale, with a web of faint veins visible through the skin on my thighs, a fuzz of three-day-old shaving stubble. My toes, with chipped blue nail polish, are curled under my feet, as though they're cringing.

I open Eshal's door and wander across the hallway, the magnolia carpet scratching against the pads of my heels, into the bathroom. Eshal is sitting on the toilet with the lid down, her legs tucked under her. She is leafing through a stapled wad of photocopied paper. The bath is running, and steam vapour rises from the gushing water. The bathroom is already a few degrees hotter than the rest of the house. It seems unnatural, considering how hot it is outside, and how everyone has been taking cold showers through the heatwave. I feel my heart rate go up.

Are you ready? Eshal asks me.

I say, I suppose so, quickly, before I have time to think about it and change my mind.

I lift one leg over the side of the white bath and dip my foot into the water.

Shit, it's hot! I say.

Well, that's kind of the point.

I lower my body into the water, gasping at the heat as it envelopes me. The temperature is scorching. I struggle for breath.

You'll get used to it in a minute, Eshal says with confidence, but her face looks worried.

It hurts, I say. I lift an arm out of the water and show her the angry pink colour my skin has turned from the elbow down, a sharp line showing the contrast between the skin that has been in the water and the skin that hasn't. It looks like I've been sunburned and now I have terrible tan lines. Eshal relents and turns the cold tap a fraction to the left. I'm still panting. There are white spots behind my eyes.

Can you turn the lights off? I ask Eshal, aware that the fluorescent bulb is causing my head to pound. Eshal pulls the light cord, and drags the blackout blind down over the small frosted window above the toilet too. She takes the bottle of Gordon's gin off the windowsill. The glass clinks against the tiles. She unscrews the lid and hands me the bottle. As I take a swig, she turns the water off. I take three gulps of the gin, and cough as it stings its way down my throat.

I hand the bottle back to Eshal. She sits back down on the toilet, picking up her papers again and examining them.

You need to take another drink in five minutes, she tells me, not looking at me.

The dolphin T-shirt is clinging to my skin, the top half of it, which is wet but not submerged in the water, already turning cold.

My skin feels like it is covered in tiny blisters. Eshal looks worried.

What? I ask her. She doesn't answer.

I twist around in the bath, every movement feeling like someone is sticking needles in my skin, and watch the clock. After five minutes, Eshal picks up the bottle and hands it to me. I take another swig. Its passage is made real by how it burns its way down my throat. I wonder what kind of damage this is all going to do to my body. Hopefully enough to eject a foetus from my womb, I think to myself, and I'm surprised by my own callousness. But that is what we're here for, after all.

We wait some more. The water is marginally cooler than it was. Slightly more bearable. After the third time Eshal hands me the gin bottle, I start to feel woozy. I stare at my legs, which are distorted underneath the bathwater. They look wobbly, the edges of my skin rippling against the white porcelain.

I spy some mould on the edge of the bath, where it joins with the tiles on the wall.

Have you got some mould remover? I ask Eshal.

She has been watching the clock and flinches as I speak, cutting through the suspended silence of the bathroom. My voice bounces off the white tiles.

What?

Mould, I say, pointing to the black spots on the sealant.

I can hear my voice rising and lowering without any real cause for it to do so. I'm slurring my words.

I think I'm getting drunk, I say out loud. Eshal watches me.

Fifth, sixth, seventh swig from the bottle. It's been almost an hour. The gin is one-third gone. Eshal keeps letting a little water out of the bath and pouring more in, scalding, from the tap. The cord for the light switch is swinging back and forth methodically even though there is no wind and no one has touched it. At the end of the cord is a little ceramic mermaid, green and purple. She's not wearing a bra.

That's a bit rude, I say.

What? Eshal says again. I don't answer.

I want to lie back and go to sleep in the bath. I inch forward a little so I can get into a more horizontal position, but I slip and lose my grip on the sides of the tub. The bath mat shifts, and I fall backwards, and the hot water slops up to my shoulder blades and I gasp at the pain. Something hard hits the back of my head. I think it's the tap.

Fuck, Bess, are you okay?

I'm fine, I say, struggling to focus on her face. It's very important that I show her that I'm fine. I'm fine, I'm fine, I'm fine.

Bess?

I touch my hand to the back of my head and bring it to my face. There's a small amount of shiny blood on my fingertips. At least I think it's blood. Everything is swimming. It could just be a pink patch of skin.

Eshal is talking about stopping and getting me out the bath. My skin is raw. She is talking frantically. Maybe we should go to A and E.

No no no no don't stop no.

Eshal looks frightened: Bess, you can't see yourself. You're not well.

I point at my stomach. Prod it with my fingernails. One fingernail at a time.

It's not done, I say. I can feel it. We need to get it out.

I have been shouting.

I remember when we were both twelve and we found an injured starling on the side of the road near my house. I got a shoebox and Eshal ushered the bird in, and we poked air holes in it and stuffed the box with tissue paper. My mum cut up an apple and we put that in there too. It hopped around frantically and made tiny but rapid movements; it had injured its wing and couldn't fly. That's what Eshal looks like now, with her small, worried, angular motions. After some deliberation, we decided to take the starling to the vet in the high street, but on the way there, the shoebox, which I had strapped to the handlebars of my bike, came loose and thudded onto the pavement. The bird immediately escaped and ran, disorientated, into the middle of the road. Within seconds, it was squished under the tyre of a Renault Megane.

I hold my hand out to her and she gives me the bottle of gin. I drink and drink and drink, and pour the dregs into the bathwater for good measure. Maybe I can absorb it by osmosis. Eshal makes a noise like she is disgusted.

I look up at the ceiling. There's a cobweb in the corner and a money spider is sitting on it. Slowly, it spools a thread of web down to the bath taps.

Bess?

Eshal is very far away now. The other end of a church hall.

Bess, you've been sick. We need to get you out now, okay? That's it. We're done.

I look down at myself and see that the dolphin on the front of Eshal's T-shirt is now covered in putrid yellow stomach acid, little lumps for all the Vitamin C things I ate downstairs. All the tablets. Seems so long ago now, in Eshal's kitchen. And I don't remember that happening. The smell of the sick is suddenly overwhelming, like it's in my blood.

I apologise to Eshal.

It's fine, she says. Look, you don't need to cry. Please stop crying.

She turns on the shower part of the taps and holds it over my head, letting all the sick rinse off me. I scream because the shower water is boiling. Eshal shushes me, apologising over and over, and changes the temperature so that it's cooler, but I am still screaming. I can't stop. She clamps her hand over my mouth as she rinses the sick off me. It covers the water, a filmy layer, like an oil spill, the little lumps floating like air bubbles.

Eshal pulls me up by the shoulders, but I can't get up. I'm too heavy. She is worrying that I'm going to drown.

I realise that she was telling me to stop crying because I am crying. Sobbing noisily. Ugly. Ugly crying.

I think about what Boy might say if he could see me now. He probably wouldn't say anything. He would probably just leave. I am such a mess. I am so devoid of hope. I am going to die in this bathtub. I know it; I can feel it.

Eshal is crying too now, still trying to drag me out of the bath. I try to help her by lifting myself up, but I have lost control of my body. All of my limbs weigh a hundred tonnes. I'm throwing up again before I have time to realise that there is bile rising in my throat.

Eshal is shouting even louder now, but she is a mile away. My eyelids are heavy.

I

feel

so . . .

I slide back into the bath in what feels like a gentle movement, but the motion causes the sick-contaminated water to slop over the edges onto the towels, the tiles, Eshal's feet.

Eshal grips my hands and I hold onto hers like she's pulling me up from a ledge. My hands are like claws in hers.

We are suspended in this moment, tethered to each other.

We are staring into each other's eyes like lovers, hers are panicked and I can't feel mine or see them so I don't know I don't know I don't know. The tug of sleep is harder and harder to resist. I slip into it; the heat of the bath is suddenly soothing instead of blistering. It's very nearly peaceful.

It's like I'm cocooned in Eshal's bathtub. It's like I'm in a womb.

Chapter Fifteen

I dream that I've gone to heaven and everything is light.

Heaven has many rooms, each of them coming off a long corridor that's neither indoors nor outdoors, but is definitely in the sky. All of the doors are locked. But the heaven corridor is also the Maths corridor on the C Floor at Our Lady of the Assumption. And it's also a hospital corridor and the light is not a good light. It's artificial strip lighting, passing above my head like white lines on a road. Like on the M3. And there are tiny carpet beetles crawling all over my skin and the hairs on my arms, eating all my clothes, burrowing into me until the only thing left is my brain locked in my skeleton. And there *she* is. My mother. She's standing in my bedroom door in the middle of the night, her silhouette illuminated by the yellow light in the hallway. And she is saying, Are you hurting yourself? Are you hurting yourself again? Have you been hurting yourself again?

When I wake up, the first thing I see is the ceiling tiles, all pure dimpled white, hexagons fitting together. It's calming. My digital alarm clock is going off too. So, I'm at home, but this isn't my ceiling. These aren't my walls. It's not my alarm clock either, it's a machine with blue and red lights on it, and coming off the machine is a thin clear tube, and the tube connects to me, and there is a clear liquid in it being slowly syringed into my body through a needle sticking out of a bit of yellow plastic attached to my wrist.

So I guess I had my abortion after all. I went to the doctor's like I was supposed to and had a real abortion.

I look over to my left and see Mrs Bhandari (of all people) sitting in a visitor's chair, her knuckles kneading her face. I feel my own body, my dry, scratchy throat, my pounding head, my aching bones. My abdomen is sore from retching. I remember the bathtub and being dragged out of it by Eshal. Bits of paramedic green. Bits of an ambulance ride, not much else.

Where's Eshal? I ask, and my voice is sandpaper in my throat. I try to cough, and it burns, but doesn't hurt. I must be smacked out on medication. I feel like I'm floating two feet above the hospital bed.

Mrs Bhandari looks up, suddenly alert, when she hears my voice. For a second, she looks relieved to see me. But the moment passes quickly and her face contorts into something like contempt. She is wearing a dark blue sari with a grey diamond pattern on it. Her eyebrows are furrowed like how Eshal looks when she's annoyed or confused. I've never noticed how much Mrs Bhandari looks like Eshal before. Well, I suppose it's the other way around. Eshal looks like Mrs Bhandari. Except Mrs Bhandari's skin is like paper that has been folded and unfolded so many times that it has become soft and thin, with tiny fibres covering its surface and her hair is stringier than Eshal's, threaded with fine silver strands.

Where's Eshal? I ask again.

I told her to leave, she says.

What happened?

Mrs Bhandari leans back and links her hands together, her elbows propped up on the armrests of the ugly hospital chair.

She says, Eshal told us everything. The doctors and me. Your mother and father are on their way to the hospital. You're in a lot of trouble, young lady. Eshal, too.

I grip the cold metal of the bed frame and feel shame wash over me, tears pricking at the corners of my eyes.

Mrs Bhandari, I start. But she holds a hand up to stop me.

And in my house, too. *My house*. Do you understand how that makes us feel, Bess? Me and my family? Do you understand how deeply you have disrespected us? We treat you like one of our own . . .

I'm so sorry, I say quietly.

Don't, she says, and her voice is wobbly. Just don't. I'm trying very hard not to raise my voice at you, and I don't want to say something I'm going to regret later.

I can't meet her gaze. Humiliation settles over me thick and sour.

She says, quietly, I pray to God that that baby is still alive inside you.

I cry, and Mrs Bhandari relents and takes hold of my hand and strokes it softly. We are in a cubicle on a busy ward, and there are turquoise-coloured curtains separating me from the other patients. But I can still hear them. They are talking quietly to doctors and visitors. Some are crying like me. One woman is shouting.

Bess, Mrs Bhandari says, after I've composed myself, I understand that there are some things that you can't tell your parents. I understand that you girls have your secrets. I just *wish* you'd told someone, other than my daughter, about this. I wish you felt as though you could have told *me*. And now Eshal's been dragged into this mess.

I know. I know. I'm sorry.

It's too late for sorry, now.

I know.

We sit quietly and I wipe my nose on the sleeve of my hospital robe. I feel wholly pathetic.

After a while, the curtain to my cubicle is tugged aside and a tall woman steps in.

Isabelle Johnson?

Yes, I say.

The woman turns to Mrs Bhandari. Would you mind giving us some privacy?

Mrs Bhandari stands up.

We'll wait until your parents get here, she says, and then we're leaving. She doesn't have as much venom in her voice as before. Her saying 'we' makes me realise that Eshal is in the hospital somewhere too.

The tall woman is blonde and very put-together. She perches on the chair and smoothes her hands over her grey skirt.

Isabelle, my name is Dr Jacobs. I wanted to talk to you a little bit about what happened today.

I wait until it's clear that she wants me to answer her.

Okay, I say.

My colleague has already spoken to your friend Eshal, who explained exactly what's been going on. But I wanted to hear everything in your words, too. Do you want to tell me about the situation?

She has produced a legal pad, I don't know where from, and has a pen poised over a fresh page, ready to take notes.

I think about where I should even begin.

Well, I say. I found out I was pregnant.

When did you find out? Dr Jacobs asks.

I think about it. It was about a month ago. After we went on study leave.

So, let's say the second week of June. Does that sound right to you?

I think about it.

Yes, because we had a science exam on the twentieth, and me and Eshal were still revising for it.

Great, Isabelle, Dr Jacobs says. I notice that I can ever so slightly see the shape of her bra through her cream shirt.

She asks me a bunch of questions about my health, whether I have any allergies, whether I smoke, how often I exercise, et cetera.

When was the last day of your period? she asks me.

I don't know.

Can you give me a rough date?

I don't know. Maybe, like the beginning of May? I'm not sure. I'm sorry.

Don't worry, Isabelle. Just relax, okay?

I try to release the tension in my body. I'm coiled up and rigid. Every time she says 'Isabelle', it's like someone has just dragged their nails across a blackboard. It makes my innards curl up.

Dr Jacobs flips her legal pad closed.

Just so you know, we've pumped the alcohol out of your stomach today. You drank a dangerous amount of gin, Isabelle. You're very lucky that your friend had the sense to call an ambulance, otherwise it's possible that you could have died.

She pauses for dramatic effect. I think to myself how easy everything would be if that had actually happened.

I hope you're aware of the serious health risks of binge drinking. I hope you're not going to engage in this kind of behaviour again. Did you take any other substances? she asks me seriously.

No, I say, and she nods. Then I remember: Actually, wait. I had quite a lot of Vitamin C tablets.

Al right, she says, and I feel like I can see the hint of a smile on her face. You'll notice as well that you've got quite a few dressings on you.

I hadn't noticed at all, but now that I look at my arms, I see that, from the wrist up to just above the elbows, my skin is dressed in thick white gauze. It feels like there is more on my back and legs too, but I can't see it.

You've sustained several second-degree thermal burns to your body as a result of coming into contact with scalding water and steam. We're going to keep treating these burns here on the ward until you go home, where we'll give you a treatment plan and write you a prescription for a course of antibiotics. For now, we need to rehydrate you and ensure that none of your burns become infected. We're giving you intravenous antibiotics and codeine to deal with the pain. That's why you probably feel a little woozy. She says, I want to talk to you now about your pregnancy.

I feel my eyes sting again. I look up at the clean tessellating ceiling tiles and count the edges of the hexagons, tracing their shapes with my eyes.

As far as we can tell without conducting an examination, there is no evidence that you have miscarried. We'll need to scan your belly to evaluate whether there has been any damage to the foetus. And we will have a chat later today to discuss your options, all right?

I don't move.

Isabelle, were your actions today – the bath and the drink – an effort to abort your pregnancy?

Of course, she already knows the answer to this.

I nod slowly, my eyes still shut.

Are you going to tell my parents? I ask her.

We have no legal obligation to share any details with your parents or guardians, Dr Jacobs says. In this case, as you're in care, your legal guardian is Surrey County Council.

This is something I've heard before. Many social workers have told me, with triumphant, self-satisfied faces, that they're my *corporate parent*. Another stupid foster-care term that means fuck all in real life. It makes it sound like I came out of the womb in a suit and tie and I've been raised in a bank ever since. But what they really mean is that instead of having actual people as guardians, the entire local council is responsible for my care.

Dr Jacobs continues. If you like, I can be here to mediate when your foster parents arrive, how about that?

I say, Yes.

Isabelle, considering your condition, I would strongly advise that you do tell them, all right? This is a very upsetting and difficult thing to be going through – for any woman, let alone a fifteen-year-old girl. There is plenty of support available from the NHS, but the best possible help you can get is at home.

I let out a fake laugh and say, You obviously don't know my mother.

You would be surprised, Isabelle.

It's Bess, I tell her.

She tugs the curtain back open and exits my little cubicle. I watch the tube slowly pump clear liquid into the pale skin around my wrist. My hands are pink and shiny and raw. I lift the corner of one of the gauze strips covering my left arm and see a large slimy blister, the size of a two-pound coin. Shit.

I lie still and try not to think of anything. Every time an inkling of pain begins to hover at the fringes of my conscious-ness, it ebbs away quickly and is replaced by a pleasant numbing sensation. I assume it's the painkillers. There is still some pain, though, like the keening ache in my belly. I imagine pulling my fingernails out one by one. I wonder if it would hurt at all.

After what seems like hours but probably isn't, I hear my mother's voice permeating the soft humdrum of the ward. She is saying, Is she in here? Is it this one? Oh, sorry, I was looking for my daughter. Bess Johnson? Do you know where she is?

It feels weird hearing her call me her daughter, and I'm suddenly imagining a different version of myself, a new identity that is *Lisa's daughter*, in the biological sense, and it feels very safe, and unconditional, like it'll all be okay now, and I wonder about yelling to her to alert her to my location, but, really, I can't bear the thought of it, how my voice would sound calling out to her. I realise that I'm afraid. And I don't want her to think I want her.

She finally arrives at my cubicle, ripping the curtain open and casting her eyes down at me. She is windswept, red-faced, sweaty, breathless.

Oh my God, Bess.

It's just her though, not the woman outside the cubicle who said *I was looking for my daughter.*

I laugh, because I can't think of what else to do. It comes out a little maniacal.

What have you done to yourself? Jesus.

Rory walks in behind Mum, overly interested in the mottled blue lino, and pulls the curtain closed gently. Mum sits down on the squeaky blue plastic hospital chair, the one that Dr Jacobs was sitting on.

What's going on? Mum asks.

Well, I've got second-degree burns, I tell her.

Rory's looked up and now he's staring at me like I'm a dead body.

Mum says, We were so worried. Eshal's mum didn't say much on the phone, just that you were in hospital and you were getting your stomach pumped. What happened?

Me and Esh were drinking, I say.

Jesus, Bess.

And I drank a bit too much, and I ran a bath, but it was too hot. So, I burned myself.

Lisa watches me, and I can tell from her expression, which is pinched, that she doesn't believe me.

A nurse announces her presence with a cheery hello that is totally at odds with the atmosphere of my cubicle. She pulls back the curtain, dragging in a trolley covered in a greenish plastic sheet, bumping into the back of Rory.

I'm going to have to ask you to leave for a brief moment, she says to Mum and Rory, I just need to examine Miss Johnson.

We're her parents. You're really telling us to leave? We just got here!

It's only for ten minutes, the nurse says. She has a very open face and a soft, calming voice, with a sing-song tone to it, which is why I think Mum follows Rory out of my cubicle.

Hello, Miss Johnson, the nurse says, in the same Maria from *The Sound of Music* type voice. I'm going to just do a quick scan of your belly, all right?

Okay, I say.

She pulls a chair up and sets up her equipment, pulling the cover off the trolley. On it is a small TV with some wires and components coming off it.

The nurse adjusts my bed so that I'm lying in a more horizontal position. She pushes some buttons on the monitor and the machine whirs into life. She untangles a curly telephone cord with something that looks like a walkie-talkie on the end of it.

I'm going to squirt some of this gel onto your stomach, all right?

I nod. She pulls back the thin sheet covering me and it's the first time that I realise I have been dressed in a hospital gown. How weird that I didn't notice that before. The nurse pinches the hem of the gown and gently shifts it upwards, avoiding contact with my skin, which I notice is red and raw all over my thighs and hips too. Everything below my knees is covered in dressings, including my feet. I wonder how I'll walk. My body looks like an organ out of a biology book, all shiny and blotchy pink. As the nurse pulls my gown past my hips, I notice I'm wearing gross disposable paper knickers. I wonder who took my knickers off for me. Who put these paper ones on. Whether they did it gently. Whether some poor orderly got a face full of pubes.

The nurse warns me of the coldness a nanosecond before squirting a huge dollop of a clear lubey liquid onto my stomach. The initial chill makes me flinch, but as she spreads the stuff over my stomach, it actually begins to feel quite soothing. It's as though this is not my body and it's not me experiencing these things. I'm a third party, a bystander, watching everything happen from a corner of the room.

Now she's prodding my stomach firmly with the walkie-talkie device. She flicks a switch by the screen and that familiar ultrasound display that you always see in *Casualty* and *EastEnders* comes up. It is a blurry black-and-white semicircle with very little on it in terms of discernible objects. Just weird smudged masses of what I guess is tissue from inside my womb.

I crane my neck to see the screen. I don't know what I'm looking for. Or hoping for. A little kidney bean inside the static, or would seeing nothing at all be better? I don't know how many weeks I am, or anything. I still don't really know what 'how many weeks' means.

How many weeks am I? I ask the nurse.

Oh, don't worry about that now, sweetheart. Dr Jacobs is going to discuss all of that with you this afternoon.

I don't respond. The nurse prints out something from the side of the machine, I assume the scans, and I turn my head away so

I don't catch a glimpse of anything, and she wheels her trolley of equipment out of the cubicle.

Dr Jacobs will be back in a few minutes, she says.

Mum and Rory come back into the cubicle.

Dr Jacobs will be here in a few minutes, I tell them.

Will you please tell us what the hell is going on? Mum asks again.

I just look at her.

For goodness' sake, Bess.

We sit in silence, listening to the conversation in the cubicle next to us. It is a drunk man, shouting quietly at his wife. In forced whispers. I suddenly feel so exhausted, like I haven't slept in a year. I want to sleep for days and wake up a new person. Someone who is not me.

The curtain twitches again, and Mrs Bhandari half-steps in. Behind her is Eshal. We lock eyes for a moment and my face stretches involuntarily into a big grin. I'm *so* happy to see her. My stomach is singing. But she doesn't smile back at me. She's been crying, I can tell. Her hands are bandaged with the same type of material on my own legs, and shoved under her armpits, like she's hugging herself. I realise that she's burnt herself, too, trying to drag me out of the bath. Her hair is all scruffy, which is unlike her. She never leaves the house without her ritual of one hundred brushstrokes.

Esh? I ask, uncertain.

Good, you're here, Mrs Bhandari says to my parents. Eshal looks at the floor.

Nazrin, what on earth is going on? Mum asks her, slightly too aggressively. The doctors won't tell us a thing. This stupid patient-confidentiality rule. Never mind the fact that she's our daughter . . .

Your daughter is pregnant, Mrs Bhandari says, although it's

more like she shouts it. And now Eshal's crying for real.

She continues: And she and Eshal thought it would be a good idea to try a do-it-yourself abortion in *my* house.

Lisa just stares at Mrs Bhandari for a moment. I don't think I've ever seen her so completely lost for words.

And then she says very quietly, after looking from me to Eshal to Mrs Bhandari to Rory and back again, And where the *hell* were you while this was going on?

Mrs Bhandari blinks. Excuse me?

And Mum's voice raises an octave. I said, where the BLOODY HELL WERE YOU?

And Mrs Bhandari is a short woman, but the way her expression changes when Mum says that, it's like she's just grown four inches.

And she doesn't raise her voice like Mum did, but as she speaks, her voice is dripping with venom, which is worse, and she says, I think you're missing the point here, Lisa. I don't think you understand what's going on. I'll tell you. What has happened is that your daughter was so afraid of telling you this secret, so terrified of your reaction, that she almost killed herself trying to keep it from you. Have you stopped to think why that might be? Why Bess would rather give herself alcohol poisoning, and near-enough melt her own skin off, than ask for your help?

I catch Eshal's eye and she looks afraid. Her own secret plain across her face.

Think about that, Mrs Bhandari continues, before you ask *me* where *I* was while *your* daughter was trying to abort a baby in *my* bathtub.

Lisa is gripping the railing on the bed, her knuckles white.

Get out, she says.

Mrs Bhandari turns to go.

And keep your daughter away from mine, Lisa spits out.

Me and Eshal shout out at the same time.

What!

Mum! No!

We were just leaving, Mrs Bhandari replies. Come on, Eshal.

And then she's gone, and she's dragging Eshal out by the arm too, and Esh is going, Mum, *stop*. And then in the corridor, past the curtain, I hear Eshal still shouting, and getting louder and louder, and it's shocking because Eshal never, *never* raises her voice to her parents. And she's shouting through sobs, all wobbly and awful, saying, What about Bess? and We can't leave her, and *Mum*, and then they're gone, Esh's voice getting quieter and quieter as they get further and further away, until all we can hear is the hushed, shocked silence of the ward. And I so desperately want to go after her, to call her back, but I'm hooked up to this machine with three different tubes and I say to Mum, You don't mean it, do you? About Eshal staying away? She's my best friend. Can't I just go and talk to her?

And Mum says, You've done enough damage, Bess. And in some ways, now that Lisa and Rory know, it's a *relief* that it's not just me and Esh dealing with this horrendous, enormous secret alone any more. Like, now it's all out there. There's nowhere to hide at all. There's no point lying any more. But now Esh is gone, maybe forever, and it's just me.

God, says Rory, slumping into his chair.

God isn't going to help you now, Rory, I tell him.

To my surprise, Mum is crying. Her face in her hands, her shoulders gently bouncing up and down, big shuddering heaving breaths coming out of her. The skin on her neck blotchy-bright.

It catches me by surprise. I try to remember a time I saw her cry. I can't.

How long has this been going on for? Rory asks in a low voice, clearing his throat.

Has what been going on for? I ask. How long have I been pregnant or how long was I in the bathtub? How long have I been an alcoholic? How long have I been sexually active?

Bess! For crying out loud.

Sorry. I shouldn't joke about it, I'm not really an alcoholic.

I remember the drunk man in the cubicle next to mine and call out sorry to him, too.

We're going to have to ring Henry.

Oh, God, yes. Henry, I say. Social services will want to know all the intimate details for my file. What position did we do it in? What colour was my underwear?

As if on cue, Dr Jacobs sidles back into my cubicle, this time clutching a bunch of different leaflets. I read one upside-down as BURNS VICTIMS: TREATING AND MANAGING YOUR PAIN.

Ah, hi again, Isabelle.

It's Bess, I say at the exact same time as Mum does.

Sorry, Bess, Dr Jacobs corrects herself, and quickly introduces herself to Mum and Rory.

I wanted to discuss your treatment for when you go home in a few days. Burns are particularly difficult to manage. I trust that you'll be looked after by Lisa or Rory?

I glance warily at Mum.

We haven't talked about it yet, I say.

We can manage the burns, Mum says dismissively. What we need to know more about is how the hell my daughter came to be pregnant—

I think that much is pretty obvious, Mum.

And what the bloody hell we're going to do about it.

Dr Jacobs steps back out into the ward momentarily before returning with a wheelchair.

Bess, why don't you hop into the wheelchair and we can have this discussion somewhere more private?

I shrug and ease my legs over the side of the bed. The movement makes me suddenly very aware of how painful every part of my body is, especially the raw sections which are touching scratchy bed sheets.

Ouch, I say.

Mum helps me off the bed, an unreadable look on her face as she sees the dressings on my arms and legs.

Dr Jacobs pushes me out of the cubicle and through a security door. Rory is wheeling my IV drip along beside us on a coat-rack-type thing. Dr Jacobs lets us into a room marked BE-REAVEMENT and the door shuts with a loud click behind us.

Once we're all sat down, Dr Jacobs says, First of all, Bess, I think it was a very brave and mature thing to do to tell your parents about the pregnancy.

She didn't tell us, Mum says. Nazrin Bhandari did.

Dr Jacobs pauses and then says, Well, whatever the situation, this is where we are now. So, we need to discuss options. Lisa and Rory, I'm not sure if you're aware of so-called do-it-yourself abortion methods. Bess's injuries sustained today are unfortunately a result of a similar attempt.

I turn to look at them. Neither of them are displaying any emotion. Eyes wide and attentive.

It's quite clear to me that Bess is very young and not at all equipped to deal with this pregnancy, nor the possibility of motherhood, on her own.

She's got us, Mum snaps.

Yes, of course she does, Dr Jacobs says. What I'm saying is that there are several options open to Bess at this stage and it's important for her to know exactly what is available to her. Now, Bess, I've taken a look at the ultrasounds we conducted earlier and, despite the damage you've sustained today, the foetus is unharmed and perfectly healthy.

Mum claps her hands involuntarily. I've never seen her look so haggard.

Dr Jacobs goes on to talk more about the ultrasound, but I don't hear her.

You mean to say, I interrupt her, that after all that. All the shit I did today, it's fine? Are you sure?

Absolutely, Dr Jacobs says. You're young and healthy, which means that your womb is a very habitable place.

A very habitable place, I repeat.

Yes, Bess.

I swallow vomit down. I glance around the room. It's dimly lit, but tastefully decorated, with terracotta-coloured walls and a potted plant on the windowsill. Behind Dr Jacobs' head, there is an oil painting of a lake. I wonder how many people have sat in this room to be told that their mum or dad, husband or wife or kid didn't make it. That the body is going cold and rigid as we speak.

Is this where you tell people their relatives have died? I ask Dr Jacobs.

Mum goes, Bess!

No, it's all right. Yes, it is. And it's also where we offer counselling to bereaved families. Why do you ask?

I just thought that maybe you were going to tell me I killed it.

There is a moment of silence as the three of them process what I have said.

Do you mean you thought you had successfully aborted your pregnancy? Dr Jacobs asks me.

I nod yes.

Is that what you wanted, Bess?

I nod again, and hot tears are streaking lines down my cheeks.

What am I going to do? I ask her. Ask them all.

Mum and Rory look at me blankly. I wonder whether they are thinking I am a monster.

What am I going to do? I say again. And Dr Jacobs says, Bess, and I lean forward and place my forehead on the cool glass of the coffee table and close my eyes, waiting for someone to answer me.

Chapter Sixteen

Every day, a nurse called Emily comes in and re-dresses the bandages on my legs and arms. The ointment smells like peppermint chewing gum. I move to an emptier ward that has long, thin windows that reach the ceiling. Most of the time, I'm alone, apart from nurses who drift in and out to look at the machine and check the tubes pumping stuff into my body. I watch patients and visitors enter and leave the ward, but they are always far away from me, the distance stretching between us so it feels like I'm watching them on TV. I've been here the longest out of everyone.

The window next to my bed looks out onto a small courtyard, which is completely surrounded by hospital buildings. I'm on the twelfth floor out of fifteen. Sometimes there is a man in the courtyard and he runs around the perimeter in white trainers, red football socks and a hospital gown. He runs laps and laps and laps until a nurse comes into the garden to collect him. One time, I count how many laps he does before the nurse finds him. It's seventy-two. When the nurse arrives, she talks to him sternly. I can't hear what she's saying because the window is chained shut. Before the man goes with her, he stretches his neck out and stares directly up at the sky, his arms slightly pulled backwards and away from his body. It looks like his ribcage is about to break open, to reveal a whole other person underneath his skin.

Mum and Rory come and visit me every evening at 7 o'clock, dropping Clarissa at Uncle Jason's in order to do so. Rory usually brings egg mayonnaise sandwiches for me, because he thinks there are no nutrients in hospital food (I don't think egg mayo sandwiches are that much better), and when I refuse them, he eats them noisily, breathing heavily through his nose, getting egg in his moustache. Mum sits on the chair at the edge of the bed and asks me tentative questions in a quiet voice that she never uses. What did you do today? Did they let you go outside? What did you eat? Did they change your bandages? Has the doctor seen you?

I answer minimally. We are all avoiding the subject of the pregnancy like it's a social faux pas. I can't bring myself to be the one to raise it, because I feel like this is an uneasy ceasefire between her and me, and it could break at any moment. I feel as though bringing it up would be like asking them for help, like asking Mum for help. I can't bear it. She is being so soft. I wonder whether she's thankful that it was me, and not Clarissa, who got into trouble. She is probably thinking, at least it was Bess, at least it was someone else's daughter, not mine. We are all pretending, for now, that the pregnancy doesn't exist. And all the time I'm in hospital, the foetus is growing inside me.

Clarissa hasn't come, although I guess Mum and Rory think she's too young to understand. But she does. She's eleven; she knows what pregnancy is. I wonder if they've even told her. Eshal hasn't been to visit me and I hope it's because Mrs Bhandari is keeping her away rather than because she doesn't want to come. Boy doesn't know that I'm here at all. Not that I would want him to come and see me, especially when I'm looking so pathetic and my hair is plastered to my scalp because it's so lank with grease from not being able to wash it, and parts of my skin are shiny purple and seeping pus. Dr Jacobs has offered to have someone come and wash my hair for me, but the thought of someone holding my head under water makes me want to scream.

When Dr Jacobs arrives, I tell her, Sputnik was the first-ever artificial satellite and it was launched by the Soviet Union in the nineteen fifties.

Dr Jacobs says, That's not what we're here to talk about, Bess.

Henry has turned up too. A surprising addition to mine and Dr Jacobs' usual powwows. When I saw him, I must have had some kind of expression of shame come over me because he gave me a look like I was a wounded sparrow and then went, Oh Bess, oh Bess, oh Bess, and he flipped his mint green neckerchief-scarf-thing over his shoulder so that it wouldn't dangle in my face, and drew me into his bony arms. He smells of glue. I wonder whether it's his washing powder or his aftershave, or whether he's been sticking sequins onto his chest as his drag queen alter ego, who I have secretly named Chlamydia Queen.

Now we are sitting in Dr Jacobs' office, which pretty much has exactly the same layout and décor as the bereavement room. And Dr Jacobs is talking about options, or rather Options with a capital O. I examine the grain of wood on her desk while she is talking, and it's only when I reach out to stroke it that I realise it is a laminate with the pattern of wood printed onto it, not real wood.

You don't need to make a decision just now, she says, but you also need to realise that you only have a small window of time to think about everything.

She rattles off my three options like we haven't gone over them a million times. Henry takes notes.

Dr Jacobs gives me two thick glossy brochure-style leaflets. One is green and has a picture of a smiley family on the front. A mum, with long hot-chocolate-coloured hair pulled back with a headband; a dad with rolled-up sleeves and five o'clock shadow; two little kids, a boy and a girl around eight and ten, both with little chubby cheeks and glossy black eyes. All four of them are showing their teeth, in a way that seems more unnatural the more I look at it. The mum looks like she is snarling, and the little girl looks like the corners of her mouth are about to rip her cheeks open. The company's name on the pamphlet is FAMILIES FORWARD, and the letters are entwined with a leaf pattern. The second brochure I have doesn't have a picture on the front, it's plain blue and has the words MARIE STOPES UK in bold white capital letters, and underneath there is a mission statement, the words *Children are a choice, and every woman has the right to choose.*

My three choices are what Eshal already deduced: have a baby and raise it, have a baby and give it up for adoption, or have an abortion.

I wish that there was a fourth option, which is that none of this ever happened. I say this out loud to Dr Jacobs and Henry, but neither of them find it funny.

I ask Dr Jacobs who Marie Stopes is. She tells me that it's not a person, it's a clinic which provides abortions on the NHS.

Why can't you do that here?

We don't provide terminations in a hospital. There are specialist clinics for it. You'll have to go there. I can make a referral if that's what you want?

Maybe, I say, surprising myself. *Maybe?* I look at the picture of the family on the FAMILIES FORWARD pamphlet. Am I the mum or the kid?

I have to stress the time-sensitive element of all this, Bess.

I know, I say. I know, I know.

Henry clears his throat daintily. Bess, I've already spoken to your foster carers, Lisa and Rory.

He says their names for the benefit of Dr Jacobs, but it feels awfully formal and not at all like Henry. I think he's bricking it that he actually has to do his job for once.

He continues: They've both agreed that they're willing to support you through your pregnancy, if that's what you choose, and also with the adoption process. They've also said that if you want to keep the – um – baby, they would be willing to provide you with lodgings and support, too, and help with childcare if you go to college or start working.

Henry is talking more to Dr Jacobs now than he is to me.

Bess's care situation is a unique one, he explains. Most children are in care for short periods of time, or if they are in care permanently, they tend to move between several different placements. Bess has stayed in the same care placement since she was four, and we've all agreed that there is no need for her to move, unless she wants to.

I'm very lucky with my *unique care situation*, I say sarcastically, and Henry nods, smiling, not getting it, totally clueless like Brittany Murphy in *Clueless*.

These are all things that you might want to think about when you're making your decision, Dr Jacobs says. It's good to know that there is a support network there for you if you need it. And I'm sure social services will be keeping an eye on you, too, as a young person in care.

Can you stop saying care? I tell her. Why do you use the word *care*? It's so weird. The reason we're all *in care* is because our parents couldn't care *less*. Didn't *care* enough to look after us properly. And when we're eighteen, we're dumped by social services anyway. Left to fend for ourselves. We're *care leavers*. How exactly does someone *leave care*? Do our foster parents stop caring about us? Do social services stop caring about us? Where do we go after that?

Bess. Henry says my name like a warning, flicking his pen against his notebook.

No, I say, turning to him. It's fucking stupid. The whole system, it's bullshit. In six months, you'll probably be reassigned to some other case with some other poor kid whose mother is a junkie, or whose uncle is a sexual predator, or whose parents beat her, and you'll pull her into the *care system*, and then you'll forget about her too. Job done, right? I've had enough social workers to know that you're all the same. We're all just little pixelated gradients on a bar chart on a fucking PowerPoint presentation, aren't we? We're statistics for your performance review.

Henry blinks at me, the tips of his ears growing pink. He glances at Dr Jacobs.

Don't tell me, I say, breathless, that I have a fucking *support network*, okay? There is no support network. There is no *care system*. There's no such thing as care. It's a myth.

I stand up with my pamphlets and I can feel my burns searing as I leave Dr Jacobs' office, but in a good way, like all of the rotten parts of my body have been cut away and now all the skin is fresh and new.

When Mum and Rory come to collect me at the end of the week, Mum insists that I sit in the wheelchair, even though I'm capable of walking properly now. She folds my things neatly into a canvas duffel bag, and fidgets while we have our 'exit interview', where Dr Jacobs goes through my antibiotics schedule, how to change the bandages on my burns and what I need to be eating and drinking.

And we still haven't got any closer to deciding about the pregnancy, have we, Bess? Dr Jacobs says. 'We' – like this is her problem too – yeah, right. Mum nods in quick, muted movements, her eyes big, deliberately not looking at me. Rory leans back in his chair, his forearms spread across the armrests like he's at the pub. Once we're done, Mum makes Rory take the handles of my wheelchair and wheel me out into the car park and offload me into the Fiesta.

What am I supposed to do with this, then? he asks, signalling the wheelchair.

For Chrissakes, Rory, I don't care. Just get rid of it, Mum says.

He wheels it over to a parking space next to a big industrial-sized bin and leaves it there.

It's not Tesco, you know, I shout through the window, you can't leave it in the car park like it's a trolley.

He does a half-jog, half-skip to the car and quickly turns the ignition.

Who wants a Chinese tonight, then? he asks loudly.

Oh, yes, please, I say.

You think you're getting a takeaway, after *this*? Mum snaps, and the expression on her face tells me that the uneasy ceasefire we've had going is officially over.

The tone in her voice reminds me that I'm pregnant and nothing has been resolved. It's only got worse.

When we get back to the house, Rory takes my stuff up to my room for me and I slowly sort through it. Mum's perfume, called Poison, lingers on my cardigan, she must've sprayed it to mask the scent of fags on the fabric. Sure enough, my little pouch of Amber Leaf tobacco has disappeared from the pocket of my jeans, too.

Once Rory is gone from my bedroom, I pull the lever on the window and delicately manoeuvre myself out onto the porch roof. I lift a loose roof tile where my emergency baccy is stashed. It's damp, but when I roll it up and light it, the paper still burns, and I smoke it even though it tastes like mould.

I squint through the smoke and sunlight. The sun is a long way away from sinking into the reservoir and Stage H and its metal warehouse walls are casting great shadows over the faces and bodies of the kids in the park. I think about the 120-foot alien-planet-crater Stanley Kubrick built in the warehouse thirty years ago when he was making *2001: A Space Odyssey*. I turn around and look to the Pits and the pools of dark water. The dark trees. The M3. Nothing has changed. It's still there. Even when we're all dead from the nuclear apocalypse or the millennium bug or in space colonising Mars, that murky water will still be there.

I creep back into my bedroom and lie down on my bed, staring at the faces in the dots on the ceiling. I think about going downstairs and calling Eshal. Mrs Bhandari would never let me speak to her. Or Boy, but he'd probably make some excuse not to talk to me, not that I would even know what to say to him. I touch my belly and try my hardest not to think about anything at all.

When I wake up, my bedroom is black apart from the street lamp outside my window. There are tiny flies buzzing around the bulb, drifting closer and closer to it before being shocked back to a safe distance. I wander into the bathroom and check the LED clock on top of the cabinet. It's 2.24 a.m. The house is the kind of silent that is louder than any real noise. I turn the light on and the extractor fan hums into life and I look at myself in the bathroom mirror. My skin is definitely better than it was, and when I lift the gauze dressings, I can see that underneath, the skin is dry and raw, rather than the angry seeping it was doing while I was in hospital. I'm not allowed to get my bandages wet to wash my hair, so it's grossly lank and greasy, shiny and stuck to my forehead. My face looks thinner, my cheekbones more prominent. My wrists feel thinner too and when I circle my thumb and forefinger around one, I can touch them together.

I stand in the bath so I can get a better angle on the mirror and pull my T-shirt up to reveal my belly. It doesn't *look* any bigger, but it is more rounded. I don't know whether I'm just imagining it, though. Dr Jacobs said I was nine weeks pregnant, which is not long at all. I have a deadline of fifteen more weeks to decide on the fate of the blob germinating in my womb. After that, nothing can be done.

Clarissa pushes the door open and sees me standing in the bath.

What are you *doing*? she asks in a whisper.

Get out, get out!

She doesn't move. She just watches me with her flying-saucer eyes. She stares at my belly.

Is it true why Mum and Dad said you were in hospital?

I nod.

What happened to your *skin*?

I shrug.

Your hair is really disgusting, Bess. It needs a wash.

You don't think I know that? Look.

I hold up my arms to show her the bandages. She looks at them for a moment, frowning. She absent-mindedly twirls a golden curl between her fingers. She looks like a ghost. She actually looks like me, kind of.

I'll wash it for you if you want.

She shrugs like it's the most benign thing. But we both know it's not.

I clamber out of the bath and say, Okay then. So, she gets towels out of the airing cupboard and makes me lean over the bath, and I can feel myself starting to panic, like she's going to drown me, all that stuff before with the bathtub, but she doesn't, of course. She sets the shower to a lukewarm temperature, and she lathers loads of shampoo into my hair, rubbing it right into my skull, and it's so soothing and nice, I feel like I'm going to fall asleep.

And while she's rinsing out the suds, she asks, Are you really pregnant?

I say, Yes, but you're probably not meant to know that.

Clarissa says she overheard Mum and Rory talking in their bedroom after she was supposed to have gone to sleep.

She coats my hair in Mum's special conditioner that we're not allowed to use and combs it through.

You're too young to be pregnant.

Well, technically not.

Yeah, but you're fifteen. You're a kid, aren't you?

I think about it. Yes, I suppose.

Clarissa sits on the toilet and wees while we wait for the conditioner to do its work, still looking at me like I'm a science experiment. She washes her hands and rinses my hair again, combing the water through it until my hair is a smooth unbroken curtain across my face, then she wraps my head in a towel.

I'm all done, she concludes, and she shuffles out of the bathroom, leaving me with my head hanging over the bathtub, wrapped up in the towel that's still hot from where it's been sitting under the hot-water tank. A moment later, I hear her bedroom door open.

Night, Bess, she says, yawning.

Night, Clarissa, I reply. And I click off the bathroom light and sit down on the floor and hug my knees to my chest in the darkness.

Chapter Seventeen

My bedroom has begun to smell like me, my body, my dirty clothes. It's that smell from spending too much time in one place. It gets into the fabric. I take out the scrapbook I got from Mum and Rory for Christmas. I'd started sticking in photographs I've taken since last summer. Half of the pages are still empty. I flick through it and count the faces in the photographs. There are eighteen photographs of Eshal. Standing in the playground on the last day of school, a shirt scrawled with dirty words and goodbye wishes flung over her shoulder. Lying on the grass in Manor Park. Esh in her back garden with her Twiggy sunglasses and platforms, staring up at the nest box in next-door's oak tree. I can almost hear her counting the blue-tit eggs and going on about the incubation period. *Parus caeruleus*, said in the voice of an old woman.

There are pictures of Boy too. Twenty-two of them. Eight are with his long, floppy hair falling over his eyes. The rest are Boy post-shave, and there is even one of him in the bathroom the day I shaved his head. His eyes are glossy with the pale pink fleshy bits showing. He's not looking at the camera; he's looking at an object a few inches behind the camera. Me. There is a smile on his face like he knows something everyone else doesn't. So different from the last time I saw him, *Don't fucking pretend you don't know.* I think he's abandoned me.

There are four pictures of me in the scrapbook. One of them Eshal took on the train station platform. The other three photographs are all with Boy, all Polaroids with the camera turned around, my wrist bent at an awkward angle, to capture both our faces. Boy's face fills the frame and a fraction of mine peeks out from the corner in all of them. Usually my forehead or chin, sometimes an eye or a cheek. They are all hideous, out of focus, shoddy. Looking at them now makes it seem ridiculous that I ever wanted to memorialise us together. Of course he doesn't feel that deeply about me. These days and weeks apart have meant nothing to him, and I'm just this sad, desperate girl in the corner of the photograph.

I take a cotton bud from my dressing table and wipe it around the inside rim of the bottle of bleach in the upstairs bathroom. I gently rub the cotton bud over my features in the pictures. The photo paper turns burnt orange, like the skin around a sunrise, and eventually becomes white, having sapped out all the colour printed onto it. I tuck the three photographs into the back of the book, right into the binding.

Mum changes my bed sheets every other day because she is terrified of my burns getting infected. She complains about the mess, the stale food. She tries to clean up, but I sulk until she goes away. She opens the window every morning, but I close it by midday. I'm horrendously miserable.

Clarissa sometimes dithers at my bedroom door before padding away. I can tell by the sound of her footsteps, because hers are the softest out of anyone in the house. I make her go to Apollo and get all four of the *Alien* movies for me when Tyson's on shift. He doesn't check IDs and would give *Basic Instinct* to a five-year-old if they had the cash to pay for it. Me and Riss get our duvets and build a pillow fort and watch all four of them back to back, eating our weight in Frazzles, while Mum and Rory are at work. Every time the house is empty, I sneak downstairs and try to call Eshal. I one-four-one it so no other member of the Bhandari household will recognise my number in case they block it. Usually it just goes to the answerphone, and Eshal's dad's voice tells me to call back later. Sometimes Mrs Bhandari picks up, and as soon as she hears my quiet breathing down the line, she says, Bess, I know it's you. Your mother wants us to stay away and we need to respect that. You need to stop ringing my house.

After the second week, my burns have hardened into bumpy purple calluses and my skin is drying and flaking off all over the place. Mum rubs a special prescription-strength steroid cream with moisturiser onto the places I can't reach. I hate the feeling of her hands on my back and neck. Her fingernails are long and filed into neat squares, with do-it-yourself French tips, and sometimes she catches my skin with one and it hurts like hell. The pretty French tips are so unlike her, the opposite of her mauve smocks and fabric softener and sensible shoes. She always has clean nails cut short, because she hates getting dirt under them. I think one of the younger girls at the opticians did the manicure for her. They're sloppy, anyway. You can see where the polish has leaked out under the stencil and turned the crisp line into a wobbly dribbly one. I offer to redo them for her. I have a steady hand. Mum says no thanks and takes the varnish off with rubbing alcohol.

On the Sunday, they let me out of my bedroom and I'm allowed to eat with the family. Such an *honour*. Mum makes me go to the opticians with her if no one else is in the house to keep an eye on me and make sure I don't sneak off to the pub or the whorehouse or wherever it is they think I hang out. I sit at the counter and fill out my college applications, which are months too late now anyway, but I do it. Sometimes I fetch things for Mum when she's with a customer. Sometimes the optician, Mr Clump, who has an impressive snow-white moustache, sticks his head out of the little examination room and hints that he wants a cup of tea and Mum gives me a pointed look, and I go and make tea for everyone. I think Mum is quite happy for me to be here, to be honest, because I'm doing all the shit jobs she usually has to do, like bleaching the customer toilet and polishing the mirrors and going out to get Mr Clump's lunch from the bakery across the road.

One time, she pauses and looks over my shoulder to see what I'm working on.

College applications? she asks me. Don't you think it's a bit late for that?

She's whispering because she's referring to the fact that I am ten weeks pregnant now. As if every customer in the shop and Mr Clump will suddenly realise I'm pregnant simply because she is referring to it in increasingly vague terms. I can already feel a hot bubble in my throat, which I know is going to burst soon.

I shrug.

I suppose I can put them in now and ask to defer for a year.

You don't know where you're going to be in a year. You don't know what your situation is going to be. Do you?

I haven't thought about it, I tell her, truthfully. And I can feel the bubble travelling up my windpipe, trying to escape. My face goes warm.

Well, that's the thing, Bess. You don't think about anything much, do you? And she turns away.

And in my head, a game-show host is shouting, *Aaaaaaaand we're back.*

*

On Tuesday night, at home, I sit at the dinner table and the four of us eat in silence. Lamb chops and mash, my absolute least favourite dinner. Mum puts her cutlery down halfway through tearing meat off the bone.

So, Bess, have you given any more thought to what you're going to do?

Clarissa's head snaps up so quickly I'm surprised she doesn't give herself whiplash. Her eyes dart from my face to Mum's. This is the closest Riss has ever got to being involved in the pregnancy conversation.

Well? Mum asks, and Rory puts his cutlery down too.

I look at her, trying to gauge what she wants me to say.

I say, I don't know.

Because I don't. Because, in all honesty, I've been trying to pack this problem up into a tiny little box and file it somewhere in a dark corner in the back of my brain where I will forget about it and it will just go away. I keep thinking of that flyer Dr Jacobs gave me with the smiling family on it. I keep waiting for Boy to come back to me and tell me what he wants. Of course, that's not going to happen and eventually I'm going to have to deal with it. But it's a nice fantasy to have all the same.

I want to chime in, Mum says. She looks nervous. If you don't mind, that is.

Okay.

She takes a deep breath: I think you should keep the baby.

Rory says, Clarissa, can you take the plates out, please. But she doesn't move, her gob open like she's trying to catch flies.

Close your mouth, Riss, I tell her.

I think you should keep it, Mum says again.

Why, though? I ask her.

You have a family here who can support you. You'll get help from social services. You're not on the street or a drug addict or anything like that. There's absolutely no reason why you're not capable of raising a child.

I shove a spoonful of creamy mash into my mouth. Push the rest of it round on my plate, build a mashed-potato fort, *Close Encounters of the Third Kind*-style.

I can help you with all the shopping and preparation. I can show you how to do it. How to change nappies and do feeds and all that kind of thing. I can go part-time at work to help you look after the baby. We can afford it, just about. You can put college on hold for a few years and go back when the baby starts nursery.

I don't reply, swishing the mash around my mouth until it is all liquid and gooey.

Leese, Rory says. Mum looks at him and I realise that she is close to crying.

I just think you need to realise that you are carrying *life* inside you, Bess. That's a *human life* in there. She points at my belly as though I can see it through my skin, the little cell cluster all warm and cosy in my womb.

Clarissa looks too and asks me if I'm going to get fat.

Are you blind? I'm already fat, I tell her. I lift up my T-shirt and push my belly out, showing her. Mum looks mortified.

Clarissa goes, Bess, you're such an idiot. You're not *fat*. You just wear clothes that are too small for you. Look: I can see your hip bones. How long until you get *really* fat? Not fake feeling-sorry-for-yourself fat?

I don't know, Riss, and I'm saying it to Mum too. I don't fucking know, okay?

I stand up and push past Rory into the hall and take my shoes out from the cupboard under the stairs.

Where are you going? Mum asks, her voice shrill.

Out.

Oh no you don't.

What are you going to do, Mum? Tie me up? Lock me up in my bedroom and throw away the key?

Fine, she says, go out. But don't come crying to me when this all comes crashing down on you. Because it will, Bess, I promise you. That boy won't care – he doesn't already, does he? Already washed his hands of you. Hasn't been calling round at stupid o'clock recently, has he? Where is he, Bess? Does he even know what's going on? Have you told him?

I slam the door extra loud. They've locked up my bike and Mum has the key in her desk drawer, because I *shouldn't be cycling anywhere in my condition*. I could walk to Eshal's, but that will take forty minutes, and when I get there, there's a ninety-nine per cent chance that Mrs Bhandari will just tell me to go home anyway. I wander up the road towards the reservoir and think about going to Boy's but dismiss the thought almost immediately as a terrible idea. I haven't seen Boy for weeks. I don't even know if he thinks of me at all any more. It feels inappropriate to turn up at his house unannounced now, even though that was normal for us before.

I keep walking to the end of the road, watching the obelisk-esque shapes of the film studios rise up into the evening sunshine. The studios have a certain smell. It's very distinct, like hot tarmac and traffic fumes. I love that smell. I wonder whether it smells like that inside the stages, too, or does it smell like plastic and silver, which is what film reel is made of?

I glance down the road towards Mary Magdalene Church and see a woman getting out of the car and bustling into the grounds. I realise it's May, the woman who was screaming at Boy when he crashed into the church last summer. I haven't seen her since she caught me loitering in the graveyard. That was months ago, before I was pregnant. So much has changed since then. Everything is beginning to segment itself into the 'before' and the 'now'. I wonder briefly what the 'after' will look like. I check my watch, the Hello Kitty one I pinched off Clarissa.

It's almost 7 p.m. I guess she's going to the women's group at the church. I walk down the road and follow her in through the large oak door.

The inside of the church is massive, the walls reaching up to a ceiling that melts into black shadows. At the altar, the stained-glass window depicts a female saint. I wonder who she was and what she did to become so holy. There are no pews, which surprises me. Instead, a group of twelve women sit in a rough semicircle on plastic classroom chairs. May is there and some other women I recognise from around town.

The women are speaking quietly to each other, laughing occasionally, all fiddling with their knitting, nimble hands winding wool around the thick needles. I approach them, unsure, my boots scuffing against the floor tiles.

May glances up and notices me. There's a flicker of recognition in her eyes. She remembers me.

Come and join us, she says, scraping her chair to the side, although it's not strictly necessary, there's plenty of room there already for an extra chair.

Who's this then, May? A woman with thick glasses and a shock of fluffy white hair says, looking up to examine me.

Well, I don't know her name, May says.

It's Bess.

Sit yourself down, then, Bess, she says. May points to the spare chairs, stacked against the wall underneath another stained-glass window.

I pull one over to the group and take my seat next to her.

Did you bring anything with you? she asks me, and I shake my head and begin to feel as though I've made a mistake.

You can use these, the woman with thick glasses says, and she nudges a carpet bag over to me.

I run my hand across the knitting needles all nestled in together. They make a metallic noise as they jostle against each other. They feel cool and smooth. I select a pair held together by an elastic band.

The glasses lady notices my choice and shakes her head. Go for thicker ones to start with. Much easier.

I obey and take out a second pair, each needle about as wide as a pencil.

Better, she says.

Has anyone got any wool?

Someone shoves some at me, a ball of thick turquoise twine, with threads of purple in it. I take it with a small smile. No one is really paying much attention to me at all, each of them working on their own knitting. Some are referring to patterns sketched or photocopied onto sheets of paper, or from magazines. May is twisting her needles around what looks to be the sleeve of a very fiddly baby's cardigan.

I turn my attention to one of the other women, who is younger than the rest, maybe in her sixties instead of everyone else's seventies and eighties. She is working on a plain square of red wool, her tongue slightly stuck out in concentration. It looks to be the easiest option compared to what everyone else is doing, so I try to mimic her. I wind my wool around one of my needles and tie a loose knot at the end, then take my second needle and poke it through the first ring. I've seen other people do this before on television and stuff. I have a vague memory of my grandmother (my real one) sitting on the sofa in front of *Springwatch*, or something equally boring, working away at a jumper or a hat. It's clear that my second-hand knowledge of how to knit is not helping at all. I have absolutely no idea what I'm doing.

May is watching me. After the wool comes away from the needle for a third time, she takes pity.

Give it here, Bess.

I hand it over and she shows me slowly how to set up the wool by gently looping loose knots around the needle, and how to start a new row.

I make slow progress, clumsily knitting my first row, pulling the wool too tight so that the material bunches and wrinkles. It's better than nothing, though.

The other women talk amongst themselves, about their kids, their grandchildren, their husbands, their friends. May's son and his wife recently moved their family to Swindon because her daughter-in-law has been offered a new job with better pay. Deirdre, the woman with the bug-eye glasses who lent me the needles, is in the deep end of a cold war with her neighbour over the overhanging petunias in the back garden.

Every morning I go out and snip a few more twigs off, Deirdre says, my neighbour hasn't seemed to notice yet. But, once, I caught him standing at the kitchen window watching me.

At first, I'm bored by their stupid anecdotes and their tiny lives, where their biggest problems are their kids moving to Swindon and their neighbours' flowers growing over the fence. But it's intriguing, and I find myself listening to Berry (the younger woman who sticks her tongue out when she knits) debating the pros and cons of planting daisies in window boxes when, really, they're weeds, but they're also really quite pretty, especially when the yolks are big. And another woman tells her, Don't be ridiculous, Berry, you can't put weeds in the window boxes. It's embarrassing.

May reaches over and helps me unknot a piece of wool where I've managed to tangle it while trying to start a new line.

It's the wrong time of year for it, May says, while picking at the knot.

Don't listen to them, Berry, I tell her, do what you bloody well like. They're your window boxes, you plant what you want in them.

Too right, Berry says, after a pause.

When the hour is up, I ask them if I can take a photograph of them. I only have my old Polaroid camera. They all cluck about their hair and straighten their clothes and arrange themselves into a cluster, some of them bending down to let the women behind them in. I snap the picture and shake the photograph that emerges from the slot. When I show them, they say oooh and aaah and tell me it's nice to have a young lady around and won't I come back next week, they'll help me with my knitting technique and bring extra cakes, and how old did I say I was again? I say yes and I mean it, because the church is so big and grand and the knitting ladies are so small inside it and it feels safe and calm, like we are in a big barren cavern and Jesus is watching over us.

Before they leave, they ask me to join their circle and say a prayer with them. It makes me feel uncomfortable. I think of Eshal with her quick, small muttered prayers under her breath, and her slow, big monumental prayers at mosque. Do I believe in God, unquestioningly, like Eshal? I don't know whether I do. I wish I did. Maybe it would make me feel safer, like it does Esh. Like someone is watching out for me, like Grandma Emelie says in my birthday cards. But even in the belly of the church, holding hands with the ladies in the circle, looking up at the stained glass, I don't feel God is watching me at all. And, unexpectedly, I feel a stab of jealousy for Eshal.

When I get home, I brace myself for the telling-off, but it doesn't come. Mum's quiet. When I was in the church, the heavy knot in my abdomen loosened, but now I'm home it is back and it feels like a peach stone stuck in my stomach.

I sit down at the dining-room table, facing her back as she cleans the glass on the cabinets.

Fine, I say.

She keeps polishing.

I said 'fine', I say again, louder.

Fine what, Bess? I don't have time for you to mess me about with your cryptic bloody crossword.

I meant, fine I'll think about it. Fine I'll think about the pregnancy. The baby.

I think, Maybe if I do this one thing, it'll be okay between us.

She stops and turns around. She pulls a chair out and drops onto it like all the air has escaped her body. She brings her hand up to her neck.

She says, I'm proud of you, and I think she means it. She's never said this to me before. I suddenly feel very flimsy.

She stands up again and picks up the polish.

By the way, she says, someone called Keris rang a few times. I told her you were out. Where were you, anyway?

I go still. Hearing Mum say Keris's name is so weird, like when you spot a teacher in the pub.

I went to the church down the road, I tell her, keeping my voice level.

The church? Yeah, right. Good one.

There's a knitting group.

Is Eshal still grounded, then?

Yes, for the rest of her life. I haven't even spoken to her.

Hmmm. I can't imagine you knitting.

Can I call her back?

What?

Can I use the phone? Call Keris?

Who's Keris?

A friend. I hesitate, and then say, She's got a baby. He's called Zack. He's two.

That's a toddler, not a baby.

Whatever. Can I call her?

Fine. But be quick.

I snatch the phone out of its cradle and sprint up the stairs, three at a time. In my bedroom with the door closed, I dial Boy's landline. I know the phone number by heart. Keris picks up on the third ring. She sounds like she's been crying. I can hear Zack in the background.

It's Bess, I tell her.

Oh. Nice to hear your voice. It's been crazy here. I don't know what to do.

As she talks, the peach stone in my belly gets bigger and heavier and more uncomfortable.

Keris, what's going on? Are you all right?

She gives a big sniff and I can tell for sure that she has been crying.

Is it Zack?

No. No, Zack's fine.

Then what's the matter?

It's Boy. He's been arrested. He's in jail.

Chapter Eighteen

The next morning, Keris picks me up outside my house in her bashed-up Ford Sierra, which has a new dent in the passenger door, with bright red paint scraped into the metal.

How did that happen? I ask her as I slide into the passenger seat. Today she's got the *Hercules* soundtrack on blast.

How do you think?

I make a face, then check myself.

Don't worry, she says, noticing, I would be mad if I were you too. I would be mad if I were *me*. He's really ballsed up now, hasn't he?

It's a statement, not a question.

Zack is in the back, strapped into his car seat. I wave at him and he goes BESSSSS in between singing along to 'Zero to Hero', a shock of fine ginger hair exploding vertically from his head like a troll doll. He says MUMMY ARE WE GOING TO SEASIDE.

Keris puts the car into first and pulls away from the front of the house. I glance up and see Mum looking out through the slatted blinds in her bedroom window. Keris notices too.

Are your parents okay with you coming out? she asks me, and the way she says it makes me feel more Zack's age than hers. Actually, the reason I got allowed out was because I told Mum that Keris and I were going to talk baby stuff, pregnancy stuff, teenage-mother stuff.

Yeah, they're fine.

God, it must be so weird to have parents that actually care about where you're going, Keris says.

I make an 'mmm' noise. I think about explaining to her about being in foster care for all of half a second before I decide against it. I can already picture the look of pity she would have on her face, the kinds of questions she would ask. Everyone asks the same questions. And anyway, I'm not about to tell Keris – who had to grow up at sixteen, whose mum ditched her and whose dad is a total loser – how I hate how they want me to be. How Mum uses social services as a threat. At least I didn't fall out of the system.

What's your mum like? Is she really strict?

Pretty much, I tell her.

I'm going to be strict with Zack, Keris says, but not *too* strict, you know? Not so strict that he hates me. Just so that he knows the rules and knows where the line is and not to cross it. It's different for boys when they get older. When me and Boy still lived with our dad, *I* was the one with the curfew and *I* was the one who got all the questions when I went out. No one cared where Boy went, even though he was younger.

Double standard, innit, I say.

But I'm not doing that for Zack. If I have a girl at some point, she's having the same rules across the board.

I say, I heard that if your parents weren't strict then you end up being super-strict as a parent. Because everyone thinks their parents were bad at parenting.

Keris nods. Was your grandma really laid-back then?

Who?

You know. Your mum's mum, because she's so strict.

I hesitate for a moment. I think of Grandma Emelie, first. She never seemed like the strict type in her cards. I never met Mum's mum – she died when Mum was young. I know that when she was a kid, Mum's family lived in Camden in London and her dad had a good job in the City so they could afford to move out to the suburbs, because back then living in London was like living in the slums, and moving out to the suburbs was like telling everyone you'd made it. Mum, Jason and their parents moved to Wimbledon when Mum was sixteen. One day my mum got home from college around four o'clock and found her hanged in the bathroom, a dressing-gown tie around her neck suspending her from the ceiling, her black patent heels still on her stockinged feet, her pink fingernails freshly painted and filed into points.

So, was your gran strict? Keris asks again, and I wonder if she thinks I didn't hear her properly or something.

Nah, I don't think so, I say, I don't think she was bothered about parenting.

Well, there you go, then, Keris says. Point proven.

We don't speak for a moment and Zack drives his fire truck up the side of the car door.

He's got no friends, Keris says, clearly not talking about Zack.

She continues, I rang his work and told them what happened and the guy I spoke to on the phone didn't know who he was. I had to describe him before the guy twigged who I was talking about. Apparently, he doesn't bother with anyone at Tesco. No one likes him there. Now I'm freaking out because maybe I shouldn't have rung them at all, because now they know and what if they sack him? It's a criminal record, right? How are we going to pay the rent? They're remanding him in custody until his court date.

I make a sympathetic noise, but I don't know what 'remanding in custody' actually means. I feel like I would look stupid if I asked, though.

When's the court date?

I don't know. Next month, probably.

What did he even *do*? I ask.

You know his car? The one he smashed into the church last year? Well, they finally traced it back to him. That car was stolen, did you know that? I sure as hell didn't know it was stolen.

She rolls down the driver's window and spits her gum out.

I swear to God, she says, this is Joel all over again.

Joel?

Zack's dad.

I tell her I'm sorry, but all I can really think about is how my belly is fizzing up because we're on our way to see him, I'm going to see Boy, even if he is in jail. I hope I look pretty. I hope I don't look too fat.

Not your fault, is it? It's his own stupid fault. D'you know, I actually think you were good for him. You calmed him down a bit, you know? Then he messed that up as well. I'm sorry to drag you back into all of this, Bess, I know you probably want to be shot of him. But I just . . . I didn't want him to have no one. You were the only person I can think of he might be happy to see.

I wouldn't be so sure, I tell her.

Are you in a fight? What happened between you two?

Oh . . . the usual. You know. He stopped talking to me and I took the hint.

Oh my God, are you serious? I'm *so* sorry. If I'd known I wouldn't have—

Don't worry about it. This will be good for me, anyway. I can . . . get it all out of my system.

Keris cringes. What a twat.

I laugh light-heartedly, thinking maybe this being arrested thing is the whole reason he hasn't been in touch with me. Maybe he's been dealing with this and he's been desperate to see me the whole time.

The windshield glitters. I'm going to see him. I'm going to see Boy. I imagine what it might feel like to touch him, my skin against his, apart from the single thin layer of atoms between us. Despite everything, I'm excited at the prospect, but I can still feel my hands trembling. I sit on them so Keris can't see.

We drive to the police station in Staines. Zack points at the police cars outside and asks whether we're going to visit Daddy, but Keris says no, we're visiting Uncle Boy. When we get there, Keris gives our names and Boy's name to the sergeant, or constable, or whoever he is, sitting behind the desk. The man looks like he is trying to grow a beard but failing.

We're here to see Boy Mitcham, says Keris.

Who? says the policeman.

Boy Mitcham. Then she pauses and says, Oh, you probably have him down as David Mitcham.

The officer checks and confirms that he's here. Keris glances at me.

David? I say, rolling the word around in my mouth.

Yep, she says.

Isn't that your dad's name?

Yep.

The dad who started the whole 'boy' nickname in the first place?

Yep.

Wow.

Yep.

The officer tells us to sit down in the waiting area, so we go over to some cheap plastic chairs against a wall. There is a noticeboard with a bunch of leaflets pinned to it warning against the danger of knives and encouraging us to report signs of domestic abuse. There's another which asks in big purple letters: ARE YOU THE VICTIM OF A FORCED MARRIAGE? with a photograph of a girl in a hijab looking down at her own clenched fists. There is the name of a charity and a telephone number. I check my bag for a pen, but no luck. I do have a camera, though. My old Diana Mini. I wipe the lens with the hem of my T-shirt and take a photograph of the poster, hoping that there's enough light in the dingy waiting room to make the picture come out all right.

Keris and I wait, the backs of my thighs sticking to the plastic chair. Outside, the sky is grey, but the air still shimmers with heat. This summer has been the hottest for a long time. There is a small television mounted onto the magnolia wall in the waiting room and it is switched to the lunchtime news. The newscaster is talking about the *Lunar Prospector*, the moon-mapping spacecraft that NASA launched last year. I remember being late for school so I could watch the launch of the Prospector on *BBC Breakfast*. Now, on the screen, the picture switches to a grainy shot of the craft on the moon's surface. I watch the subtitles pop up beneath the newsreader.

What's happened? Keris asks me, noticing that I am watching.

They crashed it.

Crashed what? The spaceship? She narrows her eyes at the screen, trying to make out exactly what it is she's looking at.

It's not really a spaceship, I say, but yeah, they crashed it.

Wow. Idiots. You'd think that working at NASA they would know how to drive a spaceship, Keris laughs.

Not a spaceship. And they crashed it deliberately.

Why would they do that?

They think there's frozen water on the moon. That's what the

Lunar Prospector was built for: to detect water on the moon.

And they found some?

Yeah. Ice deposits. And NASA crashed the Prospector because they thought the impact would dislodge the ice and send a plume of water vapour into the atmosphere, and then they would know for sure.

There's water on the moon? Mad.

Well, no. They didn't see any cloud formation. So they still don't know.

Keris is quiet for a moment, watching the interview on the telly with a NASA scientist. He looks like he's going to cry.

All that for nothing, she says.

Yep. Total waste of time.

The police officer at the reception desk slides open his glass window, which I suppose is meant to protect him from rowdy criminals, and shouts at us that visiting hours have started so we can go through now.

Big solar eclipse soon, I tell Keris.

Really? Cool. How do you know all this space stuff?

I look at her and Zack and I realise that if I go in there, to see Boy, I'm going to have to tell him that I'm pregnant. Even if I don't want to, I will. I won't be able to stop myself.

And if I tell him, that's it. There's no turning back. That's what makes it real.

Keris, do you mind if I wait out here with Zack? It will be easier for you to talk to Boy if Zack's not there. Also, I don't know whether we should let him go into a jail. I'm not sure it's a good life experience for a little kid, you know?

He has supervised visits with Joel all the time at Pentonville, Keris responds, and her tone is spiky. And what Zack said earlier about visiting his dad suddenly makes sense.

Oh. Well, obviously. Sorry.

If you don't want to come in, you can stay out here with Zack, I don't mind.

Okay, I wasn't thinking.

It's fine, Bess. I know you're not used to these things. This kind of life.

The way she says it sounds like an accusation and I feel ashamed of myself. But she changes her mind and says, That was harsh of me.

It's fine, just go. Go! I say, jokingly shooing her away.

She heads through the heavy door that is being held open for her by an officer, waving back to Zack before it closes with a dull clang. I feel like all my nerves are twisted into knots. I watch the news, and the picture is of the *Lunar Prospector* drifting into the moon's surface, as though it's no more significant than a paper bag being shunted by the breeze. The picture shows the *Prospector* from above, grinding across the terrain to stop next to a pockmarked crater. Even from the blurred, black-and-white image, it's easy to see that there is no cloud of water vapour, no plume of dislodged ice. Just quiet and blackness.

Keris arrives back in the reception area forty-five minutes later.

Let's go.

That was quick, I say as I pack Zack's toys into Keris's travel bag. We've been doing building blocks on the floor of the waiting room. We took turns building a tower and knocking it down. I did the building and Zack did the destroying.

Keris doesn't respond to my comment. We traipse out of the station and down the road to the car park. Keris straps Zack in and within moments we're back on the road.

I ask her what happened, because I can see that she is gripping the steering wheel so tight her knuckles have turned yellow.

He, she says, is infuriating. *Infuriating.* I almost got arrested myself. I had to restrain myself from throttling him across the table.

You all right?

Not really. Shall we take Zack to the park? I don't feel like going home yet. It smells bad in there. Boy usually takes the bins out because it makes me gag. Shall we go to the park, Zacky?

Zack screams delightedly.

I say, Sure, whatever you want.

We drive to Littleton Rec and let Zack run around in the park gleefully, taking it in turns to push him on the swing.

Then Keris says, What's going on with you, Bess?

I told you. He basically dumped me. Not that we were even going out. But yeah, he dumped me.

No, I mean, what's going on with *you?*

I don't answer, and fiddle with the drawstring on my shorts while Keris lifts Zack out of the swing seat and sets him down.

I feel like I want to tell her. For the last few weeks, I have had this horrible feeling in my bones, like they are all about to splinter and my skin will melt into a puddle on the floor, and the foetus will leak out of me like the yolk from a cracked egg.

But if I tell Keris, she will tell Boy, and then it's real.

I wonder if he'll do a runner. I mean, he's in prison, so he can't run anywhere. But I bet he does.

I look back at Keris and she is fussing over Zack, and she glances at me and beams and I remember what I liked about Keris in the first place, that she is one hundred per cent a good person, one of those people who could be best friends with anyone. But the moment's passed, so I tuck everything back in and try to forget about it.

When Zack gets tired and grizzly and we're ready to leave, I ask her to drop me at Eshal's house. I jump out of the car, wave goodbye, and walk up to Eshal's door. There are no cars in the driveway, which is good, because it means that she might be home alone. I knock using the brass handle, but no response. I peer through the frosted-glass window but all I can see is the fading light from the kitchen window. I sit down on the doorstep and wait.

It's forty-five minutes before Eshal's brother Anwar pulls into the driveway on his bashed-up moped with a wonky green 'P' plate slapped onto the wheel arch.

What do you want, Bess? he asks me after he has pulled his head out of his helmet and switched off the ignition.

Anwar, so good to see you! How have you been? How's university? Managed to get that stick out your arse yet?

What do you want?

Where's Eshal?

She's in Bangladesh with my mum.

What? Why?

She's being introduced to someone. A potential match.

A potential *husband*, you mean?

Look – Bess – I know what happened. My mother said you're not supposed to be here.

I thought your parents weren't kicking off the matchmaking for Eshal until after your wedding?

Well – after the stunt you two pulled – they've decided to speed it up.

Anwar, you know how sick that is, right? She's sixteen years old. She doesn't need to be in Bangladesh picking out her husband!

Bess, look, don't get involved.

He steps past me and unlocks the front door.

You know she doesn't want it, right?

He turns around and frowns at me.

Don't be ridiculous. Of course she wants it. And even if she didn't, it's not just about her. This is our cultural heritage. It's tradition. I don't expect you to understand that.

Well, when is she going to be back? I ask him, aware of the shrill tone my voice has taken on.

I don't know. Next week? The week after? Get off my porch.

I throw my arms up in exasperation just as he slams the door in my face. The noise ricochets through my body.

I shout, FUCKSAKE ANWAR and OPEN THE DOOR. When he doesn't come back, I give up and walk into the road.

The light is almost gone, now. I think about Esh, all the signs I've missed because I've been too obsessed with myself, because my whole world goes as far north as Boy's house and as far east as the M3 as it passes by the Pits and as far west as the sodding tyre swing on the river. She's been trying to find a way out and I haven't helped her. Not one bit. I sit down on the kerb, my palms flat against the warm pavement, and think of her all alone in Dhaka, and me all alone here, and in a way we're all alone together, even though we're so far apart.

Chapter Nineteen

It's my sixteenth birthday today, and for one glorious moment when I open my eyes in the morning, I forget about everything. And for that moment I feel weightless. But then I remember that Esh is gone, that I'm pregnant and getting pregnant-er by the second, that Boy is in jail and hates me and doesn't know about me being pregnant.

I look up at the dots on the ceiling and while I'm counting the faces, I concentrate on feeling sorry for myself. I've never been so miserable in my life, and there, again, is that gnawing, aching peach stone in the pit of my stomach that won't go away.

I drag myself out of bed and into the hall, dial Esh's number on the phone, and even though I know she's on the other side of the world and she'll never pick up, I'm still hopeful. When no one answers the Bhandaris' phone, I dial again, and again, and again. Each time imagining that Esh will pick up and it will all have been a bad dream, a joke that went too far. It's not, though, and I'm still alone.

When I come downstairs, Mum has laid out a pile of gifts on the living-room table. More than what I usually get for a birthday or Christmas.

You're up early, Rory says to me. He is standing in the kitchen drinking coffee.

It's eleven forty-five, I tell him.

Mum said there's a message for you on the answering machine.

I go into the living room and pick up the phone, hoping it's finally Eshal, back from Bangladesh. But the message is from Henry, my social worker, wishing me a happy birthday. Then he says that he is moving departments, and my case has been transferred to a new social worker on the 'Leaving Care' team.

That's a bit cold, isn't it? Rory asks me, overhearing.

It's exactly what I expected, I say.

I put the phone down. I should have known that Henry wouldn't be my social worker for more than five minutes. Now I have to start all over again with someone new.

My skin is still raw. Clarissa is watching Saturday-morning TV. A cooking programme; they're making duck in sticky plum sauce with thick mashed potato. My mouth is suddenly wet with too much saliva.

Clarissa wishes me a happy birthday.

Thanks, I say, and as I say it, I vomit all over Mum's tango-pink rug that Uncle Jason got her from Amsterdam.

Fuck, says Clarissa, surprising us all, including herself. Her hand flies to her mouth and she looks at Rory, her big milk-saucer eyes sheepish.

Rory tells Clarissa to get the carpet spray and some old towels and a wet J-cloth.

I'm sorry.

Don't be, Rory says, this rug is crap. I've been waiting for a reason to get her to throw it out.

And I suddenly have this feeling like I want to throw my arms around him and cry.

She's going to be so mad.

No, she isn't. She's at work until twelve, there was an emergency appointment this morning. The funeral directors in the high street need a replica pair of glasses. They accidentally broke a pair. Open casket, as well.

Awkward.

So, we've got some time to sort this out, all right?

Clarissa comes back with all the things Rory asked for and they work together to get all of my sick out of the rug.

This rug is basically the colour of sick, anyway, Clarissa says.

Rory scoops my chun up in a towel and hands it to Clarissa, who drops it into a plastic carrier bag while pinching her nose. I sit down on the sofa, waves of nausea still rolling through me.

Good thing you haven't had breakfast yet, Clarissa says, and I nod weakly, my eyes closed. Then it would be much worse, she continues, chunks and everything.

Yeah, thanks for the imagery, Riss.

Oh . . . you're still feeling sick?

Yeah.

Oh.

After it's all cleared up and disposed of, Rory rolls the Amsterdam rug up and props it against the fence in the back garden. Then I go upstairs and shower, because I feel like the smell of it is clinging to me and embedding itself into my pores. I put on a pair of tracksuit bottoms and a cardigan, ultimate comfort clothes. As I'm combing my wet hair, the sickening feeling starts to disintegrate, and by the time I'm done, it's almost completely gone.

I hear the front door open and close and Mum's voice filling up the hallway. I wander downstairs barefoot and she catches sight of me.

Happy birthday, she says.

Thanks.

Rory has poured himself another coffee and is perched on the arm of the sofa.

Are we going to get these presents opened, then? he says.

Where's my rug gone? Mum says, staring at the empty bit of carpet where it's supposed to be.

There was an accident, I tell her. Rory shakes his head at me.

What kind of accident?

I was sick.

Mum pauses, looking at me, deliberating. I point out the window to the rug, propped up in the garden.

For crying out loud, Bess.

I'm sorry, all right? It wasn't my fault.

Never your fault, always sorry. Can we not have you ruin every single thing in this house? I bet you were stuffing your face in your bedroom until God-knows-what-time last night. With food from my cupboards. No wonder you were sick. What is *wrong* with you?

It wasn't my fault. I think . . . well, I think I'm getting morning sickness.

Bess, I had *terrible* morning sickness with Clarissa and I never *once* threw up anywhere except in the toilet. Can you not control yourself? Jesus!

I want to hit her in the face. Make her nose bleed. Make her eyeballs bulge out of her skull. Make little bits of her skull splinter off into her wispy blonde hair. I want to say to her *I'm doing this for you. I've got morning sickness because* you *want this, not me.*

I thought saying I'd think about keeping it would make things between us better. But it hasn't.

I say to her, Would you react like this if Clarissa had done the same thing?

No, Bess, because *Clarissa* would never be stupid enough to get herself pregnant.

And I would? You raised both of us, Lisa. What's so different between me and Riss? What's so special about her and so *defective* about me?

Both of you, leave it, for Christ's sake, Rory says.

And even Clarissa, who has made herself very small in the corner chair, pipes up, Yeah, it's Bess's birthday, isn't it? Everyone needs to be nice to her. Birthday privileges.

Mum looks from Rory to Riss and back again, her lips very thin.

So it's all my fault, now, is it? she asks the room, her voice wavering.

And Rory goes, Lisa!

Fine, she says. Fine. Fine. Open your presents then, Bess.

She pulls out a chair for me at the dining table. I take a seat and it feels like I've been sent to the headmaster's office for a bollocking.

Not that you deserve any of it, she says quietly, only to me, and I stand up and say, Fuck this, I'm going. And I leave the dining room and her stupid smug-turning-shocked face and I walk out the front door in my trackies and my cardic with no shoes on. And I walk down the road towards the kiddie park in the shadow of Stage H and squeeze my bum into one of the swings and I kick my legs and swing so high, imagining that I could go all the way over and wrap the swing around the top support beam until I'm all coiled up in it like a bug in a spider's web.

I swing for a while, fuming. After about half an hour, Billy from next door drifts past on his scooter, his head wound all the way round like a wind-up toy so he can watch me. His eyes are black and shiny, and I can see from all the way over here that he is staring at me. I make a wanking sign at him and he makes one back at me.

He shouts over to me from the other side of the park fence:

Did you just have a bust-up? I heard it through the wall. Why did you put that rug in the back garden?

I shout back: Because I threw up on it.

What were you arguing about?

Wind your neck in, you nosy shit.

He drops his scooter where he's standing and pushes the gate open, making it squeal on its hinges. He takes the swing next to mine, planting his feet in the baby seat and throwing his body weight backwards so that his legs kick out from underneath him.

What were you arguing with your parents about?

Billy, if you don't fuck off, I swear on my life I'll—

Nah, you won't. Got any baccy?

I shake my head no.

What happened to your arms? He points at the back of my right bicep, which is still red and raw from the bathtub. The skin is beginning to flake off. I wake up in the middle of the night and feel as though I'm sleeping in a sandpit. The skin comes off in drifts. Sometimes I forget that it looks like that until someone points it out. I wonder whether Eshal's hands have healed yet, or whether they look like my own.

You want some spliff? Billy asks me, untucking a half-smoked joint from behind his ear.

Billy, you're like, twelve.

So?

What're you doing smoking weed? Don't you have a mother who loves you?

Billy shrugs. I found a needle down the alley at the back of the woods last week.

What, a knitting needle? I respond, smiling at my own joke.

Whatever. So, do you want some?

I take the blunt from his offered hand, remembering in

passing that I'm pregnant but not caring. We sit there and smoke together, passing the joint between us, until we see a couple of mums coming into the park with buggies. Billy recognises one of his mum's friends, panics, stubs out his joint, hops out of the swing and picks up his scooter from the pavement.

I still hate you, I shout at him. He waves at me and sticks his tongue out as he scoots off. He looks like a cartoon character.

I get off my swing for the mums and their toddlers and move over to a bench at the edge of the playground. One of the mothers gives me a dirty look. I stretch out across the bench like a cat and watch the kids trying to push each other on the roundabout but not managing because it's far too heavy for them. I vaguely realise that I spend way too much time hanging out in kids' parks.

From one of the back gardens parallel to the park, I can make out the sound of a child crying, the kind of crying you hear when a kid is about to throw a tantrum. Moments later, the voice of the mother is soothing him. I look across the Studios Estate, all golden in its summer-ness, with its red-brick terraces with brown roof tiles and white window frames and its neat rows of front gardens and sprinklers. I wonder how many of these houses are just cages for mums looking after their kids, how many of them are trapped here, whether I'm about to be trapped too. Wonder if I run to the Studios gates and tell them I'm escaping, whether they'll let me in.

I think about Keris, and how every single thing about her is secondary to what Zack wants and needs and feels. And Eshal, and my neck feels too heavy to carry my head when I think about what she has ahead of her, all the things she'll never be able to do now, who doesn't even have a choice in it. I realise how selfish I am compared to everyone else.

When the sun is at its highest point in the sky, I shuffle home, my bare feet cooking against the hot concrete. The front door is on the latch, so I let myself in and tiptoe up to my bedroom. Mum is in the garden, messing about with the hanging baskets, but I can't see Rory or Riss. In my bedroom, I push the window open as wide as it can go and step out onto the porch roof. From where I'm sitting, I can see the park and the two mums playing with their kids. I make up stories about them in my head.

After a while, there's a small knock on my door and Clarissa comes in, holding the presents from downstairs in her arms and balancing them in place with her chin.

I thought you might want these.

Come here, then, I tell her, and I make room for her out on the porch roof. She brings the presents with her and makes a little pile of them near my feet. There's also a card from Henry with a ten-pound voucher for WHSmith's, and the usual card I get from my real grandmother, with a babyish Barbie design on the front which is way too young for me, and a crisp fifty-pound-note inside. I lean back through the window, pull my bedside-table drawer open, thinking I'll add the money to the envelope in the photo album, where all the other fifties are from Emelie, but from this angle I can't see the photo album in the drawer, so I just shove the new note into my pencil case, think-ing I'll add it to the rest of the cash later. I remember that Boy hasn't paid me back the money I lent him, and there is a familiar pang in my stomach when I think of him. I suddenly feel as though not seeing him at the station was the wrong thing to do. Maybe if I had seen him, and he looked into my face, he would remember how he feels about me. Maybe it wouldn't be so bad if he knew I was pregnant after all.

There are seven presents in the pile. I pick each of one up and shake it and let Riss guess what it might be before I open it. She guesses: slippers, CDs, a portable radio, an ice-cream maker, a pair of earrings and chocolate. The first gift I open is from Mum and it's small and squishy. Clarissa changes her slippers guess to a scarf or a woolly hat. I open it up, balling the paper and launching it off the porch roof into the road, aiming for next-door's wheelie bin. I miss. It's not a woolly hat or a scarf, it's a set of three pale white Babygros, the kind with little popper buttons on the crotch and the shoulders. There are little yellow embroidered ducks all over them.

Are you going to puke again? Clarissa asks me, looking at my face. I shake my head, try to smile at her.

The next one I pick up is a big box with sharp corners, wrapped in pink. The one Clarissa thought was an ice-cream machine. I open it. The picture on the box is a machine with a suction thing at one end that looks like something you would use to unblock a toilet.

What is it? Clarissa asks.

I turn the box around, looking for some writing. Then I find it.

It's a breast pump, I say.

A *what*.

A breast pump. It sucks the milk out of your—

Yeah, I know what it does. I'm not stupid.

Well . . . you were half-right. You could say that both an ice-cream machine and a breast pump make a dairy product.

You're disgusting.

Next one?

None of these presents are for you really, are they?

I shake my head and suddenly feel like giving her a hug.

By the way, only cattle make dairy, she says, her face triumphant.

She hands me a smaller box-shaped item wrapped in glittery blue paper.

This one's from me, she says, I picked it out of the Argos catalogue and Dad went and got it for me. And then I wrapped it up.

I go to shake it, but she stops me. So, I peel the paper back
carefully and peek inside. I see the writing on the box and the
corner of the logo and know immediately what is.

AS IF! I shout.

I knew you'd like it.

I scramble to rip off the rest of the paper and fling it off the
porch into the front garden. I examine the box, barely daring to
believe it. A Canon MV-1. One of the smallest and lightest digital camcorders in the world. With progressive scan technology
and digital display. I've been wanting one of these cameras since
it came out last year.

How did you know about this? I ask her, half-suspicious,
half-awed.

Clarissa shrugs. I just assumed. You like cameras, but you
don't have a digital one yet. I thought you might want one. And
my friend Jessica at school whose dad works at the Studios said
that this is the best one you can get.

Your friend Jessica is right, I tell her.

Good. I'm glad you like it.

Now I *really* don't want to open the rest of this baby stuff, I
say, looking at all the unopened gifts.

Then don't. You can do it later when we come back.

Come back from where?

The Twynersh. Mum's booked a table. Birthday dinner. She
booked it ages ago.

I groan loudly. She should've known we'd have a barney on
my birthday.

Clarissa shrugs and opens one of the other presents that I
haven't touched yet. It's a holdall type bag, yellow with little
daisies printed onto it. It's quite nice.

I suppose that's to put baby stuff in, I say.

Whatever, you can put your trainers in it instead. That way, when you go out in heels, you've got comfy shoes to change into, and a nice bag to hide them in.

Clarissa, why are you being so nice to me? I'm always such a cow to you.

Clarissa thinks for a moment and says, Well, we're sisters, aren't we?

But we're not. Not really, anyway.

It feels like we are.

I agree with her because I don't want to hurt her feelings.

And Mum can be a real B-I-T-C-H sometimes.

That I can agree with.

We've got to stick together.

Guess so.

In the evening, we all get into the car and drive to the Twynersh in Chertsey, which has a huge pub garden, so we sit outside on a bench under one of the umbrellas.

I half-listen to Rory talk about the way they cook the steak here and how much better it is than the way they do it at the Boat House, but, really, I'm watching Mum and the way she is fiddling with the corner of the menu, digging it right under her fingernail so far that it looks painful, her lips thin and tight.

She looks up and spots me watching her. She says, You're wearing the same jumper I got you for your fifteenth birthday.

I look down and she's right. It's a thin dark blue sweater with three horizontal white stripes on the chest. It's one of my favourites.

I'm surprised it still fits you, she says, and I can't work out whether she's saying that I've got fatter or that I should have a pregnancy belly by now, or just that I've changed since I was fifteen.

Rory says, They season the meat with paprika salt and then they leave it to marinate for forty-eight hours.

Mum says, Shut up about the steaks, please, Rory.

I feel like I'm getting too old for this.

The waiter comes and takes our orders. Unbelievably, Rory asks for more details about the steak. Clarissa gets macaroni cheese. Mum orders a Caesar salad and I order a steak like Rory because he's kind of convinced me.

We sit in silence, except Clarissa, who chirps about any old nonsense – school, her friends, her new favourite pop group – completely oblivious to the atmosphere, until the food arrives. As soon as the waiter sets the plate down in front of me, I realise that I have made a terrible mistake. I asked for my steak to be cooked medium-rare, and I can see the oily blood dribbling out of it and settling around it, muddy against the white china. I poke it with my knife and more blood comes out. It smells metallic even though they've tried to smother the scent with garlic and butter.

As the others start eating, I realise that it's not just my steak. Everything has a terrible smell. I push my plate away from me, feeling my mouth fill up with saliva.

It takes me ten minutes to find the bathroom and then the ladies' is out of order, so I have to shove into the disabled loo, which has a faulty lock. The restaurant's air conditioning is broken, and the heat increases the smell of disinfectant and urine. I retch into the toilet basin and a miserable dribble of sick comes out on a long thin string of spit. My stomach contracts, trying to expel food that isn't there.

I come back to the table and no one says a word for a full five minutes.

I take it you're not going to eat that, Mum says. I shake my head no. She doesn't argue. Maybe the look on my face tells her something. Rory takes my plate and scoops the contents onto his own empty one. Mum calls the waiter over and asks for a glass of milk. When he comes back with it, she directs him to set it down in front of me. I look at it.

Mum, why do I want a glass of milk?

Trust me, she says, when I was having Clarissa, it did wonders for me. Settled my stomach completely.

But I'm not you, I say, I don't think dairy is going to settle my stomach.

I'm now thinking about the breast pump, and when I glance at Clarissa, it looks like she is too. She's giving the milk a look.

Just drink it, Bess.

I look at her and say, I'm really sorry. I can't.

Silence settles over us again. I don't know what to do with my hands.

Maybe I could have a Coke, I say.

Yeah, right.

What, no Coke?

You know what kind of damage that's going to do to the baby?

She whispers the word 'baby'. I think about damage and all the extra cigarettes I've been smoking since I left the hospital.

I say to Mum, I mean, if it can survive a litre of gin—

Shut your mouth.

She shakes her head.

We are silent for a few moments and then Rory is asking what I'm doing about college.

I tell him: I missed most of the application deadlines, but I reckon I'll still get an interview in a few places. They might let me start late, or maybe defer a year but guarantee my place for next September. I heard that London Film School runs courses during term time.

Mum interrupts. You can't be serious. Of course you're not going to London Film School.

Yes, I am. If I can get in.

And how exactly are you going to raise a child and be a film student at the same time? Have you thought through anything at all? Do you *ever* think?

The milk is turning yellow in the evening sunshine.

You said you would help me through college, with the baby. That's what you said. I could study part-time, or something.

I can hear how pathetic I sound as I say this, like a whiny kid. But I don't care.

That's what you told Henry, anyway.

Now she looks at me like I'm mental.

Bess, you *really thought* you could go to college and be a mother with a newborn baby at the same time? Are you thick? Being a mother is a full-time job. Believe you me. We only said those things to Henry to appease that stupid woman, Dr Jacobs. She insisted we gave you options.

I can't deal with this, I say, trying to keep my voice level, aware of all the people on the other benches, food on forks halfway to their mouths, trying not to stare too hard.

It's a shame you weren't thinking about college when you had your knickers round your ankles, Mum spits back.

I scrape my chair across the patio and stride out of the beer garden, towards the road. For once, she follows me. I get through the car park, to the edge of the dual carriageway. The cars shoot past at sixty miles per hour. The roaring sound they leave behind fills up my head. I want to press my forehead against the ground and feel the coolness of the concrete in the shade against my skull.

She shouts to me, from her spot further down the road, I know what you're planning.

What am I planning? I shout back.

I won't let you kill a baby just so you can do what you want and have an easy life.

Life is not easy, I yell at her, and I feel tears escaping my eyes and sliding down my face.

You can't be selfish when you're a mother.

But I'm *not* a mother.

You have a child!

It's not a child. It's a cluster of cells. I told you I'd think about it, didn't I? You can stop it, now. Stop being like this. You're getting what you want.

But I know you, Bess. I know when you're lying to me.

I'm not lying.

She is almost level with me now, saying, If you do this, if you *get rid* of the baby, I can't have you in my house. I can't stand by and let you make this mistake. I won't be able to forgive you.

I look up to the road and feel tempted to step out in front of one of the cars. I say, Well, that's your prerogative.

Suddenly, nausea overwhelms me.

I touch her shoulder involuntarily and tell her I'm going to be sick.

Go, go, go.

Like she's my coach and I'm an athlete on the starting block and the gun has just gone off.

I half-jog, half-run across the car park. The pebbles are paler than they were before.

I don't make it. Bile rises in my throat and I vomit violently by a purple Renault Clio.

She follows me. I'm panting, hands on my knees, vomit in a neat pile next to me.

I can't do this, I tell her.

Nor can I.

My sweater sticks to my back. She squeezes my shoulder with something that feels like concern. I spit out the leftover bile. I can feel her shuddering next to me, both of us crouched in the car park over my sick, and I know she's crying. Her fingernails dig into my shoulder as she holds onto me, tries to steady her breath. But I can't bring myself to look at her.

Chapter Twenty

Still no sign of Eshal. I cycle to Fujifilm and pick up my developed photographs. I found the key to my bike lock in the stationery drawer in the dining room. The photographs came out well. I have one set of pictures from the Asahi Pentax and the other set came from my Diana camera. One of the photographs from the Diana set is of the poster in the waiting room at the police station. It's dark but I can still make out the telephone number for the forced marriage hotline. I tuck that photo into the back pocket of my jean shorts, folded in half, and the rest go into my backpack. Then I pedal back to Shepperton along the A308, past Tesco where Boy works – used to work – and my Walkman is on and Aretha Franklin's 'Respect' is blasting full volume, making my eardrums ache because the wind against my face as I cycle hurts too, and for a moment it's as if nothing ever happened and I'm still Bess, un-pregnant. Just a normal kid.

And then a car honks at me, right next to me, so loud that my bike wobbles and I have to stop, putting my feet down to prevent myself from toppling over, and my headphones fall out and Aretha's voice is no more, and the guy who just honked at me from a rusty Mini Metro yells at me to watch the road. I make a wanking sign at him and he revs the engine hard as he accelerates away, leaving me to inhale the exhaust fumes. And all my momentary euphoria is gone, and I remember who I am and what is happening to me. That I'm eleven weeks gone now. And how there's not a single person I can talk to about this, not Mum, not Esh in Dhaka, not Boy in jail, not Henry who's fucked off God-knows-where, and I feel like I want to die.

But I keep cycling to Eshal's, because falling into traffic isn't the romantic death I have planned for myself.

I follow the dual carriageway into Shepperton and turn onto Gaston Bridge Road, which is Eshal's road. Her driveway has no cars in it. And it hits me all over again that Esh is gone. And I feel all of the air come out of me, and I'm deflating like a sad balloon, and I get off my bike and lie down on the pavement, face down, let the warm concrete touch my cheek, smell that dirt-rain-cement smell, breathe it in, all sunshine-baked, stare at the tiny stones scattered in front of my face, splay my hands and arms wide open like an angel, feel my throat get hot and dry and tight but still don't cry. I don't know if I'm ever going to see her again.

I leave my bike and knock once. Nothing. I glance up at Esh's bedroom window, which is the left-hand window on the first floor, and see that the purple sheer curtains are drawn. There is a dreamcatcher hanging from the ceiling. I clamber onto the Bhandaris' bin, and from there hoist myself onto the bay window. It juts out slightly from the flat façade of the house, and has its own little roof on it, so I can easily find my footing, with just enough height to reach the slim outer windowsill of Esh's bedroom. I take the photograph out of my back pocket, and slide it into the space between the window and the frame. The tiny gap where the seal should be is just wide enough to shove the photograph through. I watch as it drops to Eshal's bedroom floor, next to her empty laundry basket, folded in half with just the plain white back of the photo paper showing. I kiss the window, leaving an ugly smudge on it. As I lower myself back onto the driveway, I notice that there is a woman standing in the door of the house opposite Eshal's. She is holding a watering can and watching me.

Morning, I call over to her, because this seems less suspicious than saying nothing. I pick up my bike from the ground and swing one leg over it.

If I see you here again, I'm calling the police, she says loudly, and a man emerges from the dark of the house to stand next to her, probably her husband.

I'm a friend of Eshal's, I say, struggling to keep my voice level.

A friend of whose?

Eshal's.

Whose?

ESHAL.

Oh. Paki name, is it?

I stand there for a moment, propped on my bike, stunned, then I say: They're Bangladeshi, you fucking small-brained *toad*.

And she says, What did you just say to me, young lady?

And I shout, Eat shit, and then I cycle away before she can get a good look at my face.

Later the same week, I get to meet my new social worker. Henry brings her to the house. I watch them getting out of Henry's car from my bedroom window, hear Mum open the door for them, their voices filling the hallway. Her voice – the new social worker – is gruff, almost like a man's. Her name is Shelly. I wait for a while, hear Rory go into the kitchen and boil the kettle, hear Mum talking to them in a hushed yet somehow still shrill voice. I wander downstairs and into the living room and they all look up at me, stop talking, and I feel I'm on display. Shelly shakes my hand, all formal. Up close, I can see that her pores are really, really big. I catch Henry watching me, picking at his fingernails. He looks like he has some make-up on his ear, just in front of his tragus. I *have* to find out whether he really is a drag queen.

Shelly is asking about what's been going on.

Rory comes in with cups of tea for everyone, holding two mugs in each hand.

Mum says, Well, it's been an effort. A real effort. Her neck is scarlet and she is fiddling with her wedding ring, spinning it round and round and round. And the way she says it, like *poor me*, like she wasn't screaming at me in the Twynersh car park a few days ago, makes me want to fling one of the fancy mugs at her.

Have you had any more thoughts about your pregnancy, Bess? Shelly asks, looking straight at me.

I shrug. Look at Mum, who is looking at me. I want to say, Of course I've been thinking about it, it's all I ever think about. I can't bear that there's something growing inside me, but I'm afraid of what will happen if I get rid of it. Scared of what she'll do. But I don't say anything.

How many weeks gone are you now?

I tell her eleven.

So, there *is* still time to decide. I spoke briefly with Dr Jacobs—

You *spoke* to the doctor? I interrupt her.

Well. Yes. It's my job to get all the background, you see.

No shit, I say, and Mum goes *Bess* because I swore.

Anyway. Dr Jacobs is quite happy that you're aware of all the options open to you. What I would like to know is whether you're feeling pressured in any way. Do you feel as though you're free to make a choice? Are you being influenced by your partner, or by anyone else?

I look at her and realise she's deadly serious. This is not what I expected at all. Every time I see Henry, he *literally* has a checklist of questions on a piece of paper, which he ticks off as I answer. The questions are things like: Are you healthy? Are you attending school regularly? When was your last dental check-up? Have you been arrested since the last time we spoke? Have you taken any mind-altering substances since the last time we spoke? Are you being bullied? And so on.

Bess? Shelly asks, still waiting for me to answer.

I look up at Mum, who is staring out of the window pointedly.

No. I'm not being influenced by anyone, I tell her.

And have you spoken to the father yet? Is he in the picture at all?

I haven't heard anyone call him *the father* out loud.

He's . . . not around.

She won't even tell us his name, Mum says.

He's not around, I say again. It's totally irrelevant.

I wonder briefly whether anyone ever referred to *my* dad – my biological one, who was a one-night stand and never knew about me – as *the father*. Wonder what he'd think if he found out about me now. I think I'm going to have to tell Boy, sooner or later.

Fine. That's your decision, Bess. No one needs to know except you. Right?

I say right, but I realise she was actually looking at Mum and Rory. Mum nods, her eyes watery, her neck all blotchy. Every one of these meetings I've ever had involves Mum listing all the things I've done wrong and my flavour-of-the-month social worker half-arsedly scolding me while munching on a plate of shortbread and drinking tea from one of Mum's good mugs. It makes me want to bang my head against the wall. Sometimes I do. But this time it's like Mum's the one getting the telling-off. I decide that I like Shelly.

Next, she asks me about college and my applications and I tell her about my late submissions. I haven't heard back from any of the colleges I wrote to yet, only acknowledgement letters telling me they will take six to eight weeks to review my application.

Shelly says, I read on your case report that you're keen on film-making.

I say yes, stunned again that she's bothered to read my files.

I looked into the Film School you're interested in applying to, in London. But they only do postgraduate courses, I'm afraid.

Mum says, For God's sake, Bess, you should have known that before Shelly went to the effort of finding out for you. Didn't you do your research?

Well, it's my job, says Shelly, waving her hand. She continues, Don't despair *just* yet. Because I've found another one. It's in North London. It's called Basquiat – I *think* that's how you pronounce it – the Basquiat School of Arts. It does all sorts. It runs a vocational programme in film-making. It does the works – you know, editing, directing, sound design, casting – all of it. It sounds perfect for you, Bess.

She rummages in her handbag and hands me a prospectus with some paper inserts. On the cover, there's a beautiful old terraced Victorian house, four floors and a basement, with tall windows and stairs leading up to the front door. Next to the door, there's a sign that says Basquiat School of Arts in cursive script. And then, in little insets, there are pictures of kids my age working at canvases, listening on headphones in front of state-of-the-art sound desks and, best of all, standing behind professional cameras.

It's perfect. I hold my breath as I open the prospectus and flick through the pages, drinking in all of the pictures – green screens, the latest Mac computers in dimly lit editing studios. The school does music and drama too. It has its very own professional theatre in a building on the same road in Crouch End.

I look back up at Shelly, who is watching me.

I want to go here, I say.

Well, why don't we go and have a look at it first? You know, talk to some of the teachers? See if it's right?

I nod eagerly and turn my attention back to the pages. Then I see a page that says 'Finance'. I scan through the table of prices and feel my mouth go dry. Tuition on its own for my course is four thousand pounds per year, and it's a three-year programme. Then there's equipment costs. Five hundred pounds per term. Accommodation, textbooks. Field trips. And more.

Shelly can see where I'm looking and says, Don't worry about that now, all right? Let's just go and look at the place and then we'll cross the funding bridge when we come to it.

I agree, but I feel deflated. It's been snatched away from me. I don't see how I'll ever be able to get that kind of money unless I rob a bank. Even my little stash of Grandma Emelie's birthday and Christmas money wouldn't cover the first term.

Mum is asking how I could go to a boarding school when I need to be raising a baby and Shelly is saying it's a residential college not a boarding school and let's just keep her options open, let's just . . . you know. All right? And Mum says nothing, her lips a thin line like she does when she's mad at me and I feel like I'm going to get it later just because of Shelly and suddenly she and Henry are halfway out the door, Henry exchanging pleasantries with Mum, Mum thanking him for everything he's done and blah blah blah and I sidle up to Henry because it's probably the last time I'll ever see him and I say, Just tell me this one thing. Are you a drag queen or not?

And Henry is like *What?* But luckily no one else heard, so he is left staring at me, and I can't tell whether his expression is bewildered or afraid, and Shelly says, Bess, I'll call you and we'll sort out a date to go to that college, and that's it, they're gone. And the house is dark.

Upstairs in the evening, when I'm alone and bored of drawing out faces on the ceiling with my mind, I open my bedside drawer and pull out all of the cards from Emelie, all stored together in an envelope in the back of the photo album. I wonder whether I *could* cover some of the Basquiat tuition with her money. At least for a little while until I sort a job out or something. I pull the cards out of the large Manila envelope and grope around inside for the second envelope with the money stash in it – all the cash from the birthdays and Christmases. All I feel is the smooth brown paper. I tip the envelope upside down and empty all of the papers out, sorting through them in a crescent on my bed. I check the rest of the drawer, pulling out make-up compacts and old dried-up nail polishes and half-finished notepads and exploded gel pens. I pull the whole drawer out of the unit and empty it, upside down, onto my bed too. But there's no envelope. No money, apart from the one fifty-pound note still in my pencil case from my birthday card this year. I spread everything across the floor and discard each item one by one. The money is gone. I scramble around the bed, checking and rechecking. It's definitely not here. Someone's taken it all. Clarissa's too much of a goody-two-shoes to steal. Rory never comes in here. Even Lisa wouldn't stoop that low. Then I think of Boy, in here weeks ago, months ago now, going through my stuff. I thought he wanted to know me through the objects I kept in my bedroom. But it wasn't that, was it? It wasn't that at all. I lie back on my bed and stare at the faces on the ceiling, trying not to think.

And on Tuesday night when we are eating our fish and chips in front of *EastEnders*, the phone rings and Rory answers it, listens for a moment and says, Please do not call this number again. And I've never seen him look so angry, like he's trying to stop himself from throwing something against a wall. And me, Mum and Clarissa all look at him, but he's not saying anything. Of *course* it's him.

So later, when everyone is asleep, I think of my grandmother and how Boy has stolen from her, and my stomach is curdling, and I one-four-seven-one the number and it's been more than a month since that time in the garden, since *don't fucking pretend you don't know*, and it rings four times before someone picks up and then I hear the voice.

And he doesn't even say hello he just says, Bess? like his life depends on me being on the other end of the phone.

And I say, Yes, it's me. And in those three words there are all the things I've been thinking and feeling and everything for the past few weeks. And I change my mind about him again, there's *no way* he would take that money, just listen to him now, he *needs* me. I wonder whether he's been thinking about me. Whether his whole body aches before he goes to sleep, wishing so badly that I was there with him – like I do when I think about him, wishing he'll sneak in through my bedroom window at night without Mum hearing. Whether he can hear the thoughts I send to him: where are you, do you still want me, do you miss me, are you hurting like me. Waiting for him to send his thoughts back to me but never hearing a single thing. How strange that there are another six billion people out there and he's always the one I'm thinking about. That I'm the one he thinks about.

Where are you? I ask him, trying to control the tremor in my voice.

I'm at home, I got bailed. I have a court date next month.

Oh my God.

It's fine.

Are you okay?

It's fine. Really.

It's all so scary.

No. I'm just glad I'm out. It'll be over soon. I doubt they'll give me anything worse than a slap on the wrist and some community service. First offence and all that.

Are you sure?

Bess . . . When am I going to see you?

Whenever, I say, too quickly. Whenever you want.

How about now?

Now? I ask, glancing at the clock, thinking of Mum and Rory asleep upstairs.

Yes, now. Why not? I'll come and pick you up.

Fine, just give me ten minutes to get changed.

Okay. Bess?

Yes?

I . . . love you.

And I feel like the room is spinning around me because this was the last thing I was expecting him to say, and I was so ready to be furious about him stealing the money. Now I'm too afraid to ask. And at the same time, in spite of everything, all my bones are singing and my eyes are watering and surely he can't have stolen the money because *he said he loves me* and no one has ever, *ever* said that to me before and I want to open my mouth and scream with the brilliance of it, but I can't, so I just whisper down the phone, I'll see you soon.

And I'm hanging up the phone and tiptoe-running up the stairs and throwing on a dress, a short one, a jumper, smearing my eyes with kohl, pulling a brush through my hair and realising it's too greasy to have down so trying to twist it up into a scruffy bun but failing at that too. Then I hear the quiet growl of the car engine as it pulls up outside and I close my bedroom door behind me and Mum is standing there in the corridor in her dressing gown, and I stare at her.

She says, Where the *bloody hell* do you think you're going?

And I say, Nowhere, because I can't think of a lie quick enough, even though it's stupid because it's beyond obvious that I've just been caught sneaking out to see Boy.

Get back in your room, Mum says.

And I am almost about to do it and then I think of Boy waiting in his car outside, and I say, No, Mum. I push past her to the stairwell.

She says, Think about what you're doing, Bess.

I don't respond.

She says, It's him, isn't it? *The father.*

I stop because I'm still not used to him being *the father*, and I also forgot about being pregnant for a second. It's so easy to pretend like everything is normal sometimes.

I say to her, He loves me, Mum. He *loves* me.

She says, I can guarantee you he doesn't love a single person except himself.

And I turn away from her and walk down the rest of the stairs and I am out the door and in his car, looking at his face, which hasn't changed a bit, and we're driving off. As we round the corner, I look in the rear-view mirror and Mum is running out the door in her nightie, but it doesn't matter any more. The only thing that matters is him.

We drive for a while in silence. Not to his house, just around. Shepperton. It's dead. The street lamps cast everything orange and the roads are empty. We go around the roundabout at the end of the high street three times. We drive on the wrong side of the road. I look at him. The fine hairs on his forearms. The way his forehead wrinkles when he's concentrating. How he lifts one hand off the steering wheel to brush something off his cheek.

Eventually we arrive at his house and he comes around to the passenger side to open the door for me, and I laugh because it's so unlike him to be chivalrous, it makes me feel awkward. When we're inside, he makes me sit at the kitchen table while he finds music to put on the stereo – softly, because Zack and Keris are asleep – and then he pulls me onto my feet and into him and I'm like, What are you doing, and he manipulates my arms and puts a hand on my waist and I realise we are dancing. The music is 'You and Me' by Penny and the Quarters and we sway from side to side, around the kitchen table, clumsy, stepping on each other's feet, bumping into the countertops, knocking one of the chairs over. And I keep trying to laugh, but he puts his hand over my mouth, his eyes wide and playful, saying, Shh, shh. And I bite his hand. And he kisses me hard and then twirls me around underneath his arm like a ballerina. And I try to twirl him, but he's too tall and won't fit under my arm.

And then he changes and every time he moves, it becomes more pronounced, has more intention behind it, and I know that this is going where it has always gone before, and I look up at him, try to make a joke. I say, Prison has changed you, in a voice like an old woman, and he says, Come on, Bess, I've missed you so much. And I can't help but think of the baby and maybe I should tell him, but if I told him he wouldn't be touching me like this, he *shouldn't* be, he might break up with me, but then I think how we're not even together. And meekly, in a voice like a child, I say, I don't think we should, but that doesn't stop his hands or his mouth. And I say it again, louder this time, Boy, I don't think we should, I don't want to, not tonight, pushing against him, not hard because I don't want him to be offended, but he doesn't stop. He'll throw me out at the very least, if I told him, he'll call me a liar. And I can't go home, can't face Mum telling me I told you so. So I let him keep going, even though I feel suddenly awful, even though a giggle is bubbling through my lips like I'm fucking *enjoying* it. I keep thinking to myself he is just as complex a person as I am, with all the same nuances of thought and feeling.

I let my body go limp and he's going, Bess, Bess, Bess, I love you, I love you, I love you, saying it into my hair, my neck, my belly, and I'm sure he thinks he means it, and maybe he does, and I do too, I do, so it's okay, because this is what people who are in love do, right? This is how they show they love each other. And he's pushing/pulling me into his bedroom and he sits me down on the bed. All of these thoughts are crashing around inside me, but I'm so afraid that if I articulate any of them, he will hate me, and while he undresses, the moonlight from the window turning him into a ghost, I think to myself, I wish we were still dancing, I wish we were still fucking dancing. And he climbs on top of me and I try not to cry through the whole of it and, in my head, we are still in the kitchen dancing to Penny and the Quarters and it is magical.

Chapter Twenty-One

In the morning, I can't trust myself to look at him. He looks so harmless when he's asleep. There's this metallic, tender, sore feeling in my groin and my belly and my legs that I don't want to think about. Like if growing pains drew blood out of your joints. I lay in his bed, scared to move, in case my body shatters into pieces. And after a while, when my breathing is normal, I walk into the hallway of his house, still wearing my slutty black dress, my hair scraped back into a ponytail that I had to do without a mirror so it's probably lopsided, eyes crusty with sleep. Keris is in the kitchen on the phone to someone, with Zack sitting at the table eating banana slices out of a bowl with one hand and making a fire engine drive across the terrain of the place mat with the other. I make eye contact with Keris and she doesn't smile back at me.

I let myself out, clicking the door shut quietly behind me. The sun is too bright. The cars drive by too quickly, too loudly. The thistles poking through the fences that line the farmers' fields are brown and dead, leaving long, thin scratches on the skin of my calves. The air smells like something rotten. Today is total eclipse day. I wonder if the world is going to end.

When I let myself into the house, it's dead quiet and the car is missing from the garage. I don't know where they've gone. I'm glad they're not home. I have a cool shower, standing under the shower head for what seems like an age, letting the water wash over me. I scrub and scrub and scrub, every inch of me, even the bits still tender from burns, behind my ears and the bottoms of my feet. I soap my tongue, gagging, because I feel like I can still taste him. I pull the cabinet door open so I can examine my body in the mirror. Under the water, my burns look purple and bumpy. I realise that I haven't seen Boy since the day I got them. He didn't ask about them last night when I was naked in his bedroom. I can feel the scream inside me growing. In the mirror, my belly looks bigger still. I brush my teeth vigorously until my gums begin to bleed, let the pinkish foam run down my chin and dribble down my body, gargle the peppermint mouth-wash for so long it burns the corners of my mouth and I feel as if I'm about to choke.

I vomit into the plughole and sit down on the bathroom floor, letting the water pool around me like I'm my own little island. My fingernails are throbbing, bitten down to the cuticles.

After the shower, I can still feel it coming, the scream, so I go downstairs into the living room, and I clamp my hands over my mouth because I know that if I start, I won't be able to stop. I can feel my eyes prickling and there is this horrible leftover soap taste in my mouth. Lavender. I look around the living room, at the photographs on the windowsill. I'm not in any of them – only Rory, Lisa and Clarissa.

Everything starts to click into place in my head, like those gears in the engine room in *Titanic*, and I realise that the way they see me is not how I see myself. That I will never really be a part of their family. How I can never tell them what has happened. I can never tell Mum. I already know what she'll say. That it's my fault.

And that's when I let out this awful silent gasping sob, like a whisper, a kettle boiling, a broken siren. And it happens so quickly, just once, where I let the feelings escape my body so they can't rot me up on the inside. And then I take three, four, five deep breaths and rub my eyes with the palms of my hands until I can see spots of light behind my eyelids. And then I'm back here, in this room, with the photos of these people, this family. This life.

I go upstairs and get into bed and wrap myself up in the duvet, which feels nice, but after a few minutes, it gets too hot and I start sweating, so I unwrap myself and put on a pair of shorts and a vest with spaghetti straps. I go back downstairs, pick up the landline and dial Eshal's number, my hopes not high at all. She answers.

Esh? I shout down the phone, excited.

Bess? That you?

Of course it is, you numpty.

And then she's crying. And I feel like crying, too, but my mouth is hot and dry and I feel like there's nothing left inside me to cry out.

It's happening, Bess, I'm engaged. I'm going to get married. I'm marrying this guy called Mehdi. My dad went to college with his dad, they've been friends for decades. He comes from a good family. Well educated. So. It's been decided. But he's a fucking *idiot*, Bess. He's *so spotty*, it's unreal. Like, his whole face is seeping out pus. I'm not even exaggerating.

We have to do something, I tell her. And the feeling I had before, in the living room, it's gone. Because all that matters is Esh, now.

What are we going to do? Run away? There's *nothing*. I knew it was going to happen. I've known for years what the plan is. I can't believe I didn't stop this sooner.

Well, you can stop it now, can't you? Just tell your parents you don't want to be engaged! It's not like you're getting married next month. It's going to be a long engagement, right? So there's plenty of time to stop it.

It's not that simple, Bess. If I break this off now, it's going to humiliate my parents. My whole extended family. I can't do that to them. After everything they've ever done for me. It's too late.

Well, you have to do *something*. You can't just let this happen.

I'm not going to. I just need to work out what to do.

Look, are you home alone?

Dad's at work, Mum's visiting my aunties in Ealing and Anwar's out with some of his school friends before he goes back to uni.

I'm coming over.

No, don't. I'll meet you somewhere.

Pits?

See you there in twenty minutes.

I hang up and sprint up the stairs two at a time, pick up my camera and put on my trainers. Then I go into Mum's desk in the dining room and find the key for my bike lock. I take my bike out of the shed and pedal down to the Pits. I get there before Esh, and I lean my bike against one of the trees at the edge of the lake and sit down in the shade. It's almost ten-thirty, and the place is super-crowded, with families all set up with deckchairs and picnic blankets on the banks of the water. Some of them are wearing these weird-looking cardboard sunglasses. I take out my camera, the nice digital one that Riss got me for my birthday, and take some shots of the people on the bridge.

When Esh turns up, she's still crying. She's wearing some dramatic big sunglasses. She sits down next to me under the tree I picked and puts her head onto my shoulder. I put my arm around her, feeling her silky hair underneath my palm.

What are all these losers doing here? she says between sniffs, gesturing at the families and their picnic blankets.

Eclipse, isn't it? It's supposed to start soon.

These people need jobs.

What's going on? How can I help? I ask her.

She says, I got the thing you put through my window. The helpline thing.

Okay. Should we call them?

No. I called a different number, though. One I found in the community leaflets at the library. It's a branch of social services. Part of the council, I think. But I can only do it when no one's in the house. I have to schedule times with them.

What did they say?

Well, the woman I spoke to. She said they can put me in temporary accommodation, away from my family. But I don't know, Bess . . .

That sounds great. You should do it!

What, ditch my whole family? It all seems a bit extreme. It's not like I'm being *forced*. I'm just not very happy about it. Yeah, I could run away. But the consequences are too high. Like my friend Habib. My mum and dad will cut me off.

You don't even know that'll happen.

But the point is it *might*. And then what am I going to do?

Erm, how about never get married?

But I *do* want to get married. I want to do this for my family. And for me. You know? I just want to – ugh, I don't know – I just want to get through university before I start thinking about all of that. And I want to be able to pick my own husband! And I want to be able to pick someone who's not Bengali, who's not Muslim, if I wanted to! And I can't.

Eshal, you're really missing the point here. What you're saying to me now, just *tell it to your parents*.

You don't understand this stuff, Bess, you're like—

I'm like an *orphan*, right? I don't get family stuff? I put the word 'orphan' in air quotes with my fingers.

I was actually going to say you're like white, she says. And we both laugh.

Sorry about that, I say. Speaking of, your neighbours are massive racists.

Everyone in Shepperton is a massive racist, she says. See that woman over there? She points to a lady in her mid-forties with two toddlers, on a bright orange blanket with sunglasses quite like Eshal's and a straw hat on her blonde hair. Esh goes, I was in Somerfield's a couple of months ago buying sweets and I pointed out to her that she'd pushed in the queue and she told me I can either go back to Paki-land and be at the front of the queue or stay here and let the people who were born here go first. I was like, *You mug*, my birth certificate says Ashford Hospital.

Wow.

I just don't understand how people can be that fucking ignorant and not be, like, brain-dead from lack of cognitive function.

And she's laughing, but there are tears squeezing out from the corners of her eyes. And I pull her into a hug and let her cry some more.

She asks me what's going on with Boy and being pregnant.

Well . . . I'm still pregnant.

You're keeping it, then?

I don't know. Who fucking knows. Not me. I think if I have an abortion Lisa is going to throw me off the Chubb tower.

You realise that's not a good enough reason to go through with it, yeah? And there's like an expiry date on this? What about Boy? Have you told him?

I explain to her about Boy being arrested and going to visit him and changing my mind and finally about what happened last night. I feel sick while I'm talking.

Bess, you know what he did, right?

Yeah . . . he crashed a stolen car into a church. That's why he got arrested.

No, thicko, I mean last night. What he did to you.

She looks at me meaningfully, her eyes wide, like I'm missing something obvious, and I know what she's getting at, but I don't want to, I don't want to, I don't want to. I don't want to believe that's what Boy did, that he could do that, even though it's so obvious, even to me.

You know what it was, she says.

If I know what it was, I tell her, that means it happened.

Yeah, Bess, because it—

No. Not yet. Let me just not think for a few minutes, okay? If I do, I'm going to lose it. Esh . . . please can we just not? Not today.

How about we don't talk about it, all right? she says, pulling me back into a hug, this time my head on her shoulder. We don't talk about it until you're ready to talk about it.

I might not ever be ready, I tell her.

That's fine. Then we'll never talk about it.

I say, Okay, and we sit there like that for a while, and then all the people on the field start whooping and applauding and I say, I guess this is it. The end of the world. And we look up even though we don't have the special glasses on and Esh is like, Is that it? Some fucking eclipse, this is shit. And then suddenly the whole world is black, like it's the middle of the night, and I swear I can *feel* the temperature drop. And we keep watching and it's like the sun is a halo in the middle of all the darkness. And Esh takes my hand and we look up, up, up, up, until a handful of seconds later it's all over and we're still alive, the world didn't end, and suddenly all the birds are really loud.

I turn to Esh and say, Congrats on surviving the end of the world, and she says, You too, sis, and we high-five, and I say,

I love you, Esh. And she says, I love you too, Bess, you big numpty. It's the second declaration of love in as many days, after a lifetime of none, but this one is the purest, most powerful thing and it's the only kind of love that matters.

After a while, she has to go because her mum's going to be back soon and she's supposed to be grounded and before she goes, she says, Oh, by the way I got into that vet school in Basingstoke, and I hug her and tell her I'm proud of her, like I had something to do with it. But all the time I am thinking about Basquiat and how that's never going to happen. I'm so selfish. I film her walking away through the trees with all the other people who came for the eclipse and then I'm all alone and I put my hand on my belly and think, what kind of mother am I going to be? And I think about Lisa, my 'Mum' and what kind of mother she is. How do you know whether you're going to be a good mother when you never knew your own? How do you know even if you do? I look out to the Pits, sun bouncing off its black water, and I know what I need to do next.

My mother's name is Amanda and she lives in Stanwell, which is about a six-mile cycle from Shepperton. When I was twelve, my social worker at the time, Patricia, gave me her address. She wasn't supposed to, but she said it wasn't healthy for little girls to be denied access to their mothers. I never told anyone about it. From the pictures I've seen of Amanda, she looks like a skinny version of me. With blue eyes, instead of brown. We have the same smile. Maybe the same constellation of freckles on our backs.

Amanda lives on a road of little awkward-shaped maisonettes with brown-bricked walls and white plastic-framed windows. Number 42. I haven't seen her since I was four years old.

And now I'm here. It only took me half an hour to bike it from the Pits. She's lived half an hour away this whole time. I can't believe it took me this long to try to meet her.

I lock my bike to a lamp post on the edge of the green opposite the house, and wait for something to happen. Because surely something ought to happen, now. But nothing does. The wind softly threads itself through the grass. Cars drive by, the pitch of their engines doing the Doppler effect as they pass. The world hasn't stopped turning. The sky behind the squat brown houses is blue and wide and light. Outside the off-licence down the road, some kids in Kappa tracksuits are kicking a football around, playing chicken in the road, their bikes propped against the shopfront. I watch them for a while until one of them notices me and sticks a finger up at me. And then, before I know that my feet are moving, I'm walking towards the house, my trainers scuffing at the kerb, my hands fists in the pockets of my shorts, and I'm thinking, she's probably not home though, right? She's probably not home. I mean, it's the middle of the afternoon on a Wednesday. I realise I should have put some make-up on. Made more of an effort. Picked out some decent clothes. Brushed my hair. Popped the whitehead on my lip.

It's no different to the houses either side of it. Amanda's house, I mean. My mother's house. A stubby ground-floor maisonette with dirty mottled brown brickwork and thin windows with old-fashioned net curtains. A scrubby little front garden with a simple concrete pathway leading to the front door. On the lamp post directly outside, there is a sign that warns me this is a Neighbourhood Watch area. There's no car in her driveway. All the lights are off. It doesn't look like anyone's home, but I wonder whether I should knock anyway to find out for certain. But what if I knock, and someone *is* home? What if she's home?

What would I say to her? What would I do? What if she doesn't even live here any more?

My throat is burning dry. I concentrate on breathing to calm myself down.

I walk to the door and tap the brass knocker three times.

And the noise of the knocker resonates somewhere in the back of my mind. That noise. I've heard it a thousand times before. In dreams. In another life. And the noise is opening a box in my head, one that I closed a long time ago in therapy with a woman called Bridie who smelled like humbugs. I packed all these little things into a box and I tucked them away somewhere I would never have to think about them ever again. Somewhere they couldn't hurt me. Somewhere they couldn't make me hurt myself.

Nothing happens for a minute.

Then the net curtain in the bay window moves.

A moment later, I see a shadow behind the glass. The door opens, the seal unsticking from the frame. Amanda, who is my mother, opens the door and stops. She's a lot skinnier than I imagined. I was hoping she would be fat by now like me. Her eyes are yellow and watery, with blood vessels wriggling through them. She's wearing a blue smock dress with little flowers dotted all over it, like one of Lisa's. She looks older than I remember. Although I suppose it's been over ten years, so I don't know why I was expecting her to look exactly like her photographs.

She's not ginger any more. There's so much silver streaked through her hair that it looks almost pink. Her face is sagging and blotchy, but I can see a few freckles underneath the age. The same freckles as me.

She's still on the doorstep, staring at me.

I'm like, Hi, Amanda, in my head, but it doesn't come out of my mouth. I squint at her through the sun and she squints right back at me, pushing her glasses up her nose with a spindly index finger.

I can't bring myself to call her Mum.

She looks at me a moment, perplexed, and then: Isabelle?

I nod, do a stupid half-wave.

She says, You'd better come in then, hadn't you?

I step into the house, feeling like I'm about to walk into the plot of a horror movie. *Jeepers Creepers* or *The Amityville Horror* or *Carrie*. And I notice that the carpets are immaculate. I go to pull off my muddy trainers by the door.

There's no need for that, she says, watching me, too close.

I follow her into the living room and sit down on the sofa, which is covered in that plastic cellophane shit that people deliver sofas in.

I ask her, Is this a new sofa? It's the first thing I've said to her in ten years.

She says, No, I've had this sofa for a long time.

The cellophane crackles under my bum. I can already feel my skin clamming up and my thighs sticking to the plastic. If I get up now there will be a slick of sweat left behind.

Amanda is standing by the door. I stare at her openly and she doesn't meet my eyes, self-conscious. I realise she's nervous. She keeps fiddling with the little gold cross around her neck. She asks me if I want a cup of tea.

Did I live here? I ask her, because there are things I remember.

Like how if I walk down the hall and turn right there'll be a bedroom with a weird old-fashioned fireplace in it. And in the kitchen there's a glass sliding door which opens onto a little scrub of patio. And the tiles in that kitchen are beige and it's all coming back now because the box is opening, wider and wider and wider. And I'm remembering other things, like how the bathroom is just past the bedroom and how there's a spot of black mould in the corner of the ceiling above the taps. And there's a little frosted window above the loo that's always dark because it opens directly onto the wall of the house next door. And the way she's looking is familiar now, too, and the box is opening, wider still.

She doesn't answer my question. She jerks into the kitchen to put the kettle on.

I get up and look at the pictures on the mantelpiece. None of them are pictures of humans. They're all trees. I look around the rest of the room. There are two landscape watercolours on the magnolia walls.

Do you like trees? I shout to Amanda. And my voice is level and I think, Wow, I'm managing better than she is, but then I look down at my fingers and they're still trembling, like how they have been for the last few weeks. And I bring my hand to my neck and look up at the mirror and for a moment it's Lisa staring back at me.

Again, she doesn't respond. She carries a tray of tea back into the living room. There are two teacups and saucers, a bowl of sugar lumps and a little jug of milk as well as a teapot. Amanda sets the tray on the coffee table and begins to pour. It's the fanciest tea I've ever seen.

I pluck a sugar cube out of the bowl and pop it in my mouth. Once she's done pouring, Amanda sets herself on the armchair opposite me on the sofa.

Does Meg know you're here? she asks me.

She doesn't know that I've had four social workers since Meg.

Does your social worker know you're here, then?

No.

What about Lisa?

I don't answer, picturing Mum's face as I pushed past her to get into Boy's car last night.

I say, Yeah, she knows.

And she's okay with it?

I shrug, try not to think about how Mum would feel if she really did know I was here. While Amanda talks, things are slotting into place in my brain. There is a scuff mark on the flowery wallpaper that I've seen before. The wallpaper, too. It's familiar. Patterns on the ceiling. The tremor in her hands. The way she holds things.

I say, I'm sixteen now. I can do what I want.

We don't talk for a moment while she fusses over her tea.

Well, then, how have you been, Isabelle?

I say, No one calls me Isabelle any more.

She watches me closely as she sips, her eyes small.

I remember, she says. Meg told me you go by Bess now.

I say nothing.

Well, if you don't mind, she says, I'll call you Isabelle. It's the name on your birth certificate. It's the name I gave you.

I think, You have no right to call me anything.

Her fingers go back to the crucifix on her throat and I have this urge to rip it away from her and run.

I look out the window, trying to control my breathing. This was a terrible mistake. There is a birdhouse on Amanda's front lawn. A squirrel is busy trying to get a brown apple from the cage dangling in the centre of the roof.

I say, I'm pregnant.

Amanda stops tapping. She stares at me for a moment, her eyes waterier now.

Oh my goodness, she says.

I know.

What are you going to do?

I don't know.

Do you want money? I don't have any.

I splutter. Of course not! How can you even ask that?

Why are you here, then?

I don't know. I don't know.

What do you expect me to do? I can't . . . I'm technically not meant to be within a hundred feet of you.

She looks like she's going to cry.

I go to the mantelpiece and look at the trees in the photo frames.

Don't you have any photographs of me?

Yes. They're in the loft.

I say, I lived here, didn't I?

She is quiet. The clock chimes.

I say, I remember this house. I remember it.

And I've never been more angry in my life.

And I take my cup and pour the tea inside deliberately onto the carpet.

And Amanda is saying, I'm sorry I'm sorry I'm sorry.

And I'm saying, It was a mistake to come here.

She says, No, no, it wasn't.

How? I hate you.

I think we both knew this, but saying it out loud feels blasphemous.

Her big stupid doe eyes spill over and tears slide down her blotchy old face.

I say, I know why I had to go into care. They told me.

She says, You're old enough to know.

I just want to know why you did it. Are you mentally ill? Why didn't you go to prison?

Amanda says, breathing loudly, I was very ill, but I'm better now.

You don't look better to me. Your whole house is covered in fucking plastic.

I had postnatal depression.

People with postnatal depression don't want to kill their children.

Sometimes they do.

You know I remember some of it?

She has her hands in her hair now, pulling at it too hard. She's pulled some of it out and the strands are knotted up between her knuckles. She says, I was afraid you would.

I want to use the bathroom.

Amanda's face jerks up.

I don't think that's a good idea, Isabelle.

I don't give a shit what you think. And my name isn't Isabelle any more.

Muscle memory tells me where I need to go. I traipse along the hall and swing round the door frame. The movement feels familiar to me, like I've done it a million times before. On the wall next to the bathroom, there is a very old photograph of her, a formal one, in front of a blueish photographer's backdrop. It's the woman I remember, climbing out of the box in my head, alive, in my mind. The edges of her face are blurry.

The bathroom is at the end of the hall with the door closed. I stop before it and look up at the ceiling. The paint is all puckered, same as mine. The little dots spell out a thousand happy faces. I push the door open.

Inside, the tiles on the wall haven't changed. Blue with cartoon fish swimming through them. Two fish to a tile. Interspersed with ordinary white tiles. The flooring is new. The shower head is new. I picture being underwater in the bath and staring up at a different shower head, trying to reach for it.

I step into the bath and sit down on the cold porcelain. I lean back and watch the tiles with their dancing cartoon fish.

I think about the thing that is growing in my belly. I imagine it as a newborn baby. I imagine it as a toddler. I imagine it as a little girl.

I imagine running this bath to the brim and holding the girl under the water while fish dance around us.

Chapter Twenty-Two

I stay there in the bath, my neck pressed against the white-enamelled metal of the tub, the tap dripping cold water onto my feet, soaking through my socks until they're freezing and damp, until she comes in and tells me to get out. She's crying and her hair is crazy and she's screaming at me, Get out get out get out. Pushing me out the door with forceful hands, even though I'm already going, already putting distance between the two of us, she doesn't need to push me. The places she touches on my body cringe away from her. The house smells of bleach. And I'm in the hallway with eyes stinging until they water and it feels as though there is thick fog clogging up my throat. She slams the white plasticky door behind me.

As I round the corner onto the main road, I see that she's watching me from the living-room window.

Pedalling my bike feels like pedalling through custard. I can't bear the thought of going home, so I cycle around Shepperton aimlessly for hours, my mind doing cartwheels. I go to Manor Park, the train station, the M3. I stop at the top of the bridge when the sun is starting to set and breathe in the traffic fumes. I wonder what Boy is doing. He scratched his initials into the frame of my bike when he stole it. They're still there.

I cycle past the church. The custodians have installed conspicuous floodlights. They illuminate the statue of Mary at the south end of the church. She's opening her hands out to me. I spit on the ground and wonder if she hated God for the Immaculate Conception. Maybe later she hated Jesus as he was fertilising away in her womb. She didn't even have a choice.

I slip my key into the lock and heave the front door open. The living-room light goes on. The house is dark – I can't quite believe it was only this morning that I left Boy's house – but someone's awake.

Mum comes into the hallway in her slippers and dressing gown. She's got a cup of tea and I think, I should pour that one on the floor too.

I look at Mum.

I say, I'm sorry for running off like that.

She says, I know, I'm sorry for shouting. I've been too hard on you.

I go to sit in the living room. The television is on mute. It's the news and they are showing more footage of the eclipse. People looking up at the sun.

Mum sits down next to me. Her eyes are red.

She says, A long time ago, before Riss, before you, before Rory even. When I was seventeen.

She carries on, My mum had just died. Did I ever tell you about how she died? When we lived in Wimbledon? At the time, I was pregnant.

She says, Back then. It wasn't a question of choice. They didn't have the sort of medicine you get nowadays. And anyway, it was the nineteen sixties. There was no such thing as the sexual revolution yet. I mean, there was barely such a thing as feminism.

I wonder if the baby (my baby) can hear what she's saying. Wonder whether it knows what's coming.

I wonder if God can hear me.

Mum says, The boy – the dad – wasn't worth the dirt on the bottom of my shoe, you know? But, Bess, I *worshipped* him. I followed him everywhere. I tried to get him to notice me *constantly*. There was about a year of my life when I was your age, when my whole world revolved around him.

And then, when he found out I was pregnant, he bolted. Obviously. Everyone in the world told me that's exactly what he would do. And that's what he did. It was like something out of *EastEnders*.

Uncle Jason and I were organising Mum's funeral. Going from meetings with the coroner to meetings with the florist. Picking out the photograph for the newspaper notice and finding a reasonably priced electrician to mend the light fixture in the bathroom because when her neck snapped the force of it pulled the wiring out. Trying to get rid of the smell. She wasn't there for long, but there was a *smell*. I'm so sure of it. Meanwhile, Dad was drinking himself to death down the working men's club and Jason was going through his own stuff because he never told Mum he was gay, having some sort of crisis, and while all that was going on, in the middle of all of it, I lost the baby.

Mum says, It was the day before the funeral. I lost the baby.

She is crying. I don't know what to do.

She says, I wasn't thrilled about the idea of being pregnant, you know? I was in the same situation as you. Bright academic future, I suppose. Accepted into some great universities. Could've been a jeweller's apprentice if I didn't fancy doing more school. The job was all set up. Being pregnant ruined all of it, of course. It was a different situation for women back then. Young women, especially, who got pregnant. But, you know, I'd sort of *resigned* myself to it. I was even excited about it. I knew I could get by with my savings and Jason helping me, and the welfare system and so on. And then when Mum died and my boyfriend had buggered off God-knows-where, I thought to myself, thank God for this baby. Thank God, because without it I would have no one and nothing. And then next thing I know I'm in the chip shop picking up dinner and then I'm coming around from passing out and someone has pulled my tights off and I see the blood all smeared up in the nylon, and then all on my legs too, and my tights had a diamond pattern on them, you see? And all up my legs the blood had been impressed into my skin in pretty diamonds, and blood all over my dress. And I knew right away, because I felt the emptiness inside me. This big gaping hole.

She sobs in big broken gasps, like she's been holding the air in for twenty years.

I can't think of anything to say, so I ask if Rory knows.

Mum says yes.

I don't know why this makes a difference, but it does.

Rory's a good guy, really, I say. I know I give him shit.

That's the understatement of the century.

I laugh and Mum laughs through her snot.

A car drives by the house and illuminates us briefly, the white light bouncing off the polished windowsill onto our faces.

We sit quietly for a long time while Mum calms herself down and I watch her, her narrow shoulders all shivery, and I still can't think of a single thing to say to her except I'm sorry and I'm so sorry and I'm trying to be a better person.

She says, I know you are. I can tell.

I'm scared.

So am I. But we have so many people around us to help us. Social services can help us out, and Rory and I can look after the baby sometimes too. I've been too hard on you. I was all caught up in what it was like when this happened to *me*. I was too young. I was thinking of all the sacrifices I had to be prepared to make in order to have a baby. But it's not like that now. I can see that. Shelly explained a few things to me about the help that would be available to us, financially, when you have the baby. You could do a part-time course locally and still get a degree. Or do a study-at-home degree.

I nod. Yes, I could do that.

And I'm thinking, *When you have the baby.* And, *The help that would be available to us, financially.*

We're all here to help you, Bess. You are so loved. And this baby will be loved too. I know it doesn't feel like it sometimes. But it's true.

I know, I say. I know.

In this family we don't talk about love. We just don't. It's a care thing; against the rules, for starters, the ones that say foster carers can't hug you or take you for a haircut without permission. The love that Mum's talking about is different to the love me and Eshal have, or even the love between me and Boy. With Boy, to love someone is more like having power over them, which isn't love at all, I've realised. Eshal and I love one another unconditionally. If I have this baby, I'm sure I will love it unconditionally too, not like Amanda. But the love Lisa is talking about – it's not an unconditional love – it's a love that's based on *the help that would be available to us, financially.* At least part of it is about that. That's the bit that sticks in my throat. I need to figure out whether that matters.

Mum smiles deeply and puts her left palm flat against my stomach. I want to squirm away, because I'm still thinking about what she said, but I resist. She looks up at me and giggles, her eyes all shiny, still leaking leftover tears. I can feel a sudden influx of bile rising hot up my oesophagus. It's unexpected and in my surprise I swallow it down.

Just think, Mum says. A baby. Here.

I smile back at her. I remember Mary the Virgin at the church and wonder at all the women I know who are playing at being mothers.

Maybe it really is just about the baby. Maybe I'm wrong.

Maybe I'll have the baby and everything will be okay.

I say, Mum, I feel sick.

She gets me a glass of water from the kitchen and sits down with me as I take small sips. I think about how I was sitting in Amanda's bathtub a few hours ago imagining drowning my baby.

Mum asks me if I've thought of names yet. I shake my head. She's staring at my quivering hands.

Early days yet, she says.

Early days, I agree.

Rory's woken up and he comes downstairs.

I take it you two've made up, then?

I nod.

Rory's face creases into a smile.

Good. I can't take a house full of shouting. So no more. We're going to sort this out between the three of us. We're going to manage.

Mum puts me to bed like I'm a little kid again. Everyone is being so careful with me. I think I now understand why. They've realised shouting won't work. They need to keep me on side, at least until it's too late for me to change my mind.

My room feels smaller than it did yesterday.

We'll have to get rid of some of your stuff to fit a cot in here, Mum says.

I don't answer her.

We'll be okay, Mum says.

I nod, almost robotic now.

She goes to bed and I look up at the ceiling, watching invisible fish dance around the stagnant black air in my bedroom. I check the clock on my bedside table. It's nearly 1 a.m.

I think, If this is happening, I need to tell Boy. I do. There's no getting around it.

I slide out of bed and creep out onto the landing. I take the phone off the hook and take it into my room, dialling Boy's number as I do so, and my hands are shaking. It was only last night that the *thing* happened. I can still feel him all over me, despite the shower and the scrubbing. Mortified, I realise there's a frisson of excitement running through me, a low-pulsing electrical current, at the thought of speaking to him. What's wrong with me? The thought of hearing his voice again makes my innards curl up all ugly and painful and delicious.

This is the last thing I need to do to make everything right.

Keris picks up on the third ring.

Hi, it's Bess, I say.

Bess. How're you doing?

She sounds tired. I probably woke her up.

Is Boy in, Keris?

I'll check for you.

I hear her put the phone down and walk away slowly. There are muffled voices. Keris's slightly raised and shrill, and Boy's pissed-off and distracted.

Keris picks up the phone.

I'm sorry, Bess, he's not in right now.

I pause. I think of saying thanks and hanging up the phone, and then I think of last night, about what happened, and how love really is all about power with him. That's what he's trying to do, he's trying to keep hold of his power over me. That's really not love at all.

And my stomach is churning with all of the things Mum said, all the feelings I've ever had for Boy – how I've obsessed over him, imagining that he's going to save me, that he loves me, the feeling of him saying it, like I just shot straight through the sky and left the fucking atmosphere, that's how good it felt, but then this undercurrent of *shame* whenever I'm around him, always feeling like I'm not good enough for him, that I'll never be good enough, and then I think about last night, all of these things at once, in one big melting pot.

I say, Keris, not to be rude, but are you fucking kidding me? I heard the whole conversation you just had with him.

Keris is silent, caught in the act. I know what this means, but I don't want to.

The thing that comes out of this nightmare with Boy, the one thing that sticks in all of this, is that it's like he's betrayed me, and he's taken this piece of me away that I'm never, ever going to get back now. And he's left me with a piece of himself. And no matter what happens, I'm never going to be the same person now. I've been fundamentally altered. This is always going to be a part of me. Like it's going into my genetic make-up, my DNA, because of him.

So, how is it that I'm letting him get away with it?

And in that moment I hate him. I really, really do.

I say, *Keris*, and my voice trembles. I can feel the hysteria rising in my throat like bile, and I swallow it down like I did earlier.

I say, I don't know whether you've guessed this yet, Keris, and I strongly suspect that you have, but I am FUCKING pregnant with your FUCKING brother's child. Do you understand what I'm saying to you?

She says nothing.

I add, So can you please put him on the sodding phone?

Keris is silent, and I imagine Boy staring at her from the door of his bedroom, monitoring her every word and movement. Shaking his head, his eyes wild.

Then she says, Sorry, Bess, and hangs up.

I slam the phone into the mirror on the back of my door and the glass cracks around my knuckles.

*

I wake up late. Mum and Rory are out. I open the window because it's hot and overnight I've got all twisted up in my bed sheets and there are little lines impressed all over my body. I climb out onto the porch roof and watch the dogwalkers in the park by Stage H. I can hear parakeets, and children playing in gardens. Their little voices make me feel sick. And then I realise it's more than just a feeling and I dash to the bathroom, scraping my foot against a screw in the corner of the windowsill as I climb back in. And I'm sick in the toilet. As I flush it down, I look at my foot and see that a pool of blood has formed around it on the tiles, and there is a deep gash across the top, and that's when it starts hurting. I dab the wound with tissue and wipe up the blood from the floor, then go into the cupboard on the landing and get the first-aid kit out. Clarissa comes out of her bedroom

You've got blood on the carpet, she says, bored.

I look down and see that there are little dots of red blood soaking into the floor between the bathroom and the cupboard.

Let me wrap it up for you, Clarissa says, and I let her do it, and her hands are small and soft as she winds gauze around my foot. I say thank you, and wonder aloud whether it's worth trying to bleach the blood out of the carpet before Mum gets home.

I think you're as far up the creek as you're ever going to be, Clarissa says, parroting something that Uncle Jason says a lot. There's not really anything else you can do. Might as well leave it.

I put the first-aid kit away.

Are you having the baby, then? Riss asks me.

Looks like it.

What do you mean, *looks* like it?

Well. It's been decided, hasn't it?

Bess . . . why are you leaving it up to someone else to decide? That's so, so stupid.

You don't understand.

Of course I do. I know I'm younger than you, but I'm clever, aren't I? I know what's going on here. You're having the baby because that's what Mum wants, not you.

And what exactly would you do in my situation? I spit back at her.

Well – not that it would ever happen to me – but I wouldn't let her tell me what to do.

I look at her and wonder what it would be like to be her, to be the *real* daughter. The one who always gets asked first about how she is and what she's up to. Who, when she gets new clothes or school stuff, doesn't have to save the receipts so 'we can claim it back later'. Who doesn't have to have her every move audited by an army of adults who don't know anything about her. Who isn't a commodity to anyone.

I say to her, You do realise that there's a massive imbalance between you and me, right?

No . . . what are you on about? I don't know why she looks so guilty. It's not her fault that she was born into one set of cir-cumstances and I was born into another. We can't choose these things. I feel suddenly horrible for thinking nasty things about her. Being jealous. It's not like she asked to be the favourite.

She looks down at my foot, where the blood is slowly soaking into the bandage. It looks like there is a carnation blooming on my foot.

Maybe you should go to the doctor's, she says.

We hear the door go, meaning Mum and Rory have come back from wherever they went. Riss goes downstairs, but I don't feel like facing them. Then, at the bottom of the stairs, I hear her shout to me, Bess, come and look at this stuff.

So, I come downstairs and stand behind her in the hallway, and we watch as Mum and Rory bring in a flat-pack piece of furniture, wrapped in clear cellophane, through the door. I see the long wooden bars and I know that it's a baby's cot. Rory props it against the wall as Mum goes back to the car and retrieves several bulging Mothercare bags from the boot.

What is this? I say.

Well, we need the gear, don't we? Mum says, beaming, and then: Oh my God, what have you done to your foot?

I look down, having forgotten about it for a moment. The bandage is soaked all the way through now. And I look back up at Clarissa with this snarky look on her face like she's asking me *You're really okay with this?* And it's like a door has just shut in my brain. And I'm suddenly very calm, calmer than I've been for a while, since before being pregnant, since before I met Boy.

I say, Yeah, Riss, I think I do need to go to the doctor's.

I'll give you a lift, Rory says, so I put some flip-flops on and wait in the car while they unload the rest of the stuff. I try not to look too hard at the plastic bags. I still haven't showered. I'm in my pyjama shorts and a little vest. My legs are stubbly. No one notices these things. Rory's left his mobile phone in the car – a new Nokia, he just got it – and I pick it up and dial Eshal's house, thinking, Please don't let Rory come back yet, please, please, please let it be Esh that picks up. And sometimes I think there might actually be a God because she does.

Eshal arranges to meet me at the doctor's. Rory drives me to the high street, where the health centre is, and we don't say a single word to each other the whole way. I feel like it should be uncomfortable, but it's not. I look down at my hands and see that they're ever so slightly trembling again.

He pulls up in the car park and asks me if I want him to go in with me and I shake my head no quickly, slamming the door to the car before he has time to argue about it. After a moment he pulls away, and as he does, I spot Eshal rounding the corner by the motorway bridge and I wave to her.

What do you want? she yells.

Shut up and come in with me, I shout back, and I wait for her to catch up to me, her platforms thumping against the pavement as she runs lopsidedly, her ankles almost-but-not-quite buckling. She is wearing her big Audrey Hepburn sunglasses and she has a Fab ice lolly.

Got one for you, she says. She pulls a second out of the back pocket of her shorts.

Oh my God, you had it next to your bum?

Just bloody eat it, Bess, you div. Next time I won't bother.

I unwrap the Fab and quickly lick up all the runny bits.

Why are you in your PJs? Esh asks. Are you *not wearing a bra*?

I don't bother answering. She follows me through the automatic doors into the surgery. The waiting room looks empty. I walk up to the reception desk and knock on the glass. The woman behind it, who I recognise as one of the locals at The Three Horseshoes, slides the window up and says, Please don't knock on the glass, and then slides it back down.

I look at Esh like *what the hell* and she shrugs back at me and takes a bite out of her Fab. We sit down on two stained chairs in the corridor and wait.

Ten minutes later, the receptionist slides the window up and says in a too-sweet voice, Can I help you girls?

I shuffle back over to the window and ask her if she's got any emergency appointments available.

What's it regarding? she asks.

You can't ask me that! It's personal.

I can if it's an emergency appointment, love. You've got to prove it's an emergency.

I give her a look and lift my flip-flopped foot onto the countertop, my white thigh wobbling, almost doing the splits to make it. Esh snorts loudly behind me. The receptionist looks mortified.

I've got an issue with this, I tell her. It won't stop bleeding.

She considers me for a moment. Fine, she says. I'll see what we can do.

She takes my details and Esh and I go into the empty waiting room.

Not being funny, Bess, she says, your foot looks one hundred per cent gammy, but I'm not sure what role I have to play in all of this. You want me to hold your hand while they stitch you up or something?

I pick up a magazine and flip through the first few pages. All slim, tanned white women with whiter smiles and sparkly eyes staring back at me.

What's going on with your *situation*? I ask her, not wanting to talk about mine. She stiffens next to me, only slightly, but I notice it.

I spoke to a social worker.

And?

They're sorting out protective accommodation, she whispers.

What?!

Yep. Next week. It could be any time, they said. Someone's going to show up at my house and I have to have an overnight bag ready to go. And that's it. They're busting me out.

Oh my God. Esh. What the fuck.

It's only temporary, the woman said. Until we can resolve stuff, like, me and my parents, and if not, they're going to put me up in a council flat or something. It's social services doing it. And they've made a referral. So, I'm officially *on the books*.

Oh my God, I say again.

And, before you ask, no, I don't know where I'm going. And I don't know what else is happening. I'm supposed to start vet school in like four weeks. I've got an induction on the thirty-first. Fuck knows what'll happen about that, though. I'm shit-scared, Bess. Every time I look at my mum, I think about how I'm completely betraying her and everything she believes in, and everything *I* believe in, to be honest, and how much this is going to fuck her up. It's horrible.

You just have to think, I tell her, like, what's the alternative? You're gonna marry this Mehdi bloke, who you don't even like, and pop out eight of his babies and spend the rest of your life cleaning someone else's piss off the toilet seat? Does that sound like the person you want to become?

Well . . . yeah, exactly.

Think about that stuff, Esh. They will forgive you, they *will*, I promise.

Like how your parents are going to forgive you for getting pregnant at fifteen? Yeah, right.

It's different. They're not my family. They're not obligated to forgive me.

That doesn't mean you have to have a baby to please them, though, she says.

I know. That's why we're here.

What?

But before I have time to respond to her, the door to the

surgery opens and a nurse calls my name. She shows us into an office, and there's a doctor sitting at a desk. Me and Eshal sit down opposite him.

The GP introduces himself as Dr Scarman. I shake his hand tentatively. He glances at what I assume are my notes on his desk.

So, Isabelle, he says slowly, shall we take a look at your foot?

No, I say. That's just a ploy.

A ploy?

Eshal looks at me and understands what I'm doing and I think she almost smiles a little bit too, and that spurs me on.

My foot will need looking at too, I tell him.

Dr Scarman takes his glasses off and cleans them with his tie.

What else are you here for?

I blink, trying to steady my breathing. Eshal takes one of my trembling hands in her own and squeezes it gently and I can feel every single bone in her skinny fingers even though I know we're not really touching because there are millions of atoms between us. But it bloody well feels like we are, like there's no space at all between me and Esh, and even when she goes off to Basingstoke for vet school, or to escape her engagement or whatever, we're always going to be like this, like both of us holding onto each other for dear life, anchored together like planets in our own gravitational field, the only thing stopping us from floating up into space like paper lanterns set loose, like astronauts without spaceships, with nowhere to go until we disintegrate.

And I say to him – Dr Scarman, I mean – I need an abortion.

Chapter Twenty-Three

That night, I'm sitting at the dinner table with them. Mum asks me if everything is all right. And I look up at her and I say, Yes, everything is fine. And I try not to dig my cutlery into the table.

She doesn't know that in five days' time I'm going to take the train to a clinic in Brixton and they will give me a tablet, and then the day after that I will go back and they will give me another tablet and then I won't be pregnant any more. That's what the doctor explained, anyway. He said that as I'm sixteen, the NHS won't tell anyone – not even social services or my foster parents – what I'm doing. I wish I'd known that earlier. It still means I need to tell them myself, but only after it's done, so they can't try to talk me out of it again. Mum keeps asking me to clear space in my bedroom so Rory can set up the cot. Maybe I can throw out some of my VHSs, she says. Maybe some CDs and the cabinet. Maybe that hideous hi-fi sound system, which I got from the charity shop and balanced on the handlebars of my bike the whole two-mile cycle home. Babies don't like loud music. And, while I'm at it, maybe I should take those posters down. Uma Thurman with a cigarette in one hand and a gun in the other is hardly appropriate for a baby's room.

She's going to hate me, if she doesn't kill me first.

Somehow this doesn't bother me at all.

Esh is still at home for now, with her stuff packed into a bin liner and stashed under her bed. She doesn't sleep in case they come to get her at night, even though her support worker said that wouldn't happen: it'll be between ten and five.

Shelly, my new social worker, has called twice to see when I'm free to go and look around Basquiat School of Arts. I tell her I can't go there. I can't afford it. She says it doesn't matter, we should still go and look at it. I refuse and she asks me why, and I say, realising how ridiculous I sound as I do, that it is going to break my heart.

Me and Esh talk on the phone in whispers in the middle of the night because Mum still doesn't want us speaking to each other and Mrs Bhandari says she can't go against another mother's wishes. I say to her, I'm so afraid that you'll move really far away and I won't be able to see you.

She says, I'm afraid you'll have an abortion and die. Or you'll have an abortion and your mother kills you. Either way, you are going to die.

I already almost died once from that bath, didn't I? We're all going to die one day. There's no point being afraid of it.

I go through everything in my head over and over. I am going to get the train from Shepperton station on Tuesday at eleven twenty, and then I'll get the Victoria line from Vauxhall at twelve thirty-five. I'll arrive in Brixton at twelve fifty (at the latest), and then it's a fifteen-minute walk (at the most) to the Marie Stopes clinic I've been referred to. And the next day I'll do the whole thing again, except an hour later, and that will be it.

Except, I tell Eshal, there's this thing it says in the leaflet the doctor gave me.

Which is? she asks.

Which is that I'm not supposed to get the train home on my own on the second day, I say. Because of side effects from the tablet and stuff, right? Like, I might be vomming and stuff.

Well . . . what are you going to do, then?

I don't know, just chance it on the train. How else am I supposed to get home?

I'm telling Esh this to gauge her reaction, and her reaction will tell me how good or how bad an idea it is. It's a bad idea.

Are you loopy? You want to be sicking up all over the tube? You're deluded, Bess. Seriously. Aren't you going to be, like, gushing blood from your foo foo as well?

Well . . . yeah.

No fucking way. You're dumb sometimes. You know that?

Yeah. I know.

What are we going to do? I haven't got any money for a hotel. Have you?

The way Eshal uses 'we' makes me feel stronger.

I could ask Keris, I say after a few seconds. The thought has actually crossed my mind several times.

Esh thinks about it. It's not a bad idea, she says, but didn't you mouth off at her about Boy? Is she going to be interested in doing you a favour?

She's doing Boy a favour as well.

That's a bit dark.

True though, isn't it? And anyway, I'm pretty sure Boy robbed my grandmother's money out of my bedroom.

What?

Yep. So it's not like I can even dip into that and get a taxi or anything.

Bess, that's so fucked up. What a shithead. He *stole* from you?

Yep. I've got no proof. But, you know, it's Boy.

Yeah . . . Bess, I know now isn't the time for 'I told you so' . . .

Oh, don't worry. I'm done with him.

And I think, even saying his name out loud makes me feel like I want to punch something.

We sit in silence for a little longer until Eshal whispers, I think that's my dad going for a wee, and hangs up. And I listen to the dial tone for a few seconds, and then I hang up too.

The next morning is four days until the abortion. Eshal's parents are both at work, and so are mine; we're both free to sneak out, so we meet at the end of my road by the church. It's windy and Esh is wearing her Audrey Hepburn sunnies and a huge wide-brimmed black hat, movie-star-style, and she has to grip the edges to stop it blowing away.

We walk to Charlton Village on the road next to all the farmland. The road is dusty and in the farmers' fields there are big piles of gravel and dirt that look like they have been lifted straight out of the ground with a JCB.

What are they building here? I wonder aloud.

Probably flats, Esh says, and as we walk, we watch a pigeon fly out in front of a car coming towards us, and it smacks hard against the car's windscreen and the car squeals to stillness. The driver gets out and looks at the pigeon all smooshed up against the window. He goes into the back of his car and takes out an empty plastic bag. He peels the pigeon off the windscreen with the plastic bag covering his hand, all its guts hanging from it, its little beak half-open mid-screech, its eyes wide and black. Underneath the spot where the pigeon was, on the glass, there is a long, curved crack. The driver spots it and swears loudly. He flings the dead bird into the weeds at the side of the pavement and then harrumphs back into the car, turning on his wind-screen wipers before pulling away.

It takes us just under an hour to make it all the way to School Road. As we get to Boy and Keris's house, Esh takes my hand.

She knocks for me. Keris opens the door. She takes in me and Eshal on the doorstep, hand in hand, and breathes out an exaggerated sigh.

Boy's not here.

Good, I say.

Isn't that why you're here? she asks me.

No, we want to talk to you, Eshal says.

Let's go in the garden, Keris says, her eyes big, like Riss's when she's watching me and Mum having a fight.

I didn't want to call in case he picked up, I say quietly.

Keris shrugs and leads us through the open door in the kitchen into the garden. Zack is on the lawn going in circles on a little tricycle, and when he spots me and Esh, he shouts MUM BESS IS HERE and Keris goes, Yeah I know, mate, say hello and he shouts hello at us and we shout it back. We pull up the dirty plastic furniture on the patio. I can feel my hands trembling, so I light a cigarette.

You think you should be doing that? Keris asks.

I raise my eyebrows at her because I don't know how else to answer.

Keris goes back into the kitchen and brings out a carton of orange juice and a carton of apple juice, both Tesco Value. She pours us some into plastic beakers.

So, what's going on? she asks.

I take another puff on my cigarette, nervous. Keris waits. Eshal looks at me.

Eventually I say, I'm scheduled to go to a clinic on Tuesday.

Zack falls off his trike and starts screeching and we wait while Keris goes to sort him out.

Once she's done, I say, It's at 2 p.m.

Is that what you want?

Yes, it is.

Keris takes my fag from me and inhales on it deeply. She hands it back.

Fair enough, she says.

Are you going to tell Boy?

I suppose so. But I won't tell him until after it's done. You know. Stops him interfering. He knows about the – pregnancy – by the way, I told him after you rang me.

I say, Yeah . . . sorry about that.

But I'm thinking that even now he knows he still hasn't called me. I remember daydreaming about dying and whether he would have gone to my funeral. Now I know. Of course he wouldn't have.

Don't worry. Forget about it. I'm to blame for all this, too.

What? What do you mean?

Keris hesitates, takes another drag on my cigarette, exhales slowly, not looking at me. She says, I knew what was going on between you two. I'm not stupid. I knew what you were getting up to in his room. I wasn't born yesterday.

Eshal and I glance at each other nervously. I'm struck by how much like my mum Keris sounds.

I knew that he would end up losing interest and mess you about. Dad used to do the same. Younger girls as well. It's none of my business. Boy's an adult, technically speaking. But I just . . . you know . . . you're only just *sixteen*, Bess. You're a kid, really.

She was fifteen, actually, says Eshal.

Keris raises her eyebrows. I should've done *more*. And Boy should know better. You're a nice girl. I don't know.

You kind of *did* do more, though, I say.

Not enough, clearly, she says.

I smile weakly at her and she returns my expression, her eyes sad. All three of us, plus Zack, are quiet for a moment, all looking out into the garden, into the sky which is overcast, but there are still aeroplane lines, like slug trails, streaking through the pale clouds. A parakeet lands on a fence post at the end of the garden and cleans its feathers.

You're doing the right thing, Keris says quietly.

How can you say that? You had Zack, didn't you?

Keris lowers her voice and says, When I found out I was pregnant, I was too far gone to have the option to . . . you know. I didn't have a choice, not like you. If I'd found out earlier . . . well, things might have been really different, you know? I can't rely on Zack's dad for anything. He's even more of a loser than Boy is.

I wonder whether any of what Keris has said has registered in Zack's little brain. It doesn't look like it. He's back to making aggressive engine noises on his trike.

Has Boy said anything to you about it? About me?

Not really. When I told him that night, he just shut himself in his room. I haven't really seen him since. He spends his whole life out of the house God-knows-where doing God-knows-what or asleep. His court date's coming up in a couple of weeks. I think he might be bricking it. He might end up doing time.

What are you going to do if that happens?

Fuck knows. Sign on? Go into one of those women's shelters? We can't afford the rent without Boy's job. All of my benefits go on Zack's clothes and food and stuff.

I'm really sorry, Keris.

Don't worry. 'S'not your fault, is it? Boy's fault for nicking that car in the first place. His fault for knocking you up as well, isn't it?

Eshal picks up the carton of apple juice to refill her beaker. I'm about to say something about being old enough to look after myself when Keris's face changes, and I turn around and Boy is standing there. He's back from whatever he was doing. And he has the same expression on his face as Keris, maybe because they have the same genes and the same facial expressions, or maybe because they've both just been caught in the act. I don't know what the 'act' is, though, just that they've been caught. And before anyone has time to say a single thing, Boy has turned around and is pulling his keys back out from his pocket, and Eshal goes, Oh no you bloody don't, and she stands up and runs into the house, which is difficult for her because she is wearing four-inch platform boots and the arch of her foot can't bend in them. Then Keris and I get up and follow her. And I don't know what Esh is planning to do, and whatever she does, I don't know what I'm going to do to stop her. And I'm thinking about when I just saw him in the door looking at me like I grew an extra head for a moment. And how it felt like when I watched *Ten Things I Hate About You* this summer and it made me realise that the golden age of teen romance movies is over, John Hughes doesn't even make films any more and Heath Ledger isn't remotely convincing as a teenage heart-throb. It had to end sometime. And for a moment I forget that I'm supposed to be in love with him and I don't care that he's probably fucking someone else, and it's all quite liberating.

And now we're in the front driveway of the house and Boy is unlocking the car, but the key is a bit stuck so he's struggling and Esh is shouting at him, saying things like YOU DIRTY SCUM OF THE EARTH SKEEZY FUCKING KNOB JOCKEY BOY YOU'RE THE BIGGEST COWARD I EVER KNEW CAN'T BELIEVE YOU'RE RUNNING AWAY YOU LITTLE SHIT YOU DISGUST ME and so forth.

And Boy hasn't said anything back to her yet, but he has managed to get the door open on the Sierra and now he's in the driver's seat trying to get it started and Eshal, who is still holding the apple juice carton in her hand, lifts it high over her head and throws it at the windscreen, and it explodes apple juice all over the place and he turns on the windscreen wipers and they squeak against the glass and Keris goes, Oi, that's my car, about the juice, and I say, Sorry, Keris, and she watches for a few seconds and then she shrugs and goes back inside the house.

And now he's having trouble getting the car into reverse and Eshal is still shouting, and before I know it, Keris is back outside, and now she's got another carton from the fridge, milk I think, and she leans into Boy's open side window and pours most of it onto Boy's lap, making him go, WHAT THE FUCK, KERIS and Esh starts laughing and the whole thing is pretty funny, so I start laughing too, and Keris throws the rest of the carton onto the windscreen and milk dribbles all over it, obscuring Boy's face, and he's finally backing out of the driveway onto the road and slamming on the accelerator so violently that he stalls, which makes us laugh harder. And then he gets the ignition on again, and there's a car behind him honking, and then it's all over and he's gone.

I spend the evening in my bedroom re-reading my abortion literature. Pamphlets and website printouts, hidden under my mattress. On Tuesday, I'm going to be given a tablet called mifepristone, which blocks a certain hormone from reaching my uterus and that causes the lining of my uterus to degenerate and the egg can't stay embedded in it. Then, the next day, I get another tablet called misoprostol, which makes my uterus contract and *expels the foetus*. And then I have a really, *really* heavy period and that's that. Side effects: cramps, nausea, vomiting, diarrhoea, heavy bleeding, risk of infection. No plane journeys for six weeks in case of deep vein thrombosis. No swimming for six to eight weeks in case of infection. No sex until my next period. The thought of having sex makes me feel like my uterus is already contracting (from disgust).

Mum comes into my bedroom and sits on the end of my bed. All the leaflets are stashed under my pillow. The window is open and the breeze is pushing the blind away from the wall before it falls back, clattering against the window frame. Outside, there are noises like car engines and parakeets and the big oak trees on the green shifting around in the breeze. Mum says, You really need to clear some room in here for that cot.

You're getting a bit ahead of yourself with all this, I tell her.

Those parakeets never shut up, she says, watching them roosting in the oak branches. Making the leaves impossibly green, voluminous. They clean each other's feathers. Why don't you go out with Eshal tonight? Mum says

And I look at her, eyebrows raised.

What happened to you today? Did Rory put something in your Ovaltine?

What?

I thought you didn't want me to see Esh, like, at all?

Well. I don't know. You need a break. You're not going to have many opportunities to go out soon, are you? You might as well make the most of it. And I can tell you miss her a lot.

I shrug and feel guilty because Mum doesn't know how I've been sneaking out of the house at pretty much every possible moment to see Esh. I'm surprised she's never noticed it: it's not like I'm subtle. Or like I don't have it in me.

So I take the bus to the high street because they won't let me cycle anywhere any more. And when I get to Esh's house, I see that there are still no cars in the driveway, which means we are safe. I knock and Esh comes out and I say, Let's do one more night, just us two. And she looks at me. She's wearing glittery mascara which makes her eyes twinkle more than usual. And she says, Yes, okay, where to?

And we walk to the station and sit on the bench on the platform thinking about it. None of our ideas are right. We don't want to do what we always do – sit by the river or got to the Pits or smoke blunts with Manor Park Jesus – because that's what we *always* do. And this is our last night together for who knows how long. *Our last hurrah*. It can't be an ordinary night. It has to be special.

I bet there are no good clubs wherever I'm going, Esh says, kicking an old Dr Pepper can onto the railway tracks.

I doubt your social worker will know, I say, snorting.

Esh says, Whatever happened to your other social worker? That camp one? With the blue nail polish?

Henry? He moved offices, or quit, or something. I don't know.
I'm so sure he was a drag queen.

Me too.

The announcer comes onto the overhead speakers and tells us that the train now approaching the platform is the nineteen-fourteen South West Trains service to London Waterloo.

Esh nudges me, her eyes glittering. Let's go and find him, she says.

What?

Let's find him. You know. Gay bars. Drag queens. Soho. It's Friday night, isn't it? If he's really a drag queen, I bet he'll be in one of those bars.

Yeah, right, mate. You know how many gay bars there are in London?

Well, there's no harm in looking, is there? Look, I've got twenty squid on me. How much have you got?

I take my old *Powerpuff Girls* coin purse out of my rucksack and count out the pounds and pences. Fourteen fifty.

That's enough for a few drinks in London. That's more than enough. Bess . . . let's do it. Don't be a pussy.

I thought you didn't like using that word.

Yeah, but I make exceptions for when someone is *actually* being a pussy. Like right now.

I don't think you should be allowed to pick and choose your ethics like that, Esh.

Who's stopping me? Come *on*, you silly bint.

She pulls me by the arm onto the train, which has just come to a stop at the platform, the carriage doors grinding open in front of us. We sit down in the bike section, giggling because it's all so stupid. The train takes fifty minutes to get to Waterloo and when we arrive, we go to the off-licence across the road and buy a 330ml bottle of vodka and a bottle of Coke and we sit at the bus stop and mix it up, pouring a quarter of the Coke down a drain. Then we go back into the station and look at the underground map.

There's no station for Soho, says Esh.

I squint at the map and realise she's right.

How the fuck are we supposed to know how to get there, then?

We look at another map on the wall, this one a road map, and find the bit labelled SOHO.

Leicester Square, I say, jabbing the station with my index finger. We need to go to Leicester Square.

So we get on the escalator and walk through the turnstiles, and down another escalator, onto the Northern Line, and get lost in the tunnels for ten minutes before realising we're on a Bakerloo platform, and then eventually we are on the tube to Leicester Square, taking it in turns to swig from the plastic Coke bottle. Each of us gargling it to make the other laugh. And I read the tube map on the side of the train above the window and see that

Archway station is on this line and that's the station I would need to get off at to go to Basquiat School of Arts in Crouch End and then I don't feel quite so fizzy.

But anyway, we get off the train at Leicester Square and it's all huge luminous billboards, glowing shop windows, street performers with saxophones and electric guitars, dancers doing backflips to a stereo playing NWA. And the food: chicken chow mein, pizza, hot doughnuts, roasted cashews from street vendors sitting under umbrellas along the edges of the square. I want to stop and take in every sight and smell, but Eshal is pulling me away, through the square and out the other side, onto a wide road lined with tall terraced Victorian houses – they look like Basquiat School – with glass shopfronts and black taxis and buses crawling along, honking each other out of the way, and even more music, this time steel drummers, six of them, dancing and playing at the same time. But we don't stop for them either. We walk briskly down smaller roads and across public gardens, and we're in another square, much smaller than Leicester Square, but still teeming with people on the move – these ones wearing sparkly dresses, feather boas, crazy glasses and wigs, in high heels that would break my ankles if I tried to walk in them. Eshal lets us stop for five minutes.

Do you really think any of these bars are going to let us in? I ask her, looking at the buildings further along the road, many of which have people spilling out of them.

She shrugs. Just act like you belong here.

We sit down on a brick wall and finish our vodka-Coke and, as we stand up, I think to myself I definitely feel a bit drunk now, and I put my hand to my belly, thinking, Oh my God, the baby, how could I be so thick, of course I can't be drinking. And then I remember that no, I'm having an abortion, and on Wednesday the baby will be gone.

On Wednesday, the baby will be gone, I say out loud to Eshal. She was about to head in the direction of one of the busier-looking bars but pauses and turns back to look at me.

That's the decision you've made, she says.

I look down at my hands.

Bess?

For a moment, I feel like I'm going to cry, especially when Eshal comes back to where I'm standing and snakes her left arm through my right one.

But then she says, Aren't we here to rumble your social worker? Come on.

I nod, but then I think about it and say, I don't know. It seemed like it would be fun, but it's kind of invasive, right? Like, let's just let him live his life.

Eshal shrugs and says, Suits me, but I am still planning on drinking in one of these bars, so are you coming, or what?

I roll my shoulders and grip her arm more convincingly, and we walk.

The first two doormen we encounter both turn us away, barely looking at us as they do so. We turn onto a quieter street, this one with more late-night cafés than actual nightclub-style bars, and we easily walk into one with big leaded windows, no bouncer, and candles with three wicks in jars at each square wooden table. There are black-and-white photographs of old jazz musicians on the yellow walls. Behind the bar is a floor-to-ceiling bookshelf full of bottles of different kinds of drink. And there is a four-piece band near the back of the smoke-filled room playing acoustic versions of Stevie Wonder songs and me and Esh sit down at one of the candlelit tables and pretend we're on a date, and I take her hand across the table and stroke each one of her long delicate fingers from the knuckle to the tip of her fingernail. A waiter comes over with a drinks menu and we ask him to bring the cheapest bottle of white wine and two glasses without looking at the list, and we giggle at ourselves because it all feels so grown-up.

Jolly good, spiffing, top drawer, Esh says, taking a piece of her hair and draping it across her upper lip so it looks like she's got a long, wispy moustache. I make a Posh Man face and she laughs.

After a couple more songs, the band finishes and starts packing up and Eshal pouts because she was enjoying it, but then Tears for Fears comes on the overhead speakers – 'Everybody Wants to Rule the World' – which is one of our favourites, so we get up and dance, and soon the other people in the bar are up too and we're all dancing with one another and it's beautiful, and for a moment I forget that I'm pregnant and that sometimes in my bed at night I'm too scared to move a single muscle, listening to the parakeets, trying to find the faces in the paint, my fingers all clawed up, as if the slightest movement will make the house fall down around me. And then it's the bit where Roland Orzabal and Curt Smith are really going for it with the chorus, me and Eshal look at each other and basically scream the words at one another and I'm not thinking about being too afraid to move now because we are here, in this moment, alive, with all our fingers and toes and our minds and each other and, really, that's all that matters.

Chapter Twenty-Four

Here's what happened to Eshal.

Her social worker called her the next day and told her she was coming to get her on Sunday. Eshal already had all her things packed up: the stuff she needed, anyway. She didn't sleep. Instead she watched the birds in her garden, in the big tree that leans against the fence.

The next day, yesterday, at eight in the morning, Eshal's social worker pulled up and knocked on the door. Eshal's brother Anwar opened it and when the social worker asked for Eshal, he wanted to know what this weird, fluffy-headed white woman wanted with his sister. By this point, Esh was already hauling her bin bag and her suitcase down the stairs. Eshal's mum was in the kitchen and came to the door to see what was going on. The social worker asked Eshal if she wanted to explain and Esh said no. So the social worker told Mrs Bhandari and Anwar that Eshal had agreed to be housed in temporary accommodation because of her being made to participate in a marriage that she doesn't consent to.

Mrs Bhandari started doing her special meditation breathing and called Mr Bhandari downstairs, and then invited everyone into the living room for a cup of tea. Mrs Bhandari asked Eshal to explain to her exactly what had happened and why there were bin bags of her stuff in the hallway. And Eshal still couldn't look at her mum or her dad as she told them. She said, I know it's right for Anwar and it's what he wants. And I *know* you two had it and it worked out amazing. And Aisha and all our cousins too. But I don't want it. I don't want to get engaged to someone I don't know. I'm sorry. I just can't do it. I want to choose who I marry, and I don't want to marry them for five, maybe even ten, years after I meet them. I want to get my degrees before I even *think* about it. And I know you're going to hate this, and I'm sorry, but I want to be able to choose a non-Bengali boy. I'm not saying I *will* choose. I just want to *have* that choice. I'll do anything else you ask me to, I promise. I'll do anything. Because I love you and I know everything you've given up, how hard you've worked, so that me and Anwar can have a good life. But I just can't do this. I'm sorry. I can't. And I get how much this means to you, and if you want to cut me off, if you never want to see me again, I understand. But I can't do it.

And after Esh got it all out, and the lead balloon in her chest was gone, her mum and dad and brother kind of just sat there in a stunned silence for a bit, until eventually Mr Bhandari took a very long sip of tea and said, A *non-Bengali* boy?

And Mrs Bhandari slipped her hand into her husband's, and said, Well, we might need to talk about that bit, but I don't see why we can't compromise on all the other things.

What?

Honestly, Duck, why didn't you *tell* us you felt like this before?

You're not angry at me?

The only thing I'm angry about is the fact you felt you had to keep this a secret from us. We brought you up to have opinions, Eshal, to speak your mind. Not to go along with things that upset you.

So you're not going to disown me?

For goodness' sake, Eshal. How could you possibly think that? How could we ever live without you?

And Eshal stared at her mum and dad for a moment. And all the ugly, thick, cloying, suffocating fear that had been building up inside her over the months and years, it melted away. And she saw her parents very clearly, maybe for the first time in her life: she saw them as two people who loved her, unconditionally. And she burst into tears. And her mum pulled her onto her lap like she was still a little girl, and her dad stroked her hair and shushed her and she just couldn't stop crying and apologising and her mum said don't worry, and it's okay, and we love you.

And Eshal felt like one of those migrating birds, flying, and her whole ribcage was expanding, bursting wide open, and she was breathing in lungfuls of new air.

And the social worker stuck around to talk some things through with Mr and Mrs Bhandari and to recommend a family therapist, as clearly there had been a breakdown in communication between Eshal and her parents, and while things had worked out okay for everyone this time, it was still worrying that Eshal was prepared to run away from home rather than go against her parents' wishes. And Mr and Mrs Bhandari very reluctantly agreed to make an appointment. And after the social worker left. Eshal stepped out into the garden and she thought to herself, Bloody hell, I've only gone and done it, haven't I, and that's when she screamed. And it was a loud and long scream, the kind that makes your teeth vibrate and your tongue taste blood. Because she had been saving it up in her throat and her lungs and her diaphragm and her belly for years and years, ever since she was a little girl.

It's Tuesday afternoon now, and I'm lying on a trolley bed with plasticated upholstery the colour of the ocean. Tears for Fears is a lifetime ago. The walls are yellow: they always seem to be, in places like this, unless they're white.

The nurse comes back into the room with another trolley – a table on wheels – with a monitor on it, and tells me to pull down my denim skirt and knickers a bit, so that the waistband is in line with my pelvic bone. Then she tucks scratchy white paper towels into the waistband to protect my clothes, and squirts the cold gel stuff onto my belly like they do on *Casualty* and *Holby*. She does the same thing they did in the hospital the first time. The scan.

It feels weird to have this quiet stranger touching me like this, the feeling of her hands on me, the texture of the pads of her fingers. The nurse doesn't say anything; when she's done, she just takes her hand away, leaving the paper towels on my belly. There is something printing out of the machine on the trolley. I see that it is a reel of photographs of the scans of my womb. They look exactly like the ones Mum showed me when she was pregnant with Clarissa, not long after they started fostering me. Black, with wisps of grey cloud. Nothing decipherable, really, but Mum rubbed her lips with the hem of her sleeve and giggled at the pictures. She thought she would never have kids. She traced my finger around the mass of cloud that she said was a baby, her chest heaving up and down like she was drowning.

I look away from my own scans quickly, scared that I'm going to see the baby in the wilderness. Some kind of kidney-bean-shaped blob. An alien, like the gooey toy ones in plastic eggs, nestled into green jelly, whose heads explode when you put them in the fridge. I never looked when they did scans in the hospital. If I see them, it will become a real thing. I might change my mind. The thought scares me and makes me look away, but there's also part of me that wants to catch a glimpse of it, the little human being that is not yet quite human and not yet, even, a being.

The thing that is half my DNA and half Boy's, all mixed up together to make a new person. It's like losing a part of myself. But I don't know whether I'm losing a non-vital part, like a limb, or something that is essential to survival. A vital organ. Briefly, I think about whether the baby is a boy or a girl. Baby names. George for a boy and Lucy for a girl. I marvel at how readily the names come to me. It's because I already had them saved up, I think, in some quiet corner of my brain. I think of soft, bright-white baby clothes that smell like talc and the washing detergent Mum uses. The cot that is still boxed, propped against the wall in my bedroom.

The nurse tells me she'll be back in a minute, and exits the room, using the door I came in through. I finish wiping the gel on my belly with the paper towels and pull up my skirt. I pull my Looney Tunes T-shirt down to cover my belly, and realise that I must look like a child, wonder whether I'll be able to wear these clothes again without thinking of today. I look around for a bin in the examination room, but there is none, just an empty dark wooden desk and two chairs with a computer. The nurse comes back into the room and I ball the paper towels up in my hand, feeling the wet gel seep out of the fibres and between my fingers.

The nurse invites me to sit down at the desk with her. She has a Manila folder and from it she takes a stack of forms. She asks me my name, date of birth, address, contact telephone number, GP name, address, and so on. She fills out each of my answers in careful capital-letter black ink on the form. Finally, on the last page, she folds the papers and places them back in the folder, takes out a second form.

Now, she says. Isabelle.

Bess.

Bess, the reason I popped out just now was to see the consultant. I thought the foetus may be too large to opt for a medical termination and instead we would have to perform a surgical one.

I nod and say okay, like none of this, like the shape and size and colour of the room, is not making me want to vomit.

The nurse gives me a sympathetic look. Maybe my face has betrayed me, or maybe this is what she is trained to do. Maybe this is the look she gives to every girl that comes into this room and sits on this chair.

She says, The good news is that the foetus is *just* small enough for us to continue with the medical termination as originally planned.

I nod and say thank you, realising as I say it that 'thank you' is the wrong sentiment. I should say 'sorry' instead.

The nurse explains to me what the medical abortion involves. I will be given a tablet today before I leave the clinic, and then I will be required to come back tomorrow afternoon to take two more tablets, which I don't swallow. I am meant to hold them in the corners of my mouth until they dissolve completely. Then the nurse tells me about all the stuff I have already read in my leaflets. About how my uterus will begin to contract and the lining of my womb will break down, meaning that there is no choice for the foetus but to be expelled from my body. There will be lots of bleeding. I will feel faint and nauseous. I should bring a friend, partner or family member to support me through the experience.

Do you have someone to accompany you tomorrow, Bess?

I say yes, thinking of Keris, who told me she would drive me after Boy drove away that day, the car covered in milk and apple juice.

The nurse then reads questions to me from the second form. These questions are different. They ask me about my state of mind. Whether I have ever had suicidal thoughts. Whether I have a history of drug and alcohol abuse. Whether I have self-harmed. I say no to all of them, and she raises her eyebrows but doesn't contradict me.

Eventually the nurse asks me, And why exactly are you seeking a termination, Bess?

I knew this was coming. I have read about it on the pages Eshal printed out from the abortion websites at the library, before one of the nosy librarians peered over her shoulder, realised what she was looking at and told her to leave.

I glance at the papers on the desk in front of her. I read her name upside-down, printed in block capitals at the top of the form under the title of 'Examiner'. The word reminds me of doing GCSEs in the netball hall at school earlier this year. The sunshine, in shafts, coming through the caged windows above us. The smell of sawdust and gym shoes and the river. My exam results arrived a few days ago and are in a sealed envelope on my dressing table at home. I can't bear to open them yet. Not until this is done. My own name is next to 'Patient' on the form. The nurse's name is Trudy Bartholomew.

I start telling her about being in care. About wanting to be a film-maker. All the things that stop me from going to sleep, instead spending hours mentally joining the dots on the ceiling, and all of these dreams I have for myself. How I'll never be able to leave Shepperton, leave *care*, as a mother. Trudy nods and takes notes. I watch her fingers move and think about being held down in the bathtub, being drowned, my own fingers battling to find a grip along the smooth edges of the tub. Above me, the shower head and a face hanging over me, distorted by the ripples of water. I don't know what made her stop, what made her let go of me.

I am thinking about all of this as Trudy Bartholomew writes and it takes me a moment to realise that I'm crying, quite loudly.

Trudy doesn't seem fazed by this either, and she deftly pats me on the hand while simultaneously saying now, now and reaching into the top drawer of the desk for a box of Kleenex. Trudy says to me, It's very common to feel emotional at this stage. You've made a big decision. You've been very brave.

I nod and blow my nose noisily into a tissue she has offered me, while still holding the jellied paper towels in one hand. The scrunched-up napkins seem to have bonded themselves to the pads of my left palm. Trudy says stuff about how I'm doing the right thing for myself, and that no one is judging me, but if I were to change my mind, it's not too late and no one would be upset with me for it. I tell her that I'm not changing my mind. She pats my hand one more time.

She says, Take as much time as you need to cry it all out. We'll continue with the questions when you're ready.

She thinks I am crying because of the baby. I'm not.

The long and the short of it is this:

When Keris picks me up in the car on Wednesday at midday, Eshal is in the back seat. She holds my hand, and I'm so grateful and ashamed: my best friend who will do something so big and scary and life-changing and then dust herself off to help me do the same.

It's one of the last days of summer. It feels so different today than it did yesterday, when I went up to the clinic by myself on the train, chain-smoked on the way back, my stomach turning, until a sad man asked me to either stop or move carriage because his wife was dying of lung cancer and he couldn't bear to watch me.

I went straight to my bedroom when I got home in case some-one – Lisa – looked at my face and knew what I had done. I lay in my bed watching the faces in the ceiling, thinking, Almost made it, almost there. My whole body rigid with anticipation, feeling strongly that at any moment I was about to break apart. But today, with Eshal and Keris here, the smells of barbecue and traffic fumes and hot concrete thick in the air as we drive slowly through the South London traffic, it doesn't feel so bad. None of us mentions how strong the smell of sour milk is inside the car.

Inside the clinic, my appointment doesn't take more than five minutes. Eshal and Keris sit outside on the steps and share a cigarette. Seeing them through the window makes it a bit easier than yesterday, coming here. I'm called into a different consultation room to the one I was in yesterday, one that looks much more like a normal doctor's office. There is a big bay window with blooming flower boxes on the ledge. The sun pours in and lights up every corner of the room.

I don't see Trudy Bartholomew again, but a doctor, a man whose name I don't ask for, checks my forms again and asks me a few more questions about my medical history. Eventually, he takes a paper prescription bag from his desk, with my name printed on a little sticker on the side of it, and from it he hands me a blister pack with two pills. He explains that I must hold the tablets in my mouth until they completely dissolve, and this may take some time, up to half an hour. I nod, even though I've already been told this by Trudy. He gives me a small card with some telephone numbers on it in case I have any questions or something goes wrong. He asks me if I would like to be contacted with information about Marie Stopes' counselling services. I tell him no. He asks me to take the tablets in front of him and then, that's it. I'm done.

I leave the consultation room, walk through the waiting room where the other women are sitting, all waiting patiently to be called forward to collect their abortion. I'm surprised by how many of them have got men with them: husbands or boyfriends, I'm guessing. I wonder how Boy would react to this place. I've got the pills pushed up inside my mouth between the gums of my molars and the inside of my cheek. I can already feel them disintegrating into my saliva.

None of the women look like me. Most of them are much skinnier. Nearly all of them look older. I'm wearing a denim skirt which is a size too small for me. All of the skin around my fingernails has been chewed up and it's hot and raw-red and sore. I have three sanitary towels stuffed into my knickers. I have a sweat mark in the shape of an upside-down triangle on the back of my T-shirt.

I step out the front doors of the clinic. It's housed in what looks like a big Victorian mansion from the outside, all white pillars and fancy windowsills. Eshal and Keris are still on the steps waiting for me.

All done?

I nod.

All right?

I nod again and croak out a smile.

We wander through the big iron gates and onto the street. I try to manoeuvre my feet so that I'm not touching the cracks in the smooth slabs of pavement.

Keris and Eshal keep the mood light. Talking about gigs they've been to at Brixton Academy and the stuff they've bought at the shops around here. The pills are almost totally gone now, chalky and eroded against my teeth. It has been an hour-long car journey for a five-minute in-and-out job. Five minutes, two pills, and that's it.

Keris has parked in a little private car park behind a block of flats.

As we walk, I become aware of a dull pain in my gut, like an echo of being winded, slowly building, building, building in my body. Creeping up. And it's fine at first, but it's getting worse, until it's uncomfortable, until in a moment, it lances through me, cutting, and it suddenly feels as if someone is stamping on my stomach, trying to push it out through my birth canal and my throat simultaneously. It stuns me and I pause for a moment in our walk. I clutch at my stomach involuntarily, crumpling in on myself. The second pill is gone from the edges of my teeth.

Bess . . .?

Esh has realised what's happening and turns around.

I look up at them, half-bent against a wall. A dribble of sweat slides down my back.

I'm going to be sick.

Even as I'm saying it, the bile is rising in my throat and projecting in a crescent fountain onto the pavement, like some elaborate performance art piece. A woman with four kids hurries her offspring past me, stepping around the puddle I've just spattered all over the ground.

Just been to the clinic? she sneers as she prances delicately over my vom. You should be ashamed of yourself.

Eat shit, Eshal spits back.

I'm gasping for breath as I feel the second wave coming. I had a tomato and mozzarella panini for lunch. In the delicatessen by the train station. We had some time to kill before the abortion.

My mind merges images of mozzarella cheese, the bitchy mum eating actual shit and the trickles of sweat now sliding into my bum crack, and another wave of chunder comes out.

Eshal says, Bess . . . not being funny, but there's no way we're driving you home like this. My nursing capacity only goes so far.

I look up at Keris.

Keris says, Let's just go and find a bowl or something. She can have that for the journey.

Fine. Let's get a bowl. Or a plastic bag. There's a Tesco up this way.

I tell them, I don't think I can walk.

God, Eshal says, we'll wait here, then. You go, Keris. I'll wait.

And Keris is going. I look down at the chunks of congealed cheese decorating the concrete. There's nothing else for it. I sit on the ground. Then I lie down. And I hear Esh say, And *that*, kids, is why you don't have unprotected sex. Then I close my eyes and pretend to fall asleep.

A different woman walks past (I hear her shoes on the pavement) and asks me if I'm all right. Eshal is quiet, watching me nervously. I tell the woman that I am, opening one eyelid to acknowledge her. There is a man with her, who looks angry and impatient, with his hand wrapped around her wrist, which I notice and think is weird, that, like, he is holding her wrist and not her hand, like people do with children. She is very tall. She has to bend all the way over to get her face near to mine, like she is folding herself up. A piece of paper only folds seven times before it can't fold any more. No matter the size of the paper, it won't ever. I wonder if it's the same with the tall woman. She looks as though she can fold herself up more than seven times. And then I'm asleep and I am dreaming of the man who was holding onto her wrist, and he is breaking all of her bones – her ribs, her collarbone, her legs – to fold her up and fold and fold and fold until she has disappeared altogether.

Keris drives us home and I lie across the entire back seat, wishing that the car didn't smell so bad, that my eyes weren't so heavy, that the pads stuffed into my knickers weren't so uncomfortably damp and the cloying pain in my abdomen didn't exist. We have all the windows down because my whole body is covered in a thin sheen of fever-sweat. I let my eyes drift closed and pay attention to how the sunlight still gets through, though it flickers with shadows, warming the blood vessels in my eyelids. It's a beautiful day today. Even though I know it's not over, and it hurts, and there's more work to be done yet, I've not felt this peaceful in a long while.

In the front of the car, Keris and Eshal say little, but every now and again I feel a hand brush against mine, tuck a strand of hair behind my ear, stroke my forehead. The lightest touches.

By the time we arrive back home, I'm fast asleep on the back seat, a dull pain, like an ancient injury, throbbing in my lower abdomen, my clothes soaked in sweat. Keris shakes me awake. The first thing I see when I open my eyes is the Stage H building looming above us. I feel unsteady on my feet as I get out of the car and Eshal asks quietly if I want her to come in with me and I look up and see that Mum is standing at the window watching me.

And I say to her, No, don't worry. And she looks like she's going to argue, but Keris says, Come on, Esh, I'll drive you home. And Eshal gets in the car and they wait there to make sure I get the front door open and then they drive away.

Mum is in the kitchen, her hair falling in waves across her face, a mask, the palms of her hands placed flat against the countertop, and I think to myself that even though she is a tall woman, at this moment she looks so small.

And she sees how I'm hunched over, holding myself up by the elbows, how I'm pale and sweating and shaking, and she says to me, What have you done, and I can't answer her, mainly because the pain has become more intense since I've been standing up, and I don't know whether I can say the words without choking.

She says, What did you do? And then, You've done it, haven't you? Maybe she can smell it on me, the blood, the lacking, and then the look on my face must have told her what she already knows and somewhere, outside, through the open door, in someone's back garden, there's a dog barking and I thought I was imagining it because she's screaming and I can't quite hear, and I have this sensation that I'm spinning around faster and faster and faster until I can't see anything clearly any more. Everything is blurred around the edges, like I'm looking through a camera lens, but still I see the way her face is crumpled, like an old piece of paper, her mouth an upside-down capital D, every line on her face another fold, and she lets herself slip to the floor, the wailing, the noise of her, hovering around us like death, and I say to her, I'm sorry, I'm sorry, I'm sorry. Mum, I'm so sorry. But the truth is, I'm not sorry. Not one bit.

Later, I sit on the toilet and watch between pale thighs laced with shiny lilac stretch marks, as thick dark clots of blood fall out of me and turn the water pink, and then I bleach it all away with Domestos, nose stinging, like it was never there.

Chapter Twenty-Five

I spend that night, and all the next day, and the day after that, in my bedroom. I open my eyes and count the faces in the ceiling and fall asleep again. Someone comes to my door and puts plated-up food outside. From the looks of it (cheese sandwiches, Wotsits and a Frube), it's Clarissa. I'm exhausted. When I'm asleep, which is most of the time, I have these weird lucid dreams where I'm with Eshal and everything is lovely – we're at Manor Park or the Pits – and then I look down and my belly is bulging out, pregnant, grotesque, and you can see all these dark veins inside my skin stretched so thin, and my belly gets bigger and bigger and bigger until the skin ruptures and splits and out of my body comes an alien chestbuster, like Ripley in *Aliens* (the second one), slick with blood and gunk, and then I wake up, hot and tangled up in the bed sheets, thinking, Get it out of me, and then I remember it's already gone.

I think about trying to call Boy and talking to him, but Keris will already have told him. And what's the point. I don't want anything to do with him now. Being pregnant was the last thread tying us together and now it's gone, there's nothing to hold onto. I wonder about reporting him to the police for what he did that time. Eshal says I should. I wonder if anyone will believe me; it'll be his word against mine. At school, my whole maths class

304

saw Mr Greyson grab Lara Bennett's boob in the middle of a test – *everyone* saw it – and we all vouched for her too, and nothing got done about it. Mr Greyson still works there and Lara got suspended for lying about a teacher. So who's going to believe me when I try to tell people what my *boyfriend* did when I *willingly* got into his car, went to his house and got into bed with him, when I was already pregnant by him too? No one.

On the Saturday after the abortion, I go downstairs for the first time. I'm not in pain any more, but I'm tired constantly, like I can't get enough sleep. When I go into the living room to get the phone to call Eshal, Mum is in there waiting for me. I go to leave – I don't want to have this conversation yet; I can't face the inevitable screaming match, I'm too tired – but she tells me to wait.

What? I ask, feeling too awkward to sit down, like I'm an uninvited guest.

How are you feeling? she asks, her voice flat.

I'm just tired, Mum, I say. Really fucking tired.

You don't need to swear.

I'm sorry.

But you're not really, though, are you? That's the problem.

She's perched on the windowsill, fiddling with this thin gold bracelet she wears. She looks like she's lost weight too. She's very quiet. I look at her and think of all the things she's ever done for me: took me in on her own when Rory was in Iraq; treated me like her daughter in the best way she possibly could; made me eat three meals a day; made me go to school; sat up all night with me in the early years when I was convinced I was going to drown in my sleep; all those review meetings, all those therapy sessions, social workers and paperwork. And I think, She tried her best, I really believe that, but there's something wrong with being in care, the care *system*, and it's to do with making us into a transaction. I think Lisa loves me, I really do. I love her too, in a way. But that's what I've been trying to say this whole time. It's not right, how we're treated like a job. There's too much emotional labour involved.

And because I'm trying to be a better, more honest person, especially with her, I say to her: No, I'm not sorry.

And now she's crying. Quietly. And I sit down next to her and think about putting my arm around her, but it feels so alien, and I feel so numbed by all of this, there's no room left in me to be sad with her. I'm a xenomorph. My emotional capacity is all used up.

She says, I've spoken to Shelly. I've asked her to find another placement for you. You need to start packing your things.

I look at her, horrified. Another *placement*. Of course.

She says, I did warn you, Bess. I told you what would happen if you went through with this.

I've been here over ten years, I tell her.

I know.

This is my home. My family.

She says nothing.

And I think, This is what conditional love looks like.

I thought it didn't matter to me. But it isn't about what matters to *me*; it's about her, what *she* can live with. And, evidently, my time is up.

I stand up, still numb, still not processing things properly. At some point soon, this is all going to crash down on me at once. But for now, there's nothing. I go to the kitchen drawer and take out a roll of black bin bags. And I go back to my bedroom with the faces in the ceiling. And I start packing.

Chapter Twenty-Six

It's been six months now, since it happened. It's springtime. We survived the millennium after all. Shelly picked me up the following week (it all happens so quick when they want you gone) and drove me to a new house in Kingston, not far from the train station. Outside, the house looks narrow and claustrophobic. It's a Georgian-style terraced one with three floors and a big blue door. But, inside, there are enough bedrooms to comfortably sleep six, and the spaces are big, echoey, airy, bright. All wooden floors and gaping fireplaces. I like it here. I have my own bedroom, on the top floor, with low slanting walls for the roof, and a bathroom just for me. I like how the sun comes through all dusty in the morning to wake me up. I like my three housemates, who are all my age or a bit older, all people who've been in care like me. I like the landlady, Rupi, who lives here but her part of the house is totally separate, like a home within a home, and she doesn't really bother us, doesn't try to mother us. Everyone is in the same situation as me. Halfway out of care and halfway into being an adult, dumped prematurely because of a 'placement breakdown', but all that really means is they don't want you any more. They call it supported lodgings, for transitioning care-leavers. Social services pay the rent and help out with bills and stuff, but we're expected to make our own money too, if we're not going to college or uni, so I got a job at a stationery shop in the Bentall Centre, and I work the till at a chippie on the weekends.

I sold all the baby stuff Mum – Lisa – got for me after I found all the receipts paperclipped together in the kitchen drawer, ready to hand over to social services, and I used the money to redecorate my new bedroom. I bought a load of vintage movie posters, mainly John Hughes and Tarantino, and tacked them to the roof-ceiling. Weird that it's so good here, so peaceful, for a place where they put you when they obviously have no idea what else to do with you, when there's no temporary foster carers available to take you on.

Shelly is still my social worker, miraculously, and when she visits, we talk about what I'm going to do next. I've applied to Basquiat, to start in the autumn. I finally opened up my GCSE results, the day after Mum told me to start packing, and it turns out I didn't do that badly, all things considered. A couple of retakes, but nothing I couldn't handle. I called Shelly to tell her, and she told me she was going to support my application for a scholarship at Basquiat – a full free ride – on the basis of being in a 'vulnerable category'. I hate how these institutions put us into categories – vulnerable, at-risk, looked-after – but if they're going to let me go to film school for free, I think I can pretend it's not happening.

After that call with Shelly, I hung up the phone with a grin plastered across my face. I was still in Shepperton, waiting for Shelly to find me somewhere else to live. Mum was in the garden digging up weeds. Rory wasn't around. He wasn't talking to Mum, had been spending more and more time at work, on account of her telling me to leave. I came out onto the patio and watched as she tried to dislodge a stubborn crawler, roots and all, from the flower bed at the edge of the back fence. She was wearing yellow gloves and they were covered in dirt. She didn't look me in the face when we spoke to each other. The sky was big and bright and open.

Even if I don't get the scholarship, I'm going to work and save up and go in a couple of years' time, once I've got some cash together, as long as I'm offered a place. I can't believe I've finally got a social worker who's actually doing her job. Shelly calls it an adventure, avoids using all the jargon which always makes me itchy, makes me talk to her about my feelings, sometimes cooks dinner for all of us care leavers together to make us be social. Sometimes she just pops in and checks the fridge has stuff in it. Forces us to look after ourselves. Made me go to CAMHS once but didn't make me go back after the therapist told me I should express my early childhood trauma through art and made me draw pictures of bathtubs for an hour. It's mostly hands-off. This is the most anyone has ever trusted me. It's nice being able to look after myself for once. Shelly says we are all the most *resilient* people she's ever met.

She asked me if I wanted to meet Amanda again, after I told her what happened when I turned up at her house. I told her I didn't want to, and I thought she would argue with me. I asked Shelly whether she thought I owed Amanda an apology and she came so close to me that I could see all the pores on her nose, her eyes very serious, and said, Bess, you don't owe that woman a single thing. A single thing. I promise you that. And then she told me that the word 'progenitor' is an excellent word for a parent who doesn't deserve the title of 'mum' or 'dad', and she looked so angry about it all that I almost laughed, but in a good way.

Sometimes I wonder to myself whether there's been a day gone by that I haven't thought about it. That I have no sensation, in the middle of some mundane task, of how my life could be different now. In some other universe, I am about to give birth. I secretly thought that I wanted a girl when I was pregnant and then I changed my mind after the abortion (thinking, sometimes, when half-asleep, that it had never happened) because a boy would have an easy life in comparison, especially with my history of mothers. Especially with my history as a daughter.

Sometimes there are moments when it catches me off guard. I might be on the train or working in the chip shop or food shopping. And I see something that makes me think of it. Or maybe I notice things that I wouldn't have noticed before. Adverts that ask for women to volunteer to be egg donors to infertile couples. Sometimes it's the smell of a car exhaust on a hot and breezy afternoon, or the feeling of soapy water on my dry hands when I'm washing dishes. And then it hits me like a train and I forget to breathe for a moment, and when it's over, it feels as though I am empty, and my arms have nothing to do except be attached to the sides of my body.

And then the feeling subsides and I remember that it's only been a few months, no time at all really, but as it's got further away in time, it feels further away in distance too. Sometimes I try to remember it and my mind goes blank, like all the memories are being wiped away. I can't recall the nuances of my emotions. I don't remember the places I reached inside myself to get it done. I can't imagine ever reaching for those parts of myself again.

Chapter Twenty-Seven

I go back to Shepperton for Clarissa's birthday in April. I try not to go back to the Studios unless it's to see her or Eshal, who has started college, single, un-engaged, with no fiancé on the horizon. Clarissa hangs out with us sometimes. She's definitely less annoying, now that I don't live with her. We're kind of a threesome: Bess, Riss 'n' Esh. I avoid the house – Lisa, Rory – at all costs. I'm not ready to think about my feelings for them. But just Riss is fine. She went off on one at Mum and Rory when she discovered they were kicking me out. Screamed at them. Nowadays she says, Bess, Jesus, I am so desperate to get out of here. And it makes me want to cry. How right she was all along about making decisions for myself.

I walk to the high street for cigarettes before I meet Riss in the café. I think about how I know every inch of this place, how many times I've walked on this pavement, my footsteps fossilised imperceptibly in the paving slabs on top of thousands of old ones.

In the corner shop, I buy my cigarettes and when I turn around, he's standing there, having already spotted me, watching me.

He says, Bess, and I wonder whether I can run away. He is thinner than he was when I saw him last, back in August. Gaunt, even.

How are you doing? he asks me, his hands linked together so his knuckles stick out white.

Let's go outside, I tell him, looking at the cashier.

We go out onto the pavement on the main road. I let him hug me, compromise with one hand on his shoulder blade, brief, and I take stock of how he's making me feel, checking up on myself as Shelly calls it, and I'm surprised at how indifferent I am to him. I realise I'm not feeling anything at all. Nothing, except mild distaste for the way his eyes are a little gunky with sleep.

He asks me how I am again and I tell him, in as little detail as I can manage, about moving away, my plan to go to Basquiat when I've eventually saved up enough money. He says, Yeah, I always figured you'd end up at film school, and he says it in a way like he's mad about it, and I think to myself, Since when did you *always think* about anything in relation to me. He says, You know education is bullshit, right? You can learn everything you need to know in life out in the real world. I fix him with a look, not biting. Not sure whether he's baiting me or he's just really fucking stupid. Maybe both. I ask him what he's doing now, just to be polite, and he kind of shrugs and looks away and says, Oh, you know. Same old. Tesco and that. He doesn't tell me about the suspended sentence he got – two years – which I heard about from Keris because we talk from time to time. That she threw him out after he fucked up another car (stolen). And that he has an electric ankle monitor.

He looks at me, clearly wanting to say something. I realise, with a small curl of satisfaction, that he doesn't have any power over me any more. In fact, the way he looks so uncomfortable, like he's afraid of me, makes me think I have the power now. It feels good.

He opens his mouth, closes it again, pauses, fiddles with the hem of his shirt, before saying: Seeing you has made me think, actually, about . . . you know. What happened.

He leans against the brick wall.

I watch him as he says this. I don't look away.

I wait for him to keep talking and when he doesn't, I tell him, You know what, you've clearly got something to say, Boy, so how about you say it?

The road is busy with Saturday traffic. A bus drives past, its exhaust leaving behind thin grey fumes clouding the space between us. I wave them away from my face. Boy says, Why don't we go somewhere? Pits? Pub? This isn't a good place to talk, is it?

He looks nervous. Sheepish. Guilty. Ashamed. His hands now in his pockets. Still not looking at me properly. I turn around and see the car he's pointing to, inviting me into. Another bashed-up Ford: a Mondeo with dents in the doors and on the bumper. There is a sun-shaped air freshener dangling from the rear-view mirror.

I say to him, I don't mean to be rude, but I'm not going anywhere with you.

But you do, he says quickly. You do mean to be rude.

And his whole demeanour changes, like he was waiting to snatch something from me to hold onto, something that makes him the hurt party, something to help him reconfigure himself as a victim.

His skin is milky. His beard stubble patchy, his lips dry. I try to remember how he looked when we met, whether he's all that different now.

I say, I'm sorry if this isn't what you expected. You knew what was going on with me. You knew I was pregnant. But you still dropped me like it meant nothing to you – like *I* meant nothing. You were a really, *really*, shitty person to me. I can't think of anything else to say. Except, maybe . . . I don't know. I don't blame you, I suppose. You don't have to hold yourself accountable. I *absolve* you.

I turn away, go to walk back towards the church, but he shouts after me.

You don't *blame* me? *You* don't blame *me*? You've got some front, Bess. Let's not forget what you did. Keris told me what happened.

I spin round.

What exactly did *I* do?

You know.

No, I don't. Please enlighten me.

You *aborted* our *child*.

I flinch. My stomach feels as if it's been punched and all the air has gone out of me. I can see the blood falling out of me again, remember the thick, almost-black clots of it, wondering whether one of those blood clots coming out of me might be the foetus. My underwear and the sanitary towels in them saturated with more blood. My wrists bony. Sometimes I dream about it, I realise, but I wake up not knowing what I've dreamt, just feeling this same sensation of tight, burning injury in my abdomen.

And all that numbness upon seeing him in the newsagents is gone, and now I'm fuming, like that kind of acidic anger that sticks in your throat and makes your eyes water and your mouth go dry. I say to him, *sneer at him*, I know what you're doing. You're trying to see the bad in me to stop yourself from seeing the bad in you. But it's okay, Boy. Because I see the bad, all of it, in you. I see what you did. You were an adult, right? Maybe not in your mind – but you were – and I was a kid. I was fifteen when we met. You got me pregnant. And, worse than that, the last night I spent at your house. You *knew* I didn't want to. You knew it. You're not stupid. But you went ahead with it anyway, because you knew I would never tell you to stop. You think I forgot about that? And you think I didn't realise that it was *you* who robbed eight hundred quid out of my bedroom? I know who you really are, Boy, and the thing is, it doesn't bother me now. Seeing you now, I just feel sorry for you.

Boy's mouth is opening and closing and opening again. His face is red and blotchy. And I feel my veins thrumming with fear and power and I feel my eyes and my heart singing, and my fingertips fizzing like I just missed a step on the stairs. And I'm so desperate to hit him. To call the police. To spit on him. To scratch at his skin until the bone is exposed. But I back away, my arms folded, protecting my body.

Was that everything you wanted to say? I ask him. And when he says nothing, I say, I'm expecting that money back, Boy, I need it for film school. He just watches me as though he's afraid of me, too, and I realise that yes, he is afraid. Maybe he always was. And I turn away from him, thinking my hair is longer than it used to be, it almost reaches the bottom of my shoulder blades, and across the road, the church chimes two o'clock.

Chapter Twenty-Eight

That evening, Eshal texts me and we meet at the train station. We walk up to Manor Park, the sun almost ready to dip below the trees, and we sit by the river and, on the other side, the tyre swing goes back and forth with the breeze.

The river is black, reflecting light in its ripples, and my bones feel soft, and Eshal's bones do too, I can tell. Sometimes when we are together and she prays, I pray with her too. And I don't know who I'm praying to, really. Maybe it's God. Maybe it's Allah, if he's even a different person, or Buddha or Mother Nature or Mary Magdalene. Sometimes when I'm in Shepperton, I go to church and pray, or hang out at May's knitting group. I don't know if I believe that anyone is listening, but it feels good all the same.

During the holidays, I go and stay with Esh at her parents' house, or she comes to Kingston for a few nights, or we meet up and we go for walks and cook and watch bad TV, or if our paths cross in Shepperton, we'll meet there, like today, and we are so happy and safe and I know with my whole body that we'll be together forever.

Esh points the birds out to me on the riverbank, the big white manor house still gleaming even as the light fades. The names of the birds I know and the ones I don't. She's even better at identifying them now. They'll be breeding soon, she says. Laying eggs, having babies. And we lie in the grass with the daisies and the dandelions, carefree, my hand in hers, and we talk about everything in the world and nothing at all. We talk about all the things we did to get here, to get away from here, and how it sometimes feels as though the sky is pressing down on our chests. But we've got some air in our lungs, now, and that's all that matters. So we lie very still, our fingers intertwined, the skin on the palms of our hands calloused but not broken, and we look up.

Acknowledgements

First, I am deeply grateful to (and generally in awe of) my agent Anwen Hooson who has championed Bess and *Careless* from the very first read. Thank you to Charlotte Mursell and Lucy Frederick for your patience, commitment and faith in the book; it is an absolute pleasure to be edited by both of you.

Careless would not exist without Tom Rawlinson, who is an exceptional mentor. Tom, I cannot thank you enough for your extraordinary generosity and support.

Thank you to Helena Fouracre, Alainna Hadjigeorgiou, Maura Wilding and the incredible team at Orion.

I am indebted to my PhD supervisors at Brunel University London, Professor Bernardine Evaristo and Dr Claire Lynch, for their invaluable expertise and unwavering enthusiasm for the work.

Thank you to Siena Parker at Penguin Random House for the opportunity to develop *Careless* on the WriteNow scheme. Thanks also to H W Fisher Accountants for awarding me a scholarship that allowed me to study at Curtis Brown Creative under Charlotte Mendelson. Thank you to Anna Davies and Jack Hadley at Curtis Brown.

Thank you to Kenny Murray and Rosie Canning for lengthy discussions around the care experience and representation. My heartfelt thanks also go to the numerous women who told me their stories of teenage pregnancy, abortion and arranged marriage while writing the novel.

An earlier draft of the first pages of *Careless* was published in *Mslexia* no. 77, and is available on The Literary Consultancy's website, with thanks to Aki Schilz.

Some passages eventually incorporated into *Careless* were first published in a short story entitled *Window Shopping in Tokyo* in *TOKEN* Magazine in 2018, with thanks to Sara Jafari.

Thank you to my earliest readers: Conor Anderson, Lynda Dyson, Mark Gravil, Janine Hollingsworth, Sara Jafari, Emily Keech, Emma Millions, Lisa Milton, and Matt Wright.

Thank you, Emma Jeremy, for everything.

Finally, all my love and gratitude go to the family that chose me: Mum, Dad, Keiran, Jade, Grant and Sabine.

Credits

Kirsty Capes and Orion Fiction would like to thank everyone at Orion who worked on the publication of *Careless* in the UK.

Editorial
Charlotte Mursell
Lucy Frederick

Copy editor
Ilona Jasiewicz

Proof reader
Jade Craddock

Contracts
Anne Goddard
Paul Bulos
Jake Alderson

Design
Debbie Holmes
Joanna Ridley
Nick May

Editorial Management
Charlie Panayiotou
Jane Hughes
Alice Davis

Finance
Jasdip Nandra
Afeera Ahmed
Elizabeth Beaumont
Sue Baker

Production
Ruth Sharvell

Marketing
Helena Fouracre

Publicity
Alainna Hadjigeorgiou

Audio
Paul Stark
Amber Bates

Sales
Jen Wilson
Esther Waters
Victoria Laws
Rachael Hum
Ellie Kyrke-Smith
Frances Doyle
Georgina Cutler

Rights
Susan Howe
Krystyna Kujawinska
Jessica Purdue
Richard King
Louise Henderson

Operations
Jo Jacobs
Sharon Willis
Lisa Pryde
Lucy Brem